THE SWORD OF UNMAKING

(THE WIZARD OF TIME – BOOK 2)

G. L. BREEDON

KOSMOSAIC BOOKS

Copyright 2013 by G.L. Breedon
All rights reserved.
ISBN: 978-0-9837777-8-6

This book is available in print at most online retailers.

For more information:
www.Kosmosaicbooks.com

PROLOGUE

Fields of tall, gray-green grass undulate in the wind, rolling for miles and miles and miles until fading at the feet of an ice-capped mountain range.

Beasts roam through the grass — tall, shaggy furred, with curved tusks flashing bone-white in the bleached sun.

A man watches the past parade past a wide window. He wonders. To himself?

Can he wonder to himself anymore? Is that what he is doing? Even now with his mouth closed and his mind elsewhere, he can hear the voices. His voice. His voices. How many now? Enough? Will there ever be enough?

The man turns from the window and takes a sip of wine from a simple pewter cup.

He can hear them in his mind. Even before they speak. Words they have spoken before.

The other men sit and stand and pace and speak.

"We should kill him."

"We did kill him."

"Once."

"We should kill him again."

"Only him?"

"We should definitely kill *him*."

"There is no time."

"There is always time."

"We make time."

"We may need him."

"May need them both."

"If we can find it, we won't need anyone."

"Anyone?"

1

"You know what I mean."

"Yes, we do."

"Do I?"

"I'm not quite so sure."

"You there. You've…"

"Been very…"

"Silent."

Silence.

"Why…"

"So…"

"Quiet?"

Quiet.

"Do I need to speak? You know my thoughts. We are of one mind, are we not?"

"Which one are you?"

"Does it matter?"

"It may."

"Not this again."

"Pointless."

"We've been over this."

"No difference."

"None?"

"None that matters."

"And there are other matters that do matter."

"Where is it?"

"How can we get it?"

"Should have killed him when we had the chance."

"But we died trying."

"Not the same."

"If we can find it…"

"We can finish this."

"And kill him."

"Yes."

"And kill…"

"Kill…"

"Kill…"

2

"Kill him."

The men smile. All save one. One who turns away. One who looks out on the past, past the words of the men, words of himself, words still echoing and mating and multiplying in his mind as he stares out the window, trying…trying to see…what?…the future?…yes.

"What about the future?"

There are no words now. Only…

Stillness.

CHAPTER 1
EXTRACTION EXPEDITION

Vindobona. An exotic name for a common place. Not common in the sense of being like every other place, but common in the sense of being a place, like so many others, that would change its name, nature, and purpose throughout history.

Beginning in 500 BCE as a simple Celtic village situated along the Danube River the settlement became a fortified Roman outpost by the spring of 180 CE. Given the name *Vindobona,* or *"white base"* by the Celts and renamed *Flaviana Castra* by the Romans, the town was sacked and destroyed later that year by the "barbarian" tribes of the Quadi and the Macromanni.

By 600, the Lombards controlled the town, then the Avars, who gave it the Slavic name *Wiena.* The town soon became part of Charlemagne's empire in 795, and later the seat of the Badenburg's power in 1135, called by then *Wienne,* which became *Vienna* under the Habsburgs in 1273.

Eventually, Vienna became the seat of the Holy Roman Empire, facing down a siege in 1529 by the tenth sultan of the Ottoman Empire, Suleyman the Magnificent. Later, the city blossomed into one of the greatest cultural and musical centers in all of Europe, home to composers like Wolfgang Amadeus Mozart, Joseph Hayden, Franz Schubert, Johannes Brahms, and Ludwig van Beethoven as well as visionary artists like Gustav Klimt and Egon Schiele.

The capital of Austria by the time of World War I, and bombed extensively in World War II, the city of Vienna became, like so many of its European compatriot cities, a living museum, simultaneously a testament to 2500 years of history and the hope for a cultured and civilized future that might last equally as long.

A red-breasted flycatcher fluttered through the branches of a beech tree, sending a twig twirling down to Gabriel's head, bringing him back from his meandering historical reverie to the present — which, as usual for him, was really in the past.

March 17, 180 CE. The date of a particular death, significant not merely to history, but potentially important to the course of the War of Time and Magic. At least Gabriel hoped it was March 17. It could be hard to tell when there were no calendars or newspapers around to check the date. Time travel wasn't always an exact endeavor.

Gabriel lowered his binoculars and brushed the twig from his hair, watching it twist through the air as it fell to the ground some twenty feet below. He sat at the edge of one of several wooden platforms stretching between two large trees. Draped with camouflage fabric, the platforms composed a simple tree house functioning as the Chimera team's observation outpost. After realizing they could not pinpoint the date with any certainty, and hence could not know the exact time of their intended candidate's extraction, Ohin had instructed them to construct an observation station from which they could survey the fortified Roman outpost of Vindobona.

Heeding Sema's advice to find a location with few people, they settled on a small forest of trees right across the Danube River from the walls of the Roman fort. Gabriel had been very attentive as he watched Rajan use Stone Magic to reform fallen branches and trees into planks of wood. Using Wind Magic, Ling had floated the planks into position between two trees near the edge of the riverbank while Marcus used Heart-Tree Magic to affix the planks to the tree trunks. They each carried a large piece of camouflage netting in their packs, and among them there had been enough to conceal the entire tree house.

Gabriel found living in a tree house fun. For the first day. Now, nearing the end of the fourth day, he felt ready for a real bed and anything resembling a hot bath, much less a functioning toilet. It had taken the team three days to locate the candidate. Ohin had traveled in small jumps into the future to determine the window of extraction, but it required several days for Marcus to create the Replacement after taking a hair sample. It still left them with little to do beyond monitor the candidate constantly so they would have enough warning before the extraction, and keep Vindobona under observation in case Malignancy Mages showed up to disrupt the plan. It had not been the most exciting week in the year since Gabriel had undergone his own extraction.

"I hate these dull extractions."

Gabriel turned his head as Teresa flopped down beside him, crossing her long legs and leaning forward to rest her face on the heels of her slender hands.

"I. Am. So. Bored." Teresa sighed, and Gabriel laughed.

"How can you be bored with an entire Roman Legion to keep watch over?" Gabriel asked, struggling to keep the sarcasm from his voice.

"Seen anything interesting today?"

"A boat full of soldiers crossed to this side of the Danube."

"Exactly. Boring. Give me a good old twentieth century extraction any day. Calendars, newspapers, TV. Always something handy to let you know when and where you are. None of this watching from tree houses and sneaking through towns, trying not to be noticed. Your extraction? That was great."

"How do you always manage to find the least appropriate subject to talk about at the most inappropriate time?" Rajan lowered the book he had been reading as he leaned against one of the tree trunks supporting their outpost.

"She has an appalling lack of consideration for other people's feelings," Ling said from where she sat in a branch above them, whittling a small wooden figurine with a thin-bladed dagger.

"Ooo, irony," Teresa said.

Ling flicked a splinter of wood at Teresa's head. It evaporated into ash before it reached her. Teresa and Ling exchanged false smiles.

"Don't be such a Melinda Manners. He's fascinated by this stuff." Teresa turned to Gabriel.

"Aren't you?"

"Well, I guess it's sort of interesting," Gabriel said, not at all sure how he felt about the subject of his own extraction — his own death.

"Your extraction was both easy and exciting," Teresa said, her eyes glowing with enthusiasm.

"For you, maybe. I only remember drowning." Gabriel frowned at the memory.

"Sure, that sucked," Teresa said, "but the whole dying thing isn't the worst part of the extraction."

"I cannot believe you just said that." Rajan blinked incredulously.

"It's not," Teresa said, her tone suddenly defensive. "How could it be? He's alive, isn't he? We're all alive. We die and then Marcus brings us back to life. The easy part."

"I doubt Marcus would call reviving people after death *easy*," Ling said with a snort.

"Marcus is overly dramatic." Teresa pulled up the sleeves of her green and brown camouflage tunic. They all wore similar tunics to help them blend into the forest. "The hard part is switching the candidate with the Replacement before anyone notices."

Gabriel couldn't help but glance at the blanket-shrouded form lying at the edge of the observation platform. If he stared at it too long he might imagine it breathing.

"I will admit, the actual extraction can be exhilarating," Rajan said. "Knowing you're helping to save someone's life."

"And rip them away from their loved ones and everything they ever knew." Ling sliced deeply into the wooden figure taking shape in her hands.

"I'm trying to make an inappropriate conversation a little more bearable." Rajan looked up to where Ling perched on her branch, her lean legs dangling down. "You're not helping."

A woodchip flew in his direction. He ducked his head.

"Ignore them." Teresa turned again to Gabriel. "The point is, your extraction was easy and fun. Big headlines in the papers. Exact location. Pinpoint time for the extraction. And no witnesses."

"That's because they drowned," Gabriel said, frowning even deeper.

"I know," Teresa said, frowning herself. "Accidents are always difficult. Mine was a car crash. Very messy. A big crowd. I hear it was a very complicated extraction."

"It was," Rajan said, a frown now on his face.

"But a bus, underwater, with no bystanders around," Teresa said. "That's easy. And we got to learn how to scuba drive specifically for the extraction."

"The diving was not fun," Rajan said.

"It was great fun," Teresa said. "It's not our fault you're afraid of water."

"I can't swim," Rajan said. "Of course I'm afraid of water."

"I couldn't really swim, either," Gabriel said. "I only had a couple of lessons."

"Then why did you do it?" Ling asked, lowering herself down from the tree branch to sit beside Rajan.

"I don't know," Gabriel said.

"Knowing him, he didn't even stop to think about it, and plunged right in," Teresa said, her tone slightly teasing.

"I suppose you're right," Gabriel said, fumbling with the binoculars as he considered the question — a question he had contemplated many times in the last year. "It seemed like the right thing to do. I thought I could help. How could I not help?"

"No one else did," Teresa said.

"You died giving others life," Ling said. "That's something to be proud of."

"So did you," Rajan said softly.

"Hmm," Ling said, her gaze thoughtful. "I suppose that's true."

Gabriel remembered Ling had died in childbirth — the first time she had died. The second time had been at the hands of one of the multiple Apollyons, and Gabriel had risked the stability of the entire Primary Continuum to save her. He hoped her next death would be a long, long time ahead in her personal timeline. And in his own, for that matter.

"Saving people's lives, precise underwater extractions…that's exciting," Teresa said, doggedly sticking to the theme of her rant. "None of this sitting around for days in the trees watching someone die of smallpox. It feels cruel."

Gabriel nearly replied that the cruel part was telling the candidate they'd been saved from death so they could be recruited to fight in the War of Time and Magic when something prickled the back of his mind.

He reached out for the magical Grace imprints of his pocket watch as his time-sense expanded. He turned to the source of the space-time disturbance as Ohin appeared behind him.

Gabriel released the imprints of his pocket watch and exhaled a silent sigh. He had expected it to be Ohin, but anything could happen. It would not have been the first time Malignancy Mages appeared in the midst of a mission.

"It is time," Ohin said as he pulled a small, green fabric mask from his mouth and nose, letting it dangle around his neck. Smallpox was too contagious to tempt fate. Everyone in the team had similar masks dangling at their necks. "Marcus says he is close. It will not be long. The extraction begins now. Ling, ready the Replacement."

"Right." Ling slid to her feet and ducked under a low branch as the Replacement gently floated into the air. The blanket, seemingly of its own volition, wrapped itself tightly around the still form of the Replacement.

"Teresa, you're our eyes outside the bubble," Ohin said. "If anything seems out of place, you know what to do."

"Nothing escapes my gaze," Teresa said brightly. "I'm like the many-eyed Argus. All seeing."

Ohin narrowed his own eyes at Teresa, but she stared back serenely.

He turned to Gabriel. "You will create the time-dilation bubble."

"I know," Gabriel said.

Ohin's instructions were largely superfluous. The team had planned and rehearsed the extraction for several days. But Ohin liked to do things in an orderly fashion, and reiterating each team member's role in the mission helped keep everyone in order.

"The whole room, or only near the bed?"

"There are two attendants with him," Ohin said. "It will have to be the whole room. The quarters are tight and we will need space for Sema and Marcus and Ling."

"I'll prepare the observation platform for departure," Rajan said, putting his book in a nearby knapsack as he stood up.

"Good," Ohin said, "but wait until we return before you dissolve it completely. Marcus will need time for the revival and healing. Everyone ready?"

9

Ohin spread his gaze across his team. Gabriel felt a cauldron of excited energy bubbling up within him. Teresa was right. However morbid and morally confusing extractions might be — they were exciting.

Gabriel grabbed the Sword of Unmaking from where it rested between a yoke of branches and slid its strap over his shoulder. He had grown enough in the last year for it to fit at his waist, but now it felt too comfortable on his back to wear it any other way.

Satisfied that everyone stood prepared for their roles in the mission, Ohin pulled his mask up over his mouth and nodded for the others to do the same. Then Gabriel felt the all-too-familiar tug at his space-time sense, and blackness enveloped everything.

A brief whiteness followed, fading to reveal a long, wooden bed at the side of a small, stone-walled room. There were three windows, covered with a thin, pale fabric, allowing the afternoon sun to illuminate the chamber. Tapestries with simple geometric patterns draped the walls.

The candidate lay on the bed while two young male attendants in short white togas stood nearby, applying a cold compress to the dying man's forehead.

Sema and Marcus stood at the back of the room, clear of the bed and the attendants. Marcus winked at Gabriel, and Sema gave him a look of motherly caution. He could sense the Soul Magic she used to turn the attention of the dying man and the attendants away from herself and the others, rendering the team virtually invisible.

Ohin stood beside Sema while Teresa took up a position near the cloth-covered doorway as Gabriel stepped over beside Marcus.

"Any moment," Marcus said softly, turning his attention to the man lying on the ornately embroidered cushions of the bed. "He is very close."

"Someone else is close, as well," Teresa whispered from where she peeked through the thick, red fabric covering the doorway. "A soldier."

Gabriel sensed Sema reaching out with magic to the mind of the soldier beyond the entranceway, even as the man reached out to pull the curtain aside and step into the room. He did not notice Teresa standing a foot away, and he never even glanced at Gabriel or the others bunched up at the back of the room.

His red tunic and banded armor resembled that of nearly all the soldiers of the legion, but the fanned crest of the helmet he held in the crook of his arm denoted him as a military leader. Gabriel had seen him several times before, usually through binoculars. The camp tribune — responsible for maintaining a smooth-running outpost.

The tribune knelt near the bed, but not too close. No one wanted to catch the dying man's contagious disease.

"My liege, I have come for tomorrow's watch word," the tribune said, enunciating each word slowly so the dying man would be sure to hear.

The man on the bed opened his eyes and turned his pock-marked face to the tribune. He struggled to breathe, his voice faint as he strained to make words. "Go to the rising sun. For I am already setting."

The dying man closed his eyes, and the tribune bowed his head and rose to his feet. He stared at the dying man for a moment, his face filled with grief. He seemed deeply affected by the other man's impending death.

Straightening himself, the tribune nodded curtly to the two attendants and walked quickly from the room, the red curtain swaying with his departure. In the corridor outside, Gabriel could see two more legionaries standing guard at the end of a long hallway.

"It's time," Marcus said quietly, drawing Gabriel's attention back to the man on the bed. He watched with a mixture of sadness and horror as the man exhaled his last breath, his chest becoming still.

"Now, Gabriel," Ohin said, stepping closer to the bed.

Gabriel clasped his grandfather's silver pocket watch in his hand and reached for its imprints, using it to concentrate his own magical energy. He expanded his time-sense and focused his mind on willing into existence a small bubble that gently distorted the space-time continuum around the room. The bubble held at the edges of the walls, and Gabriel could feel the space within settling slightly out of sync with the time around it. Whatever happened in the time-bubble now would be imperceptible to those outside.

On an extraction mission like this, with so much to be done with witnesses standing nearby, a space-time bubble would help the team remain unnoticed and reduce the possibility of accidentally creating a bifurcation of the Primary Continuum.

Ohin could sense the stability of the space-time bubble, and he gave Gabriel a quick nod of approval before turning to the others.

"It is safe. Quickly."

Gabriel observed, with his magic-sense as much as his eyes, as Sema, Marcus, and Ling began the carefully orchestrated extraction procedure. Sema clouded the minds of the two attendants, who turned their faces away from the bed while Ling used Wind Magic to lift the dead man from the mattress and quickly strip him free of his robes. As the naked man floated to Marcus, a simple white sheet wrapped the body. Marcus embraced the corpse with Heart-Tree Magic, and the man slowly began to breathe again. The Replacement, looking exactly like that of the man who had been dead only moments ago, floated toward the bed.

"Someone is coming," Teresa said from the doorway. "Three soldiers."

Gabriel snapped his head around to stare at the doorway. There should be no soldiers arriving. From inside the space-time bubble, the world outside should appear frozen, or slowed to a near stop. Any soldiers should appear to be halted in mid-step.

If they were walking toward the room that could only mean one thing.

"Malignancy Mages," Ohin said, turning to face the doorway.

"I'm almost done," Ling said, magically wrapping the candidate's robes around the Replacement. "Just need a second."

"I can't see who they are with their helmets on," Teresa said, stepping back from the doorway. "They're almost here."

Gabriel felt her reach for the imprints of the golden bracelet on her wrist.

"Follow procedure," Ohin said, placing himself between Gabriel and the doorway.

"Done," Ling said as the Replacement settled beneath the covers of the bed. She turned to face the doorway as the first of the three soldiers improbably crossed the space-time bubble and entered the room.

"Now," Ohin said, and Gabriel released the space-time bubble as he felt Ohin impose his own will on the space-time continuum.

A moment of utter darkness and a flash of brilliant light, and Gabriel stood in the forest trees below their observation outpost. The rest of the team from the room stood around him, facing the three helmeted soldiers. That was procedure. If problems arose during an extraction, retreat — and take the problems with you.

The problems stood before the team and slowly removed their helmets in unison. Gabriel was not surprised to see they were all Apollyons — duplicates of the Malignancy Mage determined to destroy the Council of Time and Magic and cross the Great Barrier of Probability that sealed the past from the future in the year 2012.

He was, however, surprised with how determined they were to kill him.

CHAPTER 2
FIGHTING TO FLEE

The Apollyons attacked with a unity of thought and purpose impossible for normal human beings to achieve. As duplicates, created by doubling the original Apollyon through repeatedly splitting the Primary Continuum, the men's minds were linked throughout time. This allowed for a level of coordinated attack that even mages as experienced as the Chimera team could not hope to match. And, as fully trained True Mages, who were able to use all six magics, the duplicate Apollyons fielded a far greater range of magic than the Grace Mages assembled against them.

Gabriel strove to limit the magical power of the Apollyons by reaching out and claiming hold of all the Grace and Malignancy imprints in the surrounding land. Several battles had been fought over the town of Vindobona through the preceding centuries, and there were plentiful imprints — positive and negative — to be commanded.

Gabriel held a concatenate crystal in his pocket, as did all the members of the team. It was a precaution Councilwoman Elizabeth insisted upon when Gabriel was on missions. As he grasped the imprints flowing through the crystal and reached over his shoulder to draw the ancient, highly imbued katana from its sheath, the Apollyons began their silent attack. The attack was not quiet in the sense that no noise arose, but because the three Apollyons never uttered a word.

Gabriel simultaneously felt one of the Apollyons creating a space-time seal around the team as he sensed Ohin struggling to keep the seal from fully forming. Amber bolts of lightning erupted around Gabriel. He shielded himself against them as they formed and leapt through space.

He appeared behind the middle of the three Apollyons and stabbed his sword forward. The sword pierced nothing but air as the Apollyon

14

disappeared. Gabriel's space-time sense told him the Apollyon was appearing behind him. He threw himself to the ground and spun backwards, swinging the sword blade into the space he could feel the Apollyon appearing in.

The man gasped in surprise as the metal bit into his left thigh. The Apollyons on either side of Gabriel turned to attack, but he was already gone. He reappeared ten feet away and unleashed a simultaneous onslaught of magics against the three men — blasts of blue-white plasma energy from the tip of the sword, crushing gravitational forces to squeeze the men, vile curses to make their bodies collapse and their hearts stop, magic to cloud their minds and induce sleep, energies to turn their talismans and concatenate crystals to ash, and a space-time lock to hold them in place while the rest of his team attacked them with near identical assaults, matching and reinforcing their attacks with Gabriel's. They had practiced this kind of encounter many times. They knew the battle needed to be swift and merciless.

For a moment, while he watched the three Apollyons fight to beat back the numerous magics assailed against them, Gabriel believed he and his team might be winning...that they could defeat these three Apollyons and strike a blow against the entire army of duplicates.

Then he sensed something that frightened him. He could feel, with his magic-sense, a change in the imprints the three Dark Mages drew upon for their magic.

They were no longer only accessing the imprints available through the concatenate crystals around their necks. The imprints they touched were too numerous and powerful for that. The three Apollyons drew their powers from a large pool of strategically placed twins holding negative imprints in wars and battles throughout time. Gabriel and his team would need dozens of concatenate crystals to even approximate to the magical power the three Apollyons linked to.

As evidence of this newfound power, all of Gabriel's magical attacks shifted and turned back against him. He felt a space-time seal fall into place like an iron door slamming shut. The blade of his sword glowed as energy flowed into it and him. He felt gravity pushing at him from all sides, trying to collapse him into a miniature black hole. He struggled against the desire to sleep, even as pain like being dipped in lava erupted throughout his body. As he wrestled with the dark magic of the Apollyons, he saw his companions falling to the ground, felled by the overwhelming magical power loosed against them.

Gabriel knew he could not hold out long against the three Apollyons, and he was certain his team would be dead in seconds, if they were not already. With the space-time seal in place, there was nowhere to run. He grasped at all the imprints he could, clutching at the imprints of his own body from when he had sacrificed his life to save others. He focused his mind as best he could on amplifying his own magical energy as Akikane and Ohin had taught him.

It was useless. Not nearly enough time or magical power to mount a defense. He struggled to hold the three Apollyons at bay a few seconds longer. He would never know when they had concluded that killing him was preferable to capturing him, but that decision had clearly been made.

Gabriel panted from the effort of concentration, feeling his strength wane. He realized the War of Time and Magic was about to end for him, and for the team.

His team — people who had come to be more than family to him. Ohin, who had become a second father. Sema and Marcus, the aunt and uncle he had lost. Rajan and Ling, the cousins he would never see again. Teresa, the friend who might have become something more.

Gabriel stared through tear-filled eyes as his friends and teammates writhed on the ground, their faces turned so they could watch his demise moments before their own.

One face was missing. Where was Rajan?

The ground opened up beneath the three Apollyons and sucked them down, the soil undulating like the esophagus of some massive earthen beast. The magic afflicting Gabriel ceased, along with the space-time seal.

Gabriel looked upward to the tree house observation deck to see Rajan, hands outstretched, his face clenched in concentration.

In the confusion of the fight, Gabriel had forgotten Rajan had been above them in the trees. The three Apollyons had also failed to notice him. His well-timed attack might now give Gabriel the chance to do the thing he had trained for, the thing Ohin, Akikane, and even Teresa had insisted he do if ever such a situation arose — flee.

That's what he had agreed he would do. As the Seventh True Mage, the only mage able to control imprints of both Grace and Malignancy, Gabriel was too valuable to the War of Time and Magic to risk his life saving his team members. Escaping alone, he might have a chance to elude the three Apollyons. If he tried to take the team with him, it would be easier for the Dark Mages to track his passage through time, ghost his trail, and eventually catch up with him.

Part of him, the selfish part, the part of him that didn't want to die and would do anything to survive, wished he was the kind of person who could abandon his friends to certain death in order to save his own life. But he wasn't that sort of person. Teresa had been right when she suggested he had lost his life the first time because he had not hesitated before diving back into the water to save his classmates in that sunken bus. It was the right thing to do, so he did it. Abandoning his friends was not the right thing to do, even if they all said it was.

The image of his last death flittered through his mind as the thought of his next death solidified. Something about that last moment underwater, drowning despite all his efforts, elicited a memory. A memory of another body of water — an ocean beside a beach. A beach he had been to thanks to a coin Councilwoman Elizabeth had given him. A coin that had been beneath the water as well as beside it.

The ephemeral thoughts began to coalesce into a single idea, one Gabriel sought to implement even before it cohered in his mind. He could feel the first pricklings of his space-time sense telling him the three Apollyons were about to teleport themselves from the deep earthen grave Rajan had created for them. With no time to explain, Gabriel gestured with the blade of the Sword of Unmaking, using a hand of invisible force to knock Rajan from his perch within the limbs of the tree house. Gabriel had no time to create a soft cushion of air for Rajan to land on. He was already turning the full power of his magical energy toward another task even as Rajan plummeted, screaming, to the ground.

Rajan would not have time to dissolve the tree house that had been their observation platform for the last week. But it could not be left standing. It was too likely to create a bifurcating branch of the Primary Continuum if discovered by a Roman soldier or Celtic villager. They could not hope to come back to destroy it at some later time as the Apollyons would surely stand guard over it, waiting to ambush them yet again. It needed to be dissolved quickly and completely.

Unfortunately, Gabriel had never dissolved a structure like this before. Like the walls of the Council's Windsor Castle, the magic Rajan had used to fashion the platform made it both resilient and easily disintegrated. Gabriel had seen him make it, and watched him unmake a similar outpost, but it had been a process requiring minutes, not seconds, to accomplish.

To compensate for his lack of experience and the shortness of time available to him, Gabriel focused all of the magical energy at his disposal toward the task of vaporizing the entire platform in a single moment. A cloud of ash fell from the treetops revealing suddenly empty branches.

The three Apollyons appeared above ground as Gabriel put the riskiest part of his plan into action. Before the Apollyons could attack, Gabriel did as he had promised and withdrew from that time and place.

He reached into his pocket and clasped the familiar coin. It had become a good luck charm, always kept near at hand. He felt for a place along the timeline of the coin, and made his retreat.

His evacuation was not solitary, however.

As the blackness of time travel pervaded everything, it specifically engulfed his fallen teammates. When the blinding light of their concluding transit faded, the fullness of his retreat revealed all three Apollyons present, as well.

This had been intentional. He had taken them with him for a reason — because of the place he had taken them to.

Gabriel, his teammates, and the three Apollyons floated twenty feet beneath the surface of the Mediterranean Sea. Everyone except Gabriel struggled, gasping for air, sucking in water against their wills. Gabriel knew the feeling, and how disorienting it could be. He also knew it would not confuse the three Apollyons for long. He had little time to work his plan.

His friends were already convulsing and sinking toward the seafloor. Gabriel saw a flash of light and felt a burning sensation along his left side, but ignored it as he swung the Sword of Unmaking toward the three Apollyons, still floating together as they grappled with their sudden immersion. He focused the considerable magical energy at his command on one single task — making the water around the three men instantly boil.

The sea surrounding the three Dark Mages exploded in a ball of roiling white steam bubbles as Gabriel concentrated again on the coin, jumping through time with his companions, first to a deserted beach, then a barren desert hillside, then an empty ship deck at night. Then he switched relics, choosing a button from the same pocket. And then switched again. He took the team through several more relics and time frames until he was certain the three Apollyons had not been able to track their trail through time.

When the white light of time travel faded for the final time, Gabriel and the team rested on a small, grassy hillside overlooking a vast savanna in southern Africa sometime in the Paleolithic age.

Gabriel collapsed to his knees in exhaustion. The whole left side of his body burned with an incredible pain, but he ignored it. There was no time to see what the source of the pain might be. He scanned the hillside and his teammates.

Teresa struggled to sit up, still coughing and spitting water. "Just because I was talking about how you died drowning doesn't mean I wanted you to show me." She gave Gabriel a weary but thankful smile.

"Show her all you want, but leave me out of it," Ling said, shaking the water from her hair and blowing snot from her nose into her hand. She wiped it on the grass and gave Gabriel a wink.

"I seem to remember mentioning a fear of water." Rajan took long, deep breaths to reassure himself that air, not liquid, flowed into his lungs.

"I am thankful," Ohin said, straining to stand on his feet. "But you must learn to obey orders."

"I'm trying the best I can," Gabriel said, wincing at the pain in his side.

"What's wrong?" Ohin asked, stepping closer.

"Nothing," Gabriel said. "I'll be fine."

Sema, kneeling beside Marcus, called out.

"Gabriel! Marcus needs your help. He's wounded." She held up her hand, covered in blood, to make her point.

"No," Rajan called from over Gabriel's shoulder. "I need help over here. He's dead. Again."

Rajan crouched beside the lifeless form of the extraction candidate.

Gabriel spun around, looking between Sema and Marcus and Rajan and the candidate. With Marcus unconscious, Gabriel was the only hope of once more reviving the dead man.

Gabriel tried to stand, but a stabbing pain in his left leg brought him back down again. He crawled forward, holding the sword in his right hand, his left arm throbbing and largely useless.

"You are hurt!" Teresa said, getting to her feet and running to his side. She and Ohin reached him as his left side gave way completely and he tumbled into the grass. He yelped at the pain as Ohin rolled him over and Teresa pulled up the side of his tunic. She gasped and lurched back in surprise.

"Your whole side is burned," Teresa said, trying to hold the tunic away from his skin.

"We have to get you and Marcus back to the castle immediately," Ohin said.

Gabriel could feel Ohin reaching for the imprints of his necklace's seashells and the magical energy that would allow him to transport them through time to the castle.

"No," Gabriel said, looking at the candidate's body ten feet away. "He won't survive if we do that. Every second is important. That's what Marcus said."

"Every second may be important for you, too," Ohin said.

"He's right," Teresa said. "The burns are spreading. I don't know how, but they're getting worse."

Gabriel felt the pain dispersing farther along his left side and had a pretty good idea what the cause was — a powerful Heart-Tree curse. Untreated, it would consume his body in minutes and kill him. He could attempt to treat it himself, but he would lose the opportunity to revive the candidate, and their entire mission would have been pointless.

"No," Gabriel said, pleading with Ohin. "I can save him. There's time to save us both."

Ohin held Gabriel's eyes for a moment, then glanced to the candidate before turning back and nodding his assent.

"Quickly."

Ohin grabbed Gabriel under his good arm and helped him sit up.

"I've got him," Ling said, gesturing with her hand as she magically lifted Gabriel from the ground and carried him through the air, setting him down beside Rajan and the extraction candidate.

Gabriel knelt beside the candidate, wheezing now as he tried to ignore the burning pain spreading across his back. The old man beside his knees looked peaceful in death. Curly, gray hair and a carefully trimmed beard accented his regal features. He had a commanding presence, even in the stillness of his demise.

"Hurry," Teresa said, her voice filled with worry.

Gabriel nodded to her and took one quick look across the hillside to where Sema tended Marcus's wounds, trying to slow the flow of blood. Then he concentrated on the imprints of the sword in his hand. Magical energy flowed through him as he reached out with the Heart-Tree sense of his mind to scan the dead man's body.

First came the man's heart. Gabriel willed the heart to beat again, helping it, as only a True Mage could, with small, gentle contractions of Wind Magic as he healed the complex muscle. The heart once again began to beat, and he turned his attention to the lungs. The man breathed deeply, first once, then twice.

"That's enough," Ohin said, placing a hand on Gabriel's good shoulder.

"One more moment," Gabriel replied. "He'll die again if I stop now."

It was true. The smallpox had so ravaged the man's body that he would die again in minutes. Gabriel focused as much magical energy as he could into healing the man, eradicating the disease and repairing damaged organs and tissue. He couldn't heal the man completely, even with the enormous amounts of magical energy he devoted to the task. A complete healing would take much longer. But this would be enough. This would keep the man alive until they could get him back to the Heart-Tree Mages at Windsor Castle.

Gabriel released the magical energy and slumped to the ground. The man lying in the grass blinked and opened his eyes. He did not look around, did not seem bewildered. Although Ohin and the others stared at him, his eyes never left Gabriel's.

"Am I dead?" the man asked, his voice a sonorous baritone.

"You were," Gabriel said. "And you are to those who knew you. But now, you live."

"Thank you," the man said, trying to sit up. "I am…"

"We know," Gabriel said. "You are Marcus Aurelius Antoninus Augustus, Emperor of Rome. I am…"

Gabriel's eyes fluttered as he struggled to finish his thought, but the pain in his back had spread to his chest, and now it seemed to be inside his head. He would have screamed, but the agony felt too great. As his mind faded, he noticed the blackness of time-travel blending seamlessly with the darkness of unconsciousness.

CHAPTER 3
BALLGAMES AND BARBECUES

Gabriel's feet slapped the dark brown earth as he ran. He glanced over his shoulder and strained to run faster, gulping down air to fuel his muscles. He risked another look and dove feet-first to the ground, sliding forward into a square rock.

CRACK. The ball struck the leather mitt.

"Safe!"

The black-jacketed umpire crossed and uncrossed his arms in a nearly universal gesture as Gabriel stood to his feet, panting.

Baseball is great, he thought, smiling at Teresa, swinging a bat as she stepped up for her turn at the plate. The improvised baseball field filled the old royal gardens of the east terrace, running back to a small corn field within the boundary of the space-time barrier that prevented the castle and the surrounding grounds from slipping completely into the Primary Continuum.

At the bottom of the ninth inning, with two outs already and the other team leading 5-2, it looked like a clear loss for the Chimera team. With Gabriel on first base and Akikane on second, their best hope for not getting entirely trounced was for Teresa to get on base and then for Jan to hit a home run.

Jan, a sixteen-year-old Wind Mage from 1920s Minnesota, had eagerly volunteered for the ninth place on the team. Jan said he loved sports, but Gabriel suspected his interests lie more with Teresa than baseball.

Gabriel found his stomach increasingly uncomfortable every time he saw them together, but had had to admit — Jan hit the ball like a young Babe Ruth. Unfortunately, from Gabriel's perspective, he didn't look like a young Babe Ruth but rather a young Clark Gable.

Gabriel fidgeted with the small bracelet of granite-colored stones around his left wrist. It looked like a small mala of prayer beads, and he played with one of them absentmindedly. He edged away from the base as Teresa took her position at home plate. The pitcher from the opposing team, Marie, a Time Mage from the Dark Ages of France, threw the ball high and wide. Teresa swung and missed as the umpire called a strike.

She must be nervous, Gabriel thought as he edged a little father from the base. Teresa couldn't seem to catch a ball to save her life, but she could usually hit anything thrown her way. Gabriel risked another half-step toward second base as Teresa set her feet and positioned the bat in anticipation of the next pitch.

The pitcher leaned back, preparing for the throw, hesitated for the briefest of moments, then spun on her heel and rocketed the ball toward first base. Gabriel yelped in surprise and dove back for the base, closing his eyes as he stretched out his arms, racing to beat the speeding ball. He collided with the first baseman's legs a moment after he heard the ball strike leather.

"Out!"

Cheers erupted from the crowds of mages lining the back of the eastern terrace. Gabriel spat dirt from his mouth and wiped dust from his eyes as he stood up and sighed. Losing was bad enough, but being the *reason* the team lost annoyed him more than he could contemplate. Especially since creating baseball teams to build castle morale had been his idea in the first place.

He saw Teresa standing near home base, baseball bat resting idly on her shoulder, eyes wide as she stared at him with a look of incredulity. He shrugged his shoulders in response and started walking back to the castle. Akikane caught up with him halfway there.

"Good game, good game," Akikane said, beaming as though they had just won in a shutout.

"We lost." Gabriel sighed.

"True winning is having fun, not the highest score," Akikane said. "I had great fun."

Gabriel's mood brightened considerably as Akikane's words settled into his mind. It *had* been a fun game. He had caught two fly balls and had made one of the two runs the team managed to score.

"You're right. It was a good game."

"Yes, yes," Akikane said, patting Gabriel on the shoulder. "Next time though, maybe stand a little closer to the base. Winning can be fun, too."

Gabriel laughed at Akikane's teasing as they rejoined their teammates near the home plate.

"Nice dive for the plate." Teresa walked up beside Gabriel, still swinging her bat. "Too bad you were so far away from it you couldn't get back in time."

"Sorry." Gabriel wasn't sure how many times he'd need to apologize for the loss of the game, but he suspected it would be numerous.

"That's okay. You know I have a problem with the whole hand-eye coordination thing required for hitting the ball, and I hate running around bases, and honestly, winning is so overrated."

Teresa was well known as the best batter on the team and almost as competitive as Ling. Gabriel wondered if swinging the bat was an unconscious act, or whether she might be refraining from using it.

"My strategy was sound, but my execution was a little off." Gabriel tried to make sure his voice didn't sound too defensive. Although his voice had begun to deepen in the last year, it also had an annoying tendency to crack and jump an octave when excited.

"I find it amazing that someone who can defeat a pack of Apollyons can't figure out how to help us win a baseball game." Teresa teased. "Maybe we should challenge the Dark Mages to a baseball game. Apparently you need a life-threatening incentive to play your best."

"We could always set the baseballs on fire." Gabriel felt glad to see her happy.

"Don't tempt me." Teresa swung the bat up and rested it on her shoulder. Gabriel hadn't really thought she might swing the bat at him, but he sighed in relief nonetheless.

The crowd did not disperse with the end of the game or the setting of the sun. Rather, it doubled, as cooks from the castle wheeled out large charcoal grills and tables covered with dishes of sweet corn, potato salad, and apple pie. Gabriel had convinced Councilwoman Elizabeth and the rest of the council that an old-fashioned American barbeque would be not only a great end to their weekly baseball game, but also the perfect way to celebrate a successful extraction.

It had taken two full days for Gabriel to completely recover from the Apollyon's curse. His life had hung in the balance for several hours as Elizabeth and Akikane worked together to save him. Their combined powers and skills cleansed Gabriel's body of the curse, but the process had left him physically exhausted. Marcus's recuperation had been far swifter owing to the nature of his injuries, which a fellow Heart-Tree Mage had healed in minutes. The entire team had required healing of one form or another, but none of them suffered any permanent damage.

Gabriel discovered an increased appetite was the only side effect of the healing. An hour after the Chimera team's ignominious loss due to Gabriel's miscalculation, he sat jamming a third hotdog into his mouth as his teammates discussed the game.

"Practice." Marcus lifted his glass of beer. "We can't hope to win more games unless we practice more often."

"I must be drinking too much." Ling looked at the glass of beer in her hand. "I actually agree with Marcus."

"Great minds think alike." Marcus drained his glass of beer as he laughed at Ling.

"Yes, they do." Teresa winked at Ling. "And so do simple minds."

A potato chip launched itself from Ling's plate toward Teresa's head as Ling winked back at her. Teresa caught the chip in her mouth and chomped down on it.

"As well as violent minds." Teresa laughed around the potato chip.

"Words to remember." Marcus grinned as he, too, tossed a potato chip at Teresa. She craned her neck forward to catch the chip in her mouth and then stuck her tongue out at Marcus.

"Why must every meal devolve into a food fight?" Sema asked, sipping her iced tea.

"That's not true." Gabriel squirted more mustard onto his hotdog. "We hardly ever throw food at breakfast."

26

"That's because Teresa is always too tired to instigate anything before noon." Rajan scooped a second helping of potato salad onto his plate.

"I'm not the one who started throwing food." Teresa crunched loudly on the captured chip.

"If we're going to practice more, it'll have to be on Sundays." Ohin stroked his chin in thought. "We can't afford time away from our real training."

"You mean on our one day to sleep in," Teresa said.

"Laundry day," Ling said.

"A holy day, let's not forget," Marcus added.

"Holy for you in what sense?" Sema asked, turning to Marcus. "In that you drink twice as much?"

"It was Gabriel's idea to start the baseball team," Rajan said. "So he can do the laundry."

"Yes, he's very good at heating up water and shaking things around in it," Teresa said.

"It's not his fault he confuses you for a sock that needs washing when you're wet." Ling laughed as she ducked Teresa's impulsively thrown hotdog.

"Let's not waste food," Rajan said.

"Or entirely forget our table manners," Sema added.

"I agree with Akikane," Gabriel said. "It's not about winning. It's about how much fun we have playing the game."

"A perfectly enlightened attitude," Sema said, nodding her head toward Gabriel in approval.

"Particularly when we lose as often as we do," Ohin said with a deep chuckle.

"I think I'm going to practice having fun with a piece of apple pie," Gabriel said. "Anyone want some?"

His teammates all made gestures and comments about how full they were as Gabriel excused himself. He walked over to the dessert table, filled a thick clay bowl with a large piece of apple pie and then piled several scoops of vanilla ice cream on top. As he dipped his finger into the ice cream and stuck it into his mouth for a quick taste, a voice spoke up beside him.

"You were really good today."

Gabriel swung around, an ice cream covered finger still in his mouth, to find Justine, a pretty blonde girl with blue eyes from 1960s New Zealand. New to the castle, she had only recently begun her third month of apprenticeship as a Heart-Tree Mage. Gabriel had only spoken to her a few times. Her sapphire-colored eyes were quite dazzling. Had her eyes always been that amazingly blue?

"Mmmm." Gabriel pulled his finger from his mouth. His face felt suddenly aflame. "I got caught off-base and lost us the game."

"Well, yes." Justine frowned slightly. "But up until that point, you were really doing quite well."

"Thank you."

"I'm a big fan."

"I love baseball, too."

"No, I meant…well…yes, I do like baseball."

"You should join a team."

"Is there a spot open on your team?"

"Well, no. I meant one of the other teams."

"Oh. I see."

Gabriel suddenly realized how uncomfortable he felt and how odd it seemed. Not odd because a beautiful blue-eyed girl appeared to be a fan and wanted to talk to him, but odd because the more they talked, the more he wanted to be talking to a different girl with enchanting eyes. Looking over Justine's shoulder, Gabriel could see several of his teammates standing up from the table.

"I should probably…"

"I hear you escaped the Apollyons again."

"Uh. Yeah." Gabriel felt his face beginning to burn again, but for a different reason. Being the Seventh True Mage meant fielding many stares and questions from the other mages at the castle. Strangely, it was easier to talk about being the boy who lost the baseball game than the one who escaped three Apollyons.

"That's amazing. How did you do it?"

"I ran. And I got lucky. And I had my team. Speaking of which, I should get back to them. It was nice talking to you, ah, Justine."

Justine looked dejected as Gabriel smiled at her and walked back to the dinner table. By the time he arrived only Sema and Marcus remained, sitting next to each other and chatting pleasantly in low tones.

Gabriel had noticed over the last year that they seemed to get along much better when they didn't think anyone was watching. He looked around for the others and caught sight of Teresa sitting on a garden bench with Jan, laughing and drinking lemonade. Gabriel sat down with a sigh and looked at his dessert. Apple pie and ice cream suddenly didn't seem as appetizing.

"She's very pretty," Sema said.

"What. Who?" Gabriel took a bite of ice cream as much to cover his thoughts as to cool the heat once more rising in his face.

"Young Justine." Marcus laughed. "She seems quite taken with you."

"She was only…she likes baseball." Gabriel stuffed another bite of pie and ice cream into his mouth. He had discovered with conversations like this that the less he spoke, the better things went.

"I'm sure she does," Sema said, hiding her amusement as she dabbed her lips with a napkin. "Among other things."

"Let me give you some advice, my boy." Marcus leaned across the table, his eyes suddenly serious.

"Is that really such a good idea?" Sema furrowed her brow.

"It's simple advice. No harm can come of it." Marcus looked Gabriel in the eyes. "If you care about a woman, tell her so. Don't wait until it's too late."

"Justine is a friend. Well, sort of a friend." Gabriel thrust his spoon into the bowl again.

"Ah, yes." Marcus leaned back with a sigh. "No harm at all."

"That actually seems like sound advice." Sema's expression darkened slightly. "Odd that you never seem to follow your own advice."

"Its knowledge gained from painful experience." Marcus's eyes drifted from the table in thought.

"When I was a boy, not much older than young Gabriel here, I fell madly in love with a local farm girl. I used to walk five miles each way just to bring her flowers. We would talk while she taught me how to milk the cows.

"I must have spent weeks helping her with chores around the farm. She seemed to be interested, but I could never muster the courage to tell her how I felt. I was sure she must know my feelings. Then I fell ill and ended up bedridden for a month. When I finally managed to bring her a handful of forest flowers again, I found another local boy helping her with her chores. It seems he had the nerve to tell her his feelings. They were married a month later.

"I left home the day of their wedding and never returned. I often wonder where my life might have gone if I had only followed the call of my heart."

An awkward silence fell over the table as Marcus's words faded into the night. Sema seemed on the verge of saying something. Marcus sighed and looked up, realizing Sema still sat there. He cleared his throat and rose to his feet as she stood.

"That's a very illuminating story," Sema said, her voice sounding strained. "I'm sure Gabriel will find it most edifying. It's late. I should get to bed. I'll see you both in the morning."

Marcus sat back down as Sema disappeared onto the crowd. He placed his face on one hand and sighed. "Seems I'm still no smarter than that young farm boy I used to be."

"Well, I'll be sure to take your advice if I ever find myself in that situation." Gabriel looked down into his empty bowl and wondered if he should lick the melted ice cream from it. He was working very hard to ignore all the implications of Marcus's words and the effect they seemed to have on Sema. Maybe he needed a second dessert.

"I wanted to compliment you on saving my namesake."

"What?" Gabriel looked up from his bowl and into Marcus's eyes.

"My father named me for Marcus Aurelius." Marcus checked a nearby beer bottle, found it empty, and frowned. "He thought an imperial name might rub off on me. Seems to have had the opposite effect. Regardless, that was a fine triage the other day. You made the right call. Three lives were saved when it might have been only two."

"I don't think Ohin was so happy with my decision," Gabriel said.

"Ohin wouldn't have let you make it if he didn't agree." Marcus squinted as he looked around Gabriel's head and laughed. "Seems our leader is in need of a little saving himself right about now."

Gabriel turned around to see Ohin standing near a well-groomed shrubbery and talking with Paramata, a lovely, diminutive Indonesian woman from the 18th Century. She had joined the castle and the war shortly after Gabriel. More swiftly than most, she recognized that the castle provided an insufficiently small pool of potential mates for the mages who lived there. She had also quickly realized that Ohin was one of the most eligible men to be found. Unfortunately, she hadn't yet questioned why this might be the case.

Gabriel would never have broached the subject with Ohin himself, but it seemed to have taken decades for his teacher to get over losing his wife with his extraction from the timeline. Finally, he had opened his heart and married again, another Time Mage from the Olmec civilization of 1000 BCE. Unfortunately, she died on a mission after only a year together. Since then, he had remained resolutely single. This, of course, did not keep the single women of the castle from attempting to convince him to alter his resolution.

"Excuse me, I just remembered something I wanted to talk to Ohin about." Gabriel wiped his mouth with a nearby napkin as he stood up.

"Smart lad." Marcus laughed. "Get him in your debt."

Gabriel strolled over to Ohin and Paramata. She seemed to push the conversation along with an act of sheer will power. Ohin glanced around as she spoke, as though looking for an exit to dash through. The look on his face reminded Gabriel of an ensnared animal. He hoped Ohin wasn't considering chewing off his own leg.

"Have you ever been?" Paramata asked Ohin, who barely had time to shake his head, much less open his mouth in response. "It's a lovely place, especially in spring with the trees and flowers in bloom. The sunsets are breathtaking. I've always wanted to go back. It'd be a wonderful spot for a getaway. No people for centuries. Isolated. Very romantic."

"Well…" Ohin looked around as Gabriel stepped forward. He almost sighed with relief. "Ah, Gabriel."

31

"Hello." Gabriel presented Paramata with his most charming smile before turning to Ohin. "I'm sorry to interrupt, but there's something I need to talk to you about."

"It can't wait for the morning?" Paramata asked with a slight pout.

"Unfortunately, no." Gabriel contorted his face to its most apologetic continence. "It's mission related. Kind of important."

"Duty calls," Ohin said, trying to seem remorseful, but looking as though he'd narrowly escaped a Malignancy Mage's curse.

"Well, I'm glad we had this chance to talk again." Paramata's soft eyes looked up to Ohin's face. "We should do it more often."

"Ah…yes." Ohin blinked in surprise at his own words. "I should see what Gabriel needs. I'm sure we'll talk soon."

"I'm going to hold you to that," Paramata said, her face radiant. She winked at Ohin, then walked back into the party crowd.

"Thank you," Ohin said as Paramata stepped out of earshot.

"Teammates have to look out for each other," Gabriel said.

"You might remind your other teammates of that." Ohin frowned. "They all ignored my pleading stares."

"She's not so bad," Gabriel said. "She's nice, actually. Tough, but nice."

"Yes, she is," Ohin began. "But I'm not…" Ohin let that thought hang between them, unfinished. "You said you needed to discuss something. Or was that merely a ruse?"

"Totally a diversionary tactic."

"Well then, there *is* something I would like to discuss with you." Ohin breathed deeply and raised himself to his full height.

Gabriel felt his stomach tighten instinctively at the shift in Ohin's posture, but he relaxed a bit at the soft tone of his mentor's voice.

"What you did the other day, risking yourself to save the team, disobeying protocol, it angered me at the time. You are too headstrong, and you refuse to see how important you are in the larger strategy of the war. However, as you were recuperating, someone said something that made me realize how lucky I was. Paramata, actually."

Ohin paused for a moment and seemed to consider something.

"She said she felt glad that she didn't have the responsibility of leading a team, of making the hard decisions necessary to protect them.

I realized I am glad I do not face the decisions you must make. My primary responsibility is to the Council and the war, but my ultimate responsibility is to the team. To all of you. To make sure you all return safe from every mission. I am more than willing to risk, even give, my life to make sure you are all safe. And if the Council determined that one of you must be sacrificed to further the goals of the war, it would be an order I would not hesitate to disobey."

Ohin stopped again, thinking about his next words.

Gabriel's mind felt empty in the silence. Ohin had never spoken to him like this before. As an equal rather than a pupil. A sadness softened Ohin's eyes as he placed his hands on Gabriel's shoulders.

"I realized I am lucky that I am not you. You will face decisions I will never have to consider. You will need to make choices affecting countless lives. Mine, the team's, the castle's, the Continuum's. I realized that I cannot ask you *not* to risk your life to save the people you care about when I would do the same."

Gabriel stared up at Ohin a moment before he heard himself speaking.

"So I'm not in trouble?"

"Not today." Ohin laughed as he clapped Gabriel's shoulder. "I'm sure you'll rectify that tomorrow."

"You never know," Gabriel said as his teacher's words and advice sank in. "I may hold off until the end of the week."

"Hold off what until the end of the week?"

Gabriel and Ohin turned in simultaneous surprise to see Councilwoman Elizabeth standing behind them, smiling as she cradled a small teacup in her hands.

"Hold off getting in trouble," Ohin said, still smiling.

"I'd be surprised if he could hold off until the end of the evening," Elizabeth said.

Gabriel laughed along with Elizabeth and Ohin. The truth was, he rarely got in trouble. Of course, when he did, it tended to be for reasons that could threaten the balance of the war and the stability of the Primary Continuum. It wasn't all that funny, which is probably why they were laughing about it.

"I'll see you tomorrow morning," Ohin said as he patted Gabriel on the back. He nodded to Elizabeth as he walked away. "Goodnight."

Gabriel and Elizabeth called their goodnights to Ohin as she led him deeper into the garden and away from the revelers. His space-time sense tingled. He had a good feeling for when a Time Mage was about to jump through time or space. Thanks to his training with Akikane, he was also getting better at sensing where a mage might go when leaping instantaneously through space. He knew they were headed to the top of the Round Tower moments before flashes of darkness and brilliance delivered them there.

CHAPTER 4
TEACUP TEMPEST

As soon as they arrived at the edge of the crenellations atop the Round Tower, Elizabeth enclosed them in a magical seal of air, shutting out the night sounds of the castle and the party at the far end of the grounds. The presence of a sound seal concerned Gabriel. Why would they need to worry about being overheard atop the ancient tower? And why would Elizabeth not choose her office for a private conversation?

"Do you recognize this?" Elizabeth handed Gabriel the small porcelain teacup in her hands.

"It's a cup from the castle kitchens," Gabriel said, staring down at the blue floral pattern of the empty white teacup.

"It is," Elizabeth said. "Now put it to your ear."

Gabriel cocked his head in curiosity, but did as requested. As soon as he held the teacup to his ear, he heard Teresa's voice.

"I'm not sure."

"I figured since it was a day off for both of us, maybe we could do something together." That voice belonged to Jan. Gabriel frowned.

"What kind of something?" he heard Teresa say.

Gabriel felt a powerful temptation to continue eavesdropping on the conversation, but he wasn't sure he wanted to know how it would end. Besides, he wanted to know something else far more. He pulled the teacup away from his ear and looked at Elizabeth, her face illuminated but unreadable in the soft light of the half-moon above.

"How did you do that?" Gabriel asked.

"It's a very subtle bit of magic," Elizabeth said. "But there is a better question."

Gabriel thought about it a moment. "Why show me? Why here?"

"Exactly," Elizabeth said, her lips curling slightly. "Why don't you see if you can answer the first question before I explain the second?"

Gabriel turned his attention and magic-sense to the teacup in his hand, discovering an enchantment both elegant and brilliant. A bond of magic linked the cup through time and space to something somewhere else. He probed along that link to find what he had expected — an identical teacup on a table back at the party. A teacup Teresa and Jan happened to be sitting near.

As he continued to examine the magical space-time link between the cups, he realized they were not merely similar cups. They were the same cup. Somehow, the teacup in his hand was also the exact teacup sitting on the table beside Teresa. The original teacup had been duplicated in a manner that left the two resulting cups connected through time and space. He knew Teresa would have some mouth-mangling scientific explanation for it, but he didn't need words to understand the phenomenon — he instinctively comprehended the connection between the teacups.

"This is amazing," Gabriel said as he handed the teacup back to Elizabeth. "Did you come up with this?"

"Unfortunately, no." She sighed. "That brings us to the second question, which I will explain with a third. Do you remember the teacup on the bookshelf in my office?"

"Sure." Gabriel could picture the teacup in his mind. "The one Nefferati gave you as a birthday present."

"The very same." Elizabeth raised her eyes, but said no more. It took Gabriel a moment, but the question suddenly made a sickening amount of sense.

"Someone's bugged your office!" Elizabeth squinted at him in question and he corrected himself to compensate for the difference in slang between Victorian England and 1980s America. "Someone is eavesdropping on your office with a magically twinned teacup."

"Precisely. I only discovered it by accident when I moved the teacup to retrieve a book."

"How long has it been there?"

"How long, indeed?"

"That would explain how the Apollyons knew about the extraction for Marcus Aurelius."

"Among a number of other things, yes."

36

"So you can't speak freely in your office." Gabriel looked at the castle grounds below the tower and realized something even more shocking. "You can't trust anyone."

"Well, not exactly." Elizabeth joined him in looking over the tower parapet, the lights of the castle leaving most of the grounds in ominous-seeming shadows. "I trust Akikane, and Ohin, and your team. And clearly I trust you, as you are the only person I have mentioned this to as yet. But you are correct. I have no way of knowing who replaced my teacup with one that provides a direct means of listening in for Apollyon, assuming it is him."

"There could be twinned cups and glasses and vases all over the castle." Gabriel leaned against the stone of a tower crenel as a wave of despair swept through him. "They could know everything."

"We must assume they do," Elizabeth said as she pulled something from a deep pocket of her light blue tunic. She handed Gabriel a small, red leather notebook. "This is something I have mentioned on occasion to Akikane while in my office, which, until recently, is where I kept it."

Gabriel took the book in his hands and flipped through the first few pages. The script looked strange and unreadable — like no written language he had ever seen. Elegant and arcane.

"What is it?" Gabriel thumbed through the book, but all the pages were composed in the same indecipherable language.

"It is my notebook." Elizabeth reached out and Gabriel handed back the thin volume. "It contains everything I have ever learned about the Great Barrier of Probability. It is the only place where all of this information exists. I have been assembling it to help me consider how best to thwart Apollyon's plans to destroy the barrier."

"Does Akikane know what's in it?"

"He is familiar with some of what the notebook contains, but far from all of it. There are things I have learned very recently, on a little excursion I took yesterday, for instance, that are only known to me."

"Are you going to tell him?"

"Akikane is extraordinary in many ways. One of those ways is his ability to accept the universe as it appears rather than wonder why things are the way they are. To him, the Great Barrier is like a natural phenomenon. It simply is. I, on the other hand, am more interested in *why* things work the way they do."

"What language is the notebook written in?"

"A dead language. One that only I and one other living person know."

"A windtalker book." Gabriel saw the look of puzzlement on Elizabeth's face and explained. "During World War Two the United States needed a code that couldn't be broken. Instead of trying to create a new code, they enlisted men from the Navajo tribe and used their language as the code. Only the Navajo knew their language, so the code was never broken."

"Precisely," Elizabeth said. "Except the notebook is written in the language of the Indus rather than the Navajo, and I write using an alphabet I created myself."

"That sounds incredibly complicated," Gabriel said.

"That was the point. You'll discover how complicated when I teach you how to read it."

"It seems like that could take a while."

"Not as long as it took me to learn it. Nearly a year. Or a long lunch from the perspective of everyone in the castle. Regardless, you'll need to know everything in this notebook to help figure out how to stop Apollyon."

"Couldn't you simply tell me?"

"I could, but at some point I'll be turning this notebook over to you, and you'll want to know how to write in it as well as read it. Fortunately, I've created a secret Rosetta Stone to help you."

"Right."

Gabriel stifled the sigh bursting to escape his lungs. He spoke a little Spanish, thanks to his Guatemalan mother's insistence, but he had never had a knack for picking up languages. With the amulets all mages wore to telepathically translate their various tongues, he hadn't seen a need to address that deficiency. He knew from his history studies that the real Rosetta Stone had been discovered at the end of the 18th Century, inscribed with duplicate Greek and Egyptian text. It had been the only way modern archeologists had managed to decipher the ancient written Egyptian language. He wondered what Elizabeth's Rosetta Stone might be.

"As my office is no longer safe, we'll meet in the east terrace gardens in the afternoons. We'll begin tomorrow."

The mention of Elizabeth's office brought a thought to Gabriel's mind.

"It's possible Vicaquirao put the cup on your office. It sounds like something he would do."

"Potentially." Elizabeth considered this for a moment. "However, it doesn't seem complicated enough for Vicaquirao. Not enough layers in that cake. If it's not Apollyon, that means he's found some other means to know about our missions. Not a comforting thought, even if we must consider it."

"Kumaradevi, maybe?"

"No." Elizabeth actually laughed. "If Kumaradevi could place a cup near me, she'd make sure it killed me as soon as I touched it. The hatred she bares me for her husband's death wouldn't leave room for the restraint of something like this."

"He probably deserved it." Gabriel couldn't imagine what kind of man could love Kumaradevi. He found it even more improbable that Kumaradevi might care for someone other than herself.

"I'm sure he did." Elizabeth sighed. "However, I was trying to kill Kumaradevi at the time. She fled, leaving him in the way. I've never been quite certain if she blames me for his death or blames herself for abandoning him."

Gabriel snorted with laughter before he could stop himself. The very notion of Kumaradevi blaming herself for anything going wrong sounded ridiculous.

"Yes, you're right," Elizabeth said, laughing a bit herself. "We should be getting back. People will wonder what we're up to. And we must not let on that we know we're being listened to."

Elizabeth let the magical sound shield drop and transported them to back to the gardens, appearing behind a large tree where no one would notice their arrival.

"I should collect my other cup," Elizabeth said, wiggling the porcelain teacup in her hand. "What mischief are you contemplating?"

A large number of castle folk still sat at tables and benches or sprawled out on the lawn. Gabriel scanned the faces for Teresa and Jan. He didn't see them and didn't want to consider what that might mean. He also didn't want to consider why he should care one way or the other. But he knew he did. He felt his energy leave him in a wave as he sighed.

"I should get to bed. I have a long day tomorrow."

"As do we all." Elizabeth hesitated a moment and then kissed him on the forehead. "Goodnight, Gabriel."

Gabriel grinned at Elizabeth's restrained affection and walked back through the castle grounds to his room in the old visitor apartments. Contrary to castle custom, he had been allowed to keep a private room and forgo the tradition of new apprentices bunking with a roommate. A minor privilege of being the Seventh True Mage.

Later, after a brief shower, he lay in bed, letting the various conversations of the day drift through his mind, replaying parts of each in no particular order, pondering how they might all fit together. As he dozed, he wondered why he attempted to find patterns in things that didn't seem related. When he fell asleep, he dreamed of Vicaquirao.

Vicaquirao sat across an oaken table, a small, flat red stone held between his finger and thumb. His deep brown eyes examined the stone.

"The object of the game it is to capture as many of your opponent's stones as possible and be the first player with an entire section of the board dominated by a single color of stone." Vicaquirao gestured toward the game board.

What is this game?

Gabriel studied the square wooden board. Within the frame of the board sat six concentric rings, each smaller than the next, and each with a series of round black spaces marked for placing game stones. The circular rings were divided into four sections, each ring with a decreasing number of spaces. The outer ring had four sections of six spaces, the next ring four sections of five spaces, and so on. The final ring held four sections with only one space in each. In the center of the board sat a single, empty, uncolored circle. A small clay dish with game stones rested on the board outside the base of each section. Each dish held either red, blue, green, or yellow stones.

"At the beginning of your turn, you may place one stone or you may move one stone. Each stone may move up to three spaces at a time." Vicaquirao placed the red stone on the fourth ring of one section of the board and picked up two dice, one with six sides and the other a pyramid-shaped die with four sides.

"After you place a stone, you roll the dice. The six-sided die will tell you which ring must move while the four-sided die will tell you how far it must turn. Since there are four sections, a roll of four means the board stays as it is."

Gabriel watched as Vicaquirao rolled the dice. A three and a three. Vicaquirao touched the edges of the third ring, and Gabriel observed with fascination as he rotated the ring three turns.

"The keys to the game are learning to anticipate and plan for the subtle changes in the board, and how to arrange for minor alterations and use them to your advantage."

Why is he showing me this?

"I've never seen a game like this." Gabriel picked up one of the green stone pieces and held it before his eyes.

"I can't imagine you have." Vicaquirao's eyes appeared warm and bright. "Why don't you take a turn? The game can be played by four people, but as there are only two of us, I'll play blue and red, while you play green and yellow."

Where are we?

Gabriel looked up from the board and noticed for the first time that he and Vicaquirao sat in the grass along the edge of a swiftly flowing stream.

How did I get here? Is this a dream?

"Your move."

Gabriel brought his gaze back to Vicaquirao and the board of the mysterious game. He still had the small green stone in his hand. He placed it in the fifth ring in the section nearest himself and picked up the dice. He rolled a five and two, inclining his head in curiosity as Vicaquirao rotated the fifth ring of the board two sections clockwise, bringing his green stone next to Vicaquirao's previously placed red stone.

Vicaquirao laughed deeply.

"You have a great deal to learn about how to play this game."

Vicaquirao placed his red stone on the space Gabriel's green stone occupied, capturing it and setting it aside.

I can beat him at his game. I only need practice.

Gabriel watched as Vicaquirao rolled the dice and rotated the board once more, eager to begin his own next move, his mouth dry in anticipation. Dry as…

CHAPTER 5
LEFT BEHIND

Cotton.

Gabriel opened his eyes, blinking at the sunlight coming through the open window of his room and wincing at the ringing of his alarm clock. He reached out and smacked the clock into silence.

His throat felt dry. He must have slept with his mouth open. He sat up and grabbed a glass of water beside the bed, rubbing his eyes as images from his dreams faded from consciousness.

Vicaquirao. He'd been dreaming of the Dark Mage again. It happened sometimes. Less now than after his ordeals a year ago, however. Kumaradevi and Apollyon were more likely to be the sources of his nightmares. This hadn't been a nightmare, though. He'd been doing something with Vicaquirao. A game. Yes, they had been playing some strange board game. What an odd dream. He wondered what it meant.

Sema would probably say it had to do with his own desire to gain mastery over Vicaquirao in order to compensate for his feelings that the Dark Mage had gained power over him. That seemed as good an interpretation as any, and he let the thought fade as he prepared for the day.

Gabriel's days always began, after a hastily consumed breakfast in the Waterloo Chamber, with private lessons from Akikane. These lessons started with a period of meditation, followed by a longer period of sword training, and culminated in an extensive session devoted to learning how to blend and manipulate all six magics simultaneously for both combative and non-combative purposes.

Akikane believed meditation stilled the mind while swordsmanship helped concentrate it. With practice, the sword would become an extension of the will on an instinctive level. Too much conscious thought in the middle of a sword fight could lead to defeat. Thinking about how to use the sword took up precious time that should be used wielding the blade. The same, Akikane said, held true for magic. Just as a master swordsman or swordswoman could react intuitively and purposefully in a fight to defeat an opponent without taking the time for conscious thought, a mage could do the same. Learning to use magic in an instinctive way in combat, particularly all six magics simultaneously, consumed much of their lesson time together.

Mastering that lesson, however, usually involved collecting numerous bruises from the bokken, the wooden practice sword Akikane used to focus Gabriel's mind. Gabriel also held a bokken, but in nearly a year of practice, he had never once slipped past Akikane's defenses to make contact with more than air. He was, however, getting better at defending himself from Akikane's attacks. He'd lasted nearly a minute before one of Akikane's blows struck his arm.

"No thought, no thought." Akikane disappeared and reappeared behind Gabriel, sword swinging. Gabriel rolled and disappeared himself, appearing behind Akikane, his back to his teacher. Akikane appeared facing Gabriel, sword already outstretched to block the blow from Gabriel's attack.

"Good, good. More surprise." Akikane disappeared again. Gabriel leapt through space to the other side of the room, sensing where Akikane would appear next. He swung his bokken at the spot where he felt certain Akikane would soon occupy and felt a slap along his back, sending him sprawling to the floor. Looking up, he saw Akikane's smile, floating in midair like the Cheshire Cat, as his tutor hovered serenely above the ground.

Gabriel rolled and leapt to his feet, throwing his sword at Akikane's chest. The wooden blade burst into flame as it flew toward Akikane, guided and accelerated by Gabriel's magic. Akikane disappeared before the flaming sword could reach him, jumping through space to appear, once again, behind Gabriel, who spun and reached out with his magic, grasping and twisting space-time to deliver the bokken from Akikane's hand and into his own. Gabriel swung the bokken at Akikane even as the wooden sword materialized in his hand.

A look of beatific joy flashed across Akikane's face as he threw himself at Gabriel with incredible speed, managing to get inside the arc of the sword's trajectory, block his arm, turn into his body, and swing the young mage over his shoulder to the floor, simultaneously twisting his wrist to relieve him of the sword. To his credit, Gabriel rolled from the fall and jumped to his feet to face Akikane again, arms raised in defense — swordless and annoyed with himself.

"Wonderful, wonderful." Akikane raised the sword point to Gabriel's heart. The burning sword on the floor behind him extinguished itself in a small puff of smoke.

"What's so wonderful?" Gabriel tried to keep from panting. "I lost my sword!"

"True, true, but now comes the best lesson of all." Akikane's smile grew so dazzling, Gabriel nearly smiled himself.

"What lesson? How to lose?" Gabriel knew the point of the lesson — allowing subconscious thought to guide action — but he couldn't stop consciously thinking about how he might gain the upper hand again. Taking Akikane's sword had seemed like an act of inspiration. Now he'd have to settle for an act of desperation.

"No, no, you have already lost." Akikane stepped closer. "What options are available to you now?"

"Fight again?" Gabriel wiped the sweat from his forehead as he tried to discern the intent behind Akikane's words.

"Fight to lose more?"

Gabriel considered this. The absence of repetition in Akikane's words lent them more power. The answer was simple, but Gabriel didn't like it.

"Surrender."

"Exactly, exactly." Akikane lowered the sword. "With surrender comes the possibility of peace."

Gabriel frowned as he tried to figure out the meaning of Akikane's words. "But if I don't want peace…"

"Then you must fight," Akikane said. "Fight until you lose."

"And if neither of us wants peace?" Gabriel thought he saw where this line of reasoning might lead.

45

"The same end, the same end." Akikane stepped closer, swinging the wooden sword over his shoulder.

"You're talking about the war." Gabriel let his arms drop to his sides.

"You see, you see." Akikane flipped the sword from his shoulder and handed it, hilt first, to Gabriel.

"The more skillful opponent can force the other into surrender." Gabriel took the sword from Akikane with a slight sigh. "And you're more skillful than I am, even without a sword."

"Just so, just so." Akikane held Gabriel's eyes.

"You think that if we are strong enough, skillful enough, we can force the Malignancy Mages into peace."

Gabriel bit his lip as he considered the notion. He, like nearly every other mage, had assumed the war would be eternal, with neither side ever clearly losing nor winning.

"Not us, not us." Akikane's eyes still had not left Gabriel's.

Gabriel thought he might draw blood if he bit down any harder on his lip.

"You mean me."

"A leader must be strong enough to fight, and to make peace." Akikane looked at the sword in Gabriel's' hand. "Most importantly, a leader must know when to fight and when to make peace."

"But…" Gabriel didn't like where this lesson had lead and didn't want to know the answer to the question it left singing in his mind. "How will I ever be that strong?"

"Strength is not here." Akikane touched a finger to the wooden blade. "Strength is here." He moved two fingers to touch Gabriel's head. "And here." He placed his fingers above Gabriel's heart.

"Do you really think peace is possible?" Gabriel felt a pleasant, powerful warmth radiate through him from where Akikane touched his breastbone.

"Possible, possible." Akikane lowered his hand. "But likely? Who knows?" Akikane chuckled. "Now let us practice fighting when our opponent has a sword and we do not."

"I thought I already practiced that," Gabriel said with a laugh. Akikane laughed as well, then stopped and frowned as he turned to the door of the dojo training quarters.

Elizabeth strode through the door and headed toward them.

"I'm sorry to interrupt, but I have something I need to discuss with you both," Elizabeth said.

Gabriel lowered the wooden sword. She had never interrupted their lessons before and had never summoned Gabriel in person to discuss something. She usually sent someone to bring Gabriel to her office. He suspected why she would choose to come to them herself, but the fact that she did so made him worry about the reasons.

"Indeed, indeed," Akikane said as Elizabeth stepped before them. "We should take a break. Someplace with some more air, perhaps?"

"Yes, that would be ideal," Elizabeth said, waving gauzy remnants of burnt sword smoke from her face. "I know exactly the spot."

A moment later, the three stood atop the King Henry III tower. A magical sound barrier slipped into place as Elizabeth looked around.

"I have important news." Elizabeth seemed content that no one on the castle grounds had noticed their appearance on the tower and turned back to Gabriel and Akikane. "One of our informants believes the Apollyons will attack the Dresden outpost."

"When, when?" Akikane's joyful continence evaporated, replaced by a stern curiosity.

"The informant has provided a date and a time," Elizabeth said. "I believe we should mount a defense and use the opportunity to reduce the number of Apollyon duplicates as much as possible."

"Yes, yes," Akikane said. "We must act quickly before his own informants can alert him of our plan."

"I agree," Elizabeth said. "I want to assemble a strike team within the hour. Secretly. And I think you should lead it."

"Certainly, certainly," Akikane said. "We could have twenty teams ready to go that quickly. Maybe thirty."

Gabriel gasped slightly at the number. There were only around a hundred teams in total, and a third of them were out in the field at any given time. An assault force of thirty teams of mages would be half the complement of the castle.

"I'm glad you agree," Elizabeth said. "I'll inform the council privately. One at a time to avoid suspicion. I think it best if the teams leave at the same time and rendezvous for instructions."

"Nanjing, Nanjing," Akikane said. "The outpost there has room to hold them all for a time."

"Perfect." A glint of fury and determination filled Elizabeth's eyes. "We should begin immediately. Remember, ears could be anywhere."

Gabriel looked between Akikane and Elizabeth, feeling awkward and childish to still be holding a wooden sword while plans for the most dangerous and daring assault of the war unfolded before him.

"What about me?" Gabriel's voice brought the attention of both senior mages.

"You and I will stay here." Elizabeth's gaze softened as she spoke. "This may be a trap. I won't send to you face the Apollyons when you have only just recovered from the last encounter. That too may have been a trap. I've been looking into how we discovered Marcus Aurelius, and it seems altogether too convenient."

"But I can help."

"No doubt, no doubt." Akikane's joyousness had returned. "However, the war will not end today. You will see plenty of battles before it does."

"If it ever does." Elizabeth regarded Akikane with a hint of sadness.

"Faith, faith." Akikane slapped Gabriel on the shoulder. "We must have faith."

"I prefer certainty, but I suppose I'll take what I can get." Elizabeth waved her hand and the sound barrier vanished, the noises of the castle returning to their ears. "Well, then, we should be about it. You know what to tell Ohin and your team?"

"Yes, Ma'am." Gabriel flipped the wooden sword to his shoulder in what he hoped looked like a supremely confident gesture. "I'll let them down easy."

"Good." Elizabeth turned to Akikane. "Good luck."

"And you." Akikane nodded to Gabriel. "And you."

Akikane disappeared, followed a moment later by Elizabeth, leaving Gabriel alone on King Henry III's tower. He paused a moment to look out beyond the castle to the primeval world of dinosaurs surrounding their little fortress in time. It seemed so peaceful but really wasn't. Massive reptiles running, hunting, slaughtering, and eating each other in an endless cycle of conquest of survival.

Thinking about the battle his fellow mages were about to embark upon, it dawned on Gabriel that mammals hadn't changed the nature of life on the planet much when the dinosaurs became extinct. Different actors, same play. He wondered briefly if he might be able to rewrite one short act of that drama, but knowing he wouldn't know until he knew, he instead focused on the task before him.

He teleported from the tower and returned his bokken to its rack in the practice room, grabbing the Sword of Unmaking before heading off in search of Ohin and the rest of the Chimera team. They took the news of the impending assault, delivered discretely under and elm tree in the Lower Ward, with the usual dispassion.

"Bloody foolish leaving the best team in the castle behind on a mission like this." Marcus rubbed his hand over his bald head in annoyance.

"We always get stuck with guard duty." Teresa kicked at a rock. It tumbled through the grass, landing on Ohin's foot. Teresa blushed.

"We can find a way to be useful here." Ohin kicked the rock back to Teresa with a frown.

"There's useful," Ling spat, "and then there's *useful!*"

"It does seem like a sensible plan." Sema looked at the bracelet of small stones around Gabriel's left wrist. "We only narrowly escaped our last encounter with the Apollyons."

"But we know his weakness now." Rajan laughed aloud. "He can't swim."

"We'll meet at the usual time." The serious tone in Ohin's voice ceased any desire to bicker or complain. "If we are not part of the mission, we can at least continue training for other operations."

The team dispersed to continue on with their normally assigned tasks. Gabriel would usually have spent the rest of the morning training with Akikane. To keep himself occupied, he wandered around the castle grounds, trying to burn off his nervous energy. He always felt like a kettle boiling over with excitement before a mission. Even though this wasn't really a mission involving him directly, it might turn into an important day and a turning point in the war.

While walking along the path in the Upper Ward, he came across a man sitting on a bench beneath a maple tree. The man looked much healthier than the last time they had met.

"Aurelius."

The former ruler of the Roman Empire looked down from the cloud he stared at. "You?"

"Gabriel." He sat down beside Aurelius, leaning the Sword of Unmaking against the bench. It was unusual to meet famous people from history. The possibility of creating an alternate branch of time usually forbid any sort of interaction with people in the past. Occasionally, though, a famous person also turned out to be a mage. It was rare, both for Grace and Malignancy Mages. There were only a few dozen people living in the castle who history books had recorded in some fashion. Marcus Aurelius turned out to be most famous person ever identified as a Grace Mage.

"They tell me you saved my life." Aurelius stroked his chin. The gray-and-black curly hair of his beard matched exactly the short hair on his head. "I owe you a debt of gratitude. I suppose."

"You may change your mind about thanking me." Gabriel knew something of the inner turmoil and pain Aurelius felt. He hadn't been an emperor, but he had left behind his family to become a mage in an endless war. "It will get easier as time goes by. The first days are the worst."

"I hope you are right." Aurelius folded his hands in the lap of his gray tunic. "I was an emperor of a vast nation. A leader of millions. My laws and edicts shaped people's lives and defined justice. I led campaigns with tens of thousands of soldiers at my command. I died knowing I had done my duty and fulfilled it to the best of my ability. I died in peace, with the knowledge that my successes outweighed my failures, both as an emperor and a man."

Aurelius looked at his hands in his lap as if contemplating what they had become.

"Now I am a foot solider in a war I could never have imagined possible, surrounded by people from history and the future, wandering a fortress so far in the past I cannot recognize the wondrous beasts outside its walls, and all of us led in our struggles by a woman. A woman who, if I am honest with myself, frightens me more than a little."

"You don't need to fear Councilwoman Elizabeth." Gabriel nearly laughed at the thought, then thought of something else. "But if you ever meet Nefferati, I'd proceed with caution."

Gabriel tried for a moment to consider how odd everything must seem for a man who had been the focal point of an empire where women were considered unworthy of rights. An empire that not only condoned slavery but subsisted upon it. An empire expanded over centuries by war after bloody war of conquest.

Gabriel felt almost envious of Aurelius's sudden relegation to the sidelines of life in the castle and the war. Gabriel's journey had been the reverse. From oblivious obscurity to the center of the raging fire of at the heart of the War of Time and Magic.

"Where did you get that bracelet?" Aurelius pointed to the beads wrapped around Gabriel's wrist.

"I made it, actually." Gabriel held his wrist up so Aurelius could examine the stones more closely.

"A craftsman as well as a magician." Aurelius touched one of the beads with an outstretched finger. "I once gave something similar to my daughter, Lucilla, when she was a child."

Aurelius lowered his hand and sighed.

"I have learned she was executed by my son, Commodus, for attempting to overthrow his rule a few years after my death. Of all the mistakes I made in my life, insisting that my son become emperor was the most misguided. When I first learned of my second life, my rebirth, I felt possessed with the desire to know what had befallen my friends, my family, and my empire after my death. Now I wish I could forget everything I learned and live instead in ignorance. How long will that desire last, my young friend?"

"I don't know." Gabriel had researched Aurelius's life before the extraction and knew most historians considered his son Commudus's twelve-year reign to be one of the three worst in the entire history of Roman Empire, alongside Nero's and Caligula's. Depressing news to add to all the knowledge that came with a mage's rebirth.

"I'm lucky. I was no one when I died."

"It seems you are very much someone now." Aurelius breathed deeply and his mood seemed to brighten. "They tell me you are something rare."

"I can do things other people can't." Gabriel thought about all those things for a moment. "It doesn't make me special the way most people think it does."

"In my experience, character is what separates great individuals from people who are merely talented."

Aurelius looked into Gabriel's eyes as though searching for something. Seeming to find what he sought, he nodded, then turned away to stare back up at the clouds. "I do not envy you. I may have traded one burden for another, but mine is trivial in comparison to the weight you must carry."

"How did you bear that weight in your other life, back when you were an emperor?"

"All things are not as separate as they seem." Aurelius waved his hand. "The clouds, the sky, the sun, the castle, the trees, you, me, all the people throughout time. They are all connected. We each have a part in the grand design of the universe. And we all must play our parts. If I had abandoned my duty when my people needed me, I would have been neglecting my role in the cosmic pattern.

"In a better world, I would have been a scholar, a philosopher. I have no doubt that I would have been a better philosopher than a ruler. But that was not my part to play. My responsibilities extended beyond my own desires. I had a duty, and I could not have been true to myself if I did not discharge it, even if it meant I made choices and took actions I personally disliked. My duty was more important than my own feelings. No one thread is central to the pattern of the cosmos, but one's unraveling can unravel all the others."

"But what if, in trying to do your duty, you unravel the pattern by accident?" This was another question Gabriel often wondered about. How could he know his actions had helped rather than harmed the war?

"A leader cannot know the future." Aurelius laughed suddenly. "Well, maybe *you* can know the future, but you cannot know your *own* future. The best we can do is act upon our convictions with the hope that the results will benefit the world. Sometimes this means waging a war when you would rather sue for peace, or accepting peace when war might seem justified.

"Again, I am glad our roles are not reversed." Aurelius reached out and patted Gabriel's arm, a familiar, grandfatherly gesture that caused Gabriel's heart to clench in remembrance of the grandfather he would never see again.

"Sometimes, I wish this all had never happened to me." Gabriel held that thought a moment. "But then again, there are days when I get to sit and talk to one of the most famous men in history."

"And were I still dead, I could not sit and talk with a boy as unique as yourself. And I would not be able to do this." Aurelius pointed his finger at a fallen leaf in the lawn. It quivered and then floated into the air, hovering for a second before gradually floating down to the grass.

"That's great for your first week of training!" Gabriel smiled at the old emperor's newfound skill.

"I've always been good at focusing my mind single-pointedly on a task." Aurelius lowered his hand. "That seems to help."

"It helps a great deal."

As Gabriel looked up from the leaf, his eyes rested on the clock of the Curfew Tower. Nearly an hour had passed since his surreptitious meeting with Elizabeth and Akikane. The teams, all thirty of them, would be readying to leave. He concentrated on his space-time sense, extending it as far as he could. He felt gentle tugs at the fabric of space-time and knew the teams had begun their departures. If he had not known what to look for, and when, he would have noticed nothing. It was unlikely that any of Apollyon's potential spies would be able to warn him or his duplicates of the surprise counter-attack.

"Well, it's begun," Gabriel said out loud.

"What has begun?" Aurelius gave Gabriel a quizzical look.

"Nothing, I was thinking out..." Gabriel stopped. His time-space sense rang in his head like a fire alarm. Multiple time-space jumps erupted throughout the castle grounds. Could the assault teams be back already?

An explosion rocked the Curfew Tower. Screams and shouts filled the air. Gabriel looked around, catching sight of someone standing atop the nearby Garter Tower.

His breath froze in his lungs. How could that be? He knew then what the many space-time jumps meant. What the jumps still happening meant.

The war had come to Windsor Castle.

"What can I do?" Aurelius's eyes went to the sword beside Gabriel.

Gabriel grabbed the Sword of Unmaking, swinging the strap over his shoulder with the same motion he used to unsheathe the blade. He turned to Aurelius.

"Hide."

A nearby tree exploded in flame. Gabriel looked overhead to see three Apollyons floating above the King Henry VIII gate.

He took one step forward, claimed hold of all the imprints available to him, and launched himself upward into the sky.

CHAPTER 6
CAPTURE THE CASTLE

Gabriel soared through the air, heading straight for the three Apollyons hovering above the castle.

He did not fly often. Although slower than simply teleporting through space, it might give the advantage of being unexpected. The Apollyons did seem momentarily surprised by his arrival in the sky, but they swiftly began their simultaneous attack, nonetheless.

A wave of Malignant magic assailed Gabriel. Streams of fire from the three Apollyons' fingers wove around him as curses battered his body and mind. A space-time seal fell around him while some invisible hand tried to crush him like a frail leaf. Gabriel focused on the power of the imprints at his disposal and dissolved the magical assaults arrayed against him. The three Apollyons blinked in unison from astonishment.

Gabriel found himself surprised at how easily he had overpowered the three Dark Mages. The source of his own now considerable strength lay in the bracelet around his left wrist. The beads of the bracelet, each a miniature concatenate crystal, connected to a string of six full concatenate crystals, linked back in turn to powerfully imprinted relics and artifacts in the vast store rooms of St. George's Chapel. The resulting bracelet linked him to forty-nine objects imbued with Grace imprints and another forty-nine imbued with Malignant imprints.

The size of the tiny concatenate crystals rendered them useless beyond the confines of the castle grounds, but they bestowed upon Gabriel a massive amount of magical power within its boundaries. The idea of creating the links to both negatively and positively imbued objects in the castle had been Gabriel's, but Ohin's skill proved invaluable in making the crystals as small as possible. Teresa had helped him paint the crystals to look like stones and presented him the bracelet with some fanfare one dinner so no one would suspect its true nature.

Gabriel fought down a powerful wave of nausea from the Malignant imprints he held. They were easier to endure when balanced with Grace imprints, but it still felt like he had ingested a bucket of putrid swamp water. He relished the looks of confusion on the faces of the three Apollyons as he regained his internal equilibrium.

"It seems you have learned a few things of use in this castle, after all," the middle Apollyon said.

"A shame it won't be here for long." The Apollyon on the right scowled.

"But then again, neither will you." The Apollyon on the left glared.

Gabriel could sense them beginning to form another attack. The three of them floating before him reminded him of the last time he had faced three Apollyons. Magical energy followed his thoughts even before the idea had fully formed in his mind. A space-time seal clamped down around the three Apollyons while the air around them rushed away, leaving them trapped in a vacuum bubble.

The Apollyons gasped and struggled, combining their magical energies to attack the space-time seal Gabriel held in place. As they panicked and their mental defenses slipped, Gabriel could hear their thoughts calling to their twinned brothers for assistance.

"Help."

"Above."

"He's killing us."

Gabriel felt the bending of space-time, signaling the arrival of several Apollyons to rescue their brethren. He released the space-time seal and vacuum of air, letting the Apollyons plummet to the ground as he leapt through space to a point high above the castle grounds. The vertigo of suddenly being half a mile above the castle made his head spin, but he steadied himself and studied the scene below.

He could see five Apollyons halting the decent of their three falling companions near the castle gate. From his vantage in the sky, the castle seemed overrun with ants. Vicious, dangerous, black-clad ants intent on destroying the castle and the mages within it. With all the chaos created by the magical battle being fought, Gabriel found it hard to follow the events below.

56

He estimated at least fifty Apollyon twins were involved in attacking the castle. He could see no other Malignancy Mages. Maybe the Apollyons felt they were strong enough on their own. Maybe they didn't trust the other Dark Mages. Maybe the other Dark Mages were all involved in the attack on Dresden…if there was an attack. It seemed clear that the information on Dresden had been a double-layered trap, intended to both separate the castle forces and attack the castle itself. But why? Why take the risk?

The upper floor of the state apartments exploded in flame, bringing Gabriel's thoughts back to the fighting below. He couldn't afford to waste more time. He needed a plan. Akikane's training concentrated on learning how to unify thought and magic in battle, but he always emphasized the importance of strategy.

Gabriel watched as the castle defenders beneath him took heavy losses. A team of six Grace Mages normally proved barely a match for a single Apollyon, even when they had time to prepare and could access concatenate crystals. Caught by surprise, the teams remaining in the castle stood little chance of survival. Gabriel scanned the castle grounds for his own team, but found it impossible to discern them from his altitude. He fought back against a rising sense of panic as he watched the battle for the castle. If only he could do something about all those vile little ant-like Apollyons killing his friends and fellow mages.

Ants.

A memory bubbled up in the back of Gabriel's mind — a summer afternoon spent in the company of distant cousin intent on introducing him to a favorite cruel pastime.

Gabriel looked above to the noonday sun blazing in the pale cerulean sky. Magic formed even as he looked back down. Ling had taught him how to manipulate gravity to create a lens capable of warping and magnifying light. She used it like a massive telescope to see things at a distance. But a magnifying glass also had other uses.

Gabriel spotted five Apollyons standing atop the Round Tower casting bolts of lightning, streams of fire, and waves of other devastating magics against fifteen or so Grace Mages trapped in the yard of the Middle Ward. Uncertain how big to make the lens, or how much to bend and concentrate the light that would flow through it, Gabriel elected the most reliable option — making it as large and powerful as possible. As the magic creating the gravity lens coalesced, he estimated it stretched nearly a mile in diameter. A wave of anger rushed through him as he focused the gravity lens on the five Apollyons attacking his fellow Grace Mages.

Unimaginable brightness blotted out the landscape below, centered on the Round Tower. An explosion of stone and light followed for a second before Gabriel released the magic of the gravity lens. The whole top half of the tower had been vaporized. Stone, melted to magma-like rivulets, streamed down the side of the structure's remnants. No sign remained that the Apollyons might have escaped.

Shocked by the level of destruction he had wrought, as well as the potential deaths of the five Apollyons, Gabriel barely noticed the bending of space-time around him as a swarm of eight Apollyons appeared in the nearby air to attack him. He leapt through space himself as they arrived.

He had a strategy now. He might have to destroy the castle to save it, but the alternative would be worse.

Gabriel appeared in the middle of a magical skirmish between two Apollyons and a team of six Grace Mages in the Upper Ward courtyard outside the state apartments. The Apollyons spun to redirect their attacks toward Gabriel but found him already focusing his anger and magical energy as he materialized and raised his hand. The two Apollyons flew backward as though struck by a giant baseball bat, hurtling a hundred feet through the air like small black missiles before hitting the walls of the Prince Wales Tower with a painful sounding crunch. Even as the two unconscious Apollyons fell to the ground, Gabriel bent space around himself, catching the astonished looks of his fellow Grace Mages before he appeared again, high above the land.

As he formed the gravity lens again, Gabriel scanned the castle, looking for his next target. A flame erupted from the ground, capturing his attention. Three Apollyons in the Lower Ward fought a circle of twelve Grace Mages, attacking from the vantage of the Mary Tudor Tower. Gabriel's rage against the invaders felt like a furious fire in his breast. He focused the gravity lens and a cloud of light and earth erupted in the Lower Ward. As the dust settled, a massive crater of charred soil twenty feet in diameter smoked in the ground. Gabriel released the gravity lens and teleported through space as he felt several Apollyons jumping to his location.

He appeared in the Royal Gardens in the middle of four Apollyons fighting against a circle of nine Grace Mages. One of the Apollyons looked over his shoulder. Gabriel glared at the man he had come to despise, the bonfire of hatred in his heart taking manifest form. A wall of flame exploded around the Dark Mages, billowing into the sky as it became a cyclone of fire and wind, carrying away the four Apollyons.

Gabriel pushed the tornado of flame across the garden grounds, directly toward two other Apollyons fighting a lone Time Mage who jumped through space around them, the steel blade of his sword flashing in the sunlight. Gabriel recognized him. Hans. One of Akikane's best students. The young man stared in astonishment as the fiery whirlwind swept up the couple of Apollyons and carried them toward the edge of the grounds.

Gabriel heard two screams, which seemed distinguished amid all the other sounds of terror around him. These voices sounded entirely too high-pitched and too distraught.

Children.

He frantically looked around, knowing he needed to jump again soon. There. A boy and a girl, ages six and eight, hiding under a bench in the gardens. How had they gotten there? There were very few children in the castle, and they should have been in the school room within the private apartments.

Gabriel jumped through space to the children. They screamed even louder as he appeared suddenly, crouching down beside them. Fortunately, they quickly recognized him.

"Gabriel!" The girl threw her arms around Gabriel's neck, and he felt the flame of anger within him flare again. He had to protect them.

"The Goblins are attacking!" The boy clutched at Gabriel's arm.

With so few of them around, everyone knew the names of all the children. Leah and Liam. Brother and sister. Both born in the castle. Their parents both Time Mages. Hopefully, both still lived.

"Hiding is good, but we need to find someplace safer for you." Gabriel tried to smile reassuringly. By the children's reactions, it more closely resembled a scowl. He held them both tight, more for their comfort than practicality, and jumped again. They appeared a moment later in a dimly lit room of stone blocks and iron bars.

"The dungeon," Leah said, her voice squeaking. She held him tighter.

"The cellars," Gabriel said. "You'll be safe here." Electric bulbs flickered. The emergency generators were probably under attack. Gabriel used Fire Magic to light two old oil lamps bolted to the walls.

"But it's dark!" Liam said, his eyes filled with panic.

"Would you rather be down here by yourselves, or up there with the goblins?" Gabriel slowly and gently pulled the children's hands from his arms.

"We'd rather be with Mommy and Daddy." Leah wiped her nose on the back of her sleeve.

"You'll be with them soon." Gabriel hoped it proved true. He had seen a lot of fallen Grace Mages on the castle grounds above. "I need to go now."

"Are you going to stop them?" Liam sniffed and rubbed his eyes.

"I'm going to do my best." Gabriel hoped his best would be enough. And soon enough. He sensed the rage begin to burn brightly within him once again.

"Make sure they don't come back." Leah frowned in barely controlled anger.

"Stay here."

Gabriel warped the space around himself and once more appeared high above the castle.

As he completed the jump, he realized his mistake. A space-time seal slipped around him as a barrage of Malignant magics assaulted his mind and body in rapid succession. Eight Apollyons floated in the air around him. They had countered his strategy more quickly than he had anticipated.

He drew on all the power of the magical imprints he held yet still found himself barely able to keep the onslaught at bay. Eight Apollyons were a match for him.

Relying, as they did, on their connection to their duplicates holding negative imprints at sites of great violence, rather than concatenate crystals, the Apollyons could be extraordinarily powerful. However, their powers, like all mages' powers, came from how many imprints they could hold. If nearly fifty Apollyons were at the castle, that left few able to provide them with imprints. Especially if more were involved in the attack on the Dresden outpost. Unless there were more duplicate Apollyons than the Council suspected.

"We are stronger than you." The Apollyons all looked the same and dressed the same, so Gabriel didn't bother wondering which one spoke. He saw anger in their eyes, and, for the first time, fear. He didn't have to read their minds to know their thoughts. They wanted to kill him. Badly.

"We will always be stronger." Another Apollyon.

He hoped they could not so easily intuit the icy fear suddenly grasping at his heart, threatening to freeze the rage blazing there since the battle began. A sweat broke out along his face and back as he focused on repelling the Apollyons' magics.

"How many of you are there these days?" Gabriel might as well try to acquire some useful information while he had the opportunity. Assuming he lived through the encounter, it might prove important.

"Enough." Several Apollyons answered in unison.

"If it were really enough, the Great Barrier would be gone." The Council suspected that Apollyon would need to make at least 108 copies of himself to have any hope of destroying The Great Barrier of Probability. If he had created that many twins, why would he delay?

"It will be gone soon enough." The Apollyons spoke in unison. It felt like listening to a demented choir. "As will you."

As the Apollyons' last words faded, their magical attacks, which had not ceased during the conversation, abated momentarily. With his next breath, Gabriel discovered why. No air occupied the space surrounding him, trapping him in an airless space-time seal, exactly like he had done to the first three Apollyons he'd encountered.

The eight Apollyons still spoke, but with no air to bring the sound waves of their voices to his ears, Gabriel could only see their lips moving. They appeared to be gloating, but he could hear none of it. The physics of the situation apparently escaped them. Gabriel might have tried to read their lips if more urgent matters, like breathing, hadn't required his attention.

Through a haze of terror, his mind noticed two things simultaneously. First, suffocating from lack of air felt nothing like the sensation of drowning. Neither was pleasant, both would kill you, but lack of air seemed to create less fright. The second thing he noticed provided him a sliver of hope. The Apollyons used the same method of suffocation against him as he had against their twins, but incompletely. While they held him in place with a field of gravity, they devoted most of their energies to maintaining the space-time seal.

Gasping for airless breaths, the fiery sensation of his lungs becoming a physical manifestation of the anger burning in his breast, Gabriel abandoned his struggles against the space-time seal and focused all the power of his magic into two separate courses. He thrust himself earthward, even as he again formed a gravity lens above himself. The lens did not stretch as wide as previous versions, but it proved more than sufficient in its magnifying power.

He forced his way through the magical chains of gravity holding him aloft moments before the sky around him exploded in heat and light. The concussion from the explosion of super-heated air hit him like a crashing wave.

He tumbled through the sky, temporarily unconscious, arms fluttering, the Sword of Unmaking slipping from his grasp. He blinked his eyes with awareness, gasping in shock as he rushed toward the ground below. He concentrated on reclaiming the imprints of the concatenate crystal bracelet, using its magical energy to arrest his descent at the last possible second.

Gabriel hung inches above the ground, feeling as though he were a speeding train that had hit a mountain wall. He lowered himself to the grass of the Middle Ward lawn and sat up. The Sword of Unmaking struck the ground beside him, burying itself nearly to the hilt in the soft grass. Gabriel jumped, his heart pounding in his chest from his narrow escape and near impalement from his own sword.

In the brief moments following, he noted the absence of the rage that had so consumed him during the battle. He knew its source. The Malignant imprints he wielded to defend the castle affected his mind. He had trained to avoid their effects, but never with this many dark imprints, and never against a foe as ruthless as the attacking Apollyons.

He would have to worry about the consequences of this anger after the army of Dark Mages had been defeated.

Around him, the battle to save the castle still raged, Apollyons attacking in groups of threes and fours and hammering teams of Grace Mages with wave after wave of Malignant magic. Gabriel rolled to his feet, straining to pull the Sword of Unmaking from the ground as he tried to assess the battlefield and quickly determine a new strategy for defending the castle.

He found little time to formulate a new set of tactics. He saw something equally as important as saving the castle. Across the yard, beneath the broad branches of an oak tree, four Apollyons waged a battle of horrendous magic against Elizabeth and the members of the Chimera team.

Gabriel jumped through space, appearing beside the fallen ruins of the still-smoking Round Tower. The acrid odor stabbed at his nostrils as he raised the Sword of Unmaking above his shoulder. The four Apollyons, twenty feet away, turned like limbs of a single body to see him standing at their sides, sword raised in challenge.

Gabriel felt the rage rekindled within, searing hot as he lowered the sword in a swift arc, the mountainous wall of rubble behind him flying into the air like a million stone projectiles traveling faster than the eye could track. The wall of debris crashed through the four Apollyons, carrying them across the yard and slamming them into the North Terrace wall.

Gabriel disappeared and reappeared beside Elizabeth and his team. They looked exhausted, each sporting at least one obvious wound. He would have sworn they had been the ones hit with a wall of rubble. At least they were all still alive.

"Gabriel." Elizabeth sighed, wiping dust and sweat from her face. "At least one of us is having some success in defending the castle."

"Was that you who blew up the Round Tower?" Rajan bent over to catch his breath.

"Yes." Gabriel looked around. He didn't want to stay in any one place too long, especially near Elizabeth and the team. It presented too great a risk. He couldn't jeopardize them like that. Not with how strongly the Apollyons wanted him dead.

"That was brilliant." Teresa placed her hand on his shoulder. "But you had us worried."

"I'm fine." Gabriel looked at Teresa, grateful for her touch, but still too possessed by anger at the invaders to offer his customary smile. He turned to Elizabeth. "Do you have it?"

"Yes." Elizabeth patted the pocket of her tunic. "I thought it would be safer with me, but I'm beginning to suspect that was a mistake."

"Do you think they're here for it?" Gabriel asked, looking around.

"Among other things." Elizabeth frowned. "Yes. I'm sure of it."

"You have to protect Councilwoman Elizabeth at all costs," Gabriel said to Ohin, his voice tight with passion.

"That is what we've been doing." Ohin's voice sounded weary and annoyed.

"Not here in the open." Gabriel looked around at his friends, his heart pounding with fear for them, and also what it might mean if Elizabeth were captured. "You have to hide. Try the cellars."

"We can't hide when the castle is under attack." Ling looked like she might fight Gabriel for suggesting the notion.

"He's right." Everyone looked at Elizabeth. "It's more important than the castle."

"I'll find you when it's over." Gabriel turned to go, gently sliding Teresa's hand from his shoulder. He wanted to turn to her and tell her...tell her what? He had no time to puzzle through his feelings for her.

"What will you do?" Marcus gestured to Gabriel's singed clothes and bruised face. "You look half-dead."

"I'll think of something." Gabriel hoped he would.

"They are all sharing one mind," Sema said, reaching out to wipe a smudge of soot from Gabriel's face. "Try to use that if you can."

Gabriel felt space-time around them warping and knew the other Apollyons had found them. As he jumped away through space, he tried to grab the materializing Apollyons and take them with him. There were six of them. He managed to grab four. Hopefully Elizabeth and the team could cope with the other two and then find a secure place to take shelter.

Gabriel and his four captive Apollyons appeared on the roof of St. George's Chapel. The four were not as disoriented as he had hoped they might be, and they seemed intent on calling for reinforcements. Gabriel felt seven more Apollyons arriving via the warping of space as he jumped again himself.

Sema's idea had given him the glimmerings of a plan, but he would need to find and restrain a lone Apollyon for it to work. Unfortunately, the Apollyons knew they were vulnerable alone and only attacked in groups. Gabriel repeatedly jumped through space from one end of the castle to the other, alighting for a moment to survey the battleground before jumping again in search of a solitary Apollyon.

After twenty-plus jumps, he found one fighting three Grace Mages near the Military Knight's Lodgings, a fallen fellow Apollyon at his feet. Eight Grace Mages also lay on the ground, some far too motionless to be alive. A Time Mage held the lone Apollyon from jumping through space while one Fire and one Wind Mage attacked.

Gabriel studied the scene for a moment, feeling the anger flare in his heart. Raising his hands, he used Wind Magic to pull the Apollyon to him in a single, jarring motion. The Apollyon crossed fifteen feet in a fraction of a second, Gabriel's hands reaching out to clasp the man's skull as he came to a halt.

Remembering his lessons in Kumaradevi's arena, his fiery rage blazing even brighter at the memory, Gabriel concentrated all of his magical energy into the Soul Magic he arrayed against the Apollyon in his grasp. The Apollyon struggled for a moment, then went rigid, a high-pitched wail bubbling forth from his lips. Gabriel pressed on, reaching into the Apollyon's mind and searching for the man's connection to his twins. After a moment, he found it — a whirlwind of voices. Voices filled with concern. As Gabriel pushed farther, pouring more caustic Soul Magic into the link between the Dark Mages, the whirlwind of voices became a cyclone of screams.

Gabriel opened his eyes and looked around, trying to gauge the effect his Soul Magic had on the army of Apollyons. From his vantage on the side of the Lower Ward, he could see several Apollyons grasping their heads, immobile with pain. He could also feel them fighting back along the links that connected them to the Apollyon quaking before him.

Gabriel took to the air once more, risking the use of some of his magical energy for flight, sparing a little more for the Wind Magic necessary to hold the convulsing, lone Apollyon beside him.

He came to a halt several hundred feet above the castle grounds and looked down. The tide of the battle had changed. The Apollyons stood motionless and under attack by the remaining Grace Mages. Gabriel noticed several other people not moving.

Teresa lay on the grass where he had left her in the Middle Ward. Elizabeth lay beside her, as did the rest of the team. Three Apollyons stood clasping their heads in agony nearby. Gabriel knew he could not continue to hold the Soul Magic spell on the Apollyons for long, and could never hope to keep it in place while helping his fallen companions.

Gabriel released the Wind Magic holding the Apollyon beside him in the air at the same time he undid the Soul Magic trapping the Dark Mages like beetles in amber. He glanced at the screaming Apollyon as the man plunged to the ground. Against all his better judgment, Gabriel felt sorry for him. Not sorry enough to quell the anger still swaying him, nor enough to slow the Dark Mage's descent, but sorry, nonetheless.

Gabriel jumped through space, appearing beside Teresa and the others. He scanned Teresa's unconscious form with Heart-Tree Magic and found her mildly concussed but otherwise uninjured. Fearing an attack, he glanced up, his eyes widening in surprise as he watched the army of Apollyons disappear from the castle grounds while they recovered from Gabriel's Soul Magic.

He quickly examined his other unconscious teammates, finding nothing life-threatening in their injuries. As Ohin moaned, Gabriel knelt next to Elizabeth. He frowned as he probed her with his magical senses. A deep unconsciousness held her mind, a powerful Soul Magic curse clinging to her brain like black tar on exposed skin. The magic-induced coma gripped her mind completely.

Gabriel could not guess how much time it would take to cure her from the spell. Probing the curse, seeing how deeply it reached into Elizabeth's mind, he could not be certain that she would ever be cured. It did, however, explain the uniform state of his teammates. Close proximity to a curse that powerful could easily have rendered them instantly unconscious.

Gritting his teeth in anger, he checked Elizabeth's tunic pocket and cursed. Empty. One of the Apollyons must have it. But which one? He looked around as more of Dark Mages fled from the castle and the defensive attacks by the Grace Mages. It could be any one of them. Could be, but more likely one who had been close to Elizabeth when Gabriel started his attack. There had been several close by. Three were still left, battling off a team of Grace Mages as they tried to recover one of their fallen duplicates.

Gabriel stood up, looking around. How to make sense of the pattern? So much movement. So much activity. Except...one place. One person. Someone not moving. Someone in black, hiding behind a fallen wall. Odd. Why would one of the Apollyons be hiding? Why not simply jump through time with the others?

Then Gabriel realized the fallen wall concealed the hiding Apollyon from the view of his fellow duplicates in the courtyard. The rogue Apollyon wasn't trying to avoid capture by the Grace Mages — he awaited the retreat of the other Apollyons.

Gabriel ducked down behind a nearby fallen tree and watched the rogue Apollyon. The last of the other Apollyons had finally departed. Gabriel waited, but did not sense a disturbance in the space-time continuum for nearly a minute. As he watched the lone Apollyon, he noticed something in the Dark Mage's hand. Was that a flash of red leather? Did this Apollyon have Elizabeth's notebook?

He felt the Apollyon begin to warp time and space to jump away, free from his brothers.

Gabriel knew he only had one chance of retrieving the notebook. He would have to try shadowing the rogue Apollyon to ghost his time travel path, following him like a bloodhound tracking the scent of a fox.

He glanced over at Elizabeth, Ohin, and the others and then looked back to see the rogue Apollyon disappear. He could feel the trail with his space-time sense, but he couldn't follow too closely or the Apollyon would sense him. Too far away and he would never be able to perceive the faint trail of the relic the rogue Apollyon used to travel through time.

Gabriel waited as long as he could, nearly a full ten seconds, and then warped the fabric of space-time around himself to follow the mysterious rogue Apollyon, hoping to recover the notebook that might otherwise give the Dark Mage the long-sought knowledge of how to destroy the Great Barrier of Probability.

As Gabriel departed the castle grounds, leaping through space and time toward an unknowably dangerous destination, he felt a hand clasp around his shoulder.

CHAPTER 7
SIEGE MENTALITY

Gabriel ignored the hand on his shoulder. Whoever grabbed ahold of him wasn't trying to attack, so he disregarded the fingers grasping him tightly. He needed all his concentration to follow the rogue Apollyon. Ghosting a Time Mage, particularly a mage as powerful and experienced as the rogue Apollyon, would be no simple task. As the whiteness of space-time travel faded, Gabriel held onto it, keeping himself and his mysterious companion on the edge of materializing with the rogue Apollyon.

To surreptitiously follow another Time Mage jumping through time without their knowledge, one needed not only to sense the specific warping of space-time, but also the signature of the relic being used to determine a time and location in history.

The whiteness signaling the contraction of space-time at the end of a jump continued to linger. Gabriel could distinguish a forest beyond the horizon of the time barrier around him. He could also perceive the rogue Apollyon making another jump.

Gabriel allowed the whiteness to collapse around him for a fraction of a second, seeing the forest he had sensed, large pine trees looming overhead. His space-time sense stretched to its limit, he caught the fading tendrils of the rogue Apollyon's jump and thrust himself into the chase.

Gabriel had spent months with Ohin practicing how to avoid allowing another Time Mage to track him while making jumps. This training also resulted, not surprisingly, in Gabriel being very good at tracking Time Mages jumping away from him. He pursued the rogue Apollyon through repeated jumps in various times and places in history. His prey took no chances, using a different relic for each jump — taking them to rural China in what looked like the country's medieval period, then to a barren island in the middle of a rock-strewn sea, and to an empty apartment in what might have been New York City in the 1920s. The rogue Apollyon made eight jumps in all.

Gabriel held the whiteness at the end of the final jump long enough to make sure the rogue Apollyon would not depart again, then nudged himself back into blackness. He warped space-time ever so slightly and arrived a full thirty seconds in the past, a hundred feet from where the rogue Apollyon would appear.

Gabriel had only seconds to take in his surroundings and confront the enigmatic companion still clutching at his shoulder. He stood near the wall of what appeared to be a courtyard within a medieval castle.

He grabbed the hand at his shoulder and twisted from the wrist, as Ling had taught him in their many martial arts lessons. As he turned around to face the owner of the hand, he found his own wrist bent back in a counter move.

"Ouch, you idiot." He let go of the hand and spun on his heel at the sound of Teresa's voice.

"What are you doing?" Gabriel looked around the crowded castle courtyard beyond Teresa's shoulder.

"I'm keeping you from doing something stupid again." Teresa straightened up to her full height, which left her an inch taller than Gabriel, even after a year of male adolescent growth.

"I'm not doing something stupid, I'm tracking one of the Apollyons." Gabriel stepped between the oaken beams of an open-faced lean-to built along the stone walls of the castle so they would attract less attention. He didn't think anyone had seen them arrive, but if they continued to argue, someone would surely notice them.

"You ran off by yourself again. How is that not stupid?" Teresa stepped beside Gabriel under the edge of the lean-to and looked around. She shimmered briefly, and her clothing shifted to become similar to the dress of the medieval villagers they could see jamming the inner courtyard of the castle.

Gabriel followed Teresa's example, remembering to adjust the coloring of his skin to appear paler like the people around him. As a final touch, he made the Sword of Unmaking slung over his back appear to be a small bundle of sticks.

70

"I had no choice but to go alone." Gabriel actually felt relieved seeing Teresa, and this emotion found expression through his tone of voice. He also felt a sense of peace as he realized the anger dominating his mind since touching the Malignant imprints of the bracelet had finally begun to fade.

"I saw one of the Apollyons waiting for the others to leave. I think he had Councilwoman Elizabeth's notebook. So I followed him."

"What notebook, and where is this Apollyon?" Teresa looked furtively around the castle's bailey yard.

"The notebook contains everything known about the Great Barrier of Probability." Gabriel pointed discreetly to the other side of the castle grounds. "And the rogue Apollyon is going to arrive over there in about two seconds."

Teresa followed the direction of Gabriel's finger and they both watched as the rogue Apollyon blinked into existence in the shadowed recesses between two thatch-roofed stables. He did not bother to change his appearance as he stepped out into the throng of people working and milling about the courtyard. Gabriel could feel the Soul Magic the rogue Apollyon used to turn people's attention away from his presence.

"We have to follow him, but we can't use magic." Gabriel started to walk in the direction of the rogue Apollyon. "He might be able to sense it."

"So, what's the plan?" Teresa stepped quickly to catch up with Gabriel.

"We have to get the notebook back before the rogue Apollyon can decipher it." Gabriel tried to relax his mind while he walked. Without the aid of Soul Magic, he and Teresa would need to do everything possible to avoid attracting attention. Ohin and Akikane had taught him how to gently force the subtle energy of his being, the same energy he used to create magic, lower and lower into his body. Doing this lessened people's subconscious interest in him. Teresa called it putting her chi in her feet. Gabriel had no doubt she performed the same practice as she walked beside him.

"What kind of code is it written in?" Teresa asked.

"Elizabeth wrote it in a dead language using a special alphabet she created herself." Gabriel twisted sideways to avoid colliding with a soldier.

"Where does she find time for...never mind." Teresa ducked under a ladder carried by a man whose tool bag silently named him as a carpenter.

"We need to follow him and steal the notebook back, then escape without him tracking us." Gabriel slowed down, realizing they didn't need to follow the rogue Apollyon very far. The black-shrouded man walked through the front entrance of a small stone church built against the wall of the castle. What would an Apollyon be doing in a church?

"Now what?" Teresa asked as they stopped beside an open-sided foundry, a blacksmith's hammer strikes ringing out as he slowly forged a double-edged sword.

"We have to get inside and see what he does." Gabriel looked around the courtyard. It seemed awfully full of people from what he could remember about medieval castles. He could see soldiers high on the walls above, and several groups of them among the crowd of villagers in the courtyard. Some of the village men worked building stone and wooden structures along the walls while several women cooked in pots suspended by tripods above open fires. Children, looking even dirtier than their adult counterparts, raced through the spaces between clumps of peasants, or they sat huddled with their companions while gnawing on hard, dark bread.

"We should go back to the castle and get reinforcements." Teresa ignored their surroundings and stared at Gabriel. "We need help."

"I'd love to, but we can't." The more Gabriel looked at the courtyard and the walls of the castle, the more certain he became of that statement. "If we use magic to leave, the rogue Apollyon will sense it and flee."

"If we leave the castle, we can get far enough away. He'll never sense a thing." Teresa's voice sounded simultaneously hopeful and worried.

"We can't get out of the castle." Gabriel sighed and gestured to the mass of villagers packed into the castle's bailey. "The castle is under siege."

Teresa looked around and blinked as the truth of Gabriel's statement sank in.

"So let me sum up." Teresa sighed and raised her fingers, counting them off silently as she spoke. "We can't go back to our castle. We can't use magic. We need to steal a notebook back from one of the Apollyons so he can't use it to destroy the Great Barrier of Probability. We're trapped in a medieval castle under siege. And we have no idea what castle it is, whether or not everyone dies, or when that might happen."

"Actually, I think I do know what castle this is." Gabriel barely managed not to sigh.

"Okay, impress me." Teresa raised one eyebrow in curiosity.

"Based on the curves of those scalloped walls, I'd say we're in the middle bailey of Chateau Gaillard." Gabriel gestured to the castle walls, which curved into each other like a series of semicircular towers built right next to one another.

"Those walls are very distinctive. They were designed to make it harder to attack with projectiles. And see those arrow slits? The curves allow arrows to be fired from multiple angles. That's the inner bailey, and beyond those walls you can see a tower that has to be the keep. Behind the far walls is the Seine River. We're in the middle bailey, and back behind us, across a moat, is the outer bailey, facing the valley where the sieging soldiers are massed."

"I am so glad somebody pays attention during Ohin's history lectures." Teresa laughed lightly. "What do you know about the siege?"

"Based on the weather and the number of people still in the castle, I'd say we're near the beginning of it." Gabriel squinted as he tried to remember more details about Chateau Gaillard and the siege. He wished he had his copy of *The Time Traveler's Pocket Guide to History* with him. "The siege lasted six months, I think. This is probably sometime in December of 1203. King Philip of France won't capture the castle for a few months yet."

"Then we have plenty of time if we need it." Teresa breathed a little easier.

"Not really." Gabriel tilted his head in the direction of the villagers. "The lord of the castle, Roger de Lacy, I think, is going to realize any day now that all these people eat a lot of food. He's going to start kicking them out pretty soon."

"So…" Teresa gave Gabriel a look that worried him a little. "What are our chances if the two of us attack this lone-wolf Apollyon when he's not expecting it?"

"You mean assuming we don't use so much magic and attract so much attention that we create a bifurcation?" Gabriel had grown used to people telling him he could be impulsive and reckless. Not for the first time, he wondered how they never seemed to notice that Teresa was at least as impulsive and reckless as he. Reckless or not, her loyalty and bravery were beyond measure — as was his gratitude now at having her by his side.

"I've got the Sword of Unmaking and the pocket watch, but we have no idea what imbued artifacts he may have access to. He could have one concatenate crystal or several. It seems like he's hiding from his brothers, but if he connects with their power, we'd be lucky if we could survive a battle, much less win it."

"That's what I thought." Teresa's face brightened. "Which means we're going to have to be devious."

"Then it's a lucky thing for me that you tagged along." Gabriel found his mood had lightened considerably with the hint of assuredness on Teresa's lovely face.

"We need to sneak into that little chapel and see what this Apollyon is up to and get that notebook." She looked toward the church the rogue Apollyon had disappeared into. "So, what are we waiting for?"

CHAPTER 8
CASTLE SPIES

Gabriel and Teresa stepped though the slender doorway of the small chapel and paused for a moment, as much to let their eyes adjust to the darkened interior as to allow their nostrils to adapt to the odor.

The chapel had few windows. The outer wall of the castle dominated one whole side of the building, leaving only the opposite side to provide illumination from the sun. A handful of oil lamps, hung at strategic points around the space, added a dim, flickering yellow glow to the pale blue light of the overcast day that seeped through the heavily leaded glass windows.

No pews or benches lined the church floor. Medieval church parishioners normally stood for their weekly sermons. The majority of the forty or so refugees from the nearby village filling the chapel lay prone on the floor or leaned against the walls. The chapel housed all those too old, young, or sick to bear the strain of the frigid weather beyond its confines.

Gabriel noticed a thin man with tonsured hair and brownish-black robes kneeling in prayer beside an elderly woman coughing with some illness. Disease arising from humans crammed in close quarters with improper ventilation and poor sanitation proved a challenge for many castles under siege. If Gabriel remembered correctly, at least this castle had two interior wells. He wasn't sure about waste disposal, but he seemed to remember something about the siege ending when King Philip's men breached the castle walls by sneaking through a latrine chute.

"Not many places he could hide." Teresa stepped into the chapel and slid up against the wall. She was right. The open rafters of the chapel held no attics or balconies. Behind the altar,

Gabriel could see a door illuminated by the light of a window at the back of the chapel.

"Maybe he's in the priest's quarters behind the altar." Gabriel joined Teresa against the wall. "Or a cellar."

"I don't see any way down to a cellar, even if there is one." Teresa wrinkled her nose. The pungent smell of the oil lamps did little to cover the aroma of human sweat and excrement permeating the church. "I'd forgotten how much I love visiting the Middle Ages."

"After a couple of days without a bath, you'll hardly notice." Gabriel motioned toward the back of the chapel. "Let's see what we find."

He gingerly stepped between two women crouching with their babies on the floor nearby and focused his mind, keeping his subtle energies in control, pushing them down, making himself less noticeable. It took nearly a minute to navigate the length of the chapel in this fashion. Occasionally people glanced up from their tasks, women darning the holes of overworn clothes, children playing with small clay marbles, old men laughing at some shared memory, but inevitably their gazes slid away from the young mages like water flowing around rocks in a stream.

No villagers occupied the small vestibule behind the altar. Gabriel assumed that respect for the priest as much as their faith kept them from sprawling in the space. The side of the short corridor facing the courtyard outside held a darkly stained wooden door. A stone wall filled the other side of the vestibule. Something about this seemed a bit odd to Gabriel, but he found himself strangely unconcerned about it.

"I'll check it out," Gabriel said.

"I'll keep watch," Teresa said. "Be careful. He's probably in there."

Gabriel slowly crept down the hall. He glanced over his shoulder. Teresa stood where she could easily watch both him and the villagers in the nave.

He slipped beside the thick oak door and listened. He heard nothing from within. He pulled gently on the handle of the door, hoping the wrought-iron hinges nailed into the stone archway would prove well-oiled. The door swung toward him slowly. The hinges remained silent.

He tugged at the handle until a slender crack opened between the door and the frame.

Darkness filled the small, stone chamber. Gabriel risked pulling the door open enough to peer through, placing his eye to the opened slit. He closed his other eye and waited for his vision to adapt.

The room held nothing but a wash basin resting on a small table, a three-legged stool, a thin wooden bed, and a clay chamber pot.

Gabriel frowned and leaned back, pushing the door closed to what appeared to be the priest's private quarters. He turned to Teresa and shook his head at her questioning look. She frowned.

Gabriel mimicked her frown, but not because the room had been empty. Something else bothered him. The wall across from him seemed solid, but it lay a good seven feet from the side wall of the chapel, the outer wall of the castle. Odd, but nothing he needed to be concerned about.

Gabriel started to walk back to Teresa, but stopped. He frowned even deeper. He turned back to the wall and placed his hand on it, reaching out with his magic-sense. As he did so, the wall changed, revealing a door resting directly across from the one he had examined.

The rogue Apollyon had used Soul Magic to cloak the presence of the room. With so many villagers around, no one would know the room existed except for the priest, whose memory the rogue Apollyon could easily adjust.

The door to the hidden room sat slightly ajar. Gabriel took a long, slow breath, concentrating on his subtle energy and pushing it down into his toes. He took two quick, silent steps to the door and placed his eye to the inch-wide gap.

The room looked almost identical to the one across the hall. The rogue Apollyon sat on a rickety stool, hunched over a table. Councilwoman Elizabeth's notebook sat opened before him. He rubbed his forehead in frustration as he slowly flipped through the last pages of the thin, leather-bound book. The Dark Mage sighed heavily.

Gabriel eased away from the door, quickly retreating to Teresa's side. He guided her around the corner and out of sight of the rogue Apollyon's chamber.

"Is there a reason you were staring at that wall so closely?" A mild concern filled Teresa's face as she gently placed her hand on his chest. "You can't lose your mind on me while we're trapped in a castle under siege in the Middle Ages with an Apollyon wondering around."

"I'm not losing my mind." Gabriel found the warmth of Teresa's hand on his chest comforting — and extremely distracting at the same time.

"There's a door to another room. The rogue Apollyon used Soul Magic to cloak it."

Teresa looked around the corner of the wall to where the door should be and shook her head.

"I can't see a thing." She sounded annoyed to be so easily fooled by the rogue Apollyon's magic.

"What was he doing?"

"Nothing," Gabriel said. "He was looking at the notebook. Probably trying to figure out how to read it."

"If he had any sense, he would have gone to the future and tried to use a supercomputer to break the code," Teresa said. "Let's get out of here."

Outside the chapel, Gabriel and Teresa sat in the dirt beside a thatched-roof storage barn across the courtyard and considered their options. They had few.

"Would you like to sum up again?" Gabriel's tone sounded both teasing and tired. Exhaustion still clung to him from the battle to save their castle. It felt like he hadn't slept in days. He couldn't tell if his mind ached more than his body, but both needed rest. He longed for a hot shower, a hearty meal, and the comfort of his warm bed.

He consoled himself with the fact that he would finally have some time alone with Teresa.

"Let's see," Teresa said in a chipper tone of voice as she assumed a plastic smile. "We need to find food, but we can't disrupt the Primary Continuum, and since we're in a castle under siege, we'll be lucky to steal a few potatoes."

"No potatoes yet." Gabriel's mouthed watered at the thought of a big baked potato with melted cheddar cheese and sour cream. "Potatoes come from Peru. They don't end up in Europe until the 1700s."

"Thank you, Mr. History." Teresa nudged Gabriel playfully with her elbow. "So, to continue with the litany of our predicament, we'll be lucky to steal some old parsnips. Those *are* parsnips that woman over there is cooking, right?"

"They smell like parsnips." Gabriel swallowed to keep from drooling as his stomach rumbled.

"So, food will be hard to come by, *and* we need to find a place to sleep that's out of the cold but where we can watch that chapel in case the rogue Apollyon leaves, *and* we need to spy on him often enough to figure out how to steal the notebook back *before* he decodes it but without using magic, *and* we have to escape before he can kill us both." Teresa's plastic smile melted into a scowl.

They sat together in silence for a few minutes. Gabriel contemplated all the points in Teresa's list. The hardest part would be getting the notebook from the rogue Apollyon. But none of it would be easy. When he had imagined spending time alone with Teresa, it had been under circumstances more amorous than arduous. He suddenly found himself aware of how close she sat to him. He could feel the heat of her arm where their shoulders touched.

"What's he up to?" Teresa put her chin in the palm of her hand, staring the chapel doors.

"Plotting to take over the universe?" Gabriel could not keep himself from noticing how lovely Teresa looked, her hair falling down around her shoulders, across her cheek…

"No, why is he here?" Teresa tilted her head in curiosity and squinted.

"He's hiding from the others?" Gabriel found he could not manage to have distracting thoughts about Teresa's many attractive qualities and hold a conversation at the same time. He stared at the old chapel and tried to concentrate on the problem at hand.

"But why hide in this place?" Teresa crinkled her brow in frustration. "Why this castle at this time? Is it random? Was he planning this all along? He went right for the chapel when he arrived. He must have been here before."

"You're right." Gabriel's eyes went wide as he thought about Teresa's words. "He's not merely a rogue, he's a defector. He's been planning his escape from the others for some time."

"But why?" Teresa said. "Why now and why here?"

"This must be someplace the others wouldn't think to come." Gabriel placed his chin in his palm in unconscious mimicry of Teresa as he thought about the question. "It's a place where there are imprints he can use, but not many. Not yet, at least."

"If there aren't many imprints, the other Apollyons wouldn't be interested."

"No, they wouldn't. But their minds are connected. That's how I managed to get them to abandon their attack on Windsor Castle. This Apollyon would have needed to keep this place a secret while he was plotting his escape."

"How could he do that?"

"He'd have to suppress the connection. I've been learning how to do something similar with Sema. But the rogue Apollyon would have to do it all the time."

Gabriel suddenly realized what that might mean. "He can't sleep for fear the connection will return and the other Apollyons will find him."

Teresa turned to Gabriel. "So, we need to get the notebook before he goes crazy from sleep deprivation, or before he falls asleep and his brothers come for him."

"Exactly." Gabriel's stomach rumbled as much to protest the lack of food as the constant stress of the day. He heard Teresa's stomach growl in friendly response to his own. Ignoring the seriousness of their dilemma, he laughed aloud. "We should do something about that."

"Yes," Teresa said, laughing lightly. "I'll find us a hiding place while you rustle up some dinner. It looks like it's going to be a long, cold night."

"Deal," Gabriel said as he stood to his feet and offered a hand to help Teresa up. "I'll see if I can find something hot that the Primary Continuum won't miss much."

It took Gabriel longer to round up sufficient supplies for the night than he expected, but the process turned out to be easier than he'd feared. Village men, guarded by castle soldiers, distributed food twice a day to the villagers trapped by the siege.

He had considered trying to steal the food, but while he could escape casual notice by controlling his subtle energy, he lacked the skills of a true thief. If he were caught, it could cause trouble in a number of ways. More than once, he wished Marcus and his deft hands were there to help.

While waiting in line for the food, he tried his best to avoid attracting attention and listened to the conversations around him in hopes of better ascertaining how long the siege had been in place. A half-hour in line brought him within ten villagers of the food.

"Hi."

Gabriel turned to see a young girl about his age with long, stringy black hair and ice-blue eyes.

"Thanks for saving me a place." The girl grinned wide, her white teeth a stark contrast with her soot-smudged face.

Gabriel glanced around, eyes wide, unsure what to do. He tried to push his subtle energy down into the ground. Across the courtyard he could see Teresa staring at him, a look of curiosity falling across her face.

"Sure." Gabriel assumed she had mistaken him for some other young boy in the castle.

"I hate starting at the back of the line." The girl stepped even closer to Gabriel. He considered stepping away, but didn't want to attract attention from the men and women in line behind them. "Do you think the Lord will toss us out? That's the rumor. There isn't enough food to last, and the Lord will throw us to King Philip's wolves."

Gabriel's mind teetered between fear and panic as he tried to figure out how to respond to the girl's question. Interacting with people could be very dangerous to the timeline, easily creating alternate branches of time by throwing off the person's own timeline. He reached out with his space-time sense but could find no impending danger from speaking with the girl. He settled on something bland that might discourage further conversation.

"Maybe."

"You don't talk much do you?" The girl laughed and nudged him with her shoulder.

Gabriel could feel his face warming from the casual affections of the strange girl. Her attractiveness only helped amplify his discomfort. Something about her reminded him of Justine back at the castle. He risked a glance across the courtyard. Teresa still stared at him. The look on her face had changed from curious to incredulous.

"My name is Agrace." She stared at him until he couldn't help but return her gaze.

"Gabriel." He wanted to kick himself for using his real name, but he and Teresa hadn't had time to come up with a cover story of who they were in case they had to talk to people. The whole point was *never* to talk to people.

"Like the angel." Agrace grinned again. "We could use some angels now. We're next. You go first. For saving me a place."

"Thanks." Gabriel smiled back at Agrace, feeling like an idiot for thanking her.

The men handing out food gave him dried meat, cheese, bread, and apples. The cheese looked hard, the apples soft, but the bread seemed fresh and still felt warm against his hand. He even managed to convince the men that he had a sick sister too ill to join the line but in need of rations all the same. His space-time sense told him taking the food posed no risk of changing the time line. He assumed the castle still had enough provisions to support two extra mouths without endangering the Primary Continuum.

They handed him the food in a small piece of cloth and he turned to walk away.

"I hope your sister gets better."

Gabriel looked back, seeing Agrace waving at him.

"Thanks." He turned and walked even quicker, wandering through the crowd a bit before heading toward Teresa, checking over his shoulder to make sure Agrace couldn't see him. She left the line and disappeared onto the sea of villagers milling about the castle bailey. He hurried to find Teresa standing beside a stable not too far from the church entrance.

"Who's the girl?" Teresa asked as Gabriel handed her the rag-wrapped food.

"She came out of nowhere and wouldn't stop talking." Gabriel's frustration elicited a poorly timed squeaking of his voice.

"She's very cute." Teresa opened the cloth and inspected their supplies.

"Her name's Agrace." Gabriel regretted mentioning it when he saw the frown on Teresa's face.

"No signs of a bifurcation being created from your little chat?" Teresa took one of the apples and sunk her teeth into it.

"No." Gabriel also grabbed an apple. "Which is weird. I would have thought I'd feel something, even if a bifurcation wasn't likely."

"Not so weird if you think about it."

The sudden sadness in Teresa's eyes gave Gabriel pause. He considered the situation for a moment and felt a wave of sorrow well up within him, twinned with a painful understanding.

"Oh."

Gabriel took a sullen bite of his apple. Talking to Agrace wasn't likely to cause a bifurcation because Agrace wasn't likely to survive the siege. That knowledge gave him yet another reason to hope he didn't need to talk to the beautiful, blue-eyed girl again.

"I found a place for us to hide at night." Teresa pointed to a narrow alleyway between the stable and a small storage shack. From the scraps of broken bark on the ground, Gabriel surmised it had been used to store wood, another scarce commodity within the castle walls during the siege.

"It's perfect." Gabriel stepped inside the thin passage and turned around. They would be able to keep their backs to the castle wall and still see the front of the chapel across the bailey yard.

"It's going to be a little cold." Teresa scowled. "What's the point of being a Fire Mage when you can't create a fire to keep warm?"

"I'll see if I can find us a blanket." Gabriel took another bite of his apple and felt his mood lighten. It felt like they were making some progress in their stakeout, even if they didn't have a clear plan yet.

As shadows draped the castle courtyard and the stars began to awaken in the evening sky, he saw a number of villagers with blankets, but none who seemed to have a spare they might be willing to offer, or one he could pilfer when they weren't looking.

His search took him as far as the Outer Bailey, across a thin drawbridge above a water-filled moat twenty feet below. Eventually, he admitted he would need to use magic to get a blanket. It was too risky to access the imprints of the pocket watch, much less the Sword of Unmaking, so he settled on the imprints on his own consciousness, those he had acquired when risking his life to save his classmates in that bus at the bottom of a river. It seemed so long ago.

Gabriel had been practicing meditations with Ohin and Akikane to concentrate and amplify his own imprints and subtle energy. He would never be as strong as with his pocket watch, but after months of steady work, he could manage a time jump with nothing but his own imprints. He couldn't take anyone with him, but it gave him a modicum of peace knowing that if he were ever held captive by Kumaradevi again, he might be able to escape.

He used as little magic as possible, fearing any magic at all might alert the rogue Apollyon to his presence. He found a soldier with two blankets and, after thoroughly scanning the man with his space-time sense to make sure no bifurcations might erupt, he used of a subtle bit of Soul Magic to convince the man to hand over a threadbare bedcover.

When Gabriel returned to Teresa, he found her sitting with her back against the castle wall staring at the chapel entrance, her arms around her knees, chin resting between them. She accepted the blanket eagerly, and even more so, Gabriel's added heat beside her. They huddled close, and Gabriel ate what remained of the food, gnawing on a lump of heavily salted, dried meat while watching the chapel door and trying not to think about how warm Teresa felt beside him, or how much he wanted to put his arm around her, or how nice she smelled. How could she smell nice after the day they'd had? Could she smell him? He doubted he smelled good.

Why was he having these thoughts at all? Why was he always having these thoughts lately? Well, not lately. For months. Teresa was like a sister. The whole team felt like his family. He loved them like the family he had lost. But Teresa wasn't his sister. Not really. She was certainly a friend. A friend he kept thinking about kissing. He glanced at her, seeing her dark eyes reflecting the dim, shifting light from a nearby fire in the courtyard. She looked angelic.

Gabriel turned away. Looking at her didn't help cease the thoughts of kissing her. And what would happen if he did kiss her? Would she want that? She didn't seem to. But then, how did you know when a girl wanted you to kiss her? And wouldn't she rather be kissing Jan? Jan, the handsome, older boy.

Gabriel sighed.

"I'm bored, too." Teresa sighed, as well. "You're not the exciting company I thought you'd be on a stakeout."

"Sorry." Gabriel squinted through the darkness at the chapel door as he rephrased the question he had been asking himself — why would Teresa want to kiss the boring boy she probably thought of as a little brother?

"Let's go check up on our rogue Apollyon." That wasn't boring.

"Excellent idea." Teresa shifted sideways, excitement flickering in her eyes alongside the reflected firelight. "If he's asleep, we can sneak in, steal the notebook, and be in our nice warm beds in the castle in no time. Assuming you didn't destroy my bedroom while you were saving the castle."

"It's probably still there." Gabriel rose to his feet. "It might have some smoke damage, though."

"Everything has been so crazy since we left the castle." Teresa stood up, letting the blanket fall to the ground as she held Gabriel's eyes. "I should have told you this before, but you were amazing. You're the only reason we'll have a castle to go home to. It was very impressive."

Gabriel couldn't help himself. He fidgeted under Teresa's stare. The look in her eyes was both grateful and...and what? What was that look?

"Thanks."

"Now let's see if I can impress *you* with my abilities by sneaking into a church full of sleeping villagers." Teresa walked out of the alleyway.

"What makes you think you're going alone?" Gabriel hastily stuffed the blanket in a corner and hurried after Teresa.

CHAPTER 9
WAITING GAME

Getting into the church proved far easier than crossing its inner expanse in near darkness while avoiding the dozens of sleeping villagers strewn about the straw-covered dirt floor. Gabriel and Teresa proceeded at a glacial pace, stepping gingerly over legs and arms and snoring heads, often feeling gently with their toes to make sure their feet would land on packed earth rather than soft flesh. By the time they reached the far side of the altar they were both dripping with sweat, even in the chill air of the chapel.

Relief filled Gabriel's mind as he discovered that the short corridor behind the pulpit and altar held no sleeping villagers. Gabriel wondered if it might not be due to the volume of the priest's snoring rumbling from behind his chamber door. Gabriel pointed to the opposite wall and beckoned Teresa to follow him as he leaned closer to listen. He cleared his mind of the Soul Magic the rogue Apollyon used to camouflage the little room and placed his ear against the door. Teresa did the same, although he knew that, to her, it would seem her head rested on a cold stone wall.

Gabriel had hoped to hear snoring noises similar to the priest's to indicate that the rogue Apollyon had fallen asleep. An opportunity to try and sneak in and steal back the notebook. Instead, he heard something far more disconcerting.

"Word, words, what do the words mean? What language? Is it a language? A code, yes. But what language in code? And the symbols? Have we seen those before? No. No. Have I seen those before?"

Gabriel saw the concern he felt mirrored silently in Teresa's eyes — it was past two in the morning, and their rogue Apollyon couldn't sleep for talking to himself.

"Can't see. Not enough light. No not the light. Can't see past the darkness. Yes. The light reveals. The darkness conceals. The darkness within conceals what? What am I concealing from her? What are they concealing from me? I should rest. No. No. No. No sleep. Mustn't sleep. They can find us in our sleep. No. No. They can find me. Me. They can find me in my sleep. No sleep. Words. Symbols. Patterns. That's what he always said. Look for the patterns. See the patterns and see the whole in the part of the whole that is part of the whole. Yes. Patterns."

Gabriel slowly stepped away from the door and into to the nave of the church. Teresa followed him as they warily made their way across the church floor, out through the courtyard, and back to their hiding spot. Neither spoke until the blanket once more wrapped them and their backs rested against castle stone.

Teresa cupped her hands and blew into them slowly, rubbing them together. "You've been alone with him more than anyone else. Is he always that crazy?"

"No." Gabriel imitated Teresa's strategy, using it to warm his own hands. "I think being able to hear each other's thoughts is driving them mad. Even more mad than they were before."

"And this one more mad than most."

"He's trying to escape them for a reason. But if he's turned against them, why would he want the notebook?"

"Leverage against them? To pay them off? To blackmail the Council?"

"If he does fall asleep, the other Apollyons may find him. But if he doesn't fall asleep, he might become even more unstable."

"And then the real fun will begin." Teresa yawned. "How long do you think he can go before he collapses into unconsciousness?"

"A lot longer than me." Gabriel could not resist answering Teresa's yawn with one of his own. He realized how heavy his eyelids felt. His body, mind, and heart ached with progressively deeper intensity. He closed his eyes. He might have said goodnight. Or he might not have.

At some point, he realized his dreams held sway over his mind. In one of these dreams, he again played the mysterious and complex board game with Vicaquirao. They sat in the middle of a narrow wooden bridge spanning a small stream running through a dune-swept desert.

"How can you predict the future?" Vicaquirao's dark brown eyes glittered in the midday sun as he took a blue stone and placed it on the board. "How can you know where a piece will end up when part of its motion is driven by chance?" He rolled the dice and turned the third ring of the board.

"You can't." Gabriel took a green stone and moved it two spaces toward the center, then rolled the dice and turned the second ring.

"True." Vicaquirao moved a red stone and captured the green stone that Gabriel had placed down a moment before. "However, if you look carefully, you can discern probabilities, and within the probabilities, potentialities. By looking for recurring motifs you can begin to assemble a hypothetical image of an emergent future state."

Vicaquirao rolled the dice. The fourth ring turned five spaces as a result.

"You mean you have to imagine the pattern of the board when the game is done." Gabriel took a yellow stone and captured a red stone, now conveniently at the edge of the fourth ring.

"Yes." Vicaquirao watched with amusement as Gabriel rolled the dice and turned the innermost ring. "And you must be willing to improvise in the face of luck. Both your opponent's and your own."

Vicaquirao's delight increased as he moved a blue stone from the inner ring to the open circle in the center of the board. Gabriel frowned at the pattern of red and blue stones on the board forming a perfect cross — one line of crimson, one line of cobalt.

"How?"

"You don't simply need to envision the final state of the board, you need to know what you want that final state to be."

Vicaquirao laughed as the wind gusted around them, a wall of sand blowing across the board and obliterating everything into dusty darkness.

Gabriel awoke, working his tongue as though gritty soil filled his mouth. As he rubbed his eyes, he decided finding water would be the first mission of the day. It took him a moment to realize Teresa no longer leaned against him. He bolted to his feet, tossing the blanket aside and dashing down the thin alley. He crashed into Teresa coming from the courtyard, sending two apples rolling back along the passageway.

"Morning to you, too." She rubbed her head and handed him the heel from a loaf of bread.

"Sorry." Gabriel accepted the bread and picked up the apples, handing one to Teresa. "When I woke up and you weren't here..."

"I saw the rogue Apollyon leaving the church, so I followed him." Teresa wiped dirt from the spongy apple.

"You should have woken me up." Gabriel again found his voice uncontrollably creaking and rising in pitch.

"I tried, but I couldn't wake you." Teresa squatted down to watch the church doors again. "I figured you needed the rest."

"Where did the rogue Apollyon go?"

"Shopping. He got some food and wine. I figured I might as well do the same. I stood in line after I knew he had gone back to the church." Teresa unslung a goat's bladder water skin and handed it to Gabriel.

"How did you steal a water skin?" Gabriel took a long, satisfying drink. The earth-chilled water tasted heavy in minerals.

"Let's just say I've learned a few things hanging around with Marcus for the last couple of years." Teresa bit into her piece of bread with zeal. "So what's the plan now?"

"We watch him and wait for an opportunity to get the notebook back." Gabriel chomped on his heel of bread, realizing Teresa's enthusiasm came from hunger, not the flavor of the loaf.

"How long do think that will take?" Teresa took the water skin back and sipped.

"A day, maybe." Gabriel took a bite of his apple, hoping its juices would help to soften the dry bread in his mouth, as he contemplated how long their mission might last.

Three days later, they sat in the same spot, eating the same meal, and wondering the same thoughts. The days had passed with excruciating monotony, nearly entirely consumed with the act of huddling together beneath the blanket in an attempt to ward off the chill air while keeping the church under constant observation. Twice a day they would take turns getting food and water. Twice a day they would sneak into the chapel to spy on the rogue Apollyon. Twice a day they would hear him muttering to himself, each time more erratically and unintelligibly than the last. He rarely left to get food and always returned directly to the hidden chamber at the back of the chapel.

On the second day, Gabriel had hoped they might try picking the Apollyon's pocket under the assumption that the notebook would always be in his possession. While the bulge in the breast of the Apollyon's black shirt clearly announced the presence of the notebook, neither Gabriel nor Teresa could figure out a way to liberate it from its well-buttoned pocket without being noticed.

Their best option would have been taking a page from Marcus's past and trying to rob the rogue Apollyon like a Highwayman, knocking him unconscious from behind and fleeing with the notebook. Unfortunately, the rogue Apollyon only ventured out during the busiest part of the day. Attacking him then would have risked attracting the attention of the villagers and possibly creating a bifurcation in the timeline. They had discussed several possible plans, but abandoned them all as unnecessarily risky.

By the afternoon of the fourth day, Gabriel wondered if he would ever feel warm again. The mid-December air regularly dropped to near freezing at night and hovered not much higher during the day. The need to snuggle beneath the blanket with Teresa, arms wrapped around each other for added warmth, became his only consolation. Unfortunately, the unrelenting noise of his chattering teeth drove any possible thoughts of romance straight from his mind.

"When we get home, I'm going to build the biggest bonfire the castle has ever seen." Teresa's breath clouded the air before them. "Then I'm going to sit right in the middle of it."

Gabriel laughed and then wondered if she might be serious. If ever a Fire Mage could sit unharmed in the middle of a bonfire, it would be Teresa. Imagining himself back at Windsor Castle warmed him a little, even if only in his heart. "It's odd to think of a place so large and strange as home."

"Some days it's hard to remember my real home." Teresa sighed. "It took me a long time to realize, or to admit to myself, that I was more

90

comfortable in the castle than I had been in my family's house. Not that I didn't love my family, or don't still love my family, but I always felt out of place there. It wasn't their fault. My mom and dad were the best parents I could have hoped for. Always encouraging me. Always supporting me. Loving me. And my brothers and sisters, too.

"But I wasn't like them. And we all knew it. I was different from them and from everyone we knew. I never fit in at school. It's not being smart that makes it hard, it pretending you're not as smart as you are in hopes people will like you, because how can they like you when they always feel stupid and uncomfortable around you?"

"I never feel stupid and uncomfortable around you." Gabriel realized the truth of this statement even as he spoke it aloud. He felt more comfortable around Teresa than anyone he knew. Except maybe when she turned and looked at him with those soft brown eyes of hers as she did just then.

"Thank you." Teresa smiled and Gabriel could not help but grin back at her. "Things are so difficult as a prodigy child. You see things other kids can't. Things adults in your life don't see. And you learn and remember quicker. And even when people seem to cheer you on, you can sense resentment under it all. By the time I was ten, I was doing math equations that stumped my school teachers.

"College was even worse. A twelve-year-old at college! Finally I had people around who could challenge my mind, but I felt even more out of place, like the kid sister no one wanted. I felt alone there. And boys. No offense, but boys were the worst part. The college boys were too old and the boys my age were all afraid of me. And I can only pretend to be stupid enough to be attractive for so long."

"See, that's where they were confused," Gabriel said. "There are plenty of reasons to be afraid of you, but your brain isn't one of them."

"That's sweet." Teresa looked at Gabriel again. "That's the best part about the castle for me. Being around people so amazing...I finally feel like I fit in. No. That sounds pompous. I finally feel ordinary."

"You are anything but ordinary." Gabriel meant it in a number of ways, but Teresa seemed to only acknowledge one of them.

"But I am." Teresa seemed adamant now. "Did you know I've never beaten Akikane at chess? I'd never lost a game of chess before I met Akikane. And Ohin. Do you have any idea how much he remembers? I don't mean things and places and people. I mean whole books. And Rajan. Don't ever tell him I said this, but I get lost sometimes when he's explaining the history of some philosophy and how it relates to some development in science. And I love that stuff! That's what's so impressive."

"It's an amazing place with extraordinary people." Gabriel felt a little homesick from the mention of the people they had left behind. He hoped they were all safe.

"No, not the castle. You." Teresa stared at Gabriel, her eyes filled with intensity. "You're the one who is impressive. Being a child math prodigy is nothing compared with being the Seventh True Mage. But you make it seem easy, like it's no work at all to fit in at the castle or the Council or the team. It's amazing. No wonder all the girls like you."

"What girls?" Gabriel hadn't expected Teresa's compliment, and her observation on girls at the castle baffled him.

"Justine, for one." The look on Teresa's face changed subtly and Gabriel struggled to discern the difference and what it might mean.

"She's…well, she's very friendly," Gabriel said.

"She's not following you around the castle like a stray puppy because she's friendly." Teresa gave a small snort of laughter.

"Jan follows you around the castle." Gabriel tried to keep the note of jealousy in his voice to a minimum and largely failed.

"That's just…he likes me." Teresa wrinkled her nose as she thought about her next words. "But I don't really think of him that way. I mean the way a girl would. Or the way he hopes for."

"Oh." Gabriel reappraised all the times he had seen Teresa and Jan together and the way she behaved around him. "I thought that you…well, that you and he…or that he and you…"

"And everybody thinks the same about you and Justine." Teresa's voice sounded defensive.

"But that's silly."

"Exactly."

"I'm not interested in her."

"And I'm not interested in him."

The recipient of Gabriel's unspoken interest stared at him with her soft brown eyes, her arm over his shoulder, and his arm around her waist. He could barely form a thought in his head beyond the desire to know if she reciprocated that interest. How could he know? Could he ask her? He could simply kiss her. That wild and adventurous idea had been floating around the back of his mind for months, repressed by feelings of jealousy and inadequacy. Now the thought seemed to be the only one he could manage.

Teresa still held his gaze, her breath warming his lips. He leaned in slightly, his eyes fluttering shut as he watched hers close. He bent his neck slightly, tilting his head as he had seen others do so many times. He held his breath…

The screams filled the air and fell between them like an iron wall, thrusting their heads apart and their eyes open. Gabriel looked at Teresa for a second, knowing their moment of romantic reverie had been shattered. He saw something in her eyes. Regret?

Then they clambered to their feet and stumbled down the alleyway to discover the source of the screams in the courtyard. Men and women shouted as children ran pellmell in every direction while soldiers shouted orders and brandished their blades.

"We don't have much time." Teresa swallowed audibly beside him.

"Lord De Lacy is expelling the villagers from the castle." Gabriel and Teresa slowly backed into the shadows of the tiny alley, hoping to escape the notice of the soldiers forcing the villagers from the castle and out to face the army of King Philip of France.

CHAPTER 10
ENTERING AND BREAKING

Gabriel and Teresa hid in the hayloft of the stable as soldiers corralled the villagers toward the gates. For all the screaming and yelling and pushing and protestations, the eviction of most of the villagers happened rather quickly. Within an hour, the last villagers marched out the main gate.

Fortunately, King Philip's troops allowed them to pass their lines unmolested and flee the area. The villagers allowed to stay were mainly able-bodied men to help work the castle. The very frail, those encamped within the chapel walls, had also been allowed to remain. The children had all been expelled.

Gabriel knew from his history lessons it would not be long before the lord of the castle decided to evict even these refugees. He also knew this second lot would not be as lucky as the first. King Philip's rage at learning that his men had allowed the villagers to pass meant the final peasants expelled would be trapped between the castle walls and the soldiers holding siege around it. They would wander for days without food or water in the cold, many of them dying, before King Philip would relent and set them free.

"How long did you say before they kick out the rest of the villagers?" Teresa brushed straw from her hair.

"A few days." Gabriel leaned back in a pile of hay and sighed. "Maybe."

"We need a better plan." Teresa leaned back beside him. "With so few people, we'll have to hide all the time."

"We can steal food at night."

"But how can we steal the notebook?"

"The next time he goes out, I'll search his room."

"How will that help? He always has the notebook on him."

94

"Maybe not." Gabriel peered into the cobwebs decorating the rafters of the stable. "I've been thinking about it. If he learned anything from Vicaquirao, it would be misdirection. Maybe he carries a dummy version of the notebook in case one of his brothers shows up. If so, he'd keep the real notebook someplace safe."

"And you think he'd hide it in his room?" Teresa scrunched her nose up in thought. "That's very optimistic."

"It's the best idea I've got."

"And I've got nothing better, so it seems we have a plan." Teresa sat up, energized by the prospect of actually doing something after days of idle observation. "Let's find a new hiding place to watch the church."

Masking their presence by hiding their subtle energy didn't work nearly as well with so few people in the castle to blend in with. The fact that children were supposed to have been removed from the castle added an additional complication. It took them nearly half an hour to creep from the stable and sneak across the courtyard to hide behind some barrels twenty paces from the church entrance.

They sat in silence, as much from fear of being overheard as from lack of constructive conversation topics, while they waited for the rogue Apollyon to make his daily supply run. Late in the afternoon, the Dark Mage exited the chapel doors and strode across the courtyard.

"Good luck." Teresa squeezed Gabriel's hand quickly but firmly.

"Thanks."

Gabriel waited until a soldier crossing the courtyard turned away. Then he dashed through the shadows along the castle wall and slipped through the church door. Inside, he found much the same scene as his previous visits to the chapel. He walked slowly through the sick, feeble villagers reclining on the chapel floor, doing his best to avoid attention and keeping his subtle energy hidden in his feet.

In the back corridor, he concentrated his mind, clearing the Soul Magic spell hiding the rogue Apollyon's room. He touched the door and extended his magic-sense as deeply as possible into the room, looking for possible magical booby traps. More convinced he would run out of time than that the room held no dangers, he gently pulled the door open and stepped inside.

His previous glimpse of the room proved accurate in revealing its details. A narrow wooden bed with a thin mattress and a crumpled blanket sat against the wall, flanked by a small desk and a stool. A candleholder rested on the desk, residue from the half-melted tallow candle spilling over onto the wood. A small stone statue of a woman perched on an overturned wooden crate between the desk and bed. A bladder sack of wine hung from a wooden peg in the wall. A reeking pile of chicken bones and apple cores littered one corner of the room. The rogue Apollyon's sanitation habits seemed as impaired as his sanity.

Gabriel hurriedly searched the room, checking under the bed and the mattress, looking within the folds of the blanket, and peering at the underside of the desk. He placed the statue on the bed and flipped the crate over, running his hand through the empty interior. He replaced the crate and reached back to grab the statue, knocking it from the bed. He threw his hand after the statue as quickly as he could, but it reached the floor first.

Gabriel picked up the statue and saw a small chip missing at the base. He scanned the floor, knowing he wasted precious time that he should be using to search for the notebook. Spotting something under the bed, he bent down and picked it up. A tiny sliver of stone. He placed it against the chipped space in the base if the statue. It fell away. He held the small piece of stone in his hands, looking around for a good place to leave it, a place that would look like it had fallen naturally from the statue. Shaking his head in frustration, he jammed the splinter of stone into his pocket.

He placed the statue back on the crate. If the rogue Apollyon noticed the missing chip, hopefully he would think it had happened long ago. Why did this Apollyon have a statue in his room, anyway?

Gabriel looked at the statue more closely. The soft red stone revealed the detailed features of a woman with a sharp chin and high cheekbones. Was she someone Apollyon had known? What did the statue mean?

Gabriel could risk no more distractions. His time for searching the room exhausted, he gave a futile last look up to the rafters of the room, but could see no place where a notebook might be hidden. He retreated from the chamber, closed the door, and walked as quickly as he could down the short corridor and back to the chapel nave.

Seeing the door to the chapel swinging open, Gabriel quickly sat down between two old men dozing against the wall of the church. Hiding his face in his arm, he pretended to sleep, as well. His body screamed to run, lungs panting in anticipation of flight. He tried to slow his breathing.

Through barely open eyelids, he watched the rogue Apollyon stomp through the church door, slamming it behind him. Gabriel could feel the Soul Magic the Apollyon radiated, turning away the attention of everyone in the room. He held his breath until the Apollyon crossed the chapel hall and entered his hidden chamber.

Wasting no time, and knowing that the residual effects of Apollyon's Soul Magic would help conceal him, Gabriel dashed across the church floor, hopping over coughing old men and wheezing women to slide quickly through the main doors and out into the cold air. Pausing only a moment to make sure no one nearby might see him, he raced back along the castle wall to where Teresa waited in hiding behind several barrels of walnuts. She wrapped him in a lung-crushing embrace as he sat beside her.

"When I saw him go in, I thought..." Teresa sat back, her face a mixture of fear and anger. "I didn't know what to do."

"I'm fine." Gabriel tried to slow his breathing, realizing how loud the pounding of his heart sounded in his ears. "I hid. Like a frightened mouse."

"Like a smart mouse," Teresa said, finally beginning to relax. "Any luck?"

"Nothing." Gabriel leaned against one of the barrels. "Maybe he does have the real notebook on him when he leaves the room. If it's hidden, it'll take time to find it."

"We can check every time he's out." Teresa leaned back beside Gabriel, pulling the blanket up around them.

"We can wait outside his room at night. He has to be tired enough to sleep soon. If we can catch him dozing, we could sneak in and get the notebook before he wakes."

"It's too risky."

"We don't have a better plan."

"I didn't say it wasn't a good plan. But we need to make sure he sleeps, not wait for it to happen."

"How do we do that?"

Teresa's eyes widened with excitement. "I may not pay attention to Ohin's history lectures, but I do remember a few things Marcus taught us about herbs. Yesterday, I saw one of the women in the chapel making a tea from valerian root for some of the sick villagers. With enough of it, I can make a sleeping potion. It won't knock him out instantly, but it should make him drowsy enough to doze off. Especially since he hasn't slept in days. Once he's asleep, we sneak in and steal the notebook."

Gabriel marveled at Teresa's ingenuity. "How do we get him to drink it?"

"We put it in his wine."

"And how do we do that?"

Teresa's excitement faded. "I have no idea."

Getting the valerian-laced wine into the rogue Apollyon's hands turned out to be far less complicated than Gabriel or Teresa had presumed. Unable to mingle freely with the remaining villagers in the castle, they found themselves forced to accomplishing everything under the cover of darkness. This included stealing food for themselves in addition to securing enough valerian root to render the rogue Apollyon unconscious. After chopping and crushing the root and blending it with water, Teresa created a concentrated liquid to instill into a sack of wine. These things were relatively easy, though time consuming, to accomplish.

Figuring out how to get the wine into the rogue Apollyon's hands proved simple. The next time the rogue Apollyon went out, Gabriel snuck into his room and replaced the contents of the wine sack hanging on the wall. There could be no guarantee the rogue Apollyon would drink from the wine skin, but it was the only hope they had.

That afternoon, shortly after Gabriel made the switch with the wine, the soldiers expelled the last of the villagers from the castle. Gabriel and Teresa hid, hastily cramming themselves into a large, mostly empty barrel of chestnuts. With the lid of the barrel placed loosely above their heads, they felt relatively safe from the forced eviction.

As the sun set and the noises of the villagers' protests faded, Gabriel and Teresa crowded together in the moldy-smelling barrel, trying to arrange their limbs in some manner of comfortable alignment. They ended up with Teresa seated on Gabriel's lap, her head bumping against the wooden lid. The pain of the chestnuts digging into his hindquarters distracted greatly from the pleasantness created by Teresa's proximity.

"Whose stupid idea was this?" Teresa tried to arrange her arm so her elbow didn't poke into Gabriel's ear.

"Yours." Gabriel groaned softly as Teresa's knee jutted into his stomach while she twisted around.

"This must be what it feels like in a can of sardines." Teresa rotated her head, her hair falling across Gabriel's face. He found himself suddenly thinking far less about the pain the chestnuts caused him.

"More like a can of Spam." Gabriel blew a puff of air to dislodge a strand of Teresa's hair tickling his cheek.

"Let's not talk about food. I'm too hungry." A thin shaft of moonlight pierced the gap between the barrel and the lid, illuminating Teresa's face.

"If you're counting Spam as food, you must be hungry."

Gabriel paused for a moment, mesmerized by the beauty of her face. How did she manage to look so pretty with greasy hair and her face covered in dirt?

"Would you like a raw chestnut?"

"If you can figure out a way to slice them open with that sword and not take my hand off." Teresa's eyes went to the Sword of Unmaking shoved against the side of the barrel.

"I think it would be safer to starve a little longer." Gabriel tried to adjust himself again, sending Teresa tilting sideways.

"There must be something we can do to keep our minds off how uncomfortable this is." Teresa's eyes flickered to Gabriel's, and then away, just as quickly.

He could certainly think of something that would take his mind off their circumstance. Had she been thinking the same thing? Could she possibly have been thinking the same thing? How could he know? Was there some sign? Some signal? How did these things work? Gabriel suspected they rarely worked inside a barrel of chestnuts.

He tried to think about all the romantic movies he had seen and how the boy first kissed the girl. He realized then that he had not really seen many romantic movies. Science fiction movies, kung-fu movies, sports movies, comedies, yes, but what fourteen-year-old boy willingly watched romantic movies? This now seemed like a monumental oversight. A massive strategic blunder. How was he going to know what girls might like, one girl in particular, if he didn't at least research the subject?

As he made a mental note to create a list of romantic movies to study upon his return to Windsor Castle, he noticed the odd look on Teresa's face and how closely she seemed to be studying him.

"Is there something wrong with you?" Teresa frowned. "You've been staring at me like, forever."

Gabriel blinked. He *had* been staring at her for a considerable time. He could feel his cheeks burning. He'd been daydreaming about ways to kiss Teresa while staring at her. Idiot!

"Nope. I'm fine. Just thinking."

"What were you thinking about?"

A phrase from Akikane's training leapt to Gabriel's mind. *Less thinking, more doing.* That's what he needed — more doing. Gabriel leaned forward, tilting his head up, intending to show Teresa exactly what he had been thinking about. As he brought his lips level with hers, his eyes staring deeply into her own, a small avalanche of chestnuts collapsed beneath him. He wriggled and shifted his weight to try and compensate, but somehow overcompensated, knocking his forehead into Teresa's nose.

"Ouch!"

Teresa wiggled sideways as Gabriel tried to correct for the shifting weight and the foot suddenly stabbing into his kidney. The motion sent the barrel tilting precariously to the side. Teresa quickly leaned in the opposite direction of the sway, Gabriel instinctively leaning with her, becoming aware as he did so that his mass only enhanced the counter tilt of the barrel, sending it tipping over and rolling across the hard ground for ten feet before thudding into the side of the horse stable. As the barrel bounced back from the wall of the stable and came to a rest, Gabriel and Teresa lay half outside it, their arms entangled, heads facing away from each other.

"I'm not sure what you were thinking about," Teresa said, disentangling her arms from Gabriel's, "but maybe you shouldn't think about it again. At least not while we're in a barrel."

"Right. I'm not sure what I was thinking." Gabriel sat up, feeling like he would spontaneously combust from embarrassment. He looked around, thankful to find that their tumbling barrel trick hadn't attracted anyone's attention. He consoled himself by noting that Teresa had said not to think about it while they were in a barrel. He had no intention of getting in a barrel again anytime soon.

"We might as well sneak into the church and wait for him to fall asleep." Teresa brushed herself off as she stood up.

"Good idea." Anything to keep them both from thinking about the disastrous near-kiss could be considered a good idea. Gabriel grabbed the Sword of Unmaking from the barrel and stood beside Teresa.

They crouched low as they ran from store house to stables to the steps of the church entrance. Squeezing quietly through the church door, they found the inner nave empty. The old and sickly villagers had been expelled from the castle with all the others. It saddened Gabriel to know they would starve in the cold air outside the castle walls, and that some would surely die before King Philip would consent to let them pass. He wished he could do something for them, but knew it was impossible. One of the many aspects of his new life he could never accept — seeing injustice but being unable to act against it.

They walked silently across the nave. The sounds of the priest's snores reached Gabriel's ears before he reached the pulpit. When he stepped into the small corridor behind the altar, he realized the snoring came not from the open door of the priest's quarters, but from the magically hidden room the rogue Apollyon occupied.

Gabriel glanced inside the priest's chamber and found it empty. The clergyman had obviously been evicted along with the villagers. Or, more likely, had chosen to follow and help them as best he could.

Gabriel turned to the concealed door of the rogue Apollyon's room and focused his mind, clearing away the Soul Magic obscuring the room.

He knew Teresa was unlikely to accomplish a similar feat, so he motioned her to follow him as he slowly pulled the door to the room open and stepped through.

He stopped and held still. The rogue Apollyon lay on the narrow bed, feet dangling over the edge, his snores reverberating around the room. The flickering light from the candle on the table showed the surprise on Teresa's face as she stepped through the nonexistent wall and stood beside Gabriel. The glow of the candle also revealed the notebook, sitting open on the small desk.

Gabriel glanced at the slumbering rogue Apollyon and inched closer to the desk, trying to keep his breathing shallow and quiet. Each breath seemed like a roar of wind in his ears. Cautiously extending his arm, he reached for the notebook.

He felt a space-time seal fall into place as his finger touched the open pages.

Gabriel grasped for the imprints of the Sword of Unmaking and his pocket watch as he spun to confront the rogue Apollyon. Unable to sense the space-time seal, Teresa didn't realize what had transpired around her until the sound of the snores ceased and the rogue Apollyon sat up on the bed with a wild laugh. His curly black hair, matted and oily, gave him the appearance of a vagrant while his wild, roving eyes seemed more like those of a madman.

"Did you really think I wouldn't notice the valerian root?" The rogue Apollyon stood up, three concatenate crystals glowing on a chain around his neck. "Valerian root. It was one of the first things he taught me."

"Gabriel?" Teresa risked a glance in his direction.

He could feel the magical energy she held, waiting to be unleashed.

"I won't kill you." The Apollyon's mania faded slightly. "I need you alive."

"Gabriel?" The pitch of Teresa's voice lowered an octave, expressing more concern in that single word than a countless number of sentences might have accomplished.

Gabriel wasn't ignoring Teresa. He wasn't panicked into inaction. Not yet, at least. His mind spun in a dozen possible directions, simultaneously seeking out a possible course of action that could lead to a desirable outcome. They could attack, but could they win? Three concatenate crystals would be more than a match for the Sword of Unmaking and his pocket watch. Especially if each of the crystals were connected to six others.

Even Teresa's considerable magical power and skill would be of little consequence. With his bracelet of concatenate crystals no longer connected to the imprinted relics of the castle, Gabriel simply did not have the magical strength to defeat the rogue Apollyon. Even if they could escape, would they be able to steal the notebook? If not, they would never have a second chance to track it down. And if they did manage to escape with the notebook, the magical battle required to do so would surely create a bifurcation of the Primary Continuum, and possibly more than one new branch of time.

"Gabriel, what do we do?" Teresa turned to him, her face contorted in anger and fear.

The words of Akikane's last lesson rang clearly in Gabriel's mind like the sound of bells cutting through the noisy din of a city street. Words which revealed an unexpected path out of disaster. Words he hoped he could remember well enough to turn to his advantage.

Gabriel lowered his arms.

"We surrender."

Teresa's jaw dropped in surprise. He looked her in the eyes.

"*Trust me.*"

He planted the words in her mind via Soul Magic, and then released the imprints he held.

The rogue Apollyon laughed, high-pitched and near-maniacal, as he rubbed his hands together.

"Excellent."

CHAPTER 11
CAPTIVE AUDIENCE

Gabriel and Teresa sat on the edge of the moth-eaten mattress, their hands tied behind their backs with strips of bedding cloth, their legs bound together in a similar fashion. Gabriel's sword and pocket watch and Teresa's bracelet lay in a corner of the room. The rogue Apollyon sat on the shaky-legged stool facing the two young mages, his face sweaty, voice strained.

"You must know." The rogue Apollyon scratched at his ill-kempt beard. From his erratic motions and the desperate look in his eyes, Gabriel knew the man had not slept at all in the past few days. He wondered how the Dark Mage managed to continue to stay alert and how his state of mind might be affected by the extreme lack of rest.

"I've told you all I know." Gabriel tried to keep his voice even and calm in hopes it would elicit a similar response from the rogue Apollyon. "The notebook is written in a dead language and in an alphabet that Councilwoman Elizabeth created herself. I don't know how to read it."

"She must have told you the key." The rogue Apollyon leaned even closer. Gabriel wrinkled his nose at the man's rancid breath.

"What key?" Gabriel glanced at the notebook, still open on the table. Maybe the rogue Apollyon's mind had descended into madness more deeply than he had suspected if the man thought the notebook needed a key to open it.

"The key, the key, the key." The rogue Apollyon snatched the notebook from the table and shook in front of Gabriel's nose.

"The key to decipher the code." Teresa leaned closer to Gabriel to draw the mad Apollyon's attention. "Right? The key to decipher the code. That's what you're looking for, right?"

"Yes! The key. Exactly. Do you know? No. She'd never tell you. You're no one. Nobody. Nothing. No…but she'd tell him. They all talk to him. He's their favorite pet. You always tell the favorite pet. I was the favorite once. I know. What did he say? What did he always say? Look for the patterns. See the pieces before they are set. But how can I see the pieces without the key?"

"I'm trying to tell you, there is no key." Gabriel spoke softly and slowly, ignoring the warning look in Teresa's eyes and the subtle shake of her head. "There can be no key, because it's an alphabet, not a code. It's a written language. Only Elizabeth knows how to read it."

"No, no, no!" The rogue Apollyon put his head behind the open page of the notebook and shook it with fury. "She must have told you how to read it. She must have. You need to know what is in these pages. I need to know what is in these pages. I must. Must. Before the others find me. Find it. Before they can read it. If they read it…if they read it they will know what they need to know and then they will do it."

"You mean the Great Barrier." Gabriel began to wonder if surrender into captivity had been such a wise plan. The rogue Apollyon's mental instability frightened him more than the thought of losing the notebook. Particularly the thought of what the man might do if Gabriel felt forced to enact his option of last resort.

"Yes, yes, the Great Barrier." The rogue Apollyon sat back, lowering the book and looking at Gabriel and Teresa as if suddenly realizing they were there and that he hadn't been speaking merely to himself. "They'll destroy it if they can. And they can. They are close to the number they need. They only require the knowledge. Power is knowledge. No. Power is empty without knowledge. That's what he always said. Why didn't I see it then?"

"See what?" Teresa leaned forward slightly, trying to hold the rogue Apollyon's eyes.

"The balance." The rogue Apollyon's eyes wandered up toward the ceiling, seemingly chasing after unseen thoughts.

"The balance of what?" Gabriel asked.

The rogue Apollyon's eyes drifted down to gaze at Gabriel. "Everything."

"And they'll destroy the balance of everything?" Gabriel didn't have to ask who *they* were.

"Like children kicking over sandcastles." The rogue Apollyon blinked and looked at Teresa. "What was it she said that day? Men who cannot create, destroy. Like boys knocking down sandcastles. What kind of man are you? What manner of man will you be? Will you create or will you destroy? Create. Yes. I'll create. Create an empire. She laughed. Laughed. Why did she laugh? Did she know? Even then? Did she know even then?"

"Did who know?" Gabriel had no idea what woman the deranged Dark Mage spoke of, but he had a suspicion he hoped would prove correct.

"What?" The rogue Apollyon shook himself as though allowing some possessing spirit to escape. "Don't try to confuse me. I need to know how to read the notebook. Everything hinges on this. If they tear down the wall, the balance is lost. And once the balance is gone, there is only chaos. Chaos is a dangerous goddess. Necessary, but dangerous. To unleash her without restraint is madness."

"Yes, that sounds like madness." Teresa nodded her head sympathetically. "Too much chaos and the system falls apart. The center cannot hold. Too much structure and the system stagnates and rots. But the balance between is the golden mean."

The rogue Apollyon looked at Teresa as if for the first time, leaning closer to peer into her eyes. Gabriel had no idea what her babbling had been about, but it seemed to calm the distraught mage.

"You see." The rogue Apollyon nodded his head in approval. "Yes, you see. Did he tell you that? Have you spoken to him?"

"I've spoken to him." Gabriel held no doubts about who the rogue Apollyon referred to. He seemed obsessed with Vicaquirao. "He's told me about the balance."

"Then you know." The rogue Apollyon raised the notebook again, shaking it with renewed enthusiasm. "You know how important it is to stop them. How important this notebook is. Why I must understand. To preserve the balance. Light and dark, past and future, to save us all."

"I will stop them if you let me go." Gabriel tried to make his voice as firm as possible. For once, it did not break and crack under strain.

"You!" The rogue Apollyon spat on the floor. "You are boy. A child. They will eat you alive. They will flay you and eat you. They will

106

roast you and flay you and eat you. A child. A child he speaks to. A child they all speak to. Why? Why do they trust you? Why you more than me? Why a boy more than me? I am the one. I have seen. I have sacrificed. I must know. Not you. Not a boy. Am I not more than a boy? Yes. I am. And you will tell me. You will tell me how to read the book. I know you know, and you will tell me."

Lost in a sea of madness, the Apollyon tossed the notebook on the bed and clasped his hands around Gabriel's head. Gabriel knew what to expect even as he watched the three concatenate crystals begin to glow. He felt the Dark Mage's Soul Magic assault his mind — a flaming spear thrust into his brain. Gabriel gasped and Teresa screamed. She tried to use her shoulder to slam into the rogue Apollyon and loosen his grip on Gabriel, but she only succeeded in being thrown from the bed by a black-clad elbow to her head.

Gabriel's mind filled with thoughts. Thoughts swirling like trees uprooted in a windstorm. Not his own thoughts. The mad Apollyon's mind, reaching into his own, searching for knowledge of how to read the notebook.

"Where, where, where. Do not hide. Do not hide it from me. I will find it if I must kill you. No, I mustn't kill you. But you will tell me. You will tell me now. Tell. Me. Now!"

Gabriel focused his mind and tried to fight the wave of incoherent words and images attempting to overtake it. He could not tell the mad Apollyon how to read the notebook. He didn't know. But the Apollyon would keep looking. Tearing at Gabriel's mind, leaving behind his madness as he searched for what he could not find. Gabriel realized he would be left as insane as the man assaulting him if he did not find some way to stop the invasion of his thoughts.

He grasped the imprints within himself and focused his subtle energy on them, trying to form a shield of Soul Magic against the Apollyon's mental intrusion. The Apollyon shook his head, confused. Gabriel took advantage of the confusion and pushed back, thrusting his own mind into the Apollyon's consciousness, concentrating on the darkness that came with sleep.

"Sleep. Sleep and all will be well."

"No. How? This is…no. No!"

107

"Yes. Finally!"

"I hear him."

"Where?"

"No. Release me."

"Who is that?"

"Who is that with him?"

"Not possible."

"Where? Where are they?"

"No. Must stop. They will find us."

"Yes."

"Found them."

"Yes."

The connection with the mad Apollyon's mind broke. The Dark Mage yanked his hands back from Gabriel's head as though they had been burned in a flame. Gabriel pitched forward, nearly falling to the floor.

What had happened?

Those other voices. The other Apollyons.

His space-time sense told him someone would materialize in the room a fraction of a second before it happened. The rogue Apollyon sensed it as well, grabbing the notebook from the floor.

A single twin Apollyon blinked into existence near the door. A space-time seal cloaked the room with his arrival. Dressed in the same black clothes, a look of arrogant superiority filled his clean-shaven face. The rogue Apollyon stood before the small statue on the crate, one arm raised as though to defend himself.

"Great," Teresa growled and sat up on the floor, leaning against Gabriel's legs.

The newly arrived Apollyon twin looked at Teresa, then Gabriel, then the rogue Apollyon, curiosity filling his gaze.

"Brother?"

The rogue Apollyon said nothing, his eyes darting around the room.

"You've been missing." The Apollyon twin remained standing by the door, appearing as though he had simply stopped by for tea.

"I've been busy." The rogue Apollyon licked his lips and swallowed.

"I can see that." The new Apollyon gestured toward Gabriel and Teresa with an open hand.

"Prisoners." The rogue Apollyon's hand shook as he wiped sweat from his forehead.

"Yes," the new Apollyon said. "And you have the notebook."

"I've been…I've been working on it."

"All alone?"

"Yes. Alone."

"But why?" The new Apollyon's voice became gentle with mock concern. "Why work on it alone? Why not bring it to the rest of us? Why not share it?"

"I wanted to decode it. For us. For all of us."

"Really?" The new Apollyon took a step toward his twin. The rogue Apollyon recoiled slightly. "Why keep us from your thoughts, then?"

"A surprise. It was to be a surprise." The rogue Apollyon raised his chin as if to reaffirm his statement.

"Well, we were certainly surprised when we discovered you were not with us. And we were very surprised when we found you were hiding from us. And we were extremely surprised to find you with him." The new Apollyon nodded toward Gabriel.

"All part of the surprise." The rogue Apollyon's lips twitched.

"Then you can read it?"

"No." The rogue Apollyon frowned with the admission.

"Then the boy can read it."

"No." The rogue Apollyon's frown deepened.

"Then you have failed." A look of false disappointment filled the new Apollyon's face.

"No, no, no, I am working on it." The rogue Apollyon nearly stammered his words. "I simply need more time. More time."

"You must be weary from your efforts." The new Apollyon took another step closer to his twin. "You know what they say. Work sets you free. It's time to set you free."

"I don't want to be free." The rogue Apollyon shook his head.

"Why don't you let us in? Let us hear your voice in our minds again. We can help you. Bring you back into the fold."

"He's not coming back to you." Gabriel forced the words past the fear clenching his throat tight.

Trussed up and held captive by two Apollyons didn't suggest many pleasant possible outcomes. He needed to do something to change the situation. "He's never coming back to you and he'll never give you the notebook. He'll destroy it first." He hoped it would prove true.

"What is he talking about?" The second Apollyon tensed as he spoke to his twin.

"What? How should I know? The boy lies." The rogue Apollyon could hardly stand still, his free hand fidgeting and stoking his beard.

"He's abandoned you. All of you." Gabriel raised his voice, hoping to draw the second Apollyon's attention. Teresa looked up at him, her eyes full of questions and concern, but he ignored her and stared at the two Apollyons. "He realized he made a mistake."

"Mistake?" The second Apollyon's voice deepened. "What mistake?"

"Nothing. The boy lies. He doesn't know what he's talking about." The rogue Apollyon backed up, his heels bumping against the crate.

"Haven't you guessed? Isn't it obvious?" Gabriel knew the hunch he pursued might be wrong, but hoped it wouldn't matter, that it would give the rogue Apollyon an unguarded moment to act.

"Guess what? What does the boy mean?"

"I don't know. How could I know? *He* doesn't know what he's talking about."

"You both know." Gabriel's voice became more firm. "You both sense it, don't you?"

"Sense what? What have you done?" The second Apollyon stepped toward his twin, his eyes full of menace.

"I have done nothing, nothing, nothing!" The rogue Apollyon held up his free hand in a placating gesture.

"He made you. Made all of you." Gabriel hoped his suspicions of the rogue Apollyon's true nature proved correct. Or at least proved divisive. "He is the original and he knows that making you, making all of you, was a mistake. A mistake he needs to correct."

"You lie!" The second Apollyon turned to Gabriel, a finger stabbing forth in accusation. Gabriel noticed the rogue Apollyon's hand swing down behind him. "He is not the Prime."

The rogue Apollyon's arm swung out, the stone statue grasped in his hand, making bone-crunching contact with the back of the second Apollyon's head. As the second Apollyon stumbled to his knees, Gabriel felt the space-time seal disappear. The rogue Apollyon caught his eye.

"Thank you." The rogue Apollyon vanished into time even before the words finished crossing his lips.

The second Apollyon looked where the rogue Apollyon had been and then jumped through time, blinking out of existence from the room. Gabriel threw himself from the bed, lurching through the air toward the corner of the room even as he sensed the warping of space-time around him. The second Apollyon had not been alone. Gabriel had suspected as much. There were others.

And they were coming.

Gabriel landed on his shoulder, his head touching the sheath of the Sword of Unmaking. He reached out for its imprints, bending time and space around himself, encompassing Teresa, even as he sensed the arrival of six Apollyons into the room. The lightless void of time-travel embraced him and he sighed in relief. Dazzling white revealed a small Japanese village beneath a grassy hill before Gabriel thrust himself and Teresa back into the blackness again. He jumped several times, using the sword and the pocket watch and Teresa's golden bracelet as relics. He finally brought them to a stop on a tree-filled hill above a staggered pyramid. He had never asked where Teresa's bracelet came from. Was it Mayan? He had no time to query her.

"Tell me that was all part of your brilliant plan." Teresa sat, arms still bound, shaking her hair from her face as she glared at Gabriel.

"That was all part of my brilliant imitation of a plan." Gabriel focused on combining Stone and Fire magic, turning the bonds holding his and Teresa's limbs to ash. He stood up, slinging the Sword of Unmaking over his shoulder as he slipped the watch into his pocket. He picked up Teresa's bracelet and handed it to her as he helped her to her feet.

"Surrender to escape. I never would have thought of that." Teresa's voice oozed with sarcasm as she accepted the bracelet and slid it on her wrist. "But we lost the notebook."

"Not necessarily." Gabriel could barely restrain his enthusiasm. "I think I know where our rogue Apollyon may have taken it."

"Okay. I apologize. Maybe it was a brilliant plan." Teresa looked at him expectantly.

Gabriel reached into his pocket and withdrew a small sliver of reddish stone.

"This is going to make perfect sense when you explain it to me, right?" Teresa touched the chip of stone in Gabriel's open palm with the tip of her finger.

"This is from the statue in the rogue Apollyon's room." Gabriel held the shard of stone between his forefinger and thumb. "When I was searching for the notebook, I accidentally knocked the statue onto the floor and this chip broke off."

"You think the chip will lead us to where the rogue Apollyon is?" Teresa raised an eyebrow in skepticism.

"Why would he have a statue of a woman in his room?" Gabriel had thought about it for days. "And he kept mentioning a woman. I think this statue is of that woman. In fact, I think he carved it."

"That would explain the poor craftsmanship."

"And he hid it from the other Apollyon, remember? He stood in front of it. He didn't want the other twin to see it."

"Because it could take him someplace the others have never been."

"Exactly."

"You're right. That is a good plan. Or at least the best we're going to get. But you have to promise me something." Teresa's face looked serious as she spoke. "If we can't get the notebook back, we have to destroy it."

Gabriel thought about it for a moment. He felt certain there were secrets in the notebook known only to Elizabeth. With her in a magically induced coma there was no guarantee he would even learn what they might be. However, Teresa was right. It would be better to lose the notebook and the knowledge it contained rather than allow it to fall into the hands of any of the Apollyons.

"Deal."

"Let's go, then."

Teresa placed her arm on Gabriel's shoulder and he reached out with his time-sense to the piece of stone in his hand, searching through its timeline for a moment that seemed a plausible hiding place for the rogue Apollyon. Two things stood out as strange about the statue. It wasn't very old. A year at most. And it bent away through space-time in an odd away. It wasn't from the Primary Continuum. It came from an alternate branch of reality, possibly one the rogue Apollyon had created especially for the purpose of hiding in. Why not go there to begin with? Unless something in this new world meant a great deal to the rogue Apollyon. Enough to avoid risking discovery unless absolutely necessary.

Gabriel didn't know what the answer might be, but as the blackness formed around him and Teresa, he vowed he would find out.

CHAPTER 12
HIDING PLACE

Gabriel followed the space-time signature of the shard of statue, twisting away from the Primary Continuum. As he did so, he noticed a shroud of magic cloaking the bifurcation. The rogue Apollyon had hidden his new world well. It would be impossible to find without the chip from the statue. Images filled Gabriel's mind — a bamboo hut on a beach, a woman walking along the shoreline, a man sitting in the sand carving something, the two seated on a thin mat in the hut, a notebook in his hand, the man and woman eating roasted fish by starlight, the hut in darkness, moonlight seeping through cracks in the walls.

Alabaster light faded into moonlit darkness. Shadows of jungle trees swayed in the gentle breeze. The sound of ocean surf softly lapping against the shore permeated the air.

"Where are we?" Teresa's hand gripped a little tighter on Gabriel's shoulder.

"There's a beach hut over there." Gabriel pointed through the trees to the small bamboo structure illuminated by the moon. "I had to wait until they were asleep to make sure he couldn't sense us jumping through time."

"Them?"

"The woman is also here."

"Does he have the notebook?" Teresa pushed a palm frond to the side for a clearer view of the hut.

"I think so." Gabriel put the chipped piece of statue back in his pocket. "I'm not sure how long he's been here, though. It could be a few days. Maybe longer."

"So, we wait for morning, and when they leave the hut we sneak in and grab the notebook."

"Unless you want to try and sneak in now."

"That worked so well for us the last time." Sarcasm saturated Teresa's voice.

"Let's find a place to keep an eye on the hut." Gabriel looked around for a spot with a better vantage of the small bamboo shelter.

Teresa released the palm branch and looked up at the moon. "Probably a good five hours before sunrise. We'll take turns keeping watch."

"We can hide over there." Gabriel pointed to a clump of trees that seemed to have a good view of the beach and the hut.

When they reached their new stakeout position, Gabriel offered to take the first watch, allowing Teresa to curl up on a few fallen palm leaves and sleep. He watched as her breathing grew shallower and she drifted off into slumber. He wasn't certain where they were in the world, or in time, but at least the rogue Apollyon had chosen an idyllic hideout. It felt wonderful to be warm again after days of fighting against the cold. While slightly humid, the breeze from the ocean refreshed and calmed him. He noticed, however, the absence of icy air meant there would be no need to huddle close to Teresa. That pleasure had been worth the discomfort of the ever-present chill.

He stared at Teresa's sleeping face, painted with moonlight, and wondered again how to make sense of the feelings constantly buffeting his heart when in her company. Her safety seemed far more important than the notebook, or Windsor Castle, or the Great Barrier. But all these things would ultimately help keep her safe. Did she need to be kept safe? He might feel that, but did she need his protection, or did being near him put her in more danger?

Might the best way to keep her safe actually be staying away from her? Is that why the rogue Apollyon had not come to this tropical paradise originally? To keep the mystery woman safe? And why come here now? Was there no other place he could hide, or could he simply no longer manage to stay away from her? How long could Gabriel stay away from Teresa if he thought he needed to? Who was this strange woman and what did she mean to this Apollyon? Had Gabriel been right? Was this the original Apollyon? Did it matter?

Gabriel sighed, trying to let the weight of too many questions fall from his shoulders and his mind. He leaned back against the trunk of a coconut tree and looked up at the sky. It would still be a few hours before sunrise. He should wake Teresa soon. He should…

"You should pay attention to the game."

Gabriel looked down from a cloudless blue sky. He sat in a small boat in the middle of a nameless ocean stretching from one horizon one the other. Across from him and the familiar game board sat Vicaquirao. The old Mayan general looked pleased.

"You are losing. Again."

"I'm not sure I like this game. How about a game of checkers?"

The wooden game board shimmered and reformed into black and red squares with simple, round pieces already scattered in mid-play. Vicaquirao frowned.

"What can you learn from checkers?" Vicaquirao moved a black piece one space forward.

"How to be a gracious loser." Gabriel lifted a red game piece, hopping it over three consecutive black pieces. He collected the captured pieces with a laugh.

"Sometimes one must lose to win." Vicaquirao waved a hand and the game board shimmered in the sunlight, transforming into the lined game board of Go, white stones dominating the field of play. He placed a single black stone on the board, enclosing a ring around half the white stones, causing them to vanish from the board.

"What if it's not possible to win or lose?" Gabriel watched as Vicaquirao picked up a black stone and the game board transformed again, chess pieces populating black and white squares in the middle of a game. Gabriel moved a white bishop to capture a black rook. "What if neither side can gain advantage?"

"Stalemate." Vicaquirao's eyes narrowed as the board transformed into something Gabriel had never played but yet recognized as Senet, a box divided into thirty squares in three rows of ten. Vicaquirao moved a cone-shaped piece and looked at Gabriel. "Sometimes a stalemate is preferable. Stalemate is common in nature, but rare in games."

"I don't know how to play this game." Gabriel looked at the board and willed it to be something else. The board transformed back to its original shape. Gabriel moved a green stone and rolled the dice, turning the third ring two spaces.

"Knowing the rules is not as important as understanding the possibilities implied by the rules." Vicaquirao moved a blue stone, leaping over one of Gabriel's green stones, then an adjacent yellow stone, and finally taking the place of another green stone.

"You never said that was possible." Gabriel glared at the game board, the boat rocking in the waves.

"But did the rules imply it might be possible?" Vicaquirao rolled the dice, the rocking of the boat sending them skittering across the board.

"I don't like this game." Gabriel crossed his arms, the motion of the waves upending the game board, multicolored stones scattering along the curved hull.

"You can't stop playing this game." Vicaquirao laughed as the small vessel pitched from side to side. "This game isn't in the board or the pieces or the dice. This game is in the rules. And the rules say you must play."

"Some night watchman you are."

Gabriel blinked his eyes against the sun and the sight of Teresa's face hovering close to his. She stopped shaking his shoulder and sat back.

"I've been trying to wake you for almost a minute. Are you okay?" Teresa's deep apprehension clouded her face.

"Sorry. I fell asleep."

"You don't say."

"I had a bad dream."

"Do you want to talk about it?"

"No." Gabriel's discomfort at having fallen asleep on watch felt amplified by Teresa's concern.

"Then we should steal the notebook and get out of here." Teresa gestured over her shoulder toward the beach. "They've left the hut and he doesn't seem to have the notebook with him."

Gabriel looked at the beach and saw the rogue Apollyon seated in the sand beside a woman with long, jet-black hair that curled down to her waist. They shared what looked like a large papaya, the woman cutting slices with a small dagger.

"Right." Gabriel climbed quietly to his feet, slinging the Sword of Unmaking over his shoulder. "Stay here and keep watch. I'll go get the notebook. If it looks like they might catch me, create a diversion."

"This wasn't the plan." Teresa grabbed Gabriel's arm, fingers digging angrily into his flesh.

"It's the safest way." Gabriel winced at Teresa's grip, but made no move to dislodge it. "I can jump away if I need to and one of us needs to keep watch. You wouldn't want me to fall asleep again, would you?"

"Lame." Teresa yanked her hand back with an annoyed sigh. "That is totally lame and you know it."

Gabriel knew, but he also saw it would eliminate some of the risk for Teresa.

"I'll be back in no time." Gabriel felt an overwhelming impulse to lean over and kiss her before dashing off to do something dangerous. It felt like the absolute right thing to do. Then he saw the glare in her eyes and decided romance out of context could lead to disaster, if not bodily injury. He offered her a carefree smile and walked into the jungle.

He snuck slowly through the tropical undergrowth and came up behind the small bamboo hut. He could see the rogue Apollyon and his...what was she to him? His girlfriend? His wife? The idea of Apollyon having a wife, of being able to love someone, upended Gabriel's assumptions about the man. They sat on the beach facing each other. The sun had tanned her skin to a deep nutty brown, highlighted by the simple pale yellow dress she wore.

Rather than his customary black, the rogue Apollyon wore cutoff grey pants and a short-sleeve blue shirt. A thick, bronze bracelet wrapped around his right wrist and glittered in the sun. He had shaved, and he looked far healthier than when Gabriel had seen him last. How long had the rogue Apollyon been here?

He seemed genuinely happy with the woman. The look on his face when he held the woman's hand confused Gabriel. Could this be the original Apollyon? How could he have become so twisted? What would he become now?

Ignoring the distracting thoughts, Gabriel crept to the back of the hut.

The hut's construction consisted of a bamboo frame covered with woven palm fibers to create thin walls. A single small window covered by a thin sheet of netting sat in the middle of the back wall. Bamboo stilts raised the hut a few feet off the ground, to prevent flooding, Gabriel assumed. He pulled himself up to the window, balancing his feet along a bamboo support beam against the floor. He pushed gently at a corner of the netting over the window, hearing it rip away from the nails holding it to the frame. After creating a large enough hole, he pulled himself over the lip of the windowsill and slid slowly to the floor.

Crouching on the bamboo plank floor, Gabriel waited for his eyes to adjust to the shadows within the hut. Banners of bright orange cloth decoratively draped the ceiling. Two straw hats hung on a hook near the door. A mattress filled one corner of the room, an oil lamp on a small wooden box beside it. The familiar small statue sat next to the lamp. The opposite corner of the room held a low wooden table with two cushions around it. An iridescent purple flower floated in a glass bowl of water in the middle of the table.

The notebook sat beside the bowl.

Gabriel crossed the room at a glacial pace, patiently placing his feet where the floor looked most firm, slowly shifting his weight to avoid causing the bamboo to creak. He didn't want to make any noise that might attract the rogue Apollyon from the beach.

Finally, he stood beside the small table and picked up the notebook, rubbing his hand over the red leather cover. He hoped its contents would be worth all the effort they had gone through to retrieve it. As he turned back toward the rear window, he heard voices.

"I need to continue."

"No, you don't."

Gabriel risked a peek through the open front door. The woman took hold of the rogue Apollyon's arm as he walked to the hut. He stopped and embraced her.

"It's too important to ignore."

"There will be plenty of time for the notebook. Isn't that what you told me? We would have all the time we wanted now."

"Semele. You know what hangs in the balance."

"I know balance hangs in the balance. The balance of your mind most of all."

"I'm much better now. The voices can't reach here."

"Then take the time to relax. Sometimes the solution to a puzzle comes when we look away from it."

"Yes, maybe you are right." The rogue Apollyon kissed Semele.

"Besides." Semele guided the rogue Apollyon back to the beach. "How can you bring a woman to such a place of beauty and then leave her alone all day?"

The rogue Apollyon laughed and their voices faded into the noise of the ocean waves. Gabriel sighed and slipped back out the window. He tucked the notebook into his back pocket and walked as quickly as he could through the jungle, staying low and keeping quiet. Halfway back to where he had left Teresa, he heard something coming toward him. He stopped, watching as a shadowed shape ran through the jungle. He wondered if it might be some wild animal like a boar or a tiger.

The bright green leaves rustled and revealed Teresa. She slid to a stop, paused only briefly and then threw her arms around Gabriel.

"I thought for sure they were going to walk in on you." Teresa grinned and then did something more surprising than her sudden appearance — she kissed him.

Gabriel's brain froze.

The kiss he had thought about so many times had taken him entirely by surprise. His lips pressed against Teresa's and it felt — actually, it felt odd. Not at all what he had expected. It felt strange. Like a kiss he might have received from his grandmother as a child. As passionate as kissing a doorpost. Gabriel blinked as Teresa released the kiss, trying to sort through several layers of confusion.

"Come on."

Before Gabriel could even think of what to say, much less form words in his mouth, Teresa ran back into the jungle.

"What? Wait."

Gabriel followed Teresa through the jungle as best he could. She ran ahead, dodging around trees and between the leaves of massive tropical ferns. Gabriel turned his head as a large leaf caught him in the face. He lost sight of Teresa, but continued in the direction she had been running. A moment later he found her where he had originally left her.

"That was close." She turned from watching the beach. "Did you get it?"

"Of course." Gabriel wasn't sure what to make of Teresa's sudden kiss, much less his reaction to it. He decided it might be best not to try and understand everything girls did, especially when he seemed to only understand half the things he did himself.

"Then let's get out of here." Teresa looked back to where the rogue Apollyon and the woman Semele walked along the beach. "Before they notice it's missing."

"We need to walk as far away as we can." Gabriel looked along the beach behind them. "The farther we get, the less chance the rogue Apollyon can sense our time jump. This way."

Gabriel led the way through the jungle to a stretch of beach around a curve of land, unseen from the rogue Apollyon and Semele's hut. The couple had walked in the opposite direction along the beach, and he hoped it would be hours before they returned to the hut and found the notebook missing. Gabriel figured he needed to get at least three miles away before he could make a jump safely. He walked a little faster.

"How much farther?" Teresa quickened her pace to keep up.

"Not far."

Gabriel walked in silence trying to figure out the kiss and what it meant. Did it mean she would want him to kiss her again at some point? How would he know when to do that? Would the kiss be better the second time? Did she not like the kiss? Would there ever be a second time? Could he ask her about it? Was this the sort of thing people talked about? What could he say? He could tell her he liked it. Compliments were always a good way to start a conversation. But did he like it? He decided it might be worth trying to say something.

"You know…"

Gabriel had no time to finish the thought. The ground exploded before him, a hurricane of sand swirling around him. He felt the notebook being torn from his pocket as the wind knocked him to the ground and a space-time seal enclosed him. He seized the imprints of the sword and pocket watch as he wiped the sand from his eyes, searching for his attacker.

The miniature sand storm settled and Gabriel stood up to face the rogue Apollyon floating from the sky and landing gently on the beach. He held the book in one hand, his other outstretched as though ready to cast some spell of Malignant magic.

"It's a good thing I decided to go back to the hut for a hat." The rogue Apollyon appeared far more sane than the last time they had met.

Gabriel glanced to the side and saw Teresa getting to her knees as she brushed sand from her face.

"I told you I would not kill you, and I won't." The rogue Apollyon's eyes squinted in the sun. "However, I still need your assistance."

"Do it," Teresa whispered from beside him.

"I can't help you." Gabriel stared at the book in the rogue Apollyon's hand.

"We can help each other. We do not need to be enemies. Not in this." The rogue Apollyon lowered his hand in a gesture of peace. "How did you find this place?"

"The statue." Gabriel glanced again at Teresa's pleading eyes.

"A very astute observation." The rogue Apollyon nodded his head in appreciation. "I think you'll find my company a little more tolerable now that we are beyond the reach of my brethren."

"Creating them was a mistake."

"I know. I'm trying to correct that, but I need your help."

"I can't. I can't trust you."

"You can't trust anyone."

"That's not true."

"It is. You'll learn that eventually."

"You trust Semele."

The rogue Apollyon frowned. "You know her name. You are so much more resourceful than they assume. Good for you. Yes. You are correct. I do trust her."

"You created this alternate reality to save her, didn't you?" Gabriel didn't doubt this to be true, but he needed to stall for time in order to come up with a better plan than Teresa's.

"I failed to save her the first time." The rogue Apollyon looked away, as though remembering something painful. "It haunted me. Changed me. He convinced me it would be unwise to create a new branch of time to save her. He said we needed to learn to let things go. He was wrong. This is much better than letting go." He gestured to the beach and the sky and the jungle.

Gabriel understood. He had created an alternate reality to save Ling. Wouldn't he be tempted to do the same again to save Teresa? Would he be able to let go? Could he surrender to fate? Could he release his desires? Could he surrender again now?

"I'm sorry." Gabriel could not tell what his words were intended to express regret for. The Apollyon's loss? The unfairness of their lives, living out roles decided for them by fortune? Or for his actions? He didn't like Teresa's plan, but could see no other option.

Gabriel focused his will and magical power on the notebook. The leather-bound tome burst into flame and crumbled to ash in the rogue Apollyon's hand. The Dark Mage yelled with shock and rage, holding his charred limb with his free hand. Gabriel sensed the space-time seal flicker with the distraction of the rogue Apollyon's pain. Blackness surrounded him and Teresa as time bent around them, and they traveled back to the Primary Continuum.

Several random jumps through time eventually brought them to the edge of a forest nestled between two mountain ranges, their peaks still dusted white in the midsummer sun. From between the trees, Gabriel could see a small Japanese Buddhist temple in a nearby village. A middle-aged man wearing a simple black kimono sat in the grass across from the temple. A sword lay across his knees.

The very sword Gabriel had used to travel to this place. The gentle smile on the man's face looked the same as the one Gabriel knew from his own time.

Akikane.

He wished he could go and ask the younger version of his mentor for advice, but he knew it would only cause more problems.

"Are we safe?" Teresa took hold of Gabriel's arm and he helped her to her feet.

"For now." Gabriel looked into Teresa's eyes. "Until we need to know what was in that notebook to stop the Apollyons."

"At least none of them have it." Teresa straightened her hair.

"I can't believe we went through all that to come home with nothing." Gabriel growled and punched a nearby tree. The pain in his hand did nothing to quell the anger roiling in his chest. How could he have been so stupid? There had to have been another way. Maybe if he hadn't listened to Teresa...

"We can get it back."

"How?" Gabriel rubbed his knuckles and stared at Teresa.

"We can go back and get it."

CHAPTER 13
THE SWITCH

"How?" Gabriel realized he sounded like an idiot repeating himself, and it only annoyed him further.

Teresa flashed him a devilish look. "We sneak back to the rogue Apollyon's romantic hideaway and switch the book you stole with a copy before he has a chance to steal it back."

"Huh?" Gabriel tried to figure out exactly what Teresa suggested and how it might be possible. It sounded exactly like the sort of thing Ohin always told them to avoid. Too many possibilities of creating bifurcations.

"It's simple." Teresa slowed her words as though speaking to a child. "First, we create a dummy notebook. One that looks like the real thing from the outside. Then we go back to the beach, distract you somehow, and switch the fake notebook with the real one you took from Apollyon's hut before he finds us on the beach. Then, we get far enough away and jump someplace safe."

Gabriel blinked and shook his head. "That is an absolutely ridiculous plan."

Teresa glared at him. "Do you have a better ridiculous plan?"

Gabriel took a deep breath, preparing his response, readying his arguments for why Teresa's plan wouldn't work and could only end in disaster. He let the air out of his lungs in one long slow breath.

"Nope."

"Good." Teresa's buoyant attitude returned. "Let's find some leather we can dye red."

Finding a scrap of discarded leather proved more time consuming than altering its color. They decided feudal Japan offered as many possibilities for creating a replacement notebook as any other time, so they wandered the small village looking for a tannery. Using their amulets, they altered their appearances, adopting the plain kimonos they saw many of the villagers wearing. Gabriel knew they must be sometime during Akikane's life and guessed they were in the late 1300s. The town, composed mostly of large farmhouses with steeply sloped, thatched roofs, held fewer than a thousand citizens.

They found the tannery at the edge of the village and clandestinely searched the trash pile behind the foul smelling barn for a piece of leather the right size. Finding suitable paper took a little longer. Until the Industrial Age, paper remained relatively scarce. They decided to use one of the larger local farmhouses as a relic and travel father into the future. Unfortunately, a fire had destroyed the farmhouse in the late 1700s, forcing them to use another farmhouse to travel to the 1930s. Surprisingly, the village remained largely unchanged throughout the centuries, even as the country began to industrialize in the 20th Century.

There they changed their appearances again and, after a lunch of pilfered edamame, they found an old novel in a trash bin. Retiring to a nearby field and hiding behind a stand of trees, Gabriel used an imaginary magical blade to slice their piece of leather to match the size of the paper from the discarded book. He ripped the cover from the pages and, using a bit of subtle Stone Magic, affixed the inner pages to the new leather cover. Finally, he focused his Stone Magic on the leather, gradually changing the tint of the dried cowhide to match the reddish hue of the real notebook.

Teresa appraised the final product appreciatively. "You could have had a very good career as a forger."

"I never thought of that." Gabriel admired his own handiwork. "I could make my own money and be rich."

"Then you'd have to make your own world to spend it in." Teresa seemed intrigued by the thought.

Gabriel frowned, remembering the costs of creating worlds. "Money is too much trouble."

"Now we need to figure out how to distract you and switch the books." Teresa took the fake notebook from Gabriel.

"When you kiss me."

It seemed like the best time to Gabriel. His mind had been far from the contents of his pocket.

"When I kiss you?" Teresa said the words as though she hadn't heard him properly.

"In the jungle. After I stole the notebook. Before we got back to the hiding place." Teresa's continued look of confusion as he explained the kiss led him to a singular conclusion. "Oh."

"I see." Teresa looked down at the phony notebook in her hands. "I guess I'll be kissing you then."

"Paradox." Gabriel sighed.

Time travel could be so confusing. No wonder Teresa hadn't brought up the kiss — it hadn't happened yet for her. That explained why she had met him in the jungle suddenly and kissed him so abruptly. And why she had seemed surprised to see him when he had found her moments later at the lookout spot.

"I hate paradox."

"Let's get this over with." Teresa looked up from the book, Gabriel's heart sinking at the tone of her voice. She certainly didn't seem enthusiastic about kissing him. Or kissing the past version of him.

"Right. It'll be over before you know it." Gabriel took hold of Teresa's arm, clasping the tiny shard of stone from the rogue Apollyon's statue of Semele in his hand.

A twist through time and a moment later, they stood on the beach again, darkness surrounding them and the white light of the moon giving their faces a spectral glow. Gabriel started walking along the beach, Teresa falling in beside him.

"I brought us to a few minutes before we arrive the first time. We can find a place to watch ourselves and wait for morning."

"And then I'll...distract you, while you switch the notebooks." Teresa looked up at the moon while she walked.

"Then we wait until our previous selves escape and the rogue Apollyon chases them." Gabriel stared at the sand before his feet. "Time travel can get so bewildering."

It took them half an hour to find a spot to secretly observe their previous selves. A short while later, the slightly younger Gabriel and Teresa took up their position watching the hut. Gabriel felt a vague sense of mental vertigo, watching himself watching the hut. It felt both fascinating and disturbing at the same time. Teresa, on the other hand, seemed bored, leaning back against a tree and dozing off to sleep.

Oddly, he had no problems staying awake through the night. Too many questions plagued his mind. Questions about Teresa. Questions about the rogue Apollyon. Could he be a rogue while also being the original Apollyon? What had his twin called him? The Prime. What was this Prime Apollyon becoming? He seemed unable to stop talking about Vicaquirao. At least that is who Gabriel assumed he constantly referred to. Maybe Semele had been a good influence on his state of mind.

Was Teresa a good influence on Gabriel's state of mind? Was he a good influence on her? What would they do once they had the notebook? Return to the castle, surely. What remained of Windsor Castle? And the Council? How many casualties had they suffered? How many years had the war been prolonged? Could defeat now be a possibility? Would they be forced to surrender?

Gabriel blinked at the sunlight suddenly striking his eyes from behind a jungle leaf. When had the sun come up? How long had he been daydreaming? He gently nudged Teresa awake, pointing to the rogue Apollyon and Semele stepping from the hut. Teresa sat up and they watched their previous selves observe the man and woman on the beach.

"Nearly time." Teresa stretched the sleep from her muscles.

They waited as the older version of Gabriel snuck through the jungle.

"This way." Gabriel stood. "I'll show you where you surprise me."

He charted a course through the jungle foliage that would allow them to intercept his previous self on the way back from the hut. He found the perfect spot and instructed Teresa on how to mimic her sudden arrival as he had experienced it before. Gabriel hid behind a large jungle bush and they waited.

A few minutes later, Gabriel saw himself coming through the trees. His previous self walked right toward him. Gabriel experienced a moment of panic, fighting back the feeling they had miscalculated, and both versions of himself would come face to face. A swaying of leaves caught his attention. His previous self stopped and looked in the same direction. His older self stood only an arm's length away through the deep green leaves.

Teresa burst from the jungle and stopped in front of the previous Gabriel. She seemed to hesitate and then threw her arms around him.

Dizziness washed over Gabriel as he watched the scene before him.

"I thought for sure they were going to walk in on you." Teresa smiled, paused again, and then kissed Gabriel's previous self.

His dizziness and sense of incongruity increased to the point where he almost forgot the purpose of witnessing this bizarre romantic interlude. He reached his arms out of the leaves, slowly slipping the notebook from his previous self's pocket and gently replacing it with the fake. He could see Teresa's eyes open and watching him as he eased back into the underbrush. Gabriel allowed himself a small, inner congratulation. Marcus would be proud.

"Come on," Teresa said and dashed off into the jungle again.

"What? Wait." A confused look on his face, the previous Gabriel chased after Teresa.

Gabriel watched the older version of himself disappear into the leaves and let a long breath of relief slide past his lips.

Gabriel waited a moment and then headed for the location he and Teresa had chosen for a rendezvous. As he walked, he wondered again about that kiss. Maybe it had been so awkward because Teresa had not been the Teresa he had expected her to be? Maybe that was the source of the strangeness in the kiss? Maybe she had been distracted by the circumstances. Maybe other circumstances would prove more sympathetic. Was kissing really so distasteful?

He found Teresa exactly where he expected. She pointed to the notebook in his hand.

"Is that it?"

Gabriel flipped open the book to show her the inside, Elizabeth's cryptic script filling the pages.

"I wasn't sure it would work." Teresa looked genuinely relieved.

"Now you tell me you weren't sure." Gabriel shook his head in wonder and slipped the notebook in his pocket.

"I was mostly sure." Teresa started walking through the jungle and Gabriel followed her.

It only took a few minutes to come to a place where they could watch their previous selves fleeing along the beach. They didn't have to wait long before a small sand storm blew up around their previous selves and the rogue Apollyon appeared. Gabriel held his breath and watched the events on the beach unfold exactly as they had before.

When the notebook burst into flame he felt a twinge of compassion for the rogue Apollyon, wondering if his madness would return. Then the previous Gabriel and Teresa disappeared. The rogue Apollyon screamed in rage at the sky and then vanished himself. Those seconds of uncontrolled anger had probably been what had allowed Gabriel to escape. Every second could be essential in trying to ghost a fellow Time Mage.

Gabriel waited a few moments and then stood up.

"We did it." Teresa rose to her feet, her face triumphant.

"Yes." Gabriel laughed. "Thanks to your brilliantly ridiculous idea."

"Can I see the notebook?" Teresa offered her open palm.

"I'm not letting this thing out of my sight until we're back at the castle." Gabriel patted the notebook in his pocket.

"I only want to see it for a second." Teresa gestured with her open hand.

"We can look at it back at the castle." Gabriel furrowed his brow at Teresa's insistence.

"Hand it to me now, Gabriel." Teresa took a step forward, her voice commanding.

"Why?" Gabriel unconsciously stepped backward.

"Because I said so." Teresa glared at him with open menace. "And if you ever want to see your girlfriend alive, you'll do exactly as I say."

Gabriel instinctively grasped the imprints of the Sword of Unmaking and the pocket watch as he felt a pulsing of magic from Teresa. A pulsing of magic he should never have been able to feel from her. A magic laced with Malignant imprints. Looking down at his hands, he realized he had drawn the sword and held its tip pointed at Teresa's heart.

"Don't be a fool." Teresa shimmered and her flesh rippled as she rapidly transformed into the lovely and evil Kumaradevi. "If you kill me, you'll never know what I've done with your girlfriend."

"I don't understand," Gabriel stammered, trying to figure out what had happened.

"You rarely do." Kumaradevi's eyes twinkled with a mischievous delight. "All you need to know is that I have placed your lovely friend somewhere in time, and if you do not give me the notebook, she will die there. Alone. Most likely in some painful fashion."

Gabriel couldn't think. How had Kumaradevi managed to replace Teresa? How had she even been able to find this secret, alternate reality of the rogue Apollyon's? How had he not felt the magic used to bend space and time and take Teresa away? How had she...?

"Stop trying to tease out how you failed." Kumaradevi gestured again with her open hand. "You failed because you are pathetic. You failed because you are not half as clever as you think. You failed for the same reason you will always fail. I am superior to you in every way. Now hand me the notebook."

"Why not fight me for it?" Gabriel wasn't sure if this would be such a good idea. He could see a necklace of seven concatenate crystals glowing around Kumaradevi's neck.

"You know as well I do that my crystals are weaker here." Kumaradevi laughed. "Why would I risk fighting you when I can force you to do what I want?"

Gabriel understood her logic. Her crystals were all linked to Malignant imprints in her vicious alternate reality and would be less powerful in the Primary Continuum. In another alternate reality, they would be exponentially weaker. She was right. Holding Teresa captive gave her a much stronger position than her magic. She could easily force him to do as she wished.

"Tell me where she is first." Gabriel pulled the notebook from his pocket with one hand, still aiming the sword at Kumaradevi with the other.

"The notebook." Kumaradevi snorted in derision.

"You could take the notebook and never tell me where she is."

"I could, but then she would die."

Gabriel didn't understand Kumardevi's meaning. She laughed at the confusion clouding his face.

"If I wanted her dead, I would have killed her." Kumaradevi's genial manner evaporated. "I know what it is like to lose the one you love. I'll save that as a punishment for you, not a reward."

Gabriel threw the notebook on the ground between them. He didn't trust handing it to her. Kumaradevi's lips curled downward as she looked at the leather-bound book in the grass. She took something from the pocket of the tunic she wore and tossed it on the ground. It looked like a stone.

"Tell Elizabeth that one day I will repay her for killing my husband while he couldn't defend himself." Gabriel doubted she would ever accept any responsibility for her husband's death. Kumaradevi pointed her hand at the notebook and it flew into her fingers. She looked at him while she held the book. "Whose death do you think would crush her the most?"

Gabriel had no time to answer. Kumaradevi blinked out of existence, a wicked smile filling her face.

CHAPTER 14
LOST IN TIME

Gabriel fell to his knees, letting the sword blade sink into the grass, his shoulders shuddering as he tried to control the anger and fear pulsing through his body. Tears filled his eyes as he reached out for the stone Kumaradevi had tossed to the ground. How could he have been so stupid? How could he not have seen this? If something happened to Teresa, it would all be his fault.

As he examined it, he realized the stone in his hand wasn't a stone. He held a piece of marble, one side smoothly carved, the other jagged and uneven. Could it be from a statue? What statue and from when? Whenever and wherever it came from, it would lead him back to Teresa. Assuming Kumardevi hadn't lied to him. It might be possible, but he didn't think so. He suspected she knew the anger of losing someone too well, and he also thought she knew what he would do to her if she had killed Teresa.

He held the walnut-sized chunk of half-carved marble in his hand as he jumped through time away from the rogue Apollyon's private world and into the black void between every moment. He appeared in darkness, damp air chilling his skin. He opened his hand, concentrating on the magic he desired, a small globe of bluish light forming in his palm and floating upward, illuminating his surroundings.

Ribbed arches supported a curved stone ceiling some thirty feet above, and frescos of pastoral scenes covered the walls between several large statues of men and women. From their looks and the style of the carving, Gabriel guessed them to be Roman emperors and their wives. The major portion of the long room contained several pools of water. A Roman bathhouse then.

From the coolness of the air, these were probably the pools the bathers used to slough off the heat of the steamier baths. The word *frigidarium* came to Gabriel's mind from his studies. He looked up at the closest of the pale marble statues, the one the fragment in his hand originated from. The statue stood fifteen feet high, the eyes of its massive three-foot head gazing up at the painted stars spread across the ceiling.

He guided the magical ball of light upward to shine on the face of the statue. Yes, he knew those eyes. That beard and those cheekbones. That face. He had seen that face not so many days ago.

Aurelius. Emperor Marcus Aurelius.

How could that be possible? Was it merely a coincidence Kumaradevi gave him a fragment of a statue of Aurelius to find Teresa? Had she known about their retrieval of Aurelius? Did she still have spies in the castle and on the Council? Could this be her idea of a joke? Did Kumaradevi have a sense of humor? Did it matter as long as he found Teresa?

At least he knew when and where he would find her. He had spent a week researching the history of Marcus Aurelius. His statue stood in the bathhouse of Sagalassos, a Roman town in the Toros mountain range of what would eventually become southeastern Turkey. The town had been settled as far back as 8000 BCE, and over time had become an important center of trade, conquered by Alexander the Great in 333 BCE.

Power changed hands several times before it became part of the Roman Empire in 39 AD. The town suffered a major earthquake in 518 CE, and eventually fell to Persian raiders and more earthquakes around 640 CE, which, Gabriel suspected, had also destroyed the statue of Marcus Aurelius.

Gabriel found all of this important, not because of his love for history, but because it meant Teresa, whenever in time she might be, would be trapped in a town large enough for her to hide and find food and water until he could track her down.

Locating her posed certain problems. The entire team had been trained to stay in one place when lost in time. Normally, Teresa would have tried to remain as close to the statue as possible, but with the statue in a bathhouse, that would be almost impossible. Most likely, she would try to find a hiding place near the statue and bathhouses to wait for rescue. However, he knew Teresa's methodical mind. She would visit the statue at least once a day to make sure he could find her.

Gabriel stepped to the corner of the room, behind the leg of another Emperor, Hadrian, possibly. He touched the wall and used the bathhouse itself as a relic to scan through time for some sign of Teresa. Images filled his mind. The bathhouse during the day with sunlight streaming through the arches. Nighttime with oil lamps burning in torchieres along the walls. Crowds of men and women bathing and relaxing.

One image began to repeat. A girl near the statue of Marcus Aurelius. Gabriel jumped through time to a day when the girl sat at the foot of the statue, using his Soul Magic to render himself invisible to the people splashing in the pools.

Gabriel felt his heart swell as the girl turned her head toward him. Teresa! He nearly allowed his Soul Magic veil to drop and run to her, but he noticed something. Her face looked tan, but thin. Very thin. How long had she been here? He had hoped to find her within days of her arrival. An awful thought occurred to him, but he forced it from his mind. He needed to be certain before he allowed himself to contemplate something so painful.

Gabriel used the bathhouse to travel backward through time. One day. Then two. Then three. Teresa always sat at the foot of the statue. The same time every day. He adjusted his travel slightly, seeing her enter on one day and leave on another. She seemed to stay for two hours at a time. Long enough to bathe and sit by the statue, but not long enough to attract attention. As he skipped back in time, day by day, she looked less tan and less thin. Finally, a day arrived where she did not appear.

He had half expected to see Kumaradevi delivering her to the statue but knew the old Dark Mage would never have been so sloppy as to appear where Gabriel might find her easily. He had counted over three weeks of days into the past. Fearing what he would find, he skipped ahead a month. Teresa still sat at the foot of the statue. Another month. His hopes began to fade. Another month. When he saw her then, he knew the extraction would be painful.

A mage lost in time would, as long as they did nothing to create a bifurcation, gradually become part of the Primary Continuum. This

135

natural and somewhat unpredictable process could take as little as a month, but it rarely took more than two. Teresa had been lost in the Primary Continuum for at least three months. If he simply snatched her from the timeline now, her sudden absence from it would create a bifurcation.

The only way to save her without accidentally manufacturing a new alternate branch of the timeline would be to extract her the same way she had been removed originally — at the moment of her death. But when would her new death come? How old would she be? How many years would she be trapped in this Roman town before she died thinking Gabriel had abandoned her? How old would she be before he could save her?

The sadness gripping Gabriel's heart made it hard to breathe, much less see through the tears in his eyes. She might be an old woman before she saw him again. He took a deep breath and let it out slowly, trying to calm the swirl of emotions battering him. He jumped through time an hour until Teresa left the bathhouse. He followed her outside, keeping a safe distance, his Soul Magic making him as invisible to her as everyone else.

Outside, she crossed a wide plaza doubling as a market place. The Greek name for a public plaza had been *agora,* and the name had often been retained into Roman times, although it could also have been called a *forum*. A building with fountains in homage to the water nymphs sat across the plaza from the bathhouse. Unsurprisingly, the Romans called the temple a *nymphaeum*.

Teresa dodged a horse-drawn cart. Gabriel watched as she paid for some fruit with a coin. She knew. Of course she knew. Teresa understood time travel better than most Time Mages. She would have been counting the days, knowing each one brought her closer to being integrated into the Primary Continuum. She would never use money and make purchases so freely unless she felt certain she had already crossed that threshold. Now she would only have one way of escaping the timeline while still young, and Gabriel feared that option as much as her gradual aging.

Only by taking her own life could she hope to be rescued while still a young woman. But that would bring other risks. Primarily, the risk of never being found and ending up dead — for the final time.

Gabriel continued to follow Teresa down a street to an alley between two stone houses. He watched with admiration as she used the uneven surface of one wall to scale the taller of the two buildings, climbing onto the roof. Gabriel jumped through space to the rooftop and stood beside her as she leaned on a stone ledge. Her eyes regarded the city with sadness.

"Any day now. Please."

Gabriel stepped back, afraid he might lose control of himself and embrace her. He needed to find out how long she stayed here in this town. How long she lived. He could use her own body to guide him to that time, but he felt too afraid to touch her. A glint of gold beneath her tunic sleeve caught his eye. Her talisman bracelet. That would do fine.

Cautiously, he reached out and placed his finger on the edge of the bracelet. He looked at Teresa. She appeared oblivious to his presence. He knew she would never willingly part from the bracelet. It could only be taken from her by force, which would require more force than any average Roman might suspect. He felt certain she would wear it throughout her life.

Gabriel scanned the bracelet, looking for clues to tell him what Teresa's future might hold. His mind flickered with images of Teresa in the market, by the statue, on the roof, in the street, and then…

Gabriel gasped and staggered back. Teresa glanced around and though she heard him, but turned back to the town below. An icy chill fell over Gabriel's limbs. He couldn't breathe. Couldn't move. Even his mind felt frozen. He had seen Teresa's death.

It couldn't be. It would not be. He would not accept it.

He gently touched her bracelet again and jumped forward in time. He appeared, still shrouded in an unnoticeable cloak of Soul Magic, two weeks later in the middle of a street near the market by the bathhouse. He stood by the corner of a building watching Teresa as she walked along one side of the street.

A block away, an ox-drawn wagon filled with freshly felled logs rumbled down the street. Two men rode atop the logs, one using a long, thin stick to drive the four oxen harnessed to the wagon while the other man sat chatting with him, a large axe balanced on his shoulder as…

From the other end of the block, on the opposite side of the street behind Teresa, two black stallions raced ahead of a chariot, a lone soldier urging them forward with a crack of the reins as…

Up ahead of Teresa, a woman tossed a basin of water onto the stones of the street as….

Nearby a small, sandy-haired boy ran barefoot down the lane, kicking a red wooden ball as…

The chariot sped by Teresa. She followed its path with her eyes. Looking back, she focused on a large, gray dog gnawing on a bone in the shade of the building not far away as…

The boy's foot landed on the side of the ball, sending it rolling across the lane. The boy never looked up from the ball and dashed after it, into the street, into the path of the galloping horses and their chariot as…

The soldier in the chariot yanked back the reins, pulling the horses to the side, into the street, away from the boy as…

The chariot's frame collided with the side of the lumber wagon, crushing its rear wheel as…

Teresa's head snapped toward the sound of the crashing vehicles, sending her feet veering toward the dog. The gray dog noticed Teresa and growled, baring its teeth. Teresa stepped into the street to avoid the hound as…

The oxen, spooked by the collision with the chariot, charged as the wagon tilted toward the middle of the street, buckling under the weight of the logs and the loss of the rear wheel as…

Teresa looked from the dog to see the charging oxen and spun around, leaping toward the side of the street as…

The wagon slammed into the ground, logs bouncing and rolling into the middle of the street, the driver falling to the ground with them as splinters of wood from the falling logs struck the thigh of the woman who had tossed the water into the street as…

The second man on the wagon ran nimbly across the logs churning beneath him, leaping to the side of the street, the axe tumbling from his grip while he fell as…

Teresa hit the ground on her knees, hands outstretched, to stop her momentum as…

The wooden axe handle struck the ground, sending it spinning in a violently rapid arc as…

Teresa looked up as…

The axe blade struck her in the neck as…

Gabriel closed his eyes.

The sounds of the street — the screams, the shouting, the braying of horses, and the wild snorting of oxen — faded from Gabriel's ears. He heard only the pounding of his own heart and the swift, deep gulps of his breathing.

Teresa.

Gone.

Forever.

The primary lesson he had learned while preparing for his first extraction with the team filled his mind. Extractions were not always possible. There were circumstances when it proved impossible to save the potential mage at the moment of his or her death. In order to prevent a bifurcation, the candidate needed to be extracted after their actual death. A Heart-Tree Mage would then repair the damaged flesh of the body and bring the person back to life.

However, there were times when this simply could not be accomplished. If too much time passed between death and resuscitation, or the cause of death damaged the body beyond repair, the person would remain dead. Usually this did not present a problem. Most people died of accidents or natural causes. But while the damage from a sword to the heart could be repaired, a bullet to the brain would always be permanently lethal. Any death a Heart-Tree Mage could not repair would be a permanent death.

Decapitation always remained fatal.

Gabriel opened his eyelids to find Teresa's eyes staring back at him from the ground. Her dead eyes. Her body lay several feet away.

He turned and vomited against the wall of the building behind him. He felt his concentration begin to collapse. He didn't know how long he could keep the Soul Magic hiding his presence in place. He needed to flee. He wanted to jump through time. To get as far away in space and time as possible from where he stood. Where Teresa had died.

Unable to think of where to flee to in time, he ran. Sprinting up the street, he dodged men and women and carts and dogs and children, tears filling his eyes, making it difficult to see where he headed.

He ran until the road ended and his breathing burned his lungs. He stood at the top of the Sagalassos *Theatre*, an outdoor amphitheater built into the sloping hillside, stone seats buried into the ground in a near-full circle. The seats angled down and ended in an open, horseshoe-shaped space. Behind this stood the stage, constructed of stone, tall columns supporting the roof. Only a handful people sat scattered throughout the seats, some eating, some talking, some napping in the warmth of the sun.

Gabriel stepped into an aisle and sank down on a hard seat. He altered his appearance with the amulet to blend in with the citizens and slowly allowed the Soul Magic protecting him to fade. If anyone noticed him, they would think he arrived while they had been looking away. As the magic evaporated around him, his weeping turned to sobs and his head fell forward into his hands.

His tears fell in memory of Teresa. For all she had been. For all she meant to him. For all she might have become. For what they might have become together.

His tears fell in shame. For his role in her death. For leaving her alone to be kidnapped and stranded.

His tears fell in anger. For Kumaradevi and her treachery. For her carelessness with human life. For leaving Teresa to die alone in a strange place and time.

His tears fell in despair. For the fruitless hope he could change time and save Teresa. For the impossible desire to once again ignore Ohin's guidance and create a bifurcation to save her.

His tears fell with the pain of knowing he could not bring himself to create and destroy an entire world again to save one person, even a person he loved as much as Teresa.

When his tears had burned away the sadness of memory and the self-loathing of shame, he found his desperation fading into a desire for revenge, fueled by the anger still consuming his heart. Kumardevi would regret her hand in Teresa's death. Gabriel would make certain of that. She would not escape retribution.

For too long he had thought of the war as a game, with different sides and factions, and with himself as the most coveted piece on the board. He couldn't afford to think like that anymore. The war held no real resemblance to a game. People did not die in games. The loss of a game only provided a lesson for the next turn of play. Even Vicaquirao's game only…

Vicaquirao's game.

Gabriel sat up.

Vicaquirao's game.

A hazy memory from a half-forgotten dream rippled through his mind just beneath conscious perception.

Gabriel wiped his eyes and looked up to the sky. He had seen a sky like it in a dream. A dream with Vicaquirao. A dream where they played a strange game.

The game!

Was it only game? Did it matter? Could the game be the key? Could his past dreams have shown him a way forward in the present?

Gabriel held his breath, thinking of Vicaquirao's game, imagining the board and the pieces, remembering the way of thinking that would predict how the board might change. That's what he had thought the game to be about. Prediction. But in the dreams, Vicaquirao had emphasized placement. How to place the pieces so even a random outcome would eventually work in your favor. What had he said?

The keys to the game are learning to anticipate and plan for the subtle changes in the board, and how to arrange for minor alterations and use them to your advantage.

Could it be possible?

Gabriel stood up and walked along the curved row of stone benches.

He thought back to what he had seen on the street. How Teresa had died.

When he came to the end of the row, he reassumed his cloak of Soul Magic and jumped back to the street near the bathhouse. He took himself backward in time to a nearby rooftop and waited for Teresa and himself to arrive on the street below. He made sure his previous self could not see him. If his hunch proved possible, he'd be crossing his own personal timeline a number of times, with each occasion increasing the possibility of creating a paradox. It pained him beyond what he thought possible, but he made himself watch, extending his space-time sense and slowing the events down in his perception. As the axe struck, he moved again to another rooftop and back a little further in time and waited to see the accident from a different angle.

After the third time of seeing Teresa's death, he looked up to the clear sky above and laughed, tears rolling from his eyes once more.

It was possible. It could be done, if planned and executed precisely. However, it couldn't be done alone. He'd need the rest of the Chimera team's help and they would need to make sure to avoid the notice of any of his previous selves viewing the accident on the street.

He felt as certain as he had ever felt about anything. His heart swelled and he laughed again in relief. He could save Teresa. He could unmake her death. Thanks to his dreams of Vicaquirao, he could change time.

Of course, he'd have to kill her to do it.

CHAPTER 15
THE PLAN

Gabriel returned through time to the Council's Windsor Castle, arriving a few minutes after he had left with Teresa to chase the rogue Apollyon and the notebook. By his estimate, he had been gone for ten minutes relative to the time in the castle. The days he had experienced with Teresa felt eaten by time as he examined the castle grounds. Nothing had changed in the minutes he had been gone. The Round Tower and much of the nearby castle structures still billowed smoke. He walked across the grass of the Lower Ward, ignoring the burning trees. He held a roll of papers in his hand.

Ohin and the rest of the team still congregated around Councilwoman Elizabeth's unconscious form. Marcus and Sema bent over her body, their hands resting on her forehead. Gabriel could sense the Heart-Tree and Soul Magic they used to try to healing her.

As he approached, their eyes turned to him. He brought a magical barrier against sound into existence as soon as he reached Elizabeth's side.

"How is she?" Gabriel stared down at Elizabeth, her face contorted in a rictus of silent agony.

"I don't know." Marcus leaned back from Elizabeth with a sigh, keeping his hands in contact with her head. "I've healed her body as best I can, but she's under the influence of some very dark Soul Magic."

"I don't know what to do." Sema, tears in her eyes, looked down at Elizabeth. "It will take many mages to lift this curse. If it is even possible."

"Where's Teresa?" Ling frowned at Gabriel as she glanced around behind him.

"Teresa is dead." Gabriel kept his voice steady. Sema gasped and Ling cursed. Gabriel waited until all their eyes held his. "But I have a plan to save her."

Gabriel told them the story of his and Teresa's pursuit of the rogue Apollyon and Elizabeth's coded notebook. He told them about their time in Chateau Gaillard, their capture by the rogue Apollyon, the arrival of the twin Apollyon, and of their escape.

As he recounted the complicated events in the rogue Apollyon's world, Gabriel's recitation became slightly confusing for his listeners. He explained how he stole back the notebook from the rogue Apollyon, but then how he lost it again, and how Kumaradevi, pretending to be Teresa, helped him recover it before revealing her true nature and extorting the notebook from him in return for a hint at the real Teresa's location in time.

When he came to the tale of finding Teresa in Sagalassos and following her, only to witness her eventual death, he found he had trouble breathing, as though he were reliving the moment all over again, watching it one more time from yet another rooftop. He described quickly and succinctly how Teresa had died. Before he could explain his plan to save her, the others interrupted.

"Gabriel." Ohin's deep voice reverberated with sadness, tears filling his eyes. "There is no way back from a death like this."

"But there is." Gabriel tried to remain calm. He needed to present his case as clearly as possible for them to believe his plan would work.

"Nothing can be done, boy." Marcus rubbed his bald head in frustration, trying to hold back his emotions.

"You don't understand." Gabriel took a deep breath.

"Sometimes we must let go." Tears stained Sema's face.

"But we don't have to." Gabriel nearly laughed as he tried to contain his zeal. He knew he must look maniacal. "I've figured out a way."

"There is no way that won't create a new branch of time." Ohin placed his hand on Gabriel's arm.

"Gabriel saved me, why can't we save her?" Ling wiped tears from her defiant eyes.

"She would never accept that." Rajan stared blank-faced at a burning tree. His mind seemed unable to encompass the news of Teresa's death.

"Stop." Gabriel furrowed his brow, his voice passionate. "We don't need to create a bifurcation to save Teresa. I've figured out a way to alter the timeline of the Primary Continuum slightly, just enough to allow us to extract Teresa at the moment of her death without creating a new branch of time."

"Gabriel, what you suggest isn't possible." Ohin's hand tightened on Gabriel's arm, trying to convey the importance of his words. "The Primary Continuum cannot be changed. It might accept and incorporate small alterations over time, like Teresa gradually becoming part of the timeline, but not something like this."

"No. It's possible. I've thought it all out." Gabriel had spent two days drawing diagrams and making lists of every moment leading up to Teresa's death and the sequence of events they would need to alter in exactly the right order so as to change the timeline without breaking it.

"You can't simply make one small change. It needs to be a series of tiny variations that result in a new outcome."

"It sounds like madness," Marcus said.

"It's grief," Sema said.

"If it can be done, we have to do it," Ling said.

"Ling is right. We can't abandon her if there is a chance, even a small chance, to save her," Rajan said.

"A small chance that carries great risks," Ohin said. "Even if what you say is possible, a miniscule mistake could be disastrous."

"Not if we plan it out." Gabriel's excitement caused his voice to crack.

Ling and Rajan were convinced. He could see it on their faces. He had to convince Ohin. Sema and Marcus would follow his lead if Ohin believed Gabriel. He held out the roll of papers in his hand. "We have to be careful, but I watched it again and again and worked out everything. The key came to me in a dream where I was playing this strange board game with Vicaquirao."

"You had a dream of Vicaquirao?" Sema looked at him, sudden concern filling her eyes.

145

"Yes." Gabriel rushed on. "We kept playing this game where the board would change and you needed to place your pieces so they would be in the right spots at the right times. The dreams would change locations, but the game always remained the same."

"You had more than one dream with Vicaquirao?" Sema stood up and placed her hands on Gabriel's head. He tried to move away, but she clasped his skull tightly. "Did it never occur to you that Vicaquirao might be placing himself in your dreams?"

"No." Gabriel felt confused by the question. For that to happen, Vicaquirao would have needed to be in the castle. He would have needed to follow Gabriel through time. That didn't seem possible. The dreams were only dreams. "I've had dreams of Vicaquirao before. These dreams seemed the same."

"I don't sense anything." Sema lowered her hands, but continued to hold Gabriel's eyes with her own. "But that doesn't mean he didn't place the dreams in your mind."

"For what bloody purpose?" Marcus asked.

"We may never know the purpose, but if Vicaquirao did give Gabriel these dreams, you can be certain there is a reason." Ohin stroked his chin as he looked at Gabriel.

"It doesn't matter what Vicaquirao's purpose might be or if the dreams were real dreams, all that matters is whether Gabriel's plan will work." Ling nearly growled her words.

"Whatever we do, we need to do it quickly." Rajan gestured toward the castle grounds. "We'll be needed here whenever we come back."

For the first time, Gabriel noticed that the expedition Akikane had led against the Apollyons to defend the Dresden outpost had returned. He had been so focused on the others and convincing them of his plan that he'd been oblivious to the additional wounded mages filling the Lower Ward courtyard.

"What happened to Akikane and the others?" Gabriel saw anger in the eyes of his teammates and knew the answer before it could be spoken.

"An ambush," Ohin said.

"A massacre is more like it," Marcus said.

"The whole thing was a trap," Ling said.

146

"They drew away half our forces to make it easier to attack the castle," Sema said.

"Akikane?" Gabriel made no attempt to control the pitch of his voice as emotion and concern broke through.

"He's fine. Wounded, but he'll recover." Ohin's face became harder with the strain of his words. "The castle will take longer to repair. And the Council. We have no idea what is left of our forces or who has survived."

"And we've lost the notebook." Gabriel looked up at Ohin. His words were meant for his mentor now, not the others. "We lost too much today. We can't lose Teresa, as well. I can't. I won't. This plan will work. I know it will."

Ohin stared at Gabriel for a moment, then looked up to the faces of the team. "If we fail, we fail twice. We'll lose Teresa and create a bifurcation."

"And if we don't try?" Sema raised her eyebrows slightly with the question.

"We'll never know." Marcus turned to Ohin. "Can you imagine knowing we could have tried something but yet leaving the poor girl to die? How would we ever be able look at each other again?"

Ohin remained silent for so long, Gabriel feared he might not answer.

"Show me your plan." Ohin reached for the rolled papers in Gabriel's hand. "If it seems possible, we will make the attempt, but you must convince me it's possible."

"It is possible." Gabriel handed Ohin the papers. "We'll need someone else, though."

"Who?" Ohin asked.

"Another Wind Mage. And someone who knows the time period." Gabriel found himself smiling with excitement again. "I'll explain. It's part of the plan. And we'll need someplace to prepare. Someplace safe."

"I think I know somewhere we will be safe," Ohin said.

"What about Elizabeth?" Marcus asked, his hands again resting gently on her forehead.

"She shouldn't travel unless it's absolutely necessary," Sema said.

"I have an idea." Gabriel's gaze fell on a young mage across the yard. "I'll be right back."

Gabriel walked around the others and headed for one of the few trees not scorched by flames. As he crossed the magical barrier against sound, it dispersed. On the other side of the yard, Justine sat against the unblemished tree, her knees pulled up to her chest, tears streaking her soot-smeared face.

Gabriel knelt beside her and she turned to him, noticing him for the first time. Her eyes flared with surprise and she threw her arms around him.

"Oh, Gabriel, I thought you were dead. It's so awful. All of it. Everyone dying. All the people dying. I know I should be helping, I tried to help, but I'm so new, and they were so powerful, I hid. And then it got quiet and I came out and then…" She seemed unable to go on.

"You did exactly the right thing, Justine." Gabriel slowly pulled her arms from around him. "I need your help. There's something only you can do."

"Anything. Anything." Justine's eyes brightened slightly at the hope concealed in Gabriel's words.

"Come with me." Gabriel stood and offered Justine his hands. She accepted and he pulled her to her feet, guiding her back to the rest of the team gathered around the unconscious Elizabeth.

"Oh, no!" Justine gasped as she saw Elizabeth lying prone in the grass.

"It's okay." Gabriel patted her hand reassuringly. "She's in a coma, but she's not going to die. I need you to watch her for me."

"We can't leave her here in the open," Sema said, looking confused at Gabriel's suggestion.

"I'll take them someplace safe," Gabriel said, his voice still soothing as he turned to Justine. "I need to you watch over her for a few minutes. It won't be long. You're a very good Heart-Tree Mage, and she'll be fine as long as you're with her. Can you do that for me?"

Justine hesitated a moment and then nodded her head.

"Good." Gabriel turned to Ohin. "I'll be right back."

A whirl of colorlessness and brilliance and Gabriel stood in the castle cellars, Justine at his side, Elizabeth at their feet. The children, Leah and Liam, yelped in surprise.

"Gabriel!" The children yelled in unison and leapt to him, clinging to his legs.

"We were so worried." Leah's big eyes stared up at him.

"We thought you forgot us." Liam's words were muffled from burying his head in the side of Gabriel's thigh.

"I haven't forgotten about you." Gabriel bent down to one knee. "I have a special mission for you. Something I need you to help me with."

"We can help." Leah's voice sounded far more certain than the look on her face.

"We're good helpers." Liam wiped his nose with the corner of his small tunic.

"Good. I need you to help Justine keep watch over Councilwoman Elizabeth." The two children looked at Justine and then turned their stares to Elizabeth's comatose body. Gabriel could read on their faces the thoughts beginning to form in their minds. "She's in a very deep sleep, and she can't wake herself up."

"I need you to help me keep an eye on her." Justine sat down beside Elizabeth and smiled at Leah and Liam. "Can you do that?"

"We can do that." Leah sat down next to Elizabeth. "Did you see Mommy and Daddy?"

"Not yet." Gabriel tried to keep his tone reassuring. "We can look for them together when I come back."

"You promise to come back?" Liam stared upward as Gabriel stood.

"I'll be back before you know it." He looked to Justine, his voice filled with gratitude. "Thank you."

Justine nodded silently as Gabriel vanished from the room, appearing in the Upper Ward courtyard. He looked around, scanning the destruction, searching through faces, trying to ignore the dead and wounded. They all needed saving, but Teresa needed him more. He saw a man help carry a wounded mage across the yard near the state apartments. Gabriel ran to the familiar face, a face he had seen so much of lately.

"Aurelius!" Gabriel called to the ex-emperor, now impromptu field medic, as he ran up.

"You've survived." Aurelius helped place the wounded man on a bench that had become a makeshift triage station. He stared at Gabriel with weary eyes. "This was not the afterlife I had imagined. I'd hoped I'd be done with war."

"I need your help." Gabriel squinted as he looked up at Aurelius.

"Whatever you need." Aurelius wiped his bloody hands on his pant legs.

"Good. I need your knowledge and your magic." Gabriel jumped through space with Aurelius to rejoin his team in the Lower Ward.

"Aurelius?" Ohin looked at the man with surprise.

"We don't have time to research the extraction point and he lived close enough to the date." Gabriel looked around at the team, feeing his excitement grow. This would work. He would save Teresa. "And we need him for the extraction."

"Extraction?" Aurelius looked confused. "Now?"

"I'll explain," Gabriel said.

"Where is Elizabeth?" Sema asked.

"Safe in the cellars," Gabriel said.

"With Justine?" Marcus asked.

"Yes," Gabriel answered. "We need someone we can trust. I trust Justine. Elizabeth will be safe with her until we return."

"Where are we going?" Rajan asked.

"A place I prepared long ago for a time when I might need it," Ohin said. "Near the day the Great Barrier divides time."

"Well, let's stop yammering about it and go already." Ling spat into the grass, her patience exhausted.

"Agreed." Ohin looked around at the team and paused for a moment. "Even if Gabriel is right, this may still end in disaster."

No one said a word in reply.

Ohin reached into his pocket and removed a tarnished brass key. Then the black void of time swallowed them whole, and Windsor Castle vanished from sight.

CHAPTER 16
HOUSE AT THE EDGE OF TIME

Gabriel blinked his eyes, shadows clouding his vision. He stood with the others in the middle of a large, dimly lit room. He looked around. A long, dust-caked table told him they stood in a dining room. Heavy red velvet curtains partially covered three large bay windows with cracked glass.

Ohin slipped the key back into his pocket and pulled the curtains wide to let sunlight into the room. Dark wood panels covered the walls. A chandelier of curved glass hung above the table. Ten chairs sat scattered around the room.

"Where are we?" Rajan sneezed at the dust, covering his nose.

"The middle of a forest in Maine in August of two thousand-twelve, right before the Great Barrier arrives." Ohin gestured to the room and the house. "This house has been abandoned for years and remains empty until the Great Barrier begins two months from now. I thought we might need a safe house no one else knew about. As long as we stay in the house and near the grounds, no one should notice us."

Ohin's foresight and planning impressed Gabriel. An abandoned house near the point where the Great Barrier divided time on October 28, 2012, would make it much easier to avoid accidentally creating a bifurcation.

"Not the cleanest hideout we've ever had." Sema wiped her finger through the dust on the dining table.

"Not the worst, either." Marcus opened the door to the kitchen. "At least there's a table to sit at."

"The amenities are unfortunately Spartan," Ohin said. "There is no electricity. However, there is an old hand pump out back for water. I also laid in several weeks of supplies. There are crates of canned goods in the kitchen. And you'll be happy to know, I took the time to hunt down some mattresses for the beds. There are linens in the first room at the top of the stairs. I suggest you all take a little time to clean this place up a bit. We'll be here a few days while we review Gabriel's plan and prepare for the extraction."

"Rajan and I can deal with the dust." Ling began to use Wind Magic to push the dust coating the table into a pile. Rajan joined her, using Stone Magic to keep the dust from floating into the air.

"And I'll deal with our house guests." Marcus pointed to a small, brown field mouse running along the baseboard beneath the window before it ducked into a crack in the wall.

"I suppose I'll unpack the food and see what I can prepare for dinner." Sema headed for the kitchen. She stopped at the door and turned back to look at Ling and Rajan. "Maybe you two should start in the kitchen. It's…disgusting."

Rajan and Ling laughed and followed Sema into the kitchen.

"I'll give you a hand." Marcus walked after the other three. "I wouldn't want you to accidentally toss out the beer if Ohin had the foresight to provide some."

"You might find a case under the sink." Ohin watched with amusement as Marcus quickened his pace.

"What can I do to assist?" Aurelius looked between Gabriel and Ohin. "I'm not even certain why I'm here."

"When we perform an extraction, like the one we did for you, we try to learn as much as we can about the location and the period of history." Ohin took Gabriel's rolled papers and began to spread them out on the now dustless table.

"We'll also need you to help with some magic before the extraction." Gabriel helped Ohin flatten his drawings and notes.

"I see." Aurelius looked down and the sheets of paper covering the table. "Who are we extracting?"

"Our teammate, Teresa." Gabriel looked up from the papers to Ohin's face.

"Assuming you can convince me your plan will work," Ohin said.

"I'm confused." Aurelius pulled a chair to the table and sat down. A small cloud of dust erupted from beneath him. "How can she be a member of your team already if we need to extract her?"

"It's complicated." Gabriel grabbed the nearest sheet of paper, a hand drawing of the street in Sagalassos where Teresa died, and turned it to Ohin and Aurelius. "Let me show you what happened and how we can change it."

Gabriel's time spent creating the maps, drawings, and notes of the accident proved invaluable, not only in convincing Ohin of the feasibility of the plan but also in preparing for it. While the rest of the team spent the remainder of the day cleaning the house, making beds, and cooking dinner, Gabriel and Ohin refined the plan. They peppered Aurelius with questions about the construction of chariots and wagons, and gathered any small details that might influence the outcome of the alterations they intended to make to the Primary Continuum.

Later that night, after a meal of canned soup, heated in a large pot with Fire Magic provided by Gabriel, he and Ohin went through every detail of the plan with the rest of the team. Gabriel first explained all the events leading up to Teresa's death, and then how he intended to alter each moment, ever so slightly, to create a different outcome. They discussed the plan while eating a dessert of apples Rajan had procured from an old orchard behind the house.

"Something is still not clear to me." Aurelius held his apple, uneaten, in his cupped hands. "Why must we kill the girl in a different way in order to save her?"

"She's part of the Primary Continuum now." Gabriel hastily chewed and swallowed a bite of apple. "She has to die now or it will create a bifurcation. But we can't save her from a death by axe. It's too final."

"I still say we could change the angle or direction of the axe and skip all these complicated and risky changes." Ling gestured to Ohin with an apple core. "I can put the axe anywhere we need to."

"No, the boy's right." Marcus sat slouched in his chair, drinking a bottle of beer, ironically chilled by the heat dispersing power of Gabriel's Fire Magic. "An axe blade can create too much damage no matter where it strikes, and the handle is too small to be fatal. The real problem is the body. I'll need at least a week to create a Replacement. And I have nothing to create it with."

"Use this." Gabriel pulled a folded piece of paper from his pocket and handed it to Marcus. "I can help you speed up the process of making the body. With two of us, it won't take as long."

"You really have thought of everything." Marcus pulled a dark black hair from the folded paper and held it up. As part of his planning, Gabriel had taken a stray hair from Teresa's shirt.

"Yes, Gabriel has considered all the possibilities." Ohin frowned and looked around the table. "I believe his plan will work. I would never have considered it possible before, but in examining every detail and knowing the timeline of the Primary Continuum to be somewhat flexible, enough so to accept Teresa becoming a part of it, I believe we can change it and save her. However, we cannot control every event. We cannot plan for every contingency. There is a chance, and I don't know how large or small, that we will fail, both in attempting to rescue Teresa and in avoiding the creation of a bifurcation. There will be consequences for that failure, and we all need to accept them before we begin."

"I'd rather face the consequences of failure than the alternative of not trying, simply so we can say we followed the rules." Rajan looked across the table to Gabriel, altering the tone of his voice slightly to indicate his next words were quoted and not his own. *"Be not disgusted, nor discouraged, nor despair, if thou dost not succeed in doing everything according to right principles."*

Aurelius turned his head toward Rajan and squinted in curiosity. Gabriel recognized the words Rajan had quoted. They came from Aurelius's *Meditations*, a posthumously published book of his thoughts and sayings.

"I agree." Sema folded her hands on the table. "We've lost too many friends and allies this day to lose one more. Especially Teresa."

"Here, here." Marcus raised his bottle.

"The sooner we get her back, the sooner she can start annoying me." Ling put her chin in her hand. "I actually miss her annoying me."

Ohin looked at Aurelius, and the others slowly followed his gaze. Aurelius met their eyes, then brought his own to rest upon Gabriel. "We have a duty to those we love, even when there is danger to the world in fulfilling it."

"Then we are agreed." Ohin sat back in his chair and seemed to relax for the first time. "It's been a long and painful day. We'll rest tonight and begin training and organizing first thing tomorrow."

Preparations for the extraction took little less than a week. They spent their days practicing each element of the mission, going over every action on paper and rehearsing them in the backyard during the day or in the massive living room of the house at night. Gabriel wanted to take the team back in time to witness the accident for themselves, but Ohin decided against it. Gabriel would already suffer the effects of the paradox they were about to create, remembering both a death that no longer happened as well as one that did. It would be unwise to submit the entire team to such cognitive distress.

Gabriel cursed himself for not thinking to grab a camera to film the accident and view it later. The idea tempted him in retrospect, but he agreed with Ohin — the risks to his mind from paradox could not be taken lightly. He also had no desire to see the accident again. He found it painful enough to think about it all the time.

As the days passed, they debated possible flaws in the plan and potential anomalies that could be capable of creating a bifurcation. Gabriel and Marcus tended in turns to the rapidly growing simulacrum of Teresa in the downstairs study. They also practiced the methods they would need in order to revive Teresa from the alternate death they planned for her. The gruesomeness of the work weighed heavily on all of them, but on Gabriel in particular. A permanent knot of anxiety gripped his stomach. He found it hard to think about anything beyond the mission, but this only yielded thoughts about Teresa and contemplations of what could go wrong, or worse, condemnations of his failure to protect her in the first place.

Late in the afternoon of the third day, Gabriel sat at the large dining room table, golden autumn sunlight spilling over his plans and drawings as he reviewed the rescue strategy for what seemed like the hundredth time. While he strove to keep the plan from being overcomplicated, he knew he needed to anticipate and compensate for every variable. If they made the slightest mistake in their alterations of the Primary Continuum, not only would a bifurcation be created, but Teresa would likely remain dead forever.

Dead to *him* forever. He could not escape the recurring thought, the constant self-recrimination, that he alone carried the responsibility for her death. He had accepted that responsibility, but would he be able to rectify the result of Teresa's close acquaintance with the most dangerous individual in all known realities, the Seventh True Mage, Gabriel Salvador?

"Something to eat?"

Gabriel looked up from where a single drop of salt water stained the parchment paper spread across the table to find the dark brown eyes of Aurelius steadily meeting his own. Gabriel rubbed his eyelids and took a deep breath.

"Yes. Thank you."

Aurelius slid a worn wooden tray across the table. A half loaf of bread Rajan had baked the day before sat beside a small round of brie Ohin had somehow scavenged from the local town, along with a crystal bowl filled with dark purple kalamata olives from a can.

"I thought you might need some fortification." Aurelius sat down across from Gabriel. "I always found a light snack at midday to be of considerable aid when planning my campaigns."

"I'm fourteen. A snack is always a good idea." Gabriel pulled a hunk of bread free from the loaf and cut a slice of the soft cheese, its pungent odor filling his nose and making his mouth water in anticipation.

"I seem to remember that from my youth, as well." Aurelius plucked an olive from the dish and plopped it in his mouth. Spitting out the pit, he looked at Gabriel, seeming to think while he chewed the delicate meat of the olive. "One can, of course, *over* plan a campaign."

"One mistake could mean disaster." Gabriel stuffed a bite of cheese and bread into his mouth as he stared down at his map of Sagalassos.

"Mistakes can arise while implementing even the best of plans." Aurelius watched Gabriel flinch slightly at his words.

"That's not reassuring." Gabriel glanced up, his eyes a mixture of worry and annoyance.

"I mean, simply, that the universe is dynamic, and therefore, we cannot control every moment of it." Aurelius folded his hands, his voice soothing.

156

"I only need to control a few seconds." Gabriel put his head in his hands as he looked back down at the papers, his hunger evaporating as his anxiety condensed.

"And have you found any mistakes in your plan?"

"No."

"And do you trust your teammates?"

"Of course."

"Then maybe you should trust yourself."

"How can I trust myself when I'm always the cause of death for my friends?" Gabriel looked up again, his voice breaking under the strain of the emotion he struggled to hold in check.

"Are you truly the cause for young Teresa's death?" Aurelius's soft, questioning eyes seemed to peer into Gabriel's heart.

"Being near me makes death more likely." Unable to hold Aurelius's gaze, Gabriel looked out the window, watching the multicolored fall trees sway gently in the wind.

"We cannot despise death, our own or others. It is the will of nature. We are all some aspect of nature's will, whether we die in old age, or on the battlefield, or from some fateful, common accident." The tone of Aurelius's voice brought Gabriel's gaze back from the window.

"I can't watch my friends die because of me. I don't care if it's part of some natural order."

"Would you instead turn your friends away? Banish them from your company? Could you manage without them? Without her?"

"I…"

Gabriel choked as his words dissolved in frustration. Would Teresa and Ohin and the others be better off without him? He knew *he* needed them, needed them for more reasons than he could contemplate, but did they need him? He swallowed back the words and emotions straining his throat.

Aurelius placed his hands flat upon the table, seeming to weigh his thoughts and their possible impact before he spoke them aloud.

"The universe is as one living being, of one substance, like the many strands of a spider's web. This is the truth beneath the truth of our human lives. In our lives, some strands of this universal web hold the others in place. They cling to this central filament for support and

157

structure. Sometimes an emperor is such a strand, binding a nation together. Sometimes it is a boy, gifted beyond all others, the outcome of a war hinging upon his actions. But a single strand is not a web. The web needs both the central and tangent strands, or it simply dissolves in the wind."

"And how many strands will perish because of their connection to me?" Gabriel's jaw ached with the expression of that question, a query his heart fought to avoid answering.

"How many will *live* because of their connection to you?" Aurelius placed his finger on the papers before Gabriel. "Could anyone else save Teresa? Would anyone even dare? Is she in more danger for being close to you or safer because of it?"

"I don't know." Gabriel frowned as he considered the notion.

"It has been my experience that when one goes to war, the safest place to be is next to the best swordsman." Aurelius pulled a piece of bread from the loaf on the tray.

"I'm not a very good swordsman yet." Gabriel eyed the dish of olives, feeling his hunger return as Aurelius's words sank into his mind.

"Sometimes it is better to be the sword than the swordsman. And you are both." Aurelius winked and tossed the chewy bread into his mouth.

Gabriel spent much of the rest of that day and the next considering Aurelius's advice. He felt an odd kinship with the man, one Aurelius also seemed to acknowledge. Both had found themselves at the heart of extraordinary events affecting vast numbers of people, their decisions impacting lives near and cherished, as well as those distant and unknown. Few people could truly understand the weight of the decisions Gabriel had faced and would face. Aurelius knew the costs, personal and collective, of leadership. Gabriel found it a comfort knowing someone who could fathom the depth of the doubt and apprehension accompanying the choices he confronted. He felt thankful fate had thrown the wise Roman emperor into his life.

The night before the attempted extraction, Gabriel sat at the edge of the rickety back porch, staring up at a handful of clouds lazily drifting through the star-filled sky. Gazing at the night sky always calmed his mind. The stars were not nearly as bright as those seen from Windsor

Castle so many millions of years in the past. The light pollution inherent to the 21st Century dimmed the night sky even in a place as remote as the woods surrounding the derelict house.

He counted the handful of constellations Teresa had taught him, remembering starry nights like this as they talked in the castle courtyards or sat waiting for some mission to start. She knew all the constellations. Even in the southern hemisphere. She even knew constellations from Mayan and Egyptian astronomy. He studied Polaris, the North Star, the brightest star in the constellation Ursa Minor, known as the Little Bear. He wondered if Teresa would ever feel for him the riotous mixture of emotions his heart held for her.

Gabriel heard someone step from the house and cross the porch to sit beside him. He continued to stare at the stars, knowing from the way his magic-sense rippled in his mind who sat alongside him.

"It must feel weird for you."

Gabriel thought about the statement and wondered what about his life *didn't* feel weird.

"What do you mean?" Gabriel turned his head to look at Ling.

"Worrying." Ling laughed and punched Gabriel's shoulder lightly before throwing her arm around it. He felt his stomach relax for the first time in days under the strength of her arm. "Normally you plunge ahead and follow whatever wild idea or strange instinct has entered your head without taking the time to consider the possible consequences and dangers. Now you've spent a whole week thinking about what might go wrong and what it will mean for Teresa and us and you. The worrying must feel weird to you."

Gabriel considered Ling's words for a moment. "Is that a compliment or a criticism?"

Ling laughed. "An observation."

"It feels awful." Gabriel knew he tended to act too quickly, without waiting to think through the complications of his decisions. He had been trying to work on that fault, but he realized now that deliberative deeds could carry a set of problems absent from decisive action.

"It's awful for all of us. But not as awful as it could be." Ling raised her eyes to the stars above. "When Teresa first joined us, she was miserable. She sulked. She cried constantly. It made us all depressed to see how wretched she felt. Nothing Sema did seemed to help. For weeks, I resisted comforting her. I told myself she needed to learn to accept her new life in her own way. And I am not a person who finds affection easy to express. Don't give me that look. Anyway, that's what I told myself.

"It wasn't the truth. The truth was I wanted to comfort her, but I didn't want to face the feelings it would bring. It would remind me of the children I had lost. The husband I had to leave behind. I feared those feelings. I thought they would overwhelm me. But I was wrong. I found that when I did offer Teresa comfort, it also gave me solace. Helping her heal the wounds of her loss helped me heal my own."

"How did you comfort her?" Gabriel couldn't quite imagine Ling playing the role of consoling companion.

"The same why I comfort everyone," Ling said. "By giving her unrelenting grief until she'd forgotten how much she ached for her family."

"Like stomping on someone's toe to help them forget they've bumped their head?" Gabriel asked.

"Exactly." Ling laughed again.

"She's wrong about you," Gabriel said. "You're not like a caramel chocolate that's all hard and chewy on the inside, you're more like a cream-filled chocolate that's soft and gooey inside."

Ling sniffed and seemed to think about this for a moment. "You may be right." She lowered her eyes from the stars to look into his. "But don't forget that outer shell of chocolate is rock hard and will break your teeth if you're not careful."

"It's an observation, not a criticism," Gabriel said.

"Well, here's another observation." Ling squeezed her arm around Gabriel's shoulders. It felt like a panther had caught him in its grip, but it filled him with warmth. "I've seen you do amazing things. Things I never thought I'd see any mage accomplish. If you say this plan will work, I have complete faith in you. And you have the best team in the castle to help you. Why worry?"

Ling slipped her arm up around Gabriel's head and brought her free hand around to rub her knuckles lightly against his skull. Gabriel laughed and squirmed away as Ling chuckled in his ear. Her method of comforting might not be conventional, but Gabriel found it compelling in ways that brought tears to his eyes.

He found he slept better that night than he had all week.

The next morning, after a quick breakfast, the team assembled in the backyard and used their amulets to alter their appearances to blend in with the citizens of a Roman town. Gabriel looked at the team, his friends, his new family, as they waited for him to take them into the past, back to Sagalassos, and Teresa.

"Thank you. Thank you for believing."

No one spoke. They didn't need to. The stern smiles on their faces said more than could ever be articulated aloud. Gabriel took the chunk of statue from his pocket and looked at Aurelius, wondering how the man would respond to seeing himself carved in stone in the bathhouse. Then he focused on the magical energy of the imprints in the Sword of Unmaking, attuned his space-time sense to the piece of statue in his hand, and transported the team through time to save Teresa from her death.

CHAPTER 17
RETURN TO RESCUE

Cloaked in Sema's Soul Magic and rendered nearly invisible to the patrons of the Roman bathhouse of Sagalassos, Marcus Aurelius squinted as he stared up at the fifteen-foot statue of himself.

"Not the best likeness I've ever seen." Aurelius turned to Gabriel and the others. "There are far too many of those around."

"Is everyone prepared?" Ohin watched as the others nodded agreement of their readiness. He placed his hand on Gabriel's shoulder. "Let's begin."

Gabriel jumped through space, taking them all to the rooftop of the Nypheum, across the forum plaza from the bathhouse and near the street of Teresa's deadly accident. He jumped far enough back in time to avoid being seen by any of his previous selves who were watching the street and ultimately, Teresa's demise. He then jumped through space with each team member to their designated positions along the street, slowly releasing the cloak of Soul Magic around them. Except for Sema, they would each need to rely upon their training to remain unnoticed. They also relied upon their amulets to alter their appearances so there would be no chance of Teresa spotting and recognizing them by accident. Aurelius, with his limited training received at the safe house over the past week, blended in as well, if not better, than the others, appearing to be merely an old Roman man resting against the wall of a home.

When he had finished, Gabriel floated up through the air, hovering above the street to survey the extraction and await his part in the rescue. He observed as previous versions of himself warped space and time, popping into existence along the rooftops of the street. If he had not known when and where to look, they would have remained invisible.

Eventually, Gabriel caught sight of Teresa walking across the stones of the forum, followed by the original version of himself.

Gabriel looked up the street and saw the log-filled wagon shuddering along the stones of the lane, the two men perched atop the tree trunks, one driving the oxen, the other talking as he held the axe against his shoulder while...

Sema, leaning against a nearby wall, consciously unseen by all who passed, reached out with Soul Magic to the mind of the man holding the axe, making a gentle subconscious suggestion that the man accepted and acted upon without a pause in his monologue to his companion, lowering the axe from his shoulder and wedging its blade into a log beside him, while...

At the far end of the street, the soldier urged the horses pulling the chariot onward with a crack of the reigns, while...

Aurelius turned his head, following the chariot as it passed him, his face pulled tight as he pressed his precarious Wind Magic knowledge to its limit, using it to push back against the chariot, slowing its passage by almost exactly a second, while...

Back along the street, Sema looked after the passing wagon, using Soul Magic again, touching the mind of the driver, convincing him to hold his hand, to pause in his constant flicking of the driving stick against the backs of the oxen, allowing them to act upon her magically induced direction to lessen their pace, reducing the wagon's speed by nearly a full second, while...

Exiting from her home, a woman emptied a clay bowl of water onto the street, never noticing Rajan walking idly past as he focused Stone Magic upon the flowing water, altering its viscosity, making it thicker while gradually slackening its descent to the ground, adding practically a second to the time it took to fall across the stones, while...

The chariot thundered passed Teresa, her eyes falling on a large gray dog ahead of her, meeting the animal's eyes, while...

Across the street, Marcus used Heart-Tree Magic to coax the dog into a vicious growl, causing Teresa to alter her path by stepping into the street a second sooner, while...

A sandy-haired boy kicked his wooden ball along the side of the street, running past Ling, who wrapped the rolling toy in a cloud of

Wind Magic, slowing it down slightly as the boy's foot made sideways contact and sent it skipping into the street, where he quickly followed it a second later than he would have, while…

The soldier standing in the speeding chariot strained at the reins, steering the horses around the oblivious young boy and into the street, while…

The side of the rear wheel of the wagon slammed into the chariot, while…

Teresa, walking across the street, looked up to the sound of the collision, her feet hesitating, uncertain which way to turn, while…

The frightened oxen charged, the wheel collapsing under the strain, the wagon rolling, logs tumbling into the street, while…

The gray dog, urged again by Marcus's magic, barked and yelped, diverting Teresa's attention for a second, while…

A slender log struck the ground, bouncing end over end, propelled and guided by Gabriel's Wind Magic, hurtling through the air, while…

Teresa turned away from the barking dog and back to the street, exactly as the well-timed and expertly guided log struck her in the chest, knocking her to the ground, her body bouncing with the impact, the log rolling away as her head hammered into the stones of the street, her heart stopping, her eyes closing as she died, while…

Ohin stepped from the shadows of a building carrying a slender form wrapped in a sheet, enveloping the area around Teresa with a space-time bubble as Marcus strode over and knelt beside her.

Gabriel floated down from the sky and stood beside them.

Time within the bubble slowed and Gabriel reached out with his magic-sense to observe as Marcus placed his hand on Teresa's chest, resuming the beating of her heart with a small pulse of Heart-Tree Magic.

Ohin lowered the Replacement body to the ground and removed the sheet while Gabriel used Wind Magic to lift a still-unconscious Teresa into the air.

Ohin adjusted the Replacement body and stood up. The slender form lying in the street looked exactly like Teresa, but had never possessed the possibility of life.

164

Gabriel glanced across the street and saw his older self. He felt an odd twisting of his space-time sense, a bizarre blending of memories filling his mind, memories of seeing Teresa dying from an axe blow, memories of grieving, memories of seeing himself save Teresa with Ohin and Marcus.

He looked away before his mind could become overwhelmed by the paradox of his actions. His space-time sense gave no indication that a bifurcation threatened to form. So far, they had succeeded. He removed a rusted nail he had taken from the back door of the abandoned house in Maine and jumped through space and time, taking Marcus and Teresa with him.

The three appeared beneath the shadowed branches of a chestnut tree in the backyard behind the abandoned house. Gabriel lowered Teresa to the grass with his Wind Magic and sat beside her. Marcus, still kneeling at her side, flooded her body with Heart-Tree Magic. Gabriel watched as the bruised flesh of her face and arms healed, turning from plum to nut brown. Behind them, Ohin and the rest of the team appeared. It had been Ohin's responsibility to collect the other team members and bring them back to the house.

"She's coming around." Marcus pulled his hands away as Teresa's eyes fluttered.

Teresa blinked and looked around, seeing Marcus, Ohin, and the team. Her eyes finally settled upon Gabriel. He felt his hands shake and his heart pound.

Teresa lived.

"Took you long enough." Teresa frowned and leaned up on one arm.

He laughed as tears ran down his cheeks. Without thinking, he threw his arms around her and pressed his lips to hers. If the sudden kiss startled her, the surprise did not last long. She sat up, wrapped her arms around him, and pulled him closer.

Gabriel's mind could not hold the tumult of thoughts colliding with it any more than his heart could contain the welter of emotions struggling to escape all at once. Time seemed suspended as Gabriel and Teresa kissed, a year of unspoken desires unleashed in a single, simple human act.

"Well, at least someone follows my advice on romance." Marcus laughed, his deep baritone rumbling in Gabriel's ears, soon joined by laughter from the rest of the team.

Their public display of affection finally registering to each of them at the same time, Gabriel and Teresa broke apart, eyes still locked together.

"Now that is the way to rescue a girl!" Teresa sighed, finally looking around at the others, bashful but excited.

"Sorry it took so long." Gabriel held Teresa's hand.

"I thought I was dead." Teresa's bewildered smile flickered away and then returned. "But I'm not."

"You were," Ling said.

"So we had to kill you," Rajan said.

"A second time," Aurelius added. "Or a third time. I find it confusing."

"And by altering the time line slightly to do it," Ohin said.

"Let me guess whose idea that was." Teresa turned and frowned at Gabriel.

"I had to." Gabriel squeezed her hand. "I couldn't let you die if I had a chance to change it."

"You're an idiot." Teresa shook her head.

"Maybe," Gabriel said. "But, you'd never kiss anyone who wasn't smart enough to figure out how to save you from being dead."

"He's got you there, lass." Marcus laughed again.

"You're right." Teresa laughed, as well. "How did I end up in that Roman town? The last thing I remember is heading to meet you for the notebook switch."

"Kumaradevi." Gabriel felt anger return at the mention of her name.

"Naturally." Teresa made a sour face. "Anyway, after I knew I had become part of the Primary Continuum, I thought for sure I would die there for good. I even considered trying to take my own life so there might be a chance I could be extracted, but I couldn't bring myself to do it. I don't know how you managed it, I don't know how you could alter time without creating a bifurcation, but you found a way to save me. Thank you. Thank you all."

Teresa squeezed Gabriel's hand hard as she wiped her eyes and looked at the tearful faces of her friends and teammates. Gabriel rubbed his eyes, as well. Teresa lived. She hadn't died, trapped in the past. He and the team had freed her from what had once appeared to be an irrevocable death in the ancient Roman Empire.

Gabriel frowned.

Free.

Some tenuous thought sought his attention from the hinter regions of his mind, clawing its way through subconscious darkness and braying quietly for attention.

Something about being free. What was freedom? What was the nature of freedom?

No.

Something else.

Who was free? Were we free? How did we become free?

No. Not quite right.

Teresa had been freed. What about her freedom was important? How they had freed her? Why they had freed her?

No. Still not right.

What sets someone free? What makes the difference between freedom and servitude or freedom and captivity?

Work?

Why work?

Work will set you free.

Yes.

That was it.

Gabriel realized his eyes had not moved from the grass at his feet for quite some time. He looked up into the concerned faces of Teresa and the team.

"What is it?" Teresa's voice quavered with a hint of fear. "What's the matter?"

"I realized something." Gabriel took a deep breath and exhaled to calm himself.

"I know where the Apollyons who found us at the medieval castle are hiding. We have to find out what they know about the Great Barrier...and how close they are to destroying it."

CHAPTER 18
PREPARATIONS

An ant crawled across Gabriel's arm, tickling the skin as it clambered over fine black hairs. He raised his arm and sent the ant flying into the grass with a short puff of breath. The team sat amid the tall grass behind the abandoned house, sheltered by dense trees from any potential passersby. They ate a simple lunch of tuna sandwiches, canned baked beans, and potato chips. Ling had used Wind Magic to mat the grass down in a swirling pattern Teresa laughingly referred to as a crop circle. She had pouted and complained that no one ever understood her jokes.

"We can't trust the Council." Rajan raised his tuna sandwich to his mouth and paused before taking a bite. "We don't know who we can trust at the castle anymore."

"All the more reason to act alone until we know more." Marcus, to the surprise of everyone, drank a slender bottle of Coca-Cola rather than his preferred beer.

"I agree." Ling shooed a curious bee away from her plate of baked beans. "We risk a spy in the castle informing the Apollyons that we may know one of their hiding places."

"You're certain it's Auschwitz?" Sema took a slice of apple from a dish sitting in the grass.

"It makes sense." Teresa snatched a potato chip from Gabriel's plate. "The Apollyon who appeared while we were captured definitely mentioned the phrase 'Work will set you free' to the rogue Apollyon."

"It's not the kind of phrase that comes up in conversation very often." Gabriel held a spoon of beans to his mouth. "*Arbiet macht frei.* Work sets you free. It's the phrase on the gate to Auschwitz. It'd be a perfect place for them to hide and maintain a link to an enormous supply of Malignant imprints."

"What is this Auschwitz?" Aurelius sat with his hands in his lap, his food as yet untouched on the plate resting in the grass before him. He had been too focused on following the conversation to think about eating.

"A camp for working strong people to death and for killing the weak and the old in large numbers." Sema's lips twitched as she spoke.

"You've had little time to come to terms with how much history has happened since your extraction point." Ohin sat his plate down while he spoke.

"One thing never seems to change. War. There is always war. In the Twentieth Century, there were two great wars that engulfed nearly every nation on Earth. In the second of these World Wars, the ancestors of the Germans you died fighting invaded much of Europe and parts of northern Africa. A man named Adolf Hitler led them.

"He and his senior officers were obsessed with killing the Jews in Germany, Europe, and the world. They created a series of camps where they worked healthy Jews and gypsies and political prisoners to death as slaves. The rest they killed in chambers filled with poison gas and then cremated the bodies. They killed over a million people that way in Auschwitz alone.

"The castle maintains an observation base there, but the team guarding it was pulled away to help with the attack on the Apollyons at Dresden, a German city that was fire-bombed to near-oblivion in the same war."

Ohin's brief history lesson brought a haze of silence to the picnic.

"I can't imagine the people I fought would be proud of their descendants." Aurelius frowned. "A great deal may have happened since my time in the world, but you are right, certain things change very little."

"Some things do get better," Rajan said. "But not quickly, and not for everyone."

"Things will be a lot worse for everybody if the Apollyons manage to break through the Great Barrier," Ling said.

"Yes," Ohin said. "Gabriel and Teresa are right. We need to follow this hint of a trail to where it leads. We'll return to the castle once we've learned what we can and inform Akikane alone. I know we can trust him."

"If we can't trust Akikane, we might as well all slit our own throats now." Marcus frowned with the thought and took a sip of his cola, scowling when he realized it wasn't beer.

"It's the second part of the plan that worries me." Ohin focused his deep brown eyes on Gabriel and Teresa.

"We don't really have any choice," Gabriel said.

"There is always a choice," Sema said.

"You can choose to be stupid and put yourselves in danger," Ling said.

"We won't be in danger," Teresa said. "Well, not much."

"*Too* much danger," Marcus said.

"It seems the best way and an acceptable risk, given the stakes," Aurelius said.

"Says the man with the least experience in the field," Rajan said.

"I may not have a great deal of experience in these endeavors," Aurelius said, "but I have some considerable experience in war. War is risk. And if this subterfuge works, it advances the war considerably."

"I agree." Ohin's voice brought the attention of the others back to him. "It is a risk. We'll mitigate it as much as we can, but if Gabriel and Teresa can pull it off, it may give us the time we need to defeat the Apollyons."

The rest of the team looked unhappy, but refrained from voicing any further concerns.

"Can you have it ready by tomorrow?" Ohin asked Gabriel and Teresa.

"It'll take a little longer than the last time, but I think we can do it by then," Gabriel said.

"We can find most of what we need here in the house," Teresa added.

"Good," Ohin said. "We'll need to prepare for this mission like any other. There's a library in a town not far away. We can make a trip there tonight and see if they have any useful books."

"We're in the year two thousand-twelve," Teresa said, looking at Ohin like a slightly dim uncle. "The library will have a computer we can use to search the Internet. We can find everything we need to know in a few minutes."

"We can use what to access what?" Aurelius's confusion clouded his face.

"It's a device for storing and using information. It also allows you to connect to other devices that store information."

Teresa sighed. Being one of the few people at the castle from so far along the timeline of the Continuum, she was one of only a handful who knew how to use a computer. Even Gabriel had only seen computers on TV and in movies since he had been taken from the timeline before the explosion of personal computers in the late 1980s.

"At this point in time, you can access nearly any information from history," Teresa said. "I keep telling them to let me create a computer network at the castle, but they think there aren't enough people to help, and it's too big a job to create a database large enough to be useful. Memory storage is also a problem. I'd need a decent-sized server, which wouldn't be easy to sneak from the timeline, but I could probably daisy-chain a bunch of old desktop computers together to create a server.

"People threw out computers like used Kleenexes at the time. You see, I think I could download and adapt a few online encyclopedias and create our own intranet, which would allow us to have data terminals around the castle. I could even install a wireless network and we could get laptops and…No one has any idea what I'm talking about, do you?"

Blank faces stared at Teresa. Gabriel managed a supportive and admiring smile, but he really had no clue what she'd been rambling on about, either. For reasons he could not fathom, he found that incredibly attractive. Once again, he realized he found her intellect far more striking than her beauty.

"Whatever it is you were babbling about, I'm sure it's very brilliant…and completely irrelevant to the task at hand." Rajan chuckled.

"As usual." Ling snorted in laughter.

"I'll 'as usual' you." Teresa glared at Rajan and Ling.

"Have another potato chip." Gabriel offered Teresa his plate. She flicked a potato chip at Gabriel. He tried to catch it in his mouth, but it bounced off his nose.

"It sounds as though you've volunteered to lead the research expedition," Ohin said to Teresa.

"Happily." Teresa grabbed one of Gabriel's potato chips and winked at him.

"Good." Ohin brushed a few stray crumbs from his shirt. "If I have my calendar correct, this should be a Sunday and the local library will be closed. That should give us plenty of time to prepare for tomorrow."

A closed sign hung in the window of the library in the small town nearby when Ohin led them to it. Inside, thin wedges of light seeped through curtained windows, hiding their presence from the few people who passed on the street, and leaving the interior of the room heavily shadowed.

Teresa amazed the team, Aurelius in particular, with how much information about Auschwitz she could find in such a short period of time. They hovered around her, faces illuminated by the colorful screen of the computer as she pulled up maps, photos, and page after page of information, seemingly from nowhere.

Gabriel had seen Teresa research a subject from a computer once before, but it still felt to him as though he were momentarily a character in a science fiction film. So much information, so easily accessible. Everyone in the future must be so literate and informed, he thought. How could they not be, with so much history and culture of the world so easily accessible? When he voiced this opinion aloud, Teresa snorted, but said nothing more.

Construction of Auschwitz began in 1940 in southern Poland under German occupation. Three separate, large camps composed the majority of the Auschwitz complex with dozens of smaller satellite camps nearby. Two of the camps sat very close to each other, separated by a railway that carried the ill-fated victims of Hitler's "final solution" to the complex — and their eventual deaths.

After studying war time aerial reconnaissance photos of the area, the team determined that the most likely place for the Apollyons to create a base for harvesting Malignant imprints would be between the two close-set camps, called Auschwitz I and Birkenau-Auschwitz II. Thousands of local residents had been evicted from the area to make way for the complex of camps. Some of the houses between the two main camps had been taken over by the SS-Totenkopfverbände, the German Nazi soldiers responsible for administering the horrors of the

172

camps. Their name meant "Death's Head Units" and referred to the skull and cross bones symbol used in their uniforms.

A weariness fell upon Gabriel as they looked through the maps and photos and read the details of Auschwitz. Sometimes he could not escape the thought that history simply equaled suffering. The knowledge that some of his own Jewish relatives had not escaped that suffering added extra emotional weight to the pain that beleaguered his heart. While his grandfather's father had immigrated to the United States at the turn of the century to escape the historic oppression of Jews in Spain, his grandmother's family had come from Austria. She had often told him stories of the aunts and uncles lost in the Holocaust.

He could understand how a lone mad man might be so cruel, but how did a mad man convince perfectly normal people to become so barbaric? A person like Hitler could insulate himself from his orders to kill, but what of the people who carried them out? Were they evil to begin with, or did they become evil in the process of carrying out genocide? How could so many people's hearts become so dark? Did the imprints of their actions destroy their souls? And if he touched those dark imprints, as he so often did, would they destroy his own soul?

He tried to push the thoughts away, but flashes of the battle at Windsor Castle came to his mind. To the best of his knowledge, he had not killed any Apollyons while defending the castle. He had not witnessed any deaths. But it seemed impossible that all of them had escaped his attacks. At the time, he had felt only anger at them. Only the desire to protect the castle and destroy the army of the Apollyon duplicates. How much of his mind had been influenced by the Malignant imprints he had been using to create his magic? What would have happened if those dark imprints had not been balanced with Grace imprints? Would he have wantonly killed every Apollyon he encountered?

He accepted he might need to kill in order to protect himself or those he cared about in the war, but following Akikane's tutelage, he hoped to avoid it. Akikane constantly cautioned him that violence used with a mind of anger would destroy the defender as much as his attacker. Gabriel agreed with him. He knew what anger could do, but he didn't know if he would ever be able to use violence to defend himself with only a mind of love and compassion.

Maybe such things were only possible for rare people like Akikane. He wondered if Elizabeth worried about such notions. It seemed Nefferati did, or else she would have returned from her retreat to help fight the war.

Gabriel forced these thoughts from his head and helped the team finish their research. They all agreed the best time to look for the Apollyons' base would be after the end of the war, when the most Malignant imprints would be present and there would be less likelihood of discovery.

However, they would also want to stay near the camps in time. The imprints would be stronger the closer they were along the timeline to when the events creating them took place. Ohin assumed they would be no farther than a year from the end of the war. Probably within six months. That gave them a wide window of time, but a narrow stretch of space to search.

CHAPTER 19
UNDER THE STARS

After a dinner of canned soups and a dessert of fresh berries that Sema and Ling had picked in the bushes behind the abandoned house, Gabriel joined Aurelius for a walk in the nearby woods.

"I, too, was groomed from a young age to rule." Aurelius pulled a branch aside as they passed between two trees.

"I'm not being groomed to rule." Gabriel watched his feet, the setting sun casting thick shadows through the tree limbs.

"Not to rule an empire, no, but certainly to lead," Aurelius said. "The Council will no doubt ask you to join its ranks at some point. You are young, but you carry the weight of this strange war squarely on your shoulders."

"I wish I didn't." Gabriel allowed a sigh of frustration to escape his lips along with his words.

"Do not say that." Aurelius looked down at Gabriel with a surprising intensity. "Nothing befalls us which by nature we are not created to bear. You are honored by the Parcae, the sisters of Fate, and by your fellow mages, that you should bear this burden. And from what I have seen, you carry it well."

"But I don't want to carry it." Gabriel had given up the fanciful idea that he could ever have a normal life again. But speaking to Aurelius rekindled that yearning in his heart.

"I did not want to rule an Empire." Aurelius laughed. "Except, of course, I did. Yes, I would have preferred to live my life buried in my scrolls and discussing philosophy, but ruling the Empire was more important. I was responsible not only for my own desires, but for the wellbeing of millions, and the continuation of a way of life, of a culture, of a nation. Although I found it painful at times, it was a reward I could not have anticipated. My only wish is that I could have been the tutor to my son, Commodus, that Junius Rusticus had been to me."

Aurelius looked up into the evening sky beyond the tree branches for a moment before returning his gaze to Gabriel.

"Do not fear the yoke of responsibility. Lean your shoulders into it. In time, you'll find the weight more comfortable. Even when responsibility requires sacrifice."

"Why can't being responsible be enough of a sacrifice?" Gabriel found himself thinking of nearly losing Teresa in Sagalassos.

"Sacrifice is the test of a true leader." Aurelius sidestepped a wide tree. "No one thing is separate from any other. All people of an empire are bound together. You sacrifice the things you love, the things you care about, to maintain the whole of the empire, much like the way one must often sacrifice a wounded limb on the battlefield to save the rest of the body.

"This is a very difficult lesson to learn, especially when you are sacrificing someone you know rather than some faceless solider at a distance. Seeing the value of those you have never met and will never meet and balancing their lives against the lives of those you love will wrench your heart in pieces, but you must sometimes makes these choices…and then calmly sew the pieces of your heart together again."

As they stepped from the woods, Gabriel caught sight of Teresa sitting on the back porch alone. Seeing her as his mind absorbed the meaning of Aurelius's words unsettled him. Would he be able to sacrifice those he cared about if it meant an end to the war? Could he sacrifice Teresa if it meant peace between the Malignancy and Grace Mages? He hoped he would never be faced with that question, but he knew Aurelius spoke the truth — there would come a time when he would need to make hard choices and sacrifice those he cared for.

Again, and not for the last time, he knew, he wished he had stayed at the bottom of that river.

No. No, he didn't. Then he would have never met Teresa.

He felt warmth embrace his heart as she waved to them.

"You risked time itself to save her," Aurelius said as they crossed the yard. "I am grateful you asked me to join you. She is worth risking time and the world."

"Oh, I know," Gabriel said.

"Ready to get to work?" Teresa stood up. "I have everything set up on the dining room table."

"The sooner we start, the sooner we'll be finished." Gabriel climbed the stairs of the porch.

"Half an hour walking in the woods with the most famous philosopher king in history and that's the best aphorism you come up with?" Teresa teased as she took Gabriel's hand.

"He doesn't really speak in aphorisms," Gabriel said.

"Am I really that famous?" Aurelius asked, his eyes suddenly shy.

"People still read your book *Meditations* after almost two thousand years." Gabriel had seen Rajan reading the slender tome constantly before the extraction mission to save Aurelius.

"I find that both gratifying and humbling." Aurelius opened the door for Gabriel and Teresa.

"Well, enjoy it while you can, because nothing you do from now on will be recorded by history, no matter how wonderful and amazing," Teresa said.

"I remember every wonderful and amazing thing you do," Gabriel said, reveling in how wonderful it felt to say extraordinarily cheesy things to the girl he loved.

"As long as you remember to forget every annoying and bumbling thing I do," Teresa said with mock seriousness.

"You never do anything annoying or bumbling," Gabriel said. He stared into Teresa's eyes and tried to hold a straight face. He lasted two whole seconds before he burst out laughing. Teresa gave him a fake pout and then giggled as well, Aurelius joining their laughter as they entered the house.

Gabriel and Teresa spent the rest of the evening preparing what they would need for the next day. They worked by the light of two oil lamps on the dining room table. Sitting side by side, focused intently on their task, they rarely noticed when other members of the team passed through the room. It took most of the night, and when they were finished, they retired again to the back porch, sitting under the stars and holding hands.

"I like this," Teresa said after several minutes of silence spent staring at the stars.

"So do I," Gabriel replied. He wasn't exactly certain what Teresa referred to, but he suspected he would agree if he knew.

"I like knowing I can tell you how I feel about you without worrying that you won't feel the same way or that the rest of the team will judge me. I like that a lot." Teresa turned and kissed him.

"Have you told me how you feel about me?" Gabriel tried to think of anything Teresa might have said.

"Nope."

"Were you planning to?"

"Maybe."

Gabriel thought about that. "I could tell you how I feel about you."

Teresa laughed and kissed him again. "After risking the Primary Continuum and creating a massive paradox around yourself, I think I have a pretty good idea."

"It might be nice to hear it."

Teresa turned back to the stars. "Then I would have to worry."

"Worry about what?"

"What do you think?"

Gabriel gave this some thought. "That you might change your mind?"

Teresa laughed, her eyes twinkling in the starlight. "You are so..." She sighed and wiped the heels of her hands across her eyes.

Gabriel considered Teresa's hidden tears and decided he should be as honest as possible. "I think I'm confused."

Teresa turned back to Gabriel, squeezing his hand. "I don't want to worry about losing you. You're the Seventh True Mage. Your life is constantly in danger. People are always trying to kill you. If I tell you how I feel and you tell me how you feel, then it's real. Get it? This, what we have now, is like a bifurcation in the first thirty-seven hours. A potentiality that hasn't collapsed into a reality. But people can live in a potentiality until it collapses or it's severed. That's where we are, in an unstable probability, where we don't have to worry all the time."

Gabriel cocked his head and frowned. "You might as well be talking about computers and quantum physics, because that makes no sense at all."

"Gabriel…"

"No, seriously. How can you be so smart and not see? I need to worry about *you*, not the other way around. I'm the Seventh True Mage. I'm not that easy to kill. You may be the best Fire Mage ever, but you don't stand a chance against a couple of the Apollyons, much less Kumaradevi, and she's already threatened to kill you. Hell, she *did* get you killed. Once they know we're together, they'll try to kill you just to hurt me."

His conversation with Aurelius came back to him then.

"Or worse. They'll capture you and torture you to make me help them. Or versions of you from alternate realities, like the Apollyons did with Chimali's wife. And then I'll have to choose between you and everyone else. I have much more to worry about."

Teresa looked down at her hand clasped around his.

"Then we should stop. Before anything bad can happen."

Gabriel squeezed her hand so hard her head snapped up, eyes glaring.

"Don't be ridiculous. You've already been dead. If I can save you once, I can save you again."

"And if you can't? Or if I can't save you?"

"I have no doubt you're smart enough to figure out a way to save me from anything."

Teresa suddenly laughed. "Anything but yourself."

Gabriel laughed, as well, because it was probably true.

"I love you."

They stared into each other's eyes. Who had spoken first? Had they spoken at the same time?

They kissed again, and such questions ceased to matter.

Later that night, he sat alone in his room, staring at the flickering shadows cast by a small candle on a weathered nightstand beside the bed. He let his mind wander, flitting from thought to thought with no particular purpose. While exhausted from the day's events, his brain could not relax enough to sleep. He assumed it had something to do with kissing Teresa. And the next day's mission. And the knowledge that Windsor Castle lay partially in ruins. He sighed and leaned over to blow out the candle. Thinking about things never helped him sleep. He'd probably dream about them, anyway, so what was the point?

As he inhaled to blow out the flame, he noticed the drawer of the nightstand setting slightly ajar. Curious, and looking for any excuse to postpone slumber, he pulled the drawer open, examining its contents by candlelight. The drawer held few treasures — a couple of old coat buttons, three coins from the 1960s, a length of string, and an old photo. Out of habit, he used his space-time sense to probe the objects from the drawer. He did this now whenever encountering possible relics for time travel. One never knew when a forgotten or lost object might lead to an interesting time period or turn out to be a powerfully imprinted artifact.

Disappointingly, the buttons, coins, and string all seemed to have remained near the house for most of their existence. In contrast, the small, frayed, black-and-white photo of a woman in a white dress kissing a young soldier had traveled far. A handwritten inscription on the back read *All my love, forever. Harriet. 1916.*

By the look of the soldier's uniform, Gabriel guessed the photo had accompanied the man to the French front lines of World War I. The images flooding his mind as he probed the photo's timeline confirmed his suspicions. Wood-lined trenches. Barbed wire. Mud and smoke. Fallen soldiers. He had spent enough time studying the major battles of history to guess the location. The Battle of the Somme in the late summer of 1916. The rest of the photo's timeline focused on Paris, then London, and finally the abandoned house in Maine. It had probably been passed from one family member to another, ultimately ending up in the bedside drawer. Oddly, for an object carried during a war, it held few Grace or Malignant imprints.

Gabriel sat the photo next to the watch on the nightstand. It never hurt to have an extra relic in his pocket. Blowing the candle out, he let his head sink into the pillow. It smelled a bit musty, like the rest the house, but he found something about the odor comforting. An earthiness that reminded him of simpler aspects of life, far removed from wars of time and magic.

He fell asleep far quicker than he anticipated, and any dreams he had mercifully faded away when he awoke the next morning. One of the first to rise, he found Sema in the kitchen and helped her prepare a simple oatmeal breakfast for the team.

"Dreams?" Sema stirred the oatmeal while Gabriel provided a constant magical flame beneath the pot.

"None I remember." Gabriel added a little water to thin the rapidly congealing oatmeal.

"Still no more dreams of Vicaquirao?" Sema asked. She asked a similar question nearly every morning.

Gabriel shook his head.

Sema frowned. Then sighed. Stopped stirring. Then started again.

"I...hmmm." Sema looked at Gabriel. Then back to the pot.

Gabriel stared at her. She seemed flustered. Gabriel had never seen Sema anything less than composed, even when fighting a horde of Malignancy Mages.

"It's not really my place to say, or to ask, but..." The spoon in Sema's hand paused again. "Have you considered the consequences of a...relationship with Teresa?"

Now Gabriel felt flustered. "I...well...you mean if something bad happens."

"Something bad?" Sema turned to Gabriel.

"Like if one of us gets killed," Gabriel said.

"No." Sema looked horrified at the thought. "No, I meant if one of you...loses interest. We'd still be a team. It's hard to imagine what would happen to the team if one of you left because of...what would happen to you... or to her, or...it would be devastating, really...and you know change is very difficult for some of us and...this is all...

"You see, when I was a girl, there was a boy...before the boy who became my husband...but this other boy, he came from a family my father didn't approve of...I saw him in the market...but it was impossible...that's what I told myself...he asked me to run away with him...but how could I? What would have happened if a year passed and my heart changed? Things can never go backward. The egg breaks, but is never remade. So you see...no, you don't. How could you? I barely see myself. I'm sorry. I shouldn't..."

"Morning." Marcus sauntered into the kitchen. "I see I've been replaced as the kitchen help today."

Sema glanced over her shoulder at Marcus and focused intently on the mushy oatmeal beneath her spoon.

"Morning." Her voice seemed strained. She tasted the oatmeal and silently shook her head.

"Morning," Gabriel said to Marcus. In a lower voice, he turned back to Sema. "It's all fine."

"Forget I said anything," Sema said.

"Forgotten." Gabriel sighed, glad for the awkward conversation to be at an end. Receiving romantic advice from Sema made him profoundly uncomfortable. Almost as uncomfortable as Sema seemed giving it.

"What did I forget now?" Marcus asked as he took clean bowls from the dish rack and headed to the dining room to set the table.

"Nothing," Gabriel said, suddenly reminded of the uncomfortable romantic advice he'd received from Marcus not long ago. He wondered if anyone ever followed their own advice. And he wondered who'd be offering it next. The thought of talking about his love life with Ling or Rajan or Ohin nearly eliminated his hunger.

After breakfast, the team assembled in the living room, ready for departure. Everyone carried a backpack of supplies. They had raided the remaining provisions stashed at the house and had come up with nearly a week's worth of food. It might take a few days to locate the Apollyons, assuming they were really there.

"Ready?" Ohin asked. He held up a tiny sliver of wood. He had taken a trip the night before with Sema and Ling to the National Holocaust Museum in Washington D.C. to procure a relic capable of transporting them to their destination. They had found a book published in D.C. at the local library and used it as a relic to take them to the city. They had taken the sliver of wood from a reconstructed exhibit of the barracks the Jewish captives of Auschwitz had been crammed into. It would lead them through time to the camps.

Everyone voiced their assent to Ohin's query, and the blackness of time travel swirled around them, depositing the team with a flash of white outside the fences of the main Auschwitz camp in the spring of 1945.

CHAPTER 20
RECONNAISSANCE

Their methodical searches of the Auschwitz camps lasted longer than anticipated. They tried to focus on the land near the railway between the two main concentration camps, but the amount of effort required to cover the entire area proved time consuming. They were less worried than usual about alerting any potential Apollyon twins to their presence by warping space with time travel. The Apollyons would be aware that an outpost team from the castle might be observing the area. That team would normally have focused on the camps themselves, but following Gabriel and Teresa's suspicions, the Chimera team looked for places and times where the Apollyons might hide in plain sight.

They broke into two groups, the first consisting of Ohin, Sema, Ling, and Marcus while Gabriel, Teresa, Aurelius, and Rajan comprised the second. Gabriel and Ohin scanned the timelines of houses and buildings near the camps looking for any sign of the Apollyons. It turned out to be a fruitless search, taking days to complete. Most of the buildings were now occupied either by former Jewish prisoners or the Soviet Russian soldiers who had liberated them.

After seeing the physical state of many of the victims of the camps, Gabriel felt profoundly thankful their searches did not need to take place while the mass executions of Auschwitz had been occurring. His grandmother's stories of family members, those who had escaped death in the camps, as well as those who hadn't, came back to him, adding an extra poignancy to the painful emotions elicited by being near that hateful place.

Finally, after three days with no results, Gabriel suggested a daring plan. As the team gathered for dinner around a table in one of the few unoccupied houses in the fields near the camps, he explained his idea by the light of an oil lantern.

"Ridiculous." Ling's grip on her spoon tightened.

"It's perfectly safe," Gabriel said in his most reassuring voice.

"Will not happen." Ling tapped the table with her spoon to emphasize her words.

"We're the only two who can fly." Gabriel tried to sound placating. He hadn't realized how deeply Ling feared heights.

"I'll gladly fly a volunteer." Ling looked around the table as though expecting someone to eagerly raise a hand. No one did. "No volunteers? See? No one wants to fly."

"It's not that we don't want to fly," Teresa said in an overly sweet voice. "It's that we don't want you flying us. We're not kites."

"Same thing." Ling glared at Teresa. "Either way, I'm staying on the ground."

"I'll fly alone then." Gabriel sighed in resignation. "It'll still be quicker than searching on foot the way we have been."

"You'll still be visible if someone looks up." Aurelius hadn't yet touched his food. He never seemed to eat when an important discussion erupted over dinner.

"Not a problem," Gabriel said. "I can bend the light around myself." Gabriel gave a brief demonstration using Wind Magic to force the light from the oil lantern to curve around his body.

It took him a moment. It wasn't the kind of magic he'd become most proficient in. After a few seconds, he seemed to shimmer and disappear. His outline could still be seen if looked for carefully, but to all appearances, he had vanished. Aurelius gasped, and Teresa applauded enthusiastically.

"You're getting better at that." Ling waved her spoon appreciatively.

"Not nearly as good as you." Gabriel released the magic and reappeared. "I can cloak myself, but I can't manage to do it for anything else yet. It's too complicated to figure out how to bend the light with gravity. Especially if there's more than one light source."

"Anyone else have any crazy ideas?" Ohin looked around the table.

"What could be crazier than trying to fly while invisible?" Rajan laughed as he took a sip of water from a canteen.

"It's not crazy, it's ingenious." Teresa gave Gabriel a peck on the cheek and threw her arm around his shoulder. Gabriel felt his face grow warm as he tried to hide the pleasure elicited by Teresa's words and affection.

"There were times I wished I could have made myself invisible." Marcus took another bite of soup from his can.

"There were a number of times I wished I could have made you invisible, as well," Sema said with a straight face. Marcus glowered sideways at her, but then burst out laughing, coughing as he tried to keep soup from shooting out of his nose. Sema chuckled and patted him gently on the back as the others laughed along.

As no one had a better idea than Gabriel's, which he preferred to think of as a subtle combination of Superman's flying and Wonder Woman's invisible plane, they decided to try it the following morning. While Teresa took her turn clearing the table and cleaning up after dinner, Gabriel retreated to the small yard behind the abandoned Polish house. They had sealed the house from any escaping light to prevent being noticed by the patrolling Russian soldiers, so only starlight illuminated the backyard. He waited a moment to allow his eyes to acclimate to the darkness. As he crossed the yard in search of a place to sit, he tripped over something large in the grass and fell to the ground.

"Ouch!" Rajan sat up, rubbing his head.

"Sorry." Gabriel rolled off his stomach and sat beside Rajan. "Didn't see you."

"You're not the only one who likes to watch the stars." Rajan tipped his head back to gaze upward. "It's strange to think about all that beauty hovering endlessly above all this ugliness below."

"It's not all ugly." Gabriel could feel Grace imprints among the overwhelming Malignancy imprints in the surrounding land. "There's some beauty down here, too."

"What does it feel like?" Rajan asked. "We can only feel what's left behind from the best of human impulses. I can't imagine what it must be like to sense the imprints of the worst that humanity is capable of."

"I haven't touched the imprints here," Gabriel said. "I don't want to. Unless I need to. I can feel them. Like a swarm of bees buzzing

186

nearby. That's more than enough. It's overwhelming to touch them directly. Depressing."

"No wonder so many Malignancy Mages go mad." Rajan glanced at Gabriel. "You're not going to go mad on us, are you?"

"I'll try not to." Gabriel attempted to match the levity in Rajan's voice, but failed. The concern that came with touching negative imprints always clung to him.

"I was teasing."

"I know. But it's possible."

"I don't think so. Not you."

"You don't know what it's like. Sometimes I feel..." Gabriel faltered as he tried to express it in words. "Back at the castle, during the battle, I could feel the two imprints warring, even when I used them together. It's easier to create or heal with Grace imprints. Easier to destroy with Malignant imprints."

"Choices." Rajan's voice sounded soft, nearly a whisper. "It's always about our choices. Whether they are conscious. Whether they reflect our conscience."

"Like Auschwitz." Gabriel could see the high fences and walls of Birkenau from where they sat.

"Yes." Rajan followed Gabriel's eyes to the camps. "How could so many people do so much evil? A few evil people we can cope with. That we can understand. There's always someone with a dead soul, but for so many people to do so much evil, that's something else. How do so many people close themselves off from the part of them screaming out what is right and just and humane? Is it fear of the few truly evil people? Fear of turning back after they've started down the path of destruction?"

"I thought one of your philosophy books would have answered that question by now." Gabriel's tone teased, but his question felt serious.

"Plenty have tried." Rajan looked back to the stars.

"Philosophers. Psychologists. Theologians. Whatever the explanations, it always comes down to choices. *You* will face greater choices than any of the rest of us. You already made the choice to use Malignant imprints. I don't know what those choices must feel like. I can't imagine."

Rajan paused for a moment.

"When I was around your age, during the civil strife in India after independence from the British, there were so many people making so many choices. And so much suffering. I chose not to take sides. This wasn't a choice anyone liked, even me.

"One day, I was being chased by a gang of boys. I was always being chased by a gang of boys. Hindu boys on that particular day. I hid, but one of them found me. We fought, and surprisingly, I knocked him down. He hit his head and fell unconscious. As he lay there, I felt this overpowering desire to hit him again. To kick him. At the same time, a part of me wanted to comfort him. To make sure he was uninjured. These two sides fought within, and a choice sat between them."

"What did you do?"

"The other boys returned, and I chose to run." Rajan laughed.

"I wish I could run sometimes." Gabriel wanted to join Rajan's laughter, but couldn't.

"We're all glad you don't." Rajan turned to Gabriel. "I trust your choices, no matter what imprints might influence you. You'll make mistakes and bad decisions. We all do. But you'll regret it. That's why you'll never become like the Dark Mages, no matter what happens."

"I hope you're right."

"I'm always right. Didn't Teresa tell you?"

That did make Gabriel laugh. They were still laughing when Teresa stepped from the house to find them in the yard, which only made them laugh harder.

The next day, Gabriel soared above the camps, cloaked in a wave of gravity, bending light around his body and rendering him nearly invisible. He used a pair of binoculars to scan the woods, fields, and buildings between the main camps for any sign of the Apollyons. He focused his mind to clear any possible Soul Magic the Dark Mages might have used to conceal their location.

The results from the first few hours of searching proved uninspiring. Gabriel returned to the ground frequently, using the farmhouse the team had appropriated as a relic to jump through time by days and sometimes weeks. Ohin insisted the team accompany him on each jump. Although restricted to the ground, they could monitor his progress and come to his aid if something went wrong.

Near sundown, six months along the timeline from the liberation of the camps, on a sultry summer night, Gabriel spotted something at the edge of his vision. Closer examination revealed a large canvas tent pitched beneath the shadowing branches of a small stand of trees near the railway lines. The tent resembled the ones he had seen Soviet Russian soldiers use to store supplies.

He noticed a man in a Russian commander's uniform walking toward the tent. Gabriel recognized the Apollyon even from where he floated several hundred feet above the ground. He watched the Apollyon in Russian uniform open the tent flap. An identical man in uniform greeted him.

A good disguise. The observation teams from the castle would be looking for signs of magic, but the Apollyons, pretending to be Russian soldiers, hid in plain view. If one of the Russian troops questioned them, a simple cover story and a small amount of Soul Magic would protect them, and likely cause no disturbance to the Primary Continuum.

Gabriel slowly returned to the team, making sure to keep his use of magic for flying well away from the tent of Apollyons. He didn't want to attract any attention to himself now that he'd found their hiding place.

He shared his discovery with the team, and they put the next step of their plan into action.

Three nights later, after days of spying on the three Apollyons, Gabriel and Teresa sat in the high grass near a tree line a hundred feet from the tent, listening to yet another conversation between the Dark Mages. The team normally took turns listening to the Apollyons and following them discretely when they left the tent. The conversations between the men often sounded like a madman arguing with himself. Or three madmen arguing, Gabriel frequently thought.

Magic that might have hid the tent from the Russian soldiers would have also alerted any observation team from the castle. As a result, the Apollyons avoided sound shields and Soul Magic cloaks. Instead, they spoke quietly and stayed out of sight as much as possible.

Teresa swatted a mosquito away and leaned forward as she manipulated the small amounts of Fire Magic needed to amplify the low voices of the men in the tent. Gabriel had been impressed when Teresa had shown him how to work the magic that would intensify sound from a distance. He had never thought of sound as a form of energy before. They had taken turns with other team members over the past few days, making the magic that would reveal the Apollyons' secret conversations.

It had been dull work. The Apollyons rarely spoke of anything important. They tended to rehash the same list of grievances again and again. Gabriel sat at the top of their list of enemies, followed closely by Vicaquirao and the Council. Kumaradevi got a mention occasionally, as did individual Grace Mages like Akikane and Elizabeth. Mostly the men bickered with themselves, like a man talking to himself indecisively.

To Gabriel's annoyance, they rarely spoke of the Great Barrier, or more accurately, they spoke of it often, but only to repeat the things they already knew. Unfortunately, they seemed to know little more than Gabriel did. They often cursed him for the loss of the notebook. In the last day, they had often spoken of a group of Apollyon twins who were supposedly examining the Great Barrier closely. They also spoke of the need to move their camp. Apparently, they tried to change locations every week or so.

This final conversation topic led to Gabriel and Teresa taking up watch at night together. As they were the only mages capable of magically manipulating sound, they had seen very little of each other the last few days, alternating long shifts with the rest of the team. Now they sat side by side, appearances altered slightly by their magical amulets to conform to the plan.

After hours of eavesdropping, Gabriel occasionally found his mind wandering to topics more exciting than which Apollyon duplicate should be responsible for making dinner. Topics like how lovely Teresa looked in the dim light from the camp security lights. As he sat reflecting on this apparent truth of nature, Teresa smacked his leg.

"Stop mooning over me and pay attention." Teresa's harsh whisper accompanied a bashful turn of her eyes.

"I wasn't mooning." Gabriel wondered how she could read his thoughts so easily.

"Listen." Teresa gestured toward the tent and Gabriel turned his attention to the identical voices of the Apollyons.

"Can that be right?"

"He thinks so."

"They think so, you mean."

"We think so, you mean."

"But what does it mean?"

"And how…"

"Could it be possible?"

"Does it matter?"

"Yes…"

"Of course…"

"It matters."

"If it took both magics…"

"To create the wall…"

"It may require…"

"Both magics to destroy it."

"We'll need a different plan."

"They agree."

"They will return."

"How will we proceed?"

"We'll need to convene."

"Yes."

"Convene."

"As soon…"

"As possible."

Teresa stood up. "I think that's our cue."

"Do it." Gabriel stood next to her. "Before they have a chance to leave."

"Get ready." Teresa turned back to the tent, and Gabriel felt the power of her Fire Magic increase. The volume of the arguing Apollyons grew louder and louder.

"Where?"

"That's not important."

"How is more…"

"Do you feel that?"

"Yes."

"Nearby…"

Gabriel sensed the warping of space-time nearby and began to warp it himself. As the three Apollyons started to materialize around Teresa and Gabriel, he jumped through time. A moment later, he and Teresa stood at the edge of jungle near a towering ziggurat, thousands of people chanting in the wide, stone-lined plaza at its base. A moment later, they stood atop a lighthouse, looking out at the sun setting behind a placid harbor. Another moment took them to the rooftop of a bustling Chinese town, Imperial soldiers marching down the street. Several moments, and as many time jumps later, they stood in the middle of a large room with a vaulting stone ceiling above. Moonlight scattered through ornately cut stone screens to reveal twin, baroquely carved sarcophagi in the center of the room.

Gabriel had never been in the room before. A coin from the 19th Century British Empire had brought them there. While he had seen photos of the exterior of the Taj Mahal he had never witnessed any of the chambers within. The room stunned him with its architectural symmetry and beauty. The balance and line in both structure and decoration took his breath away. Begun in 1632 and constructed over the course of twenty years by Mughal Emperor Shah Jahan to commemorate the death of his favorite wife, Mumtaz Mahal, the burial monument became one of the most famous architectural achievements in history.

"Are we clear?" Teresa looked around the mausoleum, wide-eyed at its splendor.

"I think so." As the words left Gabriel's mouth, he felt a space-time seal fold tightly around him. His head snapped around as the air shimmered and two Apollyons revealed themselves. Apparently, they also knew the trick of invisibility.

"That was..."

"Quite a chase..."

"Fortunately we had..."

"The best instructor."

The twin Apollyons grinned wickedly in the dim moonlight as they stepped toward Gabriel and Teresa, walking around the sarcophagi of Emperor Jahan and his beloved wife. The Dark Mages, still dressed in Russian uniforms from World War II, stopped some ten feet from where Gabriel and Teresa stood. Gabriel held all the imprints of the pocket watch and the Sword of Unmaking. He tested the space-time seal and found it unbreakable. The two Apollyons could have access to untold imprints through their links with their twins.

"You've been eavesdropping."

"Poorly."

"We could have taught you…"

"Much better skills."

"Tell us…"

"What did you hear?"

The looks in their eyes implied that ignoring the request would be unwise.

"Enough to know you're clueless." Gabriel's voice, louder than he had intended, but thankfully steady and free of its recent hormonally induced changes, echoed from the domed ceiling.

"And you are all totally out of your minds." Teresa's words seemed to sting the Apollyons like wasps.

"We are…"

"Not mad…"

"Yes, *sane* people finish each other's sentences all the time." Teresa snorted in contempt.

"We are not mad…"

"Little girl…"

"We are becoming…"

"Something which has never…"

"Existed…"

"In any time."

Gabriel could sense Teresa's anger at being referred to as "little girl" and hastened to speak before she could respond to the taunt. "Release us."

"How did you find us…"

"After leaving the castle?"

"And where is…"

"The other one?"

Gabriel glanced at Teresa, dressed as she had been while trapped in Chateau Gaillard. The Apollyons had made the first assumption. So far so good.

"I've also had good instructors." Gabriel said. "You were easy to follow after we found your rogue and got the notebook back."

"You've found him…"

"Give it to me…"

"To us…"

"Tell me…"

"Tell us where he is."

"He has a private world," Teresa said.

"He's been hiding from you," Gabriel said.

"Planning," Teresa added.

"Plotting," Gabriel said.

"Tell me…us…"

"Tell us now."

The Apollyons stepped closer, their faces twitching in agitation.

"Stay back!" Gabriel reached behind, yanking at his rear pocket, thrusting the small volume forward, the red leather cover seeming black in the moonlight. "Release us, or we'll destroy the notebook."

Teresa's hand leapt with flame as the Apollyons stopped in unison.

"Give it to us…"

"Or we will kill the girl…"

"Release us and we'll tell you how to find the rogue twin." Gabriel glared at the Apollyons, no longer caring how loud his voice sounded.

"Give it to us…"

"Now!"

One of the Apollyons reached out his hand and the notebook flew from Gabriel's fingers. Gabriel focused his Wind Magic on the small book and it halted, hovering in midair between himself and the Apollyons.

"Release it, boy."

Gabriel focused all of his magical energy into the act of holding onto the notebook. It wavered in the air, moving back toward him for a moment before being pulled toward the Apollyons an inch. The Apollyon challenging him growled.

"Enough!" The second Apollyon joined his twin in the magical tug of war, reaching his hand out and adding his own magical energy to the fight. Gabriel held on a moment longer, the notebook tumbling where it floated. Then the combined strengths of the Apollyons overcame him, and the notebook sped through the moonlight into their grasping hands.

As the notebook touched the two Apollyons fingers, a flash of blue light subsumed them. When the blue light faded the two men were gone, and with them, the space-time seal surrounding Gabriel and Teresa. Teresa let the flames in her hands wink out as they cautiously looked around the room.

"That went better than expected." Teresa gave Gabriel a quick kiss.

"Since we expected them to try and kill us, I guess so." Gabriel took Teresa's hand and looked around. "Hello?"

"That did go well." Ohin's voice echoed around the room.

Gabriel and Teresa spun to see shadows shimmer as Ohin and the team appeared in the dark corners of the room. They had been hiding behind Ling's Wing Magic invisibility in the event that the plan went sour and Gabriel and Teresa required rescuing.

The plan had been Gabriel's idea, and pride swelled his chest at how successful it had been. He and Teresa had created a fake notebook, complete with pages of cypher-like gibberish, to fool the Apollyons into thinking they finally possessed the real notebook with all its secrets about the Great Barrier of Probability.

Gabriel and Ohin had enchanted the duplicate notebook with the same kind of spell the Apollyons had used on the dagger in the Aztec temple nearly a year ago. A very rare coin wedged in its pages would take the two Dark Mages to a barren stretch of arctic ice in the early 20th century. They would hopefully assume Gabriel had booby-trapped the notebook as a precaution. They were certainly paranoid enough to make that presumption.

The team had chosen the Taj Mahal because Ohin wanted a place unlikely to have many negative imprints that the Apollyons might be able to use.

The difficult part of the plan had been letting the Apollyons know they were being observed. The team had hoped to spend a week or more spying on the Dark Mages, but their lack of useful knowledge and their imminent plans to move their basecamp increased the pace of the team's schedule. Gabriel felt grateful they had managed to learn one extremely significant piece of information from the mission.

"We overheard something important." Gabriel said as Ohin and the others stepped from the shadows.

"The Great Barrier was produced using both Grace and Malignancy magic." Teresa nearly bounced on her toes with excitement as she delivered their carefully collected intelligence.

Gabriel frowned, but refrained from sighing. That small piece of information about the creation of the Great Barrier of Probability held more promise than anything they had learned so far. He couldn't blame her for being excited to share it, even if they had no idea what it might ultimately mean.

"That seems improbable." Ohin stroked his chin.

"Maybe we should change the name to the Great Barrier of Improbability," Rajan said.

"Maybe there was a time when the two sides managed to cooperate," Sema said.

"Or maybe there will be a time," Marcus said.

"You mean this wall could be created in our future, yet exist in the past?" Aurelius spoke while examining the craftsmanship of the carvings lining the two sarcophagi.

"It makes my head hurt," Ling said. "And my head can hurt somewhere else."

"Ling is right. We should go." Ohin waited for everyone to circle around him before taking them through time to the abandoned house in Maine. When the whiteness faded, they stood in the middle of the wide living area at the back of the first floor.

"Let's get to work." Ohin clapped his hands together. "We need to do a full sweep of the house and the grounds. It should be safe this close to the barrier, but we…"

Ohin frowned. Gabriel's heart seemed to stop in his chest. The black void of time travel began to surround him and the team in conjunction with a space-time seal. Gabriel instinctively drew the Sword of Unmaking, grasping its imprints as he spun around, focusing his magical energy on ending the time travel jump before it could begin. He felt Ohin's magic join his own as he spotted a man outside the window. One of the Apollyons had followed them.

Gabriel felt time moving around them, not the way it normally did in a space-time jump, but as though they were rushing through one day after another, darkness and daylight flickering outside the window. The Apollyon's magic forced them forward through time, toward the future and the Great Barrier of Probability. Gabriel's heart thundered in his chest now. If this Apollyon managed to push them over the edge of the Great Barrier, they would be trapped in the future, forever separated from the past and everyone they knew.

CHAPTER 21
MISTAKES

"The Barrier," Gabriel shouted. "He's trying to push us into the future!"

"Hold fast." Ohin clasped one hand around the ancient seashells at his neck and squinted his eyes in concentration.

Gabriel focused all the magical energy at his command upon the task of halting the bubble of time travel pushing the team toward the Great Barrier of Probability at 4:45 p.m. October 28, 2012. He could feel Ohin struggling to do the same, their magic working in concert to slow their progression through time.

As days passed in mere seconds, Gabriel saw Teresa thrust her arm toward the Apollyon outside, intending to attack him. Her hand opened, aimed at the Apollyon, but nothing happened, a looked of stunned confusion crossing her face. Gabriel saw that Ohin had reached out and clasped his hand around Teresa's wrist. He had grasped the imprints of Teresa's talisman bracelet in an attempt to increase the magical energy at his disposal. Ohin's other hand touched Ling's arm, drawing the imprints of her necklace talisman through the limb of her body. The other team members turned and assaulted the Apollyon with magic he deftly deflected.

The days and nights passing outside the windows came to a sudden halt. Gabriel could see the look of consternation filling the face of the Apollyon outside the house as he cursed aloud. Fear pulled the features of Gabriel's face tight. The team hovered at the edge of the Great Barrier, suspended in time, a fraction of a second from being pushed irrevocably into the future, beyond the wall, permanently divided from the past.

"Closer together," Ohin shouted, pushing Teresa and Ling toward the others.

Marcus and Sema leapt to the center of the room as Gabriel pushed Rajan with one hand and turned to pull Aurelius with the other. Gabriel's fingers grazed Aurelius's outstretched hand as the old Roman Emperor began to shimmer, his image wavering like stone seen through turbulent water. Gabriel lashed his Time Magic around Aurelius, trying to pull him back toward himself and the others, back to the known side of the Great Barrier.

Aurelius stared into Gabriel's eyes, a mournful curve along his lips. "Save yourself."

His voice sounded distant, as though echoing through a still forest. Aurelius's words reverberated in Gabriel's ears as he watched the unique man he had grown to know and care for fade from his sight, passing beyond the Great Barrier of Probability and into the future, never to be seen by those in the past again.

Gabriel's body shook with a depth of anger that frightened him. Aurelius had departed from his life. Gone forever. There was no possibility of rescue. No one could cross back after passing through the Great Barrier of Probability separating time.

Gabriel spun and screamed his rage, his hand reaching toward the Apollyon outside the window. Wind Magic shattered the glass window, sending a storm of dagger-like shards exploding toward the Dark Mage's face. The Apollyon yelled in fury as he turned from the flying glass, his hold on the time bubble surrounding the team weakening. The Apollyon looked back for a moment, his eyes mirroring the wrath Gabriel felt boiling within.

The Apollyon winked away, warping space-time around himself to flee. Gabriel could feel Ohin maintaining the space-time bubble, beginning to move the team backward in time, safely away from the edge of the Great Barrier. Gabriel knew he should help. Knew he should ensure Teresa and his team made it to safety.

But another thought dominated his mind.

He reached out with his space-time sense, searching for the telltale signs of the Apollyon's departure.

An image filled his mind.

He glanced briefly at Ohin and Teresa.

"Gabriel..." Ohin began to say as Teresa opened her mouth to speak.

Gabriel jumped through time, blackness surrounding him as he pursued the Apollyon who had thrust Aurelius beyond the Great Barrier of Probability and out of his life.

Caution guided the twinned Apollyon's escape as he jumped through time to a small pre-historic group of clay brick huts, then to a slender alley in a city that looked like Istanbul in the 1950s, and then to the banks of the Nile River, the Egyptian pyramids of Giza glowing white in the noonday sun. Finally, the Apollyon stopped on a hillside on an unidentifiable grassy plain.

As Gabriel followed his prey, he gave hasty thought to how to attack the man. He would need a massive number of imprints to confront the Dark Mage. As he thought through the relics in his pockets, he remembered the photograph from the drawer of the nightstand in the abandoned house. A photo some nameless English soldier had taken with him to the Battle of the Somme. A photo of his beloved to comfort him in combat. A combat that would result in over a million casualties and some 300,000 deaths in a little over four months.

As Gabriel materialized from whiteness beside the Apollyon on the grassy hillside, he wrapped the man in folds of space-time and yanked him away, appearing a moment later in the middle of the World War I battlefield near the River Somme in France. Gabriel immediately claimed the imprints of the fighting still raging around them and the deaths it had wrought. His stomach churned, and he fought back the urge to vomit as the dark imprints of thousands upon thousands of violent deaths flooded through him. He placed a space-time shield around the Apollyon and drew the Sword of Unmaking. The Apollyon turned to him, a surprising smile on his face.

"You are beginning to learn." The Apollyon shouted to be heard above the sounds of falling shells and machine gun fire. Around them lay the dead men who had fallen during of weeks and weeks of mechanized warfare.

"I've learned nothing from you." Gabriel wrinkled his nose against the caustic smoke from the exploding bombshells and the stench of bodies left to decompose in the muddy, barbwire-laden earth between the Allied French and British trenches and those of the invading Germans. The beautiful French countryside had been transformed into a desolate, crater-filled wasteland of charred, splintered trees, fallen at odd angles, much like the dead soldiers who lay beside them, weapons abandoned with death, the earth quaking and the air pulsing with the impact of every bursting shell.

"Now, you will learn how to die." The Apollyon's smile vanished as the mucky ground beneath Gabriel's feet shook and tried to suck him down.

Gabriel countered the Apollyon's Stone Magic and attacked with his own, heaving every nearby piece of metal at the Dark Mage. The Apollyon repelled the attack as Gabriel assaulted with another, lightning flaring from his free hand and striking the man in the chest.

The Apollyon stumbled as Gabriel reached out with Soul Magic and Heart-Tree Magic to attack the Dark Mage's mind and body. The Apollyon fought back Gabriel's magic and lashed out with a wave of Stone Magic, attempting to disintegrate the molecules of Gabriel's limbs. Holes dissolved in patches across his clothes as Gabriel deflected the Apollyon's magic, feeling his anger toward the Dark Mage intensify like a flame given pure oxygen to burn.

The Apollyon scrambled backward, casting a wave of Wind Magic upward and exploding a series of falling shells in midair. Gabriel sensed the space-time seal he held around the Apollyon begin to falter as a bifurcation began to erupt. The Apollyon's attempt to break the space-time seal mirrored the method Gabriel himself had used to defeat an Apollyon in the Hurtgen Forest nearly a year ago.

Gabriel split his concentration, focusing on holding the space-time seal in place while simultaneously directly magical energy through the Sword of Unmaking to sever the bifurcation, even as it formed.

As Gabriel cut the alternate branch of reality from the trunk of the Primary Continuum before it could fully be created, the Apollyon laughed and waved his hand, exploding more falling shells with Wind Magic, causing the ground to shake and soldiers to collide with Stone Magic. Flames leapt up among the trenches in the distance with Fire magic, each action creating yet another burgeoning bifurcation.

"And here is what I have learned from you!" The Apollyon cackled as he splashed through muddy puddles of stagnant water.

Gabriel chased the Apollyon, struggling to hold the space-time seal around the man and destroy the alternate worlds he wantonly created in an attempt to flee. If even one alternate world came into existence completely, it would break the space-time seal that kept the Apollyon on the battlefield. If all those alternate worlds the Apollyon was attempting to create came into existence at once, it could permanently damage the Primary Continuum.

Gabriel dodged around a charging soldier, who seemed lost and alone on the battleground. He did not even attempt the Soul Magic necessary to hide himself from the man. Stopping the Apollyon consumed all his attention. The Apollyon's next flash of Wind and Fire Magic engulfed Gabriel, sending him crashing into a tangled roll of barbed wire in a cloud of flames. Gabriel severed the final potential alternate reality as the metal wire bit into his back. He screamed in pain, feeling the space-time seal slip from his grasp while the Apollyon erected a new one around him.

Pain sliced at him in a hundred places as he rolled through the mud, trying to untangle himself from the barbed wire while magically extinguishing the flames biting at his flesh. He felt the storm of anger within him roil and spin, transforming into a whirlwind of fear as he looked up to see the Apollyon walking toward him, eyes burning with rage.

"You have learned your last lesson, boy." The Apollyon threw his arm to the side, the rusted sword of a dead German officer leaping into his hand.

Gabriel stood to his feet, the Sword of Unmaking shaking in his grip. He wiped the mud from his eyes and clasped the hilt of the blade with both hands as the Apollyon charged. Gabriel's feet slipped in the mud as he sought better footing to defend himself. He slid sideways, nearly falling, but managed to bring his sword up to block the arc of the Apollyon's attack at the last moment. Gabriel panicked, jumping back as the Apollyon continued to attack, swinging for his head, thrusting for his heart, attempting to hack at his arms.

Gabriel parried each attack, slowly regaining some of his confidence as he regained his footing. His hours with Akikane were saving his life. He blocked a blow to his neck and countered with two quick slashes at the Apollyon's midsection.

Unable to jump through space due to the seal the Apollyon held around him, Gabriel knew he had to attack with other magics. He might be able to fend off the Apollyon for a time, but he was no match with a sword against the experience and physical strength of the man he faced.

"At least the old man has taught you how to fight," the Apollyon said. "Fight old men, that is."

Gabriel jumped, Wind Magic sending him soaring over the Apollyon, the Sword of Unmaking flashing toward the man's head as Stone Magic caused the mud-soaked earth to reach up and grasp his ankles. The Apollyon ducked the blade, swinging his own sword, a flowing web of lightning reaching out to embrace Gabriel in the air. As he fell to the ground, teeth rattling, he had a moment to be thankful that their fight in the barren section of the battlefield would be unlikely to draw enough attention to create a bifurcation. It felt a paltry solace as he rolled to his feet, limping to favor a bruised knee.

"No amount of magic will save you this time." The Apollyon surged forward, his sword flashing around Gabriel in a series of brutal attacks.

Each time their sword blades met, Gabriel could feel himself being driven back, closer and closer to the water-filled pit of an exploded shell. His mind raced to think of some escape, but with his concentration split between fending off the Apollyon's sword and the curses of dark Soul and Heart-Tree Magic the man cast upon him, he couldn't spare a moment to contemplate a path out of the battlefield.

As his foot slid back under the weight of yet another bone-rattling blow from the Apollyon's sword, Gabriel realized he would die there in the mud of that battlefield, lost among all the thousands of forgotten soldiers whose bodies littered the ground between the opposing armies.

He focused on the imprints he held, weaving Grace and Malignancy energy into Wind Magic to form a shield around his body. The charging Apollyon's sword rebounded from the invisible shield, striking him in the face. The Dark Mage cursed in rage, a stream of blood running down his cheek from the cut on his forehead. He raised the sword, pointing it at Gabriel's heart, the tip of the blade pressing against Gabriel's shield of Wind Magic.

"We will give you one more lesson before we kill you, boy." The Apollyon grimaced, and Gabriel felt something odd, something he had never encountered before. His hold on the imprints of the battlefield began to waver, as though he grasped an object suddenly transforming from solid stone to wispy vapor. As the imprints of the battlefield slipped away, he sensed the Apollyon taking hold of them. Gabriel could feel his magical shield collapsing under the Apollyon's newly empowered magic.

The Dark Mage's sword blade pierced the invisible boundary of Wind Magic with ease.

"I can tell you how to find him." Gabriel said, stepping backward, the Sword of Unmaking raised before him. He felt a small pride knowing the blade held steady and did not waver from the pounding of fear in his heart.

"We don't need to know where he is." The Apollyon's sword touched Gabriel's.

"You'll want to know what he's doing." Gabriel edged sideways, hoping to find firmer ground to make a last stand. "He is the Prime."

"He is not." The cavalry sword slashed.

"He is." Steel met steel, and the ancient katana sword thrust forward.

"It will not matter."

"He will fight you."

"He will die."

The Apollyon yelled and unleashed a blazing series of attacks, his sword glowing white-hot, denting the metal of the Sword of Unmaking each time it struck. Gabriel fell backward, the flaming blade singeing his arm, burning through cloth and flesh. He cried out in pain, the Sword of Unmaking falling from his hand. He leapt backward to avoid the swing of the fiery sword, slipping in the mud and falling to the ground. Gabriel looked at the Sword of Unmaking, its blade buried in the muck. The Apollyon stepped toward him, sword point aimed at his chest.

Gabriel felt the tip of the sword draw blood where it stabbed above his thundering heart. Panting from fear as much as the fight, he stared into the Apollyon's deep, near-black eyes.

He had been foolish, and his foolishness had finally caught up with him. He would die, and with him, the best hope for saving the Great Barrier and ending the War of Time and Magic.

He sat up, leaning into the blade of the sword with a grimace as another emotion overwhelmed his fear and gave him a strange kind of strength. Shame. He might die a fool's death, but he would not die a coward.

"It's a pity you could not join us." The Apollyon wiped the sweat from his eyes with his free hand. "You will never know the future…and we will rule it."

Gabriel realized something as he lay in the mud, shells still exploding in the distance, machine gun fire filling the air, screams of dying men echoing across the barren land.

"He will stop you."

"He is not the original among us, and he cannot stop us." The Apollyon sneered and made to drive the slender blade into Gabriel's heart.

"Not your original twin." Gabriel managed a weak smile, knowing the fear and anger his next word would illicit. "Vicaquirao. He will stop you."

The Apollyon's mouth twitched, and he shook his head. "He cannot…he would not…he will never…"

The air hummed, and the Apollyon staggered to the side, spinning around, a plume of blood spurting from his chest. Gabriel looked sideways to the Sword of Unmaking as the Dark Mage fought to regain his feet. Gabriel embraced the hilt of the sword with an invisible hand of Wind Magic and threw it through the air, guiding it like a javelin into the distracted Apollyon's chest.

The Apollyon fell to his knees, the shaft of the sword jutting from his ribcage. Gabriel sensed the space-time seal around him fade away. He quickly created one around the Apollyon, grabbing the imprints of the battlefield as he felt the Dark Mage reluctantly release them.

Gabriel used his Wind Magic to pull his sword free from the Apollyon's chest and deliver it through the air into his open hand as he scrambled to his feet. He stood above the Apollyon as the man wheezed, trying to breathe. A stray battlefield bullet had punctured one of his lungs, the sword wound piercing the other. Gabriel held the Sword of Unmaking to the Apollyon's throat. The anger had returned with the imprints of the battlefield. Gabriel struggled to keep his head clear of the dark impulses filling his mind.

"Luck." The Apollyon spat blood and fell back into the mud. "Luck will win you a battle here and there, but it will never a war. You'll lose the great battle, boy."

"I'm a boy today, but one day I will be a man." Gabriel swallowed, trying to calm his shaking hands. "And I will end this war."

"You don't even have the courage to end me." The Apollyon laughed, coughing up more blood.

Gabriel realized the truth of the Dark Mage's words. Did he want to be the kind of man who killed wounded men? Could he let the Apollyon die of his wounds? He watched as the Apollyon's eyes fluttered. The Dark Mage could have healed himself if he'd been able to focus on the necessary magic.

"At least I'll die knowing you lost the other battle." The Apollyon sighed, his head rolling to the side.

"What battle?" Gabriel knelt down beside the Dark Mage, the sword blade still against the man's throat.

"The first words Alexander ever spoke to me. Always… guard… your flank."

The Apollyon's face relaxed, and his body became still.

Gabriel puzzled at the man's final words a moment, and then gasped, lunging to his feet as their import broke upon his mind.

His flank. The troops beside him. Always there to step forward into the fight and protect him. The Chimera team.

He had left the team vulnerable and open to attack.

CHAPTER 22
REPARATIONS

Gabriel looked down at the Apollyon at his feet and reached out with his Heart-Tree Magic to sense the state of the man's life. The Dark Mage's heart slowed perceptibly with each beat. He would die within seconds. Gabriel considered what to do. He could let the man die, but what would that mean for himself? He could heal the man, but what would that mean for the war? Could he take him captive? Could he hold him prisoner? To what end?

Gabriel released the Malignant imprints of the battlefield, feeling his thoughts clear of dark intentions as another option arose in his mind. He considered it. It held many risks, but there were always risks.

He wiped the blade on his pant leg, re-sheathed the Sword of Unmaking, and knelt beside the Apollyon, placing his hands on the man's wounds. Using Soul Magic to maintain the Apollyon's unconsciousness, he guided the magical energy of Heart-Tree Magic to repair the damage to the Apollyon's heart and lungs. When he had finished and knew the man would live, he placed his hands on the Apollyon's head.

He took his time, remembering his lessons with Sema and Marcus, probing with a deft blend of Soul and Heart-Tree Magic until he found what he searched for, a part of the brain capable of creating a specific effect on consciousness. He only managed to find it because of the activity it produced. Even while the Apollyon slumbered, the region of his brain seemed aglow to Gabriel's magical senses. He focused his Soul and Heart-Tree Magic on the Apollyon's brain and mind, carefully making a small alteration.

Finished, he stood up, thinking about his next steps. He would need to return to the abandoned house in Maine. It would be difficult to know what point to return to. He had departed while Ohin had been attempting to move the team back through time and away from the Great Barrier to safety. He would also need more imprints than the Sword of Unmaking and his pocket watch could provide.

He thought about the name of the sword as he drew it again from its sheath. He had used it to *unmake* history and save Teresa from certain death. He had used it to *unmake* numerous potential worlds before they could even form. He had nearly *unmade* the life of the man at his feet. In some ways, Gabriel was very much like the blade in his hand — powerful, yet dangerous when poorly controlled.

He reached out with his Time Magic as he focused on the Malignant imprints of the battlefield. Grace imprints were also present, but far fewer in number. He held those as well, using a special form of Time Magic to bind the imprints to the Sword of Unmaking, the way he would have bound them to a concatenate crystal. The magic would allow him to access the imprints of the Battle of the Somme through the Sword of Unmaking from any place in the timeline of history. The connection would not last very long, a few minutes at best. Nor would it be as strong a link as one made with a concatenate crystal, but it would give him a considerable power to wield for a short time.

He retained his hold on the imprints, forcing his mind to remain calm in the presence of such overpowering Malignancy. He had been stupid to think he could handle such massive negative imprints without a significant number of Grace imprints to counter and balance them. The imprints had clouded his judgment and left him vulnerable. He would need to remain vigilant against their insidious effects to ensure it did not happen again.

He looked down at the sleeping Apollyon and nudged the man's mind with Soul Magic. The Dark Mage's eyes blinked open. He stared up into the gray clouds for a moment before looking at Gabriel.

"You healed me." The Apollyon glanced around in confusion. "What...what have you done?"

"Like you said, I healed you." Gabriel took a step back.

"The voices...the voices are gone...the voices..."

"Consider it a gift." Gabriel pointed the sword at the Apollyon's heart. "Find your brother. He needs your help. He has saved her and she has saved him. Maybe she can save you, as well."

"Saved her?" The Apollyon's eyes lit up in sudden understanding as Gabriel gestured with the sword and a wave of Soul Magic plunged the Dark Mage back into unconsciousness.

Gabriel looked at the man a moment longer and then pulled the bent nail from the house in Maine out of his pocket. He focused on the nail and disappeared into time, leaving the Apollyon sleeping beneath a sky of smoke and ash and exploding artillery shells. The Dark Mage would regain consciousness minutes after Gabriel departed. Long enough to ensure he could not track Gabriel through time.

Gabriel appeared at the abandoned house a moment later, hovering at the edge of entering the time stream while probing the house's history. Seeing what he hoped for, Gabriel allowed the departing whiteness of his collapsing time jump to deposit him in the middle of the backyard.

Flames burst around him as he appeared. At a glance, he saw Ohin and Sema lying still in the tall grass, the side of the house ashen-black beside a collapsed Teresa. Nearby, Marcus and Rajan stood above a fallen, bloodied Ling as two black-clad Apollyons assaulted them with a barrage of magic. With Gabriel's arrival, the two Apollyons turned in unison toward him.

Gabriel attacked in a specific, precise, and simultaneous manner. His Soul and Heart-Tree Magic reached into the men's brains and minds in an unexpected and profound way. They fought back against him, but were soon overwhelmed by the power of the imprints he held and the exactness of his magical assault on their minds. After a moment, they staggered back together.

"How…" one the Apollyons said, looking to his companion in panic and confusion.

"The voices." The other twin sputtered. "The imprints."

As he had done with their twin in the mud of the Battle of the Somme, Gabriel had severed their link to the other Apollyons, a link carrying not only a psychic connection creating a din of maddening voices, but also the connection to the imprints the other Apollyons held.

"You have a choice now." Gabriel lowered the sword blade, knowing the men posed little threat. He could sense imprints of personal talismans, but nothing more, and nothing of any particular power. "You can find your creator, or you can join his creations. Choose wisely."

The Apollyons did not wait for any further words and winked away as they jumped through time to escape Gabriel. He ran to Teresa as Marcus dashed to Sema and Ohin, while Rajan knelt beside Ling.

"Where have you been?" Marcus shouted as he placed his hands on Sema's bleeding skull.

"We were barely back from the edge of the Barrier when they attacked." Rajan lifted Ling's head gently, and her eyes rolled as she blinked. "They must have been waiting for us."

"I made a mistake," Gabriel said as he fell to the ground beside Teresa.

"Tell me something I don't bloody know," Marcus growled between clenched teeth.

Teresa's wounds were extensive, and Gabriel devoted his whole attention to them. He still held the magical energy of the imprints of the Battle of the Somme fed to him by the Sword of Unmaking, and he used the full power of them to affect her healing. He knitted bone back together, fused severed tissue, repaired stricken organs, and remade burnt skin. When he finished, she opened her eyes.

"Don't leave me like that." Teresa's voice sounded weak. "I can't protect you if you run off."

"I won't leave you again." He kissed her lips briefly, gently.

Gabriel lifted her with Wind Magic and carried her to Ling. He healed Ling's wounds before taking them both to where Marcus still worked his Heart-Tree Magic on Sema. Thanks to the connection through the Sword of Unmaking to the imprints at the Battle of the Somme, Gabriel had the advantage of far more magical energy than Marcus could command. Unfortunately, that connection began to wane.

While Gabriel set about healing Ohin's wounds, he tried to keep command of the emotions the negative imprints generated within his heart. When Ohin regained consciousness, his mentor's own anger manifested the moment he saw Gabriel's face. Gabriel released all of his imprints as he saw Sema sit up nearby, held by Marcus's strong arms as he caressed her face.

"What were you thinking?" Ohin's ragged voice, torn between fury and sadness, sounded like a klaxon to Gabriel's ears.

"I wasn't."

Gabriel said no more. He had no words for his shame. For his disgrace.

"You followed him for a vendetta." Ohin's eyes burned with a wrath Gabriel had never seen before. He grabbed Gabriel's shoulders.

"Aurelius." Gabriel could feel the tears filling his eyes, but he refused to look away from his beloved mentor.

"You may have to sacrifice our lives one day for the sake of the war or the Continuum, or to save your own life, but do not throw our lives away out of vain anger and a lust for revenge. Our lives are worth more than that." Ohin nearly spat the words out, struggling to control himself.

Gabriel choked back a sob, tears streaming down his cheeks. He had betrayed Ohin's teachings and the faith of his team. He had left them to die so he could pursue a pointless revenge. He nearly died with nothing gained. A revenge left unfulfilled. And he had left Teresa, who would have surely died in another minute. A minute of time he wasted to assuage the loss of Aurelius. How would he have coped with the loss of both of them? Or the loss of all of them?

"I'm sorry." Gabriel's whispered apology hung in the still air of the yard behind the old house, seeming to quaver between himself and Ohin.

Ohin blinked back tears of his own as he pulled Gabriel into the embrace of his powerful arms. Gabriel cried as Ohin stroked his hair. "You can no longer be the impetuous boy."

Gabriel felt the hands of his friends and companions touch his back.

"We are a family." Ohin's deep voice soothed Gabriel's heart as he leaned back from his mentor's arms. "No one doubts your courage or your love for us, but you must learn to think not simply how your actions will affect you, or us, but how they will ripple out and change the course of the war, and all the lives everywhere."

"I understand." Gabriel wiped his eyes on his muddied sleeve.

Ohin looked at the mud covering him as though noticing it for the first time. "What happened to you?"

211

"Maybe we should clean him up first." Teresa wrinkled her nose as she sniffed at Gabriel.

"He does smell like a dung heap," Marcus said.

"Which is different from usual in what way?" Ling asked.

"It might be good if we all took a moment to recuperate," Sema said.

"I could use a meal," Rajan said.

"And a bath." Teresa sniffed at Rajan, as well.

"And a cold ale to ease my pains after a day like this," Marcus said.

"Can they come back?" Ling asked.

"No," Ohin said. "They ghosted our time trail. Once they've gone, they have no way back without a relic. We're still safe here."

"Good." Gabriel glanced around at his friends, landing on Teresa's face but finding it hard to look her in the eye. "Then I'll tell you how stupid I was over dinner."

Dinner consisted of a mismatched assortment of canned foods — baked beans, tomato soup, green peas, corned beef hash, Texas three-bean chili, and fruit cocktail. Gabriel ate little. At first, because he found himself too busy recounting what had happened during his encounter with the Apollyon on the Battlefield of the Somme, and later because his recitation of his foolishness had squelched his appetite.

His teammates listened to his story with a mixture of curious anger and worried disbelief. When he finished, his eyes fell to the empty place at the end of the table. The seat Aurelius would have occupied. Gabriel thought about the emperor's sad eyes, so filled with wisdom and laughter and pain. He blinked and looked away. Too soon to think such thoughts.

"I can't decide if that's brave or moronic." Teresa ground her teeth as she spoke.

"Bravely moronic." Rajan stuck a spoonful of chili in his mouth.

"Moronically brave, more like." Marcus shook his head as he pushed his bowl away.

"At least we've learned a few things." Ling leaned back in her chair.

"Like how to sever the Apollyons' connections with each other." Sema placed her napkin on the table and crossed her hands.

"Other things, as well." Ohin put his fist beneath his chin. "Even I had no idea it was possible to steal the imprints another mage held."

"Not surprising," Marcus said. "Grace Mages don't spend much time fighting each other."

"And we'd never be able to steal negative imprints from a Malignancy Mage, anyway," Rajan said.

"Gabriel can." Teresa waved her hand near a sputtering oil lamp and the wick leapt to life again.

"Assuming I can learn how." Gabriel considered the process and what it would take to accomplish the task.

"We can practice later." Teresa's smile had returned, mischievous as ever.

"I wouldn't mind observing that," Ohin said as Teresa's grin faded. "After we sweep the house and make sure it's clean. We should get a good night's rest. In the morning, we'll return to the castle. We'll be going back only minutes after we left, and there will be a great deal of work to do. Tending to the wounded. Repairing the castle and the defenses. Planning the next steps."

"Can we trust the Council to make those plans?" Marcus took a slow sip from the last bottle of beer.

"The question isn't whether we can trust the whole Council," Ohin said with a sigh. "The question is who on the Council cannot be trusted."

"There's no way to know," Rajan said.

"So we make our own plans on the side," Ling said. "Just in case."

"There is one way to know who we can trust." Sema stared at the flame of one of the lamps. "At least for everyone except Councilman Toulouse."

"How do we know Toulouse can be trusted?" Teresa asked.

"We don't." Ohin joined Sema in gazing at the flame.

"Councilman Toulouse is the only member of the Council who is a Soul Mage." Gabriel watched Sema and Ohin staring into the flicking light of the oil lamp.

"You mean you want to read their minds?" Rajan coughed in surprise.

"Not want to." Sema turned her eyes from the lamp to the others. "But it might be for the best."

"Should have done it ages ago," Ling said.

"There are rules about peeking into other people's minds," Sema said. "Without just cause, it is extremely unethical."

"Something certain mages should remember," Teresa said in a low voice to Gabriel.

"Well...of course," Gabriel said softly.

The idea of looking into Teresa's mind to discern her feelings for him had never occurred to Gabriel, which, he now realized, had probably been a good thing. Beyond the fact that his skill in Soul Magic came nowhere near Sema's, the mere thought of Teresa catching him poking around in her head made his stomach tremble with fear.

"I'll speak to Akikane about the possibility of...increasing surveillance at the castle," Ohin said, his voice lingering on the euphemism. "Until then, we'll keep the idea to ourselves."

The team sat in silent agreement.

Ohin pushed his chair back and stood up.

"Let's get to work then."

CHAPTER 23
PARADOX

Gabriel helped clear the table and clean the kitchen. Afterward, he and Teresa assisted in making the house seem as abandoned as it had been when they arrived. When they accomplished as much as could be done that night, they retreated to the backyard to practice stealing imprints from one another under Ohin's patient observation.

It took Gabriel several tries to manage wresting control of the imprints Teresa held. Once she had seen it done, she had little problem replicating the feat. As they practiced, Ohin joining in, it became clear that the process required an exceptional level of skill and concentration to be successful against a mage who knew how to fight back against the usurpation of the imprints they held.

Considering the unheard-of nature of the technique among Grace Mages, Gabriel assumed it remained a closely guarded secret among Malignancy Mages. This made a certain macabre sense. If a Malignancy Mage stole the imprints from another, it would be unlikely for both mages to survive the encounter. Gabriel doubted it would have much application among Grace Mages. At least he hoped not. It also gave him pause to think how close he came to protecting that secret with his own death.

Later, after the others had gone to bed, Teresa and Gabriel sat on the steps at the top of the worn wooden stairs, holding hands and speaking quietly.

"You have to stop being so stupid." Teresa leaned her head on Gabriel's shoulder.

"It's not as easy as it sounds." Gabriel breathed in deep, taking in the aroma of Teresa's hair, the scent of lavender and smoke.

"Are you smelling my head?"

"Ah...no."

"Weirdo."

"I don't know what you're talking about."

"Here's what you do." Teresa tightened her grip on his hand. "Next time you're about to do something stupid, stop, take a moment, and consider what I would do."

"And that's going to improve things how?" Gabriel grunted as Teresa dug her elbow into his gut.

"Okay. Point taken. Maybe think about what Sema would do. Or Akikane. Or Ohin. Or anyone but Ling." Teresa laughed.

"That's the problem." Gabriel wanted to laugh, but found he couldn't. "I can't make decisions the way they would because I'm not like everyone else."

"Don't tell me you're falling for the Apollyons' Nietzsche-inspired superman crap." Teresa sat back to look at Gabriel.

"Of course not." Gabriel struggled to find the words for his thoughts. "They will never have to make the decisions I have to make. I have to find my own way of…being me. Of making decisions without betraying myself.

"It was stupid to follow that Apollyon, but was it stupid to save him? Was it stupid to sever his connection with the other twins? Was it stupid to let him go? I don't know. Would Ohin or Sema or Akikane have made those same choices? I don't know. But those decisions feel right to me. But leaving the team alone — that wasn't a good decision. And leading that Apollyon back to the house…"

"That wasn't your fault."

"It was. I should have noticed. If I had…"

"Ohin blames himself, not you. No one blames you."

"I do. I didn't know him long, but Aurelius…"

"I know."

Teresa enveloped Gabriel in her arms. They sat silently on the steps of the stairs, gently kissing until they heard Marcus stumbling from his room, half asleep, heading for the stairs and eventually the backyard — his midnight journey to relieve his bladder. Gabriel and Teresa stood up and said goodnight as Marcus descended the stairs.

"I remember when I was young enough to stay up late kissing in stairwells." Marcus sleepily rubbed his face. "Now I'm only up to race to a makeshift outhouse."

Gabriel walked Teresa to her room and kissed her goodnight. Teresa closed the door and Gabriel retreated to his own room. He eventually fell into a fitful sleep, filled with twin Apollyons chasing him through a battlefield occupied by warriors from every age in history. Morning and wakefulness came as a relief.

After putting the final touches on the abandoned house, like magically spreading dust evenly over the furniture, Gabriel and the team assembled in the backyard one last time. A moment after Ohin took a lump of amber from his pocket, they stood in the Upper Ward of Windsor Castle, 125 million years in the past.

Their return through time deposited them a meager fifteen minutes after they had last departed. Much had happened in that short span of time as Gabriel surveyed the damage.

Fire Mages had extinguished the flames across the castle grounds, thin wisps of smoke gently rising from still-smoldering ruins. More wounded mages had been gathered into the impromptu triage area in the Upper Ward courtyard. With the return of the mages from Akikane's expedition to Dresden, the numbers seemed to have doubled. People carried wounded, or ran on various errands across the grass. Akikane stood at the center of a group of people, pointing and giving instructions on how to manage the repairs and defenses. Akikane's face did not hold its usual blissful continence, but he seemed calm, and Gabriel found that reassuring.

"I'll get Councilwoman Elizabeth," Gabriel said to the others.

"Meet us in her office." Ohin looked to Akikane. "I'll see if I can get Akikane to join us for a moment to figure out how we can be most useful, beyond trying to figure out how to revive Elizabeth."

"Don't forget to break Elizabeth's favorite teacup if we're going to meet in her office," Gabriel said.

"Yes, thank you." Ohin nodded his appreciation. "I'd forgotten about that."

Ohin patted Gabriel on the shoulder and walked toward Akikane.

"Need company?" Teresa asked.

"Um, sure," Gabriel said, happy to have Teresa with him at any time. He looked at the rest of the team. "We'll meet you in a second."

Gabriel warped space-time around himself and Teresa, delivering them a moment later to the cellars beneath the castle. Justine looked up, her bright blue eyes shining with sudden excitement at Gabriel's arrival. Her enthusiasm dimmed when she noticed Teresa standing beside him. Justine knelt beside Elizabeth, holding a wet cloth to the elderly mage's forehead. Leah and Liam sat on the other side of Justine, playing a game of checkers. The electric lights burned brightly. Someone must have fixed the castle generators.

"Gabriel." Justine stood up, smoothing out the wrinkles of her tunic.

"Gabriel!" Leah and Liam shouted in unison, jumping up from their game and running to embrace him. He knelt down to them.

"Is it safe yet?" Leah asked.

"Have you seen our mommy and daddy?" Liam asked.

"I haven't seen them yet, but it is safe now, and we'll try to find them very soon." Gabriel hugged the two children. "You've both been very brave."

"And they've been very helpful." Justine stood beside Elizabeth. She had placed some towels beneath Elizabeth's head to make her more comfortable.

"Hi, Teresa," Leah said, suddenly seeming to notice her presence. Liam beamed bashfully, but remained silent.

"I'm sure you've both been a big help." Teresa smiled warmly at the two children.

"How is she?" Gabriel nodded toward Elizabeth as he looked at Justine.

"No change." Justine's face clouded with worry. "She doesn't seem any worse, but there's no waking her."

"We learned cheppers." Liam pointed to the game board on the floor, seeming very proud of himself.

"Checkers." Leah sighed at her little brother's misstatement. "Justine taught us how to play. I won two games."

"I lost two games." Liam kicked his sister's ankle. She pulled his ear in retaliation.

"Stop it, you two." Justine stepped forward to put her arms around the two children and separated them. "I found a pile of old games in a cupboard in the back. I thought it would keep their minds off...other things." Her blue eyes looked sad as she glanced between Gabriel and Teresa.

"It was a good idea," Gabriel said.

He looked at her a moment longer, noticing again how blue her eyes were. Those blue eyes reminded him of something. Of someone? Who? When?

"Are you okay?" Justine frowned.

"Is something wrong?" Teresa instinctively looked around the room, peering into the dark shadows at the back of the cellar chamber.

"I'm not sure."

Gabriel tried to shrug off the odd feeling permeating him, but as he looked again into Justine's eyes, his body tingled with a realization — he had seen those eyes before. Eyes like hers, but not on her face.

Agrace. The girl from the food line at the medieval castle Chateau Gaillard had eyes like those he stared into now. Eyes *very* like those.

A coincidence, surely. Two girls could have similar eyes. It happened all the time.

He shook his head, convinced his wild suspicions could not be real. He looked away and caught sight of the checkerboard on the floor, causing another vague memory to bubble up from the back of his mind. What memory of a game of checkers? When had he last played checkers? And who with?

Gabriel grasped the Grace and Malignancy imprints of the concatenate crystals in his bracelet and formed a space-time seal around the room.

"Gabriel, what is it?" Teresa had felt him grasp the Grace imprints.

"Has something happened?" Justine looked concerned. Apparently, she had also felt him take hold of the imprints. Leah and Liam looked up at Gabriel, worry filling their faces.

"Everything is fine." Gabriel knelt down to Leah and Liam. "I need to talk to Justine about Elizabeth's condition. It'll only take a minute. Then we'll get Elizabeth out of here and go find your parents."

He turned to Teresa as he stood. "Keep an eye on them for a moment. Please."

"Okay." Teresa seemed unsure if she should be afraid of what had spooked Gabriel or jealous that he wanted to talk to Justine alone.

He glanced at Justine and stepped back toward the shadowed part of the cellar. "Let's talk over here."

"Okay." Justine followed Gabriel, her lips curling slightly upward as she walked past Teresa.

As he walked to the back of the room, Justine at his side, Gabriel tried to calm the multitude of thoughts whirling and exploding in his mind like firecrackers. Two girls with the exact same blue eyes. A checkerboard in a dream. It could be coincidence. But other things came to his mind now. Things that had bothered him, but which he had ignored or forgotten.

Why had Kumaradevi not seemed to know how her husband had died? How had he been dreaming of that bizarre board game so often in Windsor Castle and in Chateau Gaillard and even in the rogue Apollyon's alternate paradise world, but not one time since? Could that be a coincidence? Could it be merely coincidence the lesson he gleaned from the bizarre board game had shown him how to save Teresa's life from an otherwise irrevocable death? Did he believe in coincidences that happened so frequently and seem so connected? Could he simply be lucky? Could anyone be that lucky?

Gabriel stepped into an alcove, out of sight from Teresa and the children. He turned to Justine as she joined him in the shadows. He looked in her eyes one last time. This could not be coincidence.

"Give it to me?" Gabriel held an avalanche of magic ready to release with a single thought.

"Gabriel, what are you talking about?" Justine's voice quavered with apprehension.

"The notebook." Gabriel's breathing quickened as he tried to control the anger beginning to make his hands shake. He would not act foolishly upon his anger again.

"I don't know what notebook you're talking about." Justine moved to step closer, and Gabriel backed away.

"Gabriel, what's wrong?"

"Stop it." Gabriel pointed at Justine, fighting down the urge to draw the Sword of Unmaking. "Stop pretending. I know it's you. I know it's been you the whole time. Now give me the notebook. And tell me what you've done with Justine."

"Gabriel, I…" Justine paused, shoulders clenched, her blue eyes holding Gabriel's gaze, tears welling at the edges of her lids. Then she exhaled, a wave of calm filling her as she straightened up. He eyes no longer seemed teary, but serene. "What gave me away?"

Gabriel clenched his fists, holding back from attacking. "The eyes. The checkers. The game. Too much coincidence. Too much luck. You're too clever sometimes. Now where is Justine?"

"Asleep in the closet of her room. Probably the safest place for her, considering all that has transpired today."

"And where is the notebook?" Gabriel asked.

Justine shimmered, the features of her face and body gradually shifting, revealing the true nature of the person wearing the young girl's face. The transformation complete, deep brown eyes squinted at Gabriel.

"I don't have the notebook." Vicaquirao frowned. "And I wouldn't try to keep it from you if I did. You need to know what it says about the Great Barrier. There isn't much time to save it."

"No, you have it." Gabriel swallowed and stepped back, trying to order the bomb-like thoughts still detonating in his mind. "You have to have it. You took it from me."

"I haven't seen it to take it from you." Vicaquirao spoke slowly and calmly, sensing Gabriel's anxiety.

"You have it." Gabriel pointed again at Vicaquirao, his anger beginning to cloud his thoughts. "You took it while you were pretending to be Kumaradevi in the rogue Apollyon's world. You got the details of her husband's death wrong. You're getting sloppy. Then you kidnapped Teresa and left her to die in Sagalassos."

"Teresa looked very alive a moment ago." Vicaquirao seemed confused.

"Yes, that was clever." Gabriel could barely contain the desire to attack Vicaquirao for what he had done to Teresa. His hand ached for the Sword of Unmaking. "The dreams every night. Little lessons on how to change time. Did you intend the game as a test? Or was it some cunning joke to you, showing me how to save her after she had died?"

"Ah." Vicaquirao sighed, a look of weariness coming over him. "I hate paradox."

"Paradox isn't as bad as seeing someone you love die again and again." Gabriel felt the tears on his cheeks and hated himself for showing Vicaquirao any sign of weakness.

"No." Vicaquirao's voice became gentle. "I mean paradox for me. There's a very good reason I don't have the notebook to hand to you."

Gabriel eyes widened in surprise at the import of Vicaquirao's words. Could that be possible?

"You haven't done any of those things yet." Gabriel's tone wavered between statement and question.

"As I said, I hate paradoxes." Vicaquirao shrugged his shoulders. "However, there's nothing to be done about it. One has to play one's part, or bifurcations arise like worms after a summer rain."

Gabriel stared at Vicaquirao in silence, trying to figure out how this could all be possible and what this paradox meant.

As if reading his thoughts, Vicaquirao spoke. "If you want the notebook back, you're going to need to let me go."

"I don't trust you."

"You're finally learning."

"How do I know you will come back? How do I know you're not pretending?"

"You could read my mind, but I might change my mind about coming back."

"So... I need to trust you."

"Another kind of paradox, no?" Vicaquirao seemed amused as much as annoyed by the bizarre circumstances.

Gabriel considered Vicaquirao's demand. It would be a gamble to allow the Dark Mage to escape, and there could be no assurance he'd return with the notebook. And if he didn't? Would that change anything? It seemed Vicaquirao would obtain the notebook at some point in the future of his personal timeline. Unless Gabriel had mistaken all the signs and Kumaradevi really did possess the notebook.

Gabriel rubbed his temples with the heels of his hands. The confusion of it all strained his mind. Even his anger had faded. Vicaquirao had not left Teresa to die. Not yet. Had it been an accident, or had he done so because Gabriel had told him he would? Too many questions. Too many possibilities. Gabriel thought of the game. He would be setting Vicaquirao in motion like a game piece, attempting to predict the outcome of the move several turns in the future. Before he could do so, he needed to know a few things.

"What is the game called?" Gabriel lowered his hands.

"It has no name." Vicaquirao seemed to relax. "I created it to help me understand time."

"How long have you been pretending to be Justine?"

"Two days. I make sure she eats between naps."

"How did you follow me through so many time jumps?"

"I haven't yet. However, I find that the person who discovers an aspect of magic or time travel and who applies himself to really understanding how it works tends to be the best at accomplishing it."

Gabriel allowed the knowledge accompanying that statement to settle in his mind. It made his stomach tighten in response. Vicaquirao had been the one to discover how to secretly follow a Time Mage's path through time.

"Did you know about the attack on the castle?"

"No. It surprised me. Until I realized he was after the notebook. I expected Elizabeth to have it on her. When she didn't, I'd hoped you would have it."

"If you harmed her…" Gabriel's fingers twitched at the thought.

"You have so much history to learn." Vicaquirao seemed sad. "I would never harm Elizabeth. I don't know what curse those twinned Apollyons put on her mind, but I assure you, no one at this castle will be able to break it. I tried, but it's beyond even me."

"Go." In a decision more instinctual than logical, Gabriel released the space-time seal.

"I'll be right back." Vicaquirao's lips curled. "From your perspective."

Gabriel sensed Vicaquirao reach out to the dark imprints of a concatenate crystal hidden in the pocket of his tunic and bend space-time around himself. An instant later, he vanished.

CHAPTER 24
TRUST AND LIES

Gabriel waited. Had he made a mistake? Would Vicaquirao return? Did the Dark Mage want Gabriel to have the notebook? Did Vicaquirao want to stop the Apollyons from destroying the Great Barrier of Probability?

Gabriel peeked around the corner of the alcove. He could see Teresa distracting Leah and Liam with Fire Magic tricks. She looked up, tilting her head in silent question. He gave her a thumbs-up sign and stepped back out of sight as she glared at him. He had no idea what she thought he might be doing with "Justine" and had no desire to know.

He considered the paradox of Vicaquirao's situation and what he hoped the Dark Mage would be doing next. Vicaquirao would need to travel back several minutes in time to find Gabriel in the Middle Ward of the castle, spying on the rogue Apollyon and then…

He would then need to ghost Gabriel and Teresa's trail through time even as Gabriel ghosted the rogue Apollyon's trail and then…

He would have to follow them to Chateau Gaillard, the medieval castle under siege in 1203, changing his appearance and pretending to be the village girl Agrace, hiding in the castle and planting another dream of the mysterious board game in Gabriel's mind while he slept and then…

Vicaquirao would wait until Gabriel and Teresa's capture, and once more follow Gabriel's trail through time as Gabriel used the small stone statue of Semele to find the rogue Apollyon's private island hideaway in an alternate reality and then…

At some point while Gabriel slept, Vicaquirao would steal a relic from the rogue Apollyon's hut, something small that would remain unnoticed, so he could return to the alternate world as he needed and then…

Later that night, he would give Gabriel the final dream of the board game and in the morning he would witness Gabriel steal the notebook and eventually destroy it the in the hands of the rogue Apollyon on the beach and then...

Vicaquirao would once more follow Gabriel and Teresa's trail through time to the Japanese village and wait for them to create the fake notebook before following them back again to the rogue Apollyon's private world and then...

He would kidnap Teresa and knock her unconscious, carrying her far enough away so that Gabriel would not be able to sense the magic used to take her to Sagalassos and then...

Abandoning Teresa in the Roman town, Vicaquirao would take a piece of the statue of Marcus Aurelius from the bathhouse back with him and return to the rogue Apollyon's alternate reality using the relic he stole from the hut and then...

Vicaquirao would magically pretend to be Kumaradevi pretending to be Teresa and plant the awful kiss on the younger version of Gabriel while the older version of Gabriel switched the fake notebook in his previous self's pocket and then...

Vicaquirao would confront Gabriel, pretending to be Kumaradevi, and give him the chunk of stone that would take him to find Teresa in Sagalassos in exchange for the notebook and then...

Vicaquirao would hopefully return to cellars of Windsor Castle and give the notebook to Gabriel.

Gabriel's only solace as he waited came in knowing that because it had been Vicaquirao pretending to be Kumaradevi pretending to be Teresa who had kissed him in the jungle, at least he finally understood why their first kiss had felt so wrong.

Gabriel sensed sweat running down his sides as he began to panic, considering how gullible and foolish he had been to trust Vicaquirao, how much he had damaged his own hopes of defeating the Apollyons, how desperately he needed to know the contents of the notebook that he would likely never hold again, how he had possibly passed up the only chance for revenge for Teresa's near-death, how...

Vicaquirao appeared beside him, still wearing the simple white tunic. Startled, Gabriel fell back against the wall, his hand nearly creating a defensive spell out of reflex. Instead, he replaced the space-time seal.

"That was considerably more interesting than I had expected." Vicaquirao raised his hand to reveal the small, red leather notebook. He handed it to Gabriel.

Gabriel's hand shook slightly as he accepted the notebook. He looked up at Vicaquirao. "Thank you."

"You should thank Teresa." Vicaquirao flashed a wide grin. "As I've always said, love is a better motivator than fear."

"If you ever try to kill her again…" Gabriel's voice broke before he could finish the thought.

"I tried no such thing. Why would I? What would I gain?" Vicaquirao seemed offended. "Every time I think you understand me, you reveal your ignorance of my true intentions. I cannot decide if I am a poor communicator or you are simply too dense to grasp my meaning. I knew she would die because you told me so. The same way I knew you would save her."

"But you showed me the game to save her." Gabriel tried to ignore Vicqauirao's taunts.

"No. Think. I showed you the game before I ever knew about our little paradox." Vicaquirao sighed. "I showed you the game because I believe you will need to heed its lessons in the coming days. Saving Teresa was merely paradoxical serendipity."

"Why would I need to know how to change the Primary Continuum?" Gabriel fought back the impulse to try and physically shake coherent answers from Vicaquirao.

"Hopefully, that will become clear to you. Maybe after you read the notebook."

Gabriel glanced down at the book in his hand. "Have you read it?"

Vicaquirao chuckled. "Who do you think taught Elizabeth to speak the dead language of Indus in the first place? Although her private alphabet gave me pause for a bit. However, she's always been so good about leaving clues. And she calls me the clever one."

"Now what?" Gabriel realized Vicaquirao's return had taken him by surprise.

"Considering you are holding most of the free light and dark imprints in the castle, I suspect that depends on you." Vicaquirao crossed his arms. "You might want to take into consideration that, while I may have misdirected you on occasion, I have been completely honest with you. And I brought you the notebook."

"What will you do if I let you leave?"

"The same as I've been doing, I imagine. Keep an eye on you from a distance. Keep you safe when I can. Influence your decisions when possible. Help you save the Primary Continuum from destruction."

Gabriel looked into Vicaquirao's eyes, tempted to use Soul Magic to determine the truth of the Dark Mage's words. "Give me your relic to the castle."

"You really are learning." Vicaquirao handed Gabriel a small insect encased in amber.

"Not fast enough." Gabriel released the space-time seal for the second time, again plagued by the idea he had made yet another tragic mistake.

"Take care of yourself. There won't always be a lucky bullet to save you at the last moment." Vicaquirao winked. "And get Elizabeth to Nefferati. She's the only one who might be able to heal her."

Before Gabriel could respond, Vicaquirao disappeared into a vortex of space-time. Gabriel clasped the notebook in both hands and pondered Vicaquirao's final words. Could that be possible? Could Vicaquirao have been at the Battle the Somme? Gabriel's mind whirled, considering the implications. He shook his head, trying to calm the welter of confusing thoughts, a slightly different realization arising in the process.

Justine.

He couldn't simply leave her asleep in her closet. Who knew when she might wake up?

Gabriel slid the notebook into the pocket of his pants and warped space around himself, arriving a moment later in the second floor corridor of the old visitor apartments. While he could teleport to any place he could see directly or had been personally even without a relic, he had never been in or seen Justine's room. He did, however, know which floor of the old visitor apartments she resided on.

As he walked down the corridor, he reached out with Heart-Tree Magic, scanning the rooms for any sign of life. Near the end of the hallway, he passed a door that prickled his magic-sense. He tried the knob of the door, but it held fast. A small bit of Stone Magic altered the composition of the metal locking mechanism, and the door swung inward at his touch.

Inside the small dormitory quarters, Gabriel found Justine exactly as Vicaquirao had said, curled up in a pile of blankets, dozing peacefully in the back of her closet. He reached out with Soul Magic and studied the sleeping spell clouding her mind. She seemed fine. Dreaming deeply, but otherwise unharmed. He could wake her easily.

Gabriel squatted before the open door of the closet and stared at Justine as he considered his options. It might not be best if she woke up surrounded by her shoes and dirty laundry. And how would he explain her being asleep in the closest in the first place?

Sighing as he made his decision, he stood up, wrapping Justine's sleeping form in a cradle of Wind Magic, gently lifting her from the closet floor and guiding her to the lone, narrow bed by the window. Apparently, Justine had not yet been assigned a roommate. No doubt that had been one of the primary reasons Vicaquirao had selected the unfortunate girl to imitate for his infiltration of the castle.

As Gabriel laid Justine down on the bed with Wind Magic, he began using his Soul Magic to slowly rouse her into awareness. Her eyes fluttered briefly, and she stretched her arms above her head as she yawned. She looked very sweet and lovely, and Gabriel realized that had it not been for Teresa, he might have been swayed by her charms. Assuming she had ever really been interested in him. It dawned on him that the Justine who had flirted with him the barbecue party had actually been Vicaquirao in disguise. Had that been a plan to make Teresa jealous? Gabriel pushed the thought from his mind as Justine's eyes locked on him. She gasped and sat up in bed.

Gabriel stepped back from the bed, raising his hands in a calming gesture.

"Gabriel?" Justine looked around her room and then back to Gabriel. "What are you doing here?"

Gabriel realized he should have spent more time thinking about how to explain everything to Justine. He suspected it might not be a good idea to tell her she had been held captive in her own closet by one of the most dangerous Dark Mages of all.

"You were asleep." Gabriel decided to start simply.

"Did I oversleep? Did I miss my lessons?" Justine craned her neck to look out the window. "What time is it? Why is there so much smoke?"

So much for simple.

"You were very sick." Gabriel glanced out the window, realizing he would need to tell Justine most of the truth about the castle, even if he could hide the truth about what had happened to her. "You ate something that made you sick."

"I had food poisoning?" Justine looked back to Gabriel, her bright blue eyes filled with concern.

"It was very bad." Gabriel sighed inwardly. He hated lying. Things always got complicated when he lied. "You had a fever that even Heart-Tree magic couldn't break and were asleep for a few days."

"I've been asleep for days?" Justine placed her hand absentmindedly on her stomach. "But I feel fine."

"Yes, well, the sleep did you good, then." Gabriel needed to move the conversation away from Justine's supposed convalescence. "But while you were asleep, the castle came under attack by an army of duplicate Apollyons."

"Oh no!" Justine bolted from the bed and ran to the window, her eyes wide with panic.

"It's okay." Gabriel stepped to the window beside Justine, placing a hand on her shoulder to calm her, noticing for the first time that she smelled of lilacs. "The castle is safe now. The Apollyons were defeated."

"I slept through an attack on the castle?" Justine's shoulders slumped. "Why didn't anyone wake me? Is Heloise safe?"

"We were very busy." Gabriel tried to remember if he had seen Justine's tutor, Heloise, a Heart-Tree Mage from 1700s England, during the battle. "I'm not sure about Heloise. A lot of people are injured. That's why I came for you. We need help healing everyone."

"Yes, of course." Justine straightened up and started for the door. Gabriel smiled. Vicaquirao's impersonation of Justine had not done the young woman justice. Her single-minded concern for the castle and her fellow mages belied a depth of character he found extremely commendable. "I have a quicker way."

Justine turned to Gabriel as he enveloped them in Time Magic, warping space and depositing them a moment later in northern corner of the Upper Ward courtyard, near the impromptu triage station where the few remaining Heart-Tree Mages attended to their wounded comrades.

"They'll need your help." Gabriel watched Justine as she took in the scene before her, gasping slightly at the damage to the castle and the number of casualties.

"Of course." Justine's face assumed a mask of determination. She started toward the wounded and then paused, turning again to Gabriel. "Why did they send you to get me?"

"I, uh, I happened to be nearby." Gabriel frowned at his unconvincing lie.

"Well, thank you." Justine crossed the space between them and hugged him quickly. "I owe you one." A grim smile on her face, she turned and ran to help her fellow Heart-Tree Mages.

Gabriel watched her for a moment, admiring her enthusiasm in the face of inexperience and possible danger. An instant later, he teleported back to the cellars beneath the castle. Teresa, Leah, and Liam looked at him as he emerged from the shadows of the alcove.

"Where's Justine?" Leah asked, her small, round face pulled tight with concern.

"Yes. Where is Justine?" Teresa stood up, looking back around Gabriel.

"Justine is fine," Gabriel said. "She wanted to help with the wounded."

"Can we find Mommy and Daddy now?" Liam's voice squeaked with anxiety.

"Very soon." Gabriel looked to Teresa, silently imploring her to hold her questions.

"This had better be good," Teresa whispered. "And why do you smell like lilacs?"

Gabriel ignored the inquiry as he turned to Leah and Liam, the back of his neck warm with a sudden, confused embarrassment.

"First we need to take Elizabeth back to her office. Are you ready?" The two children nodded their heads in unison to Gabriel. Teresa squinted and crossed her arms. "Here we go."

Gabriel took the children's hands and gave them a reassuring squeeze as he teleported them all instantly through space to Councilwoman Elizabeth's office. Ohin stood next to the desk, Marcus and Sema sat in chairs, while Ling and Rajan stood next to the window. Gabriel used Wind Magic to guide Elizabeth's comatose form to the flower-upholstered settee, lowering her down gently.

"Where have you been?" Ling turned from looking out the window, her face twisted with impatience.

"We were about to send out a search party." Marcus moved from his chair to kneel beside Elizabeth and examine her. Sema joined him.

"There's been a complication." Gabriel released the children's hands and pulled the red notebook from his pocket.

"Where's Justine?" Ohin looked between Teresa and Gabriel.

"Gabriel took her to help the wounded." Teresa glared sideways at him, her eyes widening when she saw the notebook in his hand.

"She insisted." Gabriel stared back at Teresa and waved the notebook slightly. "She said she'd spent the past two days feeling like an old Mayan general and needed to help."

Gabriel didn't want to mention Vicaquirao's name with the two children in the room. They were terrified enough. No need to frighten them with the knowledge that Gabriel had left them in the care of an infamous Dark Mage pretending to be Justine.

"Oh!" Teresa gasped as she realized what had transpired.

"You mean…" Rajan began to say when Gabriel interrupted him.

"I mean we should discuss it after we find Leah and Liam's parents." He gazed down at the sister and brother. They looked worried and confused.

"There's been no change with Elizabeth." Marcus removed his hand from her forehead.

"The magic is still impenetrable." Sema brushed a stray hair from Elizabeth's face.

"We need to take her to Nefferati." Gabriel looked to Ohin, gesturing again with the notebook. "I've been told only she might be able to save Elizabeth from the curse."

"I assume this came from the usual informant." Ohin glanced at Leah and Liam and frowned. He clearly didn't like the stilted nature the conversation had taken to protect the children.

"Yes." Gabriel slid the notebook into his back pocket. "I think he wanted me to…"

Gabriel stopped as waves of massive space-time distortions erupted around the castle. So many arrivals at once could only mean one thing.

"The castle is under attack again." Ohin's normally imperturbable face reflected the panic Gabriel felt grasping his chest, making it hard to breathe.

"Hundreds of them." Rajan stared out the window at the courtyard. Gabriel and Teresa ran to his side. He instantly recognized the uniforms of the attacking Dark Mages.

"Kumaradevi." Ling's voice echoed with barely controlled rage.

"Attacking while we are weak." Ohin stepped up beside them.

"She's a coward, but she's a cunning coward," Rajan said.

"What do we do?" Teresa turned to Ohin, her eyes alight with fear and anger.

"You need to run." Gabriel spoke before Ohin could part his lips to give an order. "You need to take Elizabeth and run."

"You mean we all need to run," Teresa said.

"No." Gabriel looked past Teresa to see Leah and Liam clinging to each other as explosions began to rock the castle. "You all need to take Elizabeth and flee. You have to protect her. Kumaradevi will be looking for her. They may even know where this office is. You need to go now. I'll meet you at the emergency rendezvous point."

"I'm not leaving you here to fight alone." Teresa pointed her finger at Gabriel.

"You have to," Gabriel pleaded. "I can help defend the castle."

"He's right." Ohin stepped between Gabriel and Teresa. "This time it makes sense to abandon us to fight alone. We need to protect

233

Elizabeth." He put his hand on Gabriel's shoulder. "Go. And be careful."

As Ohin removed his hand, Gabriel jumped through space, catching for an instant the image of Teresa leaping toward him. Then he floated two hundred feet above the ground, looking down as an army of Kumaradevi's Dark Mages assaulted the castle.

A handful of Time Mages evacuated the wounded from the Upper Ward courtyard while a group of Dark Mages rained down balls of fire and tried to cause the earth to swallow people whole.

There were too many Dark Mages to count. Several times more than the number of Apollyons who had attacked the castle only a few minutes earlier. Far more than the scattered castle forces could effectively repel. Gabriel guessed at least a thousand Malignant Mages mounted the offensive. They would each possess concatenate crystals linked to Malignant imprints in Kumaradevi's vile alternate reality kingdom.

Where was Kumaradevi? How could hope he to defeat her and her army?

Gabriel's head swam with colors, his mind nearly collapsing into blackness as lightning erupted around him and the pull of gravity increased, yanking him toward the ground while a space-time seal slid into existence around him. Kumaradevi's minions had found and attacked him. Her spies had probably relayed his tactics from the previous battle with the army of Apollyons.

Gabriel focused the enormous imprints at his disposal through the bracelet on countering the magical assault and dissolving the space-time seal. He tried to see where the attack had emanated from, but there were simply too many of Kumaradevi's soldiers in the castle to ascertain its origin.

Not knowing what else to do, and having no time to formulate a plan, he jumped to the lawns of the North Terrace, appearing beside a group of three Grace Mages cowering behind a statue as two teams of Malignancy Mages bombarded them with dark magic, like cats playing with mice. As Gabriel appeared, he created a burst of gravity waves, sending the Dark Mages cascading through the air and colliding with trees and benches.

"Run!" Gabriel shouted to the three castle defenders. He didn't wait to see if they followed his advice. He jumped through space again, landing atop the Brunswick Tower in the northwest corner of the Upper Ward. A team of Malignancy Mages already occupied the tower, using it to attack the wounded castle mages and the staff still trying to flee from the courtyard below. As they spun around, Gabriel used Wind Magic again, tossing the six Dark Mages high into the sky like black-clad cannonballs arcing through the air.

He stepped to the edge of the turret wall, looking out at the Upper Ward under siege. Buildings raged with fire or collapsed under volleys of Wind and Stone Magic. Most of the castle mages fled from the overwhelming numbers of Dark Mages. Some stood their ground, but were soon overcome by the superior numbers arrayed against them.

Gabriel needed a plan. There must be some way to turn back Kumaradevi's army. He couldn't use his previous method of attacking with magically concentrated sunlight. As things stood, there would be little enough left of the castle after the battle. He needed to find a way to defeat Kumaradevi and her forces directly.

A blur of motion and a burst of lightning caught his attention. Among the ruins of the Round Tower, Akikane battled two teams of Dark Mages, jumping between them and attacking with a fluid grace Gabriel knew all too well. Gabriel drew the Sword of Unmaking from behind his shoulder and jumped through space to join Akikane's defense.

As Gabriel appeared in the smoking rubble of the Round Tower, a third team of Dark Mages joined the fray, immediately casting spells against him. Akikane gave Gabriel a look of encouragement and then leapt through space, his sword blazing like a small sun as it struck down a Dark Wind Mage. Gabriel seamlessly matched Akikane's spontaneous flow of attack and defense, surrounding the Dark Mages in a haze of magic and metal as they jumped from place to place. As he attacked and jumped again and again, Gabriel realized he recognized several of the Dark Mages.

"The boy's come for more lessons." Malik, the Dark Time Mage who had led his training in the fighting pits of Kumaradevi's palace during his captivity, smirked and spat in the dirt.

235

A wide curve of still-standing wall two stories high erupted in a burst of stone and dust, crashing into Gabriel, feeling like a small mountain had fallen upon him. Jin's handiwork, Gabriel guessed. He protected himself with a shield of Wind Magic as the weight of the stones drove him to the ground. As he fell, he felt Malik trying to place a space-time seal around him as Bob the American attempted to subdue his mind into unconsciousness.

Gabriel focused the immense power of the imprints connected to the concatenate crystals of his bracelet and repelled the Time and Soul magic attacks against him. Using Wind Magic, he held the still-falling stones of the wall in midair as he stood up.

Bob's Soul magic attack had given him an idea.

Gabriel let the boulder-like stones of the crumbled wall fall harmlessly to the ground as he reached out with a combination of Heart-Tree and Soul Magic to the brains and minds of the eighteen Dark Mages still attacking Akikane and himself. The Dark Mages froze where they stood, eyes rolling back into their heads as they slowly crumpled to the ground, deeply asleep.

"Very good, very good." Akikane's brilliantly shining sword returned to normal as he walked across a pile of debris toward Gabriel. "We are much safer when they are asleep."

"I don't think I can put all of them to sleep." Gabriel wiped dust from his face and eyes. "There are too many of them." He glanced around to see if more would attack. "Should we give the signal to abandon the castle?"

"Not yet, not yet." Akikane kept his eyes searching the battle. "Our forces are too spread out. Too easy to attack. We need to mass our troops in one place and make a stand. Tell as many as you can to assemble in the Lower Ward near the Horse Shoe Cloister. We have a chance if we act quickly."

"Right." Gabriel watched Akikane disappear as the True Mage jumped through space again. He waited only a moment, long enough to spot two Grace Mages under attack near St. Georges Gate, before doing the same himself.

He attacked the same way he had before, overwhelming the Dark Mages with a blend of Heart-Tree and Soul Magic to render them unconscious. The nature of the magic resembled the curse used upon Councilwoman Elizabeth, but would not harm the Dark Mages in any way. They would only sleep, unable to awaken, for several hours.

Gabriel turned and informed the two Grace Mages of the plan and where to rally. The two men, both in their early twenties, one African, the other Chinese, looked momentarily confused. Gabriel recognized them but couldn't remember their names. He remembered they were both Wind Mages.

"There are wounded." The African man pointed to two fallen Grace Mages in the nearby grass.

"I'll take care of them." Gabriel pointed to the Horse Show Cloister. "Go."

The two men hesitated a moment and then ran for the rallying point in the Lower Ward.

Gabriel turned to the fallen Grace Mages, noticing their hands clasped together on the soot-covered grass. As Gabriel knelt beside them, he realized he knew them. A man and a woman. Abigail and Stephen. Leah and Liam's parents. She had the same copper color hair as her children, while the man possessed their same color eyes.

The father's eyes stared lifelessly toward the heavens. The mother's eyes were closed, her face burned. Gabriel knew death when he saw it, but he reached out with Heart-Tree Magic nonetheless. He sighed. They had been dead too long. Even with all the magical imprints at his disposal, their bodies had suffered too much damage to be revived. Even if it were possible to revive them, the attempt would take precious time from fighting back the hordes of Kumaradevi's invasion.

Gabriel stood up, pushing from his mind the image of Leah and Liam when they would receive the news of their parents' deaths. As he looked up from the bodies of the children's parents, a huge explosion reverberated through the air and shook the ground. Gabriel felt the imprints of the bracelet vanish. He spun around to see billows of black smoke violently racing skyward from what had once been St. George's Chapel, the place where the imprinted artifacts connected to his bracelet had been stored.

Gabriel staggered back, the shock of the lost imprints hitting him like a fist to the gut. While he still held the imprints of the pocket watch and the Sword of Unmaking, the loss of the other imprints filled him with heart-chilling terror. The tide of the battle, already in Kumaradevi's favor, had now turned decisively toward her advantage.

Gabriel looked down to see his hand shaking as it held the Sword of Unmaking. He took a deep breath and tried to push the fear from his mind. It felt like trying to wrestle clouds of acid from a room with no windows.

He shook his head and looked up, seeking a group of Grace Mages he could assist and inform of where to mass for a last ditch defense of the castle. He spotted such a team under attack near the fire-filled ruins of St. George's Chapel. As he prepared to jump, he sensed a space-time seal enclose him. He raised the Sword of Unmaking and magically pushed back against the space-time seal as two teams of Dark Mages appeared around him.

The space-time seal held firm. He could see two Time Mages, a man and a woman, each wearing a necklace of seven concatenate crystals. Even though the origin of the dark imprints in an alternate reality lessened their strength in the Primary Continuum, their combined power proved far too strong for Gabriel to counteract. He found himself wishing the Sword of Unmaking still held a connection to the imprints of the Battle of the Somme. As that thought faded, he had no more time for thinking — the twelve Dark Mages surrounding him attacked.

Held firmly in place by the space-time seal, Gabriel swung his blade at the nearest opponent, a Wind Mage who tried to magically throw him to the ground. Gabriel fought back the Dark Magic, trying to simultaneously block the multiple magics assailing him from all sides. Fire tried to encase him, the ground grasped at his legs, the flesh of his body attempted to disintegrate, pain wracked his mind, while his heart felt as though it might suddenly freeze mid-beat.

Had he not begun his training with such multi-mage attacks in the arena of Kumaradevi's Palace, he would not have lasted long. Unfortunately, he did not have enough magical power to do more than defend against the Dark Mages. Instead, Gabriel feinted with the Sword of Unmaking at the head of a Fire Mage, only to pivot and stab a male Wind Mage in the side. He whirled, deflecting different magics while slicing toward a Time Mage who jumped through space to safety at the last moment.

Suddenly, Gabriel remembered a possible source of imprints close at hand. He reached out with his magic-sense, attempting to forcibly grab the imprints held by the Dark Mage he had wounded. The Dark Mage looked up in surprise and confusion as Gabriel stole his Malignant imprints. Gabriel pushed again at the space-time seal with his own Time Magic, but the seal held. He swung the Sword of Unmaking at another mage and concentrated on stealing the dark imprints of her concatenate crystal.

Gabriel nearly managed to wrest control of the imprints from the Dark Mage when a searing pain erupted in his side. The Sword of Unmaking fell from his hands as he reached around, feeling the hilt of a dagger blade protruding from his back.

He fell to his knees, his vision blurring as the pain in his head intensified and lightning struck him in the chest. He fell back to the ground, barely conscious — his hold on the imprints of the sword and pocket watch slipping away.

Fear cut through the pain in his mind as he struggled to breathe, panting for air that seemed to have vanished from his lungs. He looked around, the faces of the twelve Dark Mages filled with contempt and fury. Their visages blurred as the pain in his back and his mind increased.

"Not so special now, are we?" One of the Dark Mages, a man with a long gray beard, laughed and spat in Gabriel's face.

"Burn him," one of the Time Mages said.

"Let me get my dagger first." A woman Wind Mage gestured with her hand, and Gabriel felt the pain in his back double as the blade slipped from his flesh.

Gabriel struggled to remain on his knees, fighting against the pain, unable to speak as the fear of his impending death shattered his anger at the Dark Mages and Kumaradevi and his own weakness at being defeated.

He felt a wave of heat and light enclose him, building in intensity until the space-time seal faded, along with the pain in his mind and all the other magical forces besetting him. He blinked back tears and looked around as the brilliance surrounding him faded to reveal the twelve Dark Mages lying upon blackened grass, twisted arcs of blue electricity still shrouding their fallen forms. Gabriel fell sideways, his hand reaching back to cover his wound. As he looked up, a familiar face filled his vision.

"Idiot!"

Teresa reached out to grab his shirt as tears pooled in her eyes. She pulled him behind the corner of fallen stone wall and out of sight. "This is why you don't leave me behind!"

"How?"

Gabriel didn't think he could manage more than a one-word question. The ache in his head had begun to subside, but his back pulsed with pain in sync to the pounding of his heart.

"I ran from the room as Ohin jumped through time." Teresa raised her arm, displaying a variety of bracelets and necklaces. "Then I collected a few extra talismans from fallen mages. It took me a while to find enough, and to find you, but here I am. We're not even yet. Consider this the first payment of an installment plan."

"Thank you." Gabriel reached and pulled Teresa down into a kiss.

"You are such a romantic idiot." Teresa shook her head and pulled back from Gabriel's kiss. "The castle is under attack. There are Dark Mages everywhere. You're leaking blood like a punctured wine sack, and you want to kiss!"

"You are really annoying when you're right. Hand me my sword, please." Gabriel grimaced against the throbbing in his back as Teresa handed him the hilt of the blade. He embraced the imprints of the pocket watch and the sword and set about healing his wound with Heart-Tree Magic. He breathed a sigh of relief as the flesh of his back and internal organs knitted back together. When he had finished, he sat up and looked around at the twelve Dark Mages still encased in flickering miniature lightning storms.

"That is really impressive." Gabriel held out a hand and Teresa helped him to his feet.

"I may wear twenty talismans all the time." Teresa frowned and pointed to the bodies of Abigail and Stephen nearby. "That's them, isn't it? Liam and Leah's parents."

"Yes. I was too late to save them." Gabriel felt a surge of anger return to him as he thought of the death of the children's parents.

"Now what?" Teresa looked around at the battle destroying the castle.

"The plan is to assemble as many mages as possible in the Horse Show Cloister and…"

I have the old fool. Come to me now and I will spare him.

Gabriel looked around, knowing who had placed the words in his head but not knowing where they were supposed to lead. As if in answer to his unspoken question, the voice in his head spoke again.

I am on the rooftop.

An image filled Gabriel's mind.

The roof of the state apartments in the Upper Ward.

"Gabriel, what is it?" Teresa reached for his hand. Gabriel grasped her fingers tightly and tried not to let the fear in his heart fill his voice.

"It's Kumaradevi. She's captured Akikane."

CHAPTER 25
SACRIFICE

A moment later, Gabriel appeared with Teresa on the rooftop of the old state apartments and felt a space-time seal surround him. Kumaradevi stood twenty feet away, near the northern end of the rooftop. She wore a suit of finely crafted battle armor painted black with the six magical symbols of her Dark Mages etched in a red circle across her breast plate. Embedded in the armor, within the circle of crimson symbols, sat a set of six brightly glowing concatenate crystals. More embedded crystals encircled the neck and arms of the armor. A look of triumph accentuated her already frighteningly beautiful features. Around the perimeter of the rooftop stood at least fifty Dark Mages, silently staring at Gabriel with palpable loathing.

Gabriel held the Sword of Unmaking in one hand, his other still entwined with Teresa's. She refused to leave his side or let go of him for a moment. His eyes rose above Kumaradevi to where Akikane floated in a bubble of white-orange lighting, his face contorted in agony.

Looking down, Gabriel stared in to Kumaradevi's deep black eyes, struggling to keep the hatred of the woman boiling in his heart from overwhelming his thoughts. He would need his mind clear to deal with what came next. Whatever it might be.

"I understand you were instrumental in repelling the attack of our Greek friend and his duplicates." Kumaradevi stepped forward, her pleasure at his predicament evident in her every movement. "I believe I should take some credit for that, as your training began with me."

Gabriel said nothing. He knew Kumaradevi well enough to know his words were not required at this stage of the conversation.

"Of course, he made a strategic error, relying only upon himself." Kumaradevi gestured toward the Dark Mages surrounding the rooftop.

"However, his short-sightedness has allowed me to significantly expand the ranks of my own Soldiers of Light."

Gabriel frowned in surprise. He hadn't expected Kumaradevi to poach the Dark Mages from Apollyon's former army. But it made sense. As the Apollyons became more paranoid and more reluctant to rely on anyone other than fellow duplicates, their former henchmen would need to find a place to fight. Another imbalance in the war that Kumaradevi had shrewdly turned to her benefit.

"You seem very quiet." Kumaradevi's eyes glittered with malice and amusement. "Has this little girl stolen your heart, or your tongue?"

"I won't let you take him again." Teresa's voice sounded thin in the wind rushing over the roof, but Gabriel could feel the determination of it echoing in his ears.

"She is very fiery." Kumaradevi laughed. "Fiery and foolish. You have so much in common."

"I know what you want." Gabriel had to speak before Teresa could say more. "What are you offering in return?"

"What is to say I won't simply take what I want?" Kumaradevi's silky smile did nothing to conceal the venom in her voice.

"Because you are..." Gabriel searched for the right word. "Magnanimous." Another, unspoken reason made it more likely she would barter than try to take him by force.

"You flatter me." Kumaradevi nodded slightly in his direction. "I offer you a simple choice. Come with me and I will spare the castle, those within it, and even your precious mentor."

"And if I refuse?" Gabriel already knew the answer, but he needed time to think. Time to come up with a different plan from the one he held in his mind. That plan didn't end well. For anyone.

"Refuse and I will destroy the castle, slaughter everyone within it, and leave Akikane in agony for decades before I kill him." Kumaradevi's gaze knifed into him, her voice filling his head.

And what I will do to your little lovebird beside you should not be spoken aloud.

Gabriel didn't bother responding to her taunt. That would be a sign of weakness. Kumaradevi thrived on weakness. Unfortunately, Teresa didn't know the rules of this particular game.

"Why don't you take what you want if you're so powerful?" Teresa nearly shouted in anger.

"I may be powerful, but the boy does have considerable skills, even for his age." Kumaradevi seemed to relish the effect her words had on Teresa. "He knows he can kill himself before I can take him. He might even be able to kill you at the same time. It'd be very much like him to try and save you from my wrath. He couldn't, of course, save the mages still dying as he dithers, or this old fool dangling above me."

"Gabriel, you can't…" Teresa yanked at his arm.

Gabriel ignored Teresa, continuing to stare at Kumaradevi. The Dark Mage knew his mind well enough to guess his actions. Could she guess his final decision? If he surrendered to her, she would never treat him like a favored pet as she had before. No, she would use Soul Magic to twist and control his mind, turning him into a weapon to use against Grace Mages and the Apollyons alike.

He couldn't allow that. He doubted she could stop him in time from taking his own life, and probably Teresa's as well, but did that decision hold any more promise? Kumaradevi would keep her word. She would destroy the castle and every Grace Mage she could find. What would happen to Akikane hurt his heart too much to contemplate. There were no good choices.

He thought about his earlier attempt to take control of the Dark Mages' imprints and tried to figure out how it would impact his chances of survival if he could accomplish the feat against Kumaradevi. He might be able to hold enough imprints to spare himself and Teresa, and possibly enough to free Akikane, but there were simply too many Dark Mages besieging the castle to fight them all. With every moment he wasted, more Grace Mages died.

He tried to think back to the words of Akikane and Aurelius and Ohin about leadership and duty. What was his duty in this situation? To defend the castle? To protect his fellow Grace Mages? To protect Teresa and Akikane? To protect the Primary Continuum? To keep Apollyon from destroying the Great Barrier? Which duty took precedence? Could he protect only one and abandon all the others?

If only he could surrender to escape again.

Wait.

244

Could that be possible? Would it work? Did he have another choice?

"Magnanimous does not mean patient." Kumaradevi's eyes still held his own. "Have you considered all the possibilities the way our mutual friend would? Has it helped you realize you have no choice?"

"I may have no choice, but the decision is still *mine* to make." Gabriel tightened his grip on the hilt of the Sword of Unmaking.

"Semantics," Kumaradevi said. "When I leave, you will leave with me. We both know this. Now kiss the girl goodbye. You may not recognize each other when next you meet."

"Gabriel…" Teresa pulled him to face her.

His kissed her. To keep her from talking. To fulfill Kumaradevi's expectations. To steel his own nerve. When he broke the kiss, he looked in her eyes.

"Be ready."

Gabriel turned slowly back to face Kumaradevi, already beginning his plan, reaching out with his magic-sense. He could not commandeer the imprints of more than one mage at a time. However, one mage standing on the rooftop possessed far more magical imprints than all the others combined. A mage so power-hungry and paranoid no one would ever be allowed to command even remotely as many imprints in her presence.

As Gabriel's eyes locked again with Kumaradevi, she gasped aloud. Gabriel's face contorted with effort as he focused on the imprints she held, seizing control of them before she could mount a counter attack. In the space of a single breath, he usurped her command of the concatenate crystals studding her armor.

Gabriel gagged and steadied himself against the wave of nausea accompanying the ocean of Malignant imprints connected to his soul and will and desire. Kumaradevi stumbled backward in shock as the Dark Mages lining the edge of the rooftop looked about in confusion. Gabriel knew he had only a moment to accomplish his task.

"No!" Kumaradevi shrieked, seeming to guess his intent.

He swung the Sword of Unmaking in a tight arc as he focused all of the magical energy in his grasp into the blade, driving it down into the black tar of the roof, flooding it with the same Stone Magic spell he had used to destroy the observation outpost outside Vindobona while under attack from the Apollyons. The Stone Magic activated and amplified the magical spells already clinging to every inch of the castle buildings and grounds. A pool of black ash spread from the tip of the sword blade like a tsunami of ink, a crackling wave of destruction, racing away from Gabriel and engulfing the rooftop and the buildings below in moments.

Gabriel used Wind Magic to support himself and Teresa as Dark Mages all around began to fall through the roof. Kumaradevi turned and fled, fear and hatred in her eyes as she glanced back at Gabriel before leaping away from the expanding circle of ash and clasping the arm of a nearby Time Mage.

She winked out of existence a moment before the stone beneath her feet transformed to dust. As she disappeared, the connection to her Malignant imprints abruptly ceased. As they did, the storm of light surrounding Akikane vanished, and he plunged to the earth. Gabriel reached out with an invisible hand of Wind Magic and pulled his unconscious mentor to his side.

Around him, Kumaradevi's Dark Mages fled in groups, following their leader, none of them daring to attack. Perhaps they did not realize he had used Kumaradevi's imprints to destroy the castle, or that he had become vastly weaker with her departure. Possibly they simply feared anyone who could make Kumaradevi flee so swiftly. Gabriel knew he had been lucky, but he saw no disadvantage in having Dark Mages fear him.

"Gabriel, what have you done?" Teresa's voice rang with anguish and fear.

"I've destroyed the castle to save it." Gabriel floated them out over the castle courtyard, away from the rapidly disintegrating castle walls. "She might have fled after I stole her imprints, but she would have returned with more mages and more magic. With no castle left, she won't be back."

"She might come back for you." Teresa wrapped her arms around Gabriel as they floated higher.

"We won't be here much longer." He reached out with his free hand to hold the unconscious form of Akikane. Probing him with his

Heart-Tree Magic, he ascertained the extent of the damage. Reassured Akikane would survive, Gabriel pulled him close.

"Is he okay?" Teresa reached out to touch the still features of Akikane's face.

"He will be." Gabriel turned his gaze below.

He watched groups of both Grace and Malignancy mages disappearing from the castle grounds. The Dark Mages fled with their fallen comrades. The Grace Mages and the non-magical staff knew to evacuate the castle in the event that its destruction had been triggered. The magical spells Gabriel had activated and accelerated were designed to render the castle into fine dust to prevent it from ever affecting the Primary Continuum.

With its destruction, the Time Magic spells keeping the castle from entering the Primary Continuum would also dissipate. The process would normally take hours. However, empowered by the magical energy of the dark imprints Gabriel had stolen from Kumaradevi, Windsor Castle would vanish into ash within a few minutes. As he watched, towers and trees and grass crumbled to fine black dust, drifting in the wind and flowing across the ancient plains.

Gabriel looked down the blade of the Sword of Unmaking at the decomposing castle below. He had used the sword to destroy many things. Alternate worlds full of beings brought into existence through bifurcations of the Primary Continuum. Dark Mages who had confronted him in battle. And now, Windsor Castle, his home for nearly a year, the base of operations against the Dark Mages in the War of Time and Magic.

So much destruction.

An icy pain grabbed his chest as he realized this sword, this simple, centuries-old blade of folded steal, did not deserve its name. That name should be reserved for the one responsible for the destruction. He might be called the Seventh True Mage, the Destroyer of Worlds, but Gabriel understood then his real nature — He was the True Sword of Unmaking.

"What will we do now?" Teresa's tears slipped from her cheeks, catching in the wind as they fell like salty raindrops into the sea of ebony cinders spreading across the earth below.

"I don't know." Gabriel felt tears in his own eyes and fought them back.

Beside him, Akikane roused slowly to awareness, his eyes fluttering slightly before opening to stare down at the ashy ruins of the castle. Gabriel watched him, looking for any signs of anger or disappointment. He saw only the slight curve of Akikane's lips.

"Very good, very good." Akikane turned wearily to Gabriel. "Surrender the castle to win the battle. Very wise."

"I couldn't think of anything else." Gabriel could not force himself to look at his mentor for more than a second and turned back to watch the last moments of the castle's obliteration.

"Yes, yes," Akikane said. "When there is only one path forward, we must take it, regardless of where it leads."

Gabriel waited until the castle grounds completely dissolved into fine powder, looking for any signs of mages or castle staff stranded behind. Unsurprisingly, he found none. The castle residents trained several times a year in evacuation procedures.

"It's so sad." Teresa wiped her eyes. "But I'm proud of you. That wasn't easy. Aurelius would be proud of you."

Teresa's words and the thought of Aurelius, his kind actions and wise eyes, toppled Gabriel's defenses, the fortress walls of his inner resolve crumbing like the castle walls moments before. Tears streamed down his face as he held Teresa and Akikane tight. He took a deep breath to stifle a sob, and warped space-time, relieved for the blackness of time travel to carry him away from the evidence of what he had done.

CHAPTER 26
FROM THE ASHES

Shadows cloaked his eyes as the smell of dust and moldy books filled his nose. Gabriel, Teresa and Akikane stood in the back of a large antique store. In the gloom, Gabriel could see tables of items carelessly discarded by their original owners and turned valuable with the passage of time. Old dishes, aged books, jars of buttons and glass beads, small statues of ceramic and stone and wood, a box of dingy pocket watches, and hundreds of other forgotten things with small price tags attached.

This antique shop had been the one his Grandfather's friend had bought the silver pocket watch from in 1940. Gabriel and the team used it as a secret rendezvous spot. While Gabriel would always be able to return to that particular night via his pocket watch, Ohin had taken a rusted nail from the floorboards that would never be missed.

The shadows fled before the light of an old oil lamp, revealing Ohin's face. Behind him, the faces of the other team members emerged from the darkness. Ohin saw Akikane and frowned as the older man leaned against Gabriel.

"What's happened?" Ohin placed the oil lamp on a nearby table and maneuvered Akikane into an adjacent rocking chair.

"The castle is lost." Gabriel's voice creaked a bit, more from emotion than the youthfulness of his changing body. "I destroyed it."

The members of the team stared in shock.

"He had no choice." Teresa stepped slightly closer to him. "Kumaradevi had captured Akikane and she would have killed everyone in the castle."

"No, no." Akikane managed a weak smile. "There were many choices. Gabriel selected the one that would save us all."

The team remained silent until Ohin cleared his throat.

"What now?" Ohin looked at Akikane.

"Begin again, begin again." Akikane sank back into the chair.

"I know where we need to begin." Gabriel's eyes had adjusted to the dim light and he now saw Elizabeth lying on a blanket in a corner. Beside her, Leah and Liam leaned against the wall and each other, dozing quietly. He felt his breath catch as he remembered seeing their parents lying dead in the grass. Sema noticed the angle of his gaze.

"Their parents?" Sema asked.

"Dead." A chill fell over Gabriel's spine. So many had died that day. So many good people.

"Poor things." Marcus sighed, running his hand absentmindedly across his bald head.

"Where are we going?" Ling stood straight, planting her feet and looking as though preparing for battle.

"Yes, what's next?" Rajan seemed infected with Ling's energy.

Gabriel realized they probably all wanted a chance to fight back against the Dark Mages who had destroyed their home and killed their friends. He had no plans for revenge. He had few plans at all. Except one.

"I know where we need to go, but it will take a while to get there."

Gabriel explained why and where he thought they should head while the others prepared to leave. Ling carried Elizabeth with Wind Magic while Marcus hefted Liam into his arms, and Sema carried Leah, both children still deeply asleep.

It took nearly a day to reach their destination. Gabriel spent most of this time seeking out a series of relics that would lead him to the place in time he needed to go. A coin led to a scarf, which led to a hand-carved stone bowl, which led to chipped flint arrowhead, leading to a clay jar, and finally to an old fossil, which took them to a place Gabriel knew only from an image in his mind.

Gabriel led the others through a forest of pine trees swaying in a stiff breeze. A small house of rock and wood sat in a clearing a stone's throw from the ocean. As Gabriel and the others approached the house, a sturdy wooden door swung open and a woman stepped out.

"I told you this place was for you alone." Nefferati placed her hands upon her hips, her eyes fierce, her voice carrying easily across the clearing.

"Things have changed." Gabriel strode through the tall grass, gesturing as Elizabeth emerged from the forest, floating unconscious beside Ling.

"What's happened?" Hundreds of years of age seemed to vanish as Nefferati ran from the house, crossing the small glade in a matter of seconds. She placed her hands on Elizabeth's forehead. Gabriel could sense Nefferati probing her comatose friend with Heart-Tree and Soul Magic. After a moment, she pulled her hands away and looked to the others, her eyes moving between Gabriel and Akikane.

"Bring her inside. Tell me everything."

A few hours later, after informing Nefferati of all that had transpired, they sat in the grass beside the hut, eating a small meal of roasted rabbit and roots. They consumed their meal largely in silence, a deep melancholy hanging over the group as they each contemplated what the events of the last few days and weeks implied for the future. Although their tears had ceased for the moment, the children barely ate. Sema had spared Gabriel the responsibility of informing Leah and Liam about their parent's death before the team's arrival at Nefferati's retreat.

"We'll need a new base." Gabriel broke the stillness, voicing a thought that had been nagging at his mind for the last few hours.

"More than one, more than one." Akikane looked across the grass to Gabriel, smiling appreciatively.

"Yes." Ohin stroked his chin. "Forts instead of a castle. Easier to attack, but harder to find."

"And easier to abandon." Rajan gnawed on a rabbit leg.

"Where do we build these forts?" Ling asked, leaning forward.

"And where do we find the mages to run them?" Teresa reached over and grabbed a char-blackened root from Gabriel's clay plate.

"Finding the mages from the castle will take time." Sema offered a piece of rabbit to a recalcitrant Liam.

"We could use some time." Marcus handed a water skin to Leah. "Time to plan."

"Much time, much time," Akikane said. "However, if everyone followed Elizabeth's evacuation plan, we will know where to look for them. Ohin and I can gather them as we prepare each fortress."

"We can build them in the past again," Teresa said. "Farther back than before. Five hundred million years maybe. In the Cambrian period."

"With fewer fossils available from that time, it might be harder to find the forts," Rajan added.

"Yes," Ohin said. "But how will we communicate between the forts?"

"I know how we can communicate." Gabriel felt a strange sensation spread through him as he realized the ironic symmetry of the situation. "We can use the same magic the Apollyons used to spy on the castle with Elizabeth's teacup."

"Yes, yes," Akikane laughed. "Not exactly justice, but very poetic."

"You'll need help." Nefferati spoke for the first time, her voice gathering everyone's attention. "It may take months, if not years, to figure out how to lift the curse on Elizabeth's mind. That will leave you shorthanded."

"No, no," Akikane said with a hint of mockery on in his tone. "We wouldn't want to impose."

"Oh, no, you'd never do that." Nefferati threw a rabbit leg at Akikane, who laughed boyishly.

Gabriel joined the others in laughing at the elder True Mages' mock antagonism. Even Leah and Liam managed to giggle. With a plan for the future, however difficult and time consuming, the mood of the group lightened perceptibly.

Gabriel reached out and took Teresa's hand. She stretched out her free hand to wipe rabbit grease from his chin. They held each other's eyes a moment and then returned to the conversation, helping fill in the details of how to continue the War of Time and Magic.

They spent two more days at Nefferati's hut working out assignments for each person and talking through their strategy, which included tactics like using Soul Magic to scan the minds of every mage they rescued, particularly the Council members, who would each be responsible for managing a different fortress in time.

Ohin and Akikane began looking for castle evacuees, concentrating on the Council members. Surprisingly, none of the eight members they located revealed any evidence of being traitors, although they all protested greatly at Sema's Soul Magic probes of their minds. Of course, two members of the Council remained missing, so conclusions about their loyalty remained elusive but suggestive. Gabriel, Nefferati, and the others in the team began locating suitable construction sites and building the first of the fortresses.

It took Gabriel longer than he had expected to find the spot he thought perfect for a first fortress. The geography of the land had changed considerably through the millions of years preceding the time he had spent there. Eventually, he found the familiar river and the place that 500 million years later would be known as Vindobona.

A month later, Gabriel and Teresa sat on a hillside overlooking the new fortress. The basecamp resembled a real fort — orderly rows of log cabins and tents behind walls constructed of fallen timber and mud tempered by Stone Magic. A Time Mage stood watch on each of the four towers at the corners of the fort. Shifts rotated the Time Mages every eight hours. Gabriel took a watch several times a week. They would not be caught by surprise again.

The fifty mages building and inhabiting the fort moved with a sense of purpose Gabriel had rarely seen at the castle. The attacks of the Apollyons and Kumaradevi, and the loss of their friends and loved ones, not to mention the castle itself, had instilled in the survivors a determination to prosecute the War of Time and Magic with an intensity bordering on the fanatical. They did not see their losses as a reason to surrender but instead as a validation of the need to continue the fight.

One of the greatest losses of the castle had been the storehouse of relics used for time travel and imprinted objects used to create magic. As each fort reached completion, special teams were assembled to scour history for suitable replacements to the lost relics and artifacts. The library proved to be another loss, one Gabriel felt more acutely than most. Without the library, it would be difficult to accomplish the research needed for missions in time, much less the research he hoped would unlock the secrets of Elizabeth's notebook.

With Elizabeth unlikely to wake from her coma anytime soon, and Nefferati and Akikane unaware of much of what she might have written in the notebook, its decipherment became imperative. Apollyon would attack the Great Barrier of Probability soon, and they needed to know as much as possible to defend it. Attempting to break the coded alphabet and learn more about the ancient forgotten Indus language Elizabeth had written it in consumed nearly every spare minute Gabriel processed. Teresa consumed the rest. Usually his spare moments were occupied by spending time with her as she helped him attempt to untangle Elizabeth's alphabet.

"It's useless." Gabriel tossed the notebook in the sparse grass of the hillside. The more he stared at the notebook, the more he began to understand how it had driven the rogue Apollyon to such great depths of insanity.

"I'm telling you, we should try the super computer again." Teresa picked the notebook up and flipped through the pages at random. "Another trip to the future would be fun. We need some fun."

"What we need is to figure out where Elizabeth hid the clue to reading her alphabet." Gabriel had been filled with hope that a super computer in 2012 might give them a breakthrough, but after finally finding one unoccupied for a few hours, the results had been useless.

"You're sure she didn't give you any hint about the key to the code?" Teresa asked. She posed the same question nearly every day.

"No." Gabriel tried to keep the annoyance from his voice. They'd been over this dozens of times.

"What did she say again?" Teresa asked.

"She said she would show me the key, but she never had time before the attack."

"And no hint what the key would be?"

"I've told you a thousand times. No. Nothing."

"Don't get grumpy with me."

"Sorry." Gabriel reached his hand out in apology.

"I'm only trying to help." Teresa tossed the notebook back in the grass.

"All she said was that she'd show me the Rosetta Stone to unlock the text." Gabriel sighed as Teresa took his hand.

Napoleon's troops had discovered the actual Rosetta Stone in Egypt, in the town of Rosetta, in 1799 CE. A large stone stele, it carried a royal decree written in Greek and two forms of Egyptian, allowing archeologists to finally read the Egyptian hieroglyphs. Gabriel and

Teresa had concluded Elizabeth's implication suggested that she had transcribed some particular text into the notebook to use as a reference to decode her personal alphabet.

"The Rosetta Stone could be anything," Teresa said. "It could be a poem or a passage from a book or a newspaper. Anything."

Two weeks ago, they had been bubbling with excitement when it dawned on them the text they sought could be the Prophecy of the Seventh True Mage. Teresa had spent hours comparing the text of the prophecy with the passages in the notebook with no success.

"How could Vicaquirao figure it out and we can't?" Gabriel found the fact that Vicaquirao had managed to read the notebook with seeming ease frustrated him beyond words.

"He's smart." Teresa looked up at a passing cloud.

"He said the clue was obvious. Clever but obvious." Gabriel joined Teresa in watching the cloud drift through the sky.

"What are obvious things?"

"Things that are right in front of your face."

"What's right in front of our faces?"

"The notebook."

"The notebook can't be the Rosetta Stone."

They sat watching the cloud, holding hands. Teresa's last words hung in Gabriel's mind. The notebook couldn't be the Rosetta Stone. What was obvious? Could a place be the key? Could Elizabeth have hidden something in time that would function as a Rosetta Stone? Where could she hide something like that without the possibility of creating a bifurcation? Where could she hide it that was both obvious and clever? As Gabriel watched the cloud sail through the sky, he had an obvious thought.

"Oh." Gabriel heard his voice breaking with excitement, but ignored it.

"Oh, what?" Teresa noted his tone and turned to him.

"What if the Rosetta Stone is the Rosetta Stone?" Gabriel made no attempt to contain the joy that broke across his face.

"Yes!" Teresa smacked her forehead with the palm of her hand. "Why didn't we think of that? She could copy the text of the original

Rosetta Stone in her alphabet to create the key to deciphering the notebook."

"How do we find a copy of the Rosetta Stone and the translation?" Gabriel asked, again cursing the loss of the Windsor Castle library.

"I told you we needed to go to the future." Teresa snatched the notebook from the grass and beamed at Gabriel.

A quick trip to the year 2012 and some time spent in a closed New York Public Library accessing the Internet via computer, and Teresa had collected all the various translations of the Rosetta stone, as well as copies of the original text in Greek and Egyptian.

Back on the hill above the new fortress, Gabriel marveled at how swiftly Teresa managed to compare the various texts with the first passage of the notebook. Within an hour, she had determined that the notebook used an English translation of the text. Gabriel felt relieved that Councilwoman Elizabeth hadn't taken the time to learn ancient Greek.

"Here. The first paragraph is an exact match." Teresa pointed to the translation she had copied out.

"In the reign of the young one — who has received the royalty from his father — lord of crowns, glorious, who has established Egypt, and is pious towards the gods, superior to his foes, who has restored the civilized life of men, lord of the Thirty Years' Feasts, even as Hephaistos the Great; a king, like the Sun, the great king of the upper and lower regions; offspring of the Gods Philopatores, one whom Hephaistos has approved, to whom the Sun has given the victory, the living image of Zeus, son of the Sun, Ptolemy living-for-ever beloved of Ptah...

"It goes on like that for another two paragraphs." Teresa beamed with pride at the translation.

"You're a genius." Gabriel kissed Teresa. "And you're beautiful."

"I'll stick with genius, it'll last longer." Teresa's eyes softened with delight. "But you can tell me I'm beautiful all you like."

"Thanks to you...you beautiful genius...we can decode the notebook."

Gabriel realized, unsurprisingly, he liked having a genius girlfriend more than a beautiful girlfriend. Luckily, Teresa was both.

"Not really." Teresa sighed as she picked up the notebook. "I worked out the first two sentences of the notebook after the Rosetta text. I can't make any sense of it. I can read it phonetically, but it's still gibberish."

Gabriel followed her finger on the paper she had used to transcribe the notebook. *"Jee-na-ko-to-va lo-tosh."* Gibberish. One step closer, but a longer journey ahead.

"We have to learn how to speak ancient Indus." Gabriel scratched his head in frustration. He had known the notebook had been written in Indus, but had hoped for the best anyway.

"Road trip!" Teresa laughed.

"It could take months." Gabriel tried to contain his disappointment.

"You don't want to spend months with me learning a new language?" Teresa feigned offense. "Maybe you'd rather take *Lilac*. She seemed very happy to volunteer for the last trip."

By some weird quirk of fortune, Justine had been one of the first survivors of the castle to arrive at the new fort. Although she never gave any hint of rivalry for Gabriel's affections, Teresa loved to tease Gabriel with the girl's supposed infatuation, often referring to her as "Lilac" when they were alone. Gabriel had been relieved Justine expressed no interest in him, although she did tend to follow Teresa around, seeming to worship her like some exotic older sister.

"Don't be silly." Gabriel frowned at Teresa's implication. "I love missions with you, but I'm awful at learning languages."

"I'm not. Would you like to know how many I speak?" When Gabriel didn't answer, Teresa continued. "Spanish, French, Italian, German, a little Japanese, and just enough Chinese to drive Ling crazy."

"You're right." Gabriel said, his mood brightening considerably. "Road trip."

They kissed again, because they were happy, because they were young, because they were in love, and mostly, because they could.

"It had better be worth all this work," Teresa finally said.

"Elizabeth wouldn't have gone to all this trouble if what she put in this notebook wasn't likely to be the difference between saving the Great Barrier and..." Gabriel wasn't sure what would happen if the Barrier fell, but he felt sure it would be like the end of the world.

"Then we should get started." Teresa stood up as a smile spread across her lips. "Last one down cleans up after dinner!" Teresa laughed and dashed down the hill.

"But it's your turn to clean up after dinner!" Gabriel struggled to his feet, grinning as he chased Teresa down the hill and back to the imposing walls of the new fortress. Even after all they had lost, he felt happy. Even with all they faced, he felt elated. He had a purpose. He had responsibilities. He had a clear duty. He had friends. And he had Teresa.

As they ran down the hill, trying to keep from tumbling to the bottom, he realized the fort still had no name. He'd have to mention that to Ohin and the others. He knew the perfect name for a fortress fighting off a horde intent on destruction.

Aurelius.

EPILOGUE

The men walked through the trees, a dense mantle of fog obscuring them from one another. Their footsteps through the damp underbrush echoed in their ears as their words reverberated in their minds.

"There is no time."

"We must act now."

"Before it is too late."

"Before they know…"

"What we know."

"Patience is the path…"

"Of success." "Of failure." "Of wisdom." "Of cowardice."

"Action is the path…

"Of success." "Of victory." "Of triumph."

The fog grew thicker, a white-gray blanket smothering the trees and the men and the world.

"Then we act…"

"We act now…"

"We kill him…"

"Before it is too late."

The fog swallowed the men, their voices absorbed into the mist of madness obscuring their minds.

ABOUT THE AUTHOR

After a childhood spent whizzing through the galaxy in super sleek starships and defeating treacherously evil monsters in long forgotten kingdoms, G.L. Breedon grew up to write science fiction and fantasy novels. He lives with his wife in Brooklyn, NY.

For more information please visit:
www.Kosmosaicbooks.com

www.ingramcontent.com/pod-product-compliance
Lightning Source LLC
Chambersburg PA
CBHW061606170626
46811CB00001B/338